A Critical Edition of

THE
WAR
OF THE
WORLDS

H.G. Wells's Scientific Romance

With Introduction and Notes by
David Y. Hughes and Harry M. Geduld

INDIANA UNIVERSITY PRESS
Bloomington & Indianapolis

Manufactured in the United States of America

Library of Congress Cataloging-in-Publication Data

Wells, H. G. (Herbert George). 1866–1946.
  A critical War of the worlds : H. G. Wells's scientific romance /
with introduction and notes by David Y. Hughes and Harry M. Geduld.
      p.   cm. — (Visions)
  Includes bibliographical references.
  ISBN 0-253-32853-5
  I. Hughes, David Y. (David Yerkes), date. II. Geduld, Harry
M. III. Title. IV. Series: Visions (Bloomington, Ind.)
PR5774.W3 1992
823'.912—dc20   91-46741

1 2 3 4 5 97 96 95 94 93

For Jane

C O N T E N T S

PREFACE

This edition of *The War of the Worlds* has four primary objectives: to offer a detailed account of the genesis of the novel and its complex publishing history; to provide a reliable and readable text; to annotate certain words, details, and passages that have engaged the attention of critics or that might require clarification or comment for the serious reader of Wells; and to provide a selection of material extraneous to the novel but relevant either to its genesis or to Wells's thought on matters closely related to *The War of the Worlds*.

The novel's gestation, its background and themes, and its critical reception are explored in the Introduction, and Appendix I provides a transcript and collation of the oldest surviving fragment of *The War of the Worlds* manuscript. The text of the novel is (with certain modifications indicated on p. 43) that of the Atlantic edition of 1924—a reissue of the original editions of 1898 from new plates, corrected by Wells. The annotations contain much new factual material and also supply a wide range of critical perspectives by drawing freely on the wealth of published commentary on specific passages in the novel. Finally, a note on radio and film adaptations and the articles included in the appendixes augment the annotations from a variety of standpoints, ranging from episodes of pirating in the novel's publishing history to historical observation of lights on the planet Mars.

This project has been a labor of love for both of us. In undertaking it we have enriched our understanding of *The War of the Worlds* and enhanced our enjoyment and admiration of it. Our hope is that this edition will arouse new critical and scholarly interest in Wells's novel.

D.Y.H.
H.M.G.

ACKNOWLEDGMENTS

For expert help and criticism at various stages in the preparation of this edition, grateful acknowledgment is made to Bruce Harkness, Robert M. Philmus, Patrick Parrinder, David J. Lake, Philip Moses, and the anonymous reader engaged by the Indiana University Press; and special thanks go to Gene K. Rinkel, Curator of Rare Books, the University of Illinois at Urbana, for unfailing, indispensable assistance in working the resources of the Wells archive.

Material by H.G. Wells Copyright by the Literary Executors of the Estate of H.G. Wells. Limited world rights granted by the Executors and by the University of Illinois. Permissions for "Gestation" and "Appendix II" granted respectively by *Cahiers Victoriens et Edouardiens* and *Journalism Quarterly*.

D.Y.H.
H.M.G.

INTRODUCTION

Gestation[1]

H. G. WELLS began composition of *The War of the Worlds* (hereafter *W W*) in the summer of 1895, but some of his ideas went back ten years. In a student debate of 1885, he argued the case for mental giantism and physical atrophy akin to the Martians' but occurring in future human evolution,[2] and in 1893 he developed this thesis in an essay to which he referred in *W W*, "The Man of the Year Million," envisaging a humanity of mere brains and hands (see *W W* II.2.6 [in this and subsequent references to the text of the present edition, the roman numeral denotes the book, the first arabic number the chapter, and the second a note, if any] and Appendix III). In an 1888 debate, he upheld the proposition that "the surface of Mars was occupied by living beings,"[3] which, he added in 1896, would not be humanoid (see Appendix IV). However, when he left London for suburban Surrey in March 1895, Wells seems to have had no conscious inkling of the book itself. It was shortly thereafter that his brother Frank suggested the idea of a Martian invasion. The two were strolling through the peaceful Surrey countryside when Frank remarked: "Suppose some beings from another planet were to drop out of the sky suddenly, and begin laying about them here!"[4] About that time Wells and his wife had taken up bicycling, and he later recalled exploring Surrey and finding himself "marking down suitable places and people for destruction by my Martians."[5] Frank's remark had fallen on fertile ground.

Actual composition took place in three spurts in the late summer and early fall of 1895, in the first half of 1896, and in the last quarter of 1897. Two letters mark the 1895 period. W. E. Henley remarks (September 5, 1895): "I am waiting with the greatest interest, the keenest curiosity, to see what comes of the Martialist visitation: the idea is so strong, & you are working it out with so much gusto, that I have great hopes of it."[6] Wells himself, in a letter of October 15, said he had "in hand" and prospectively ready by "early in 1896" or sooner, "a scientific romance" that "will be called 'The War of the Worlds' & will run to perhaps 75000 words."[7] But some months later the story was far from finished, and the second writing spurt is marked by a letter from the Authors' Syndicate to Wells and five from Wells to the Syndicate (early January to late March 1896) that show him hard at work on it. As he said nearly two years later (November 25, 1897): "*The War of the Worlds* . . . had a whole half year to itself—the first half of 1896, & for the last month I have been rewriting it."[8] That is, he was by this time concluding the final, 1897, spurt of composition. In

April 1896, he had sold the British serial rights to *Pearson's Magazine*, promising "complete & finished copy no later than August 1st,"[9] and now, fifteen months later, he was perfecting *Pearson's* (hereafter P) for the Heinemann edition of late January 1898 (hereafter L, for London). Incidentally, whenever P is cited (it ran April–December 1897) the source is Alan K. Russell's *Collector's Book of Science Fiction by H. G. Wells* (1978), a continuously paginated, otherwise photographic reproduction of several Wells stories in their periodical form, P among them.

The surviving manuscripts came to the University of Illinois in five holograph sheaves, plus the Atlantic edition galleys. (The manuscript page numbers cited in this volume are regrettably muddled because before numeration by Illinois, the sheaves were jumbled by many users.) All the sheaves bear directions to be typed in triplicate, but no typescripts survive. Three of the sheaves constitute Wells's revision of P for book publication (initially as L). Two of these paste-ups of P correspond respectively to "Book I" and "Book II" of L, and the third (with directions to be interpolated into the second) is the manuscript of "The Man on Putney Hill." The three mark Wells's final spurt of composition of late 1897 and are here designated as PR or separately as PR1, PR2, and PR3. The other two sheaves belong to 1896, before serial publication. The shorter is a draft of the narrator's closing philosophical reflections (hereafter CD, for "coda"). The longer (hereafter MS), the fragment transcribed and collated in Appendix I, begins when the narrator leaves the ruined house (in the chapter later entitled "The Stillness") and covers his wandering in dead London and his homecoming. But between the ruined house and dead London it contains the hitherto unpublished "Marriott" segment. In due course, in L, "Marriott" would be replaced by PR3, "Putney Hill," the artilleryman episode. But meanwhile, in P "Marriott" would simply be suppressed without trace. In fact, MS is so abridged in P that the MS and CD portions of P form only the last two chapters, whereas MS is so augmented in L that the MS and CD portions of L form the last five chapters. Thus, the Illinois holdings provide a fairly complete record of the development of the last third of *W W* from the drafts of 1896 (MS and CD), through the serial of 1897 (P), to the revisions and additions of late 1897 (PR) made for the book (L), which was published in early 1898; and slight revisions continue through the Atlantic edition galleys of 1924.

On the other hand, the record of the first two-thirds of *W W* begins only with the serial, P, in 1897, and even then it is incomplete. Of twenty-seven chapters in L (seventeen in Book I, ten in Book II), the first fifteen continually diverge a little from P (rarely by more than a word or two), but few of the changes are supplied by PR. There, P is pasted up nearly untouched. Wells evidently revised later (perhaps in L's proofs), and the revision is lost. Only with the last two chapters of Book I does PR begin to provide some of L's changes; yet the two texts coincide less than ever because those changes much outpace the fraction that PR supplies. On the other hand, in Book II, while the degree of revision increases exponentially beyond anything in Book I, it is PR which is the source of virtually all of it, often verbatim. It thus turns out that the last third of *W W* is the area of dense manuscript survival, both from before P (in MS) and after it (in PR).

The interesting, and earliest, document is MS, inasmuch as the "Marriott" segment—of just seven holograph pages—comprises an alternative plot line. As noted above, in all versions the narrator progresses from imprisonment above the Martian pit, to dead London, to homecoming. In P and L, the imprisonment is near London, at Sheen. In MS, imprisonment is at Byfleet, near home in Woking and wife in Leatherhead, and when the narrator escapes, he ceases searching for his wife only when kindly folk who feed him bear witness that the Heat-Ray must have killed her. He then turns dramatically north to London—packing a bomb procured in Kingston from the formidable Marriott—bent upon dying in a single-handed assault on the Martians' Primrose Hill redoubt (where of course they lie already dead). Blood revenge is his motive. On the other hand, in P and L, the disorder of war has already removed him far Londonward from home before imprisoning him. The alien red landscape that startles him after his imprisonment—in MS purely an atmospheric touch—now plays directly upon his disoriented state of mind, which soon leads him into the necropolis itself. But by interpolating just before his entry into London his collusion with the wolfish artilleryman, L infiltrates still another note—whereby the narrator is not only ousted from domesticity but takes it as a holiday.

MS affords another striking contrast to printed texts in what the narrator "remembers" as he views the scenes of his adventures from the window of the train that carries him home after the death of the Martians. In all the texts he is reminded of his recent dangers. In the printed versions, he remembers events from both before and after passing through Byfleet en route to his accidental imprisonment in Sheen. From before Byfleet he recalls the apparition of the Martian tripod in the thunderstorm and an initial meeting with the artilleryman, and from after Byfleet the destruction of Shepperton and (in P only) the interval with the curate ending in the latter's death. On the other hand, though the MS narrator recalls the pre-Byfleet incidents of tripod and artilleryman, he has no thought of Shepperton or of the curate. One infers, therefore, that when, at some time later than MS, Wells set the imprisonment nearer London—in Sheen, not Byfleet—he opened the door to intercalate the episodes of Shepperton and the curate, the first of which served also to disorient the narrator, leading him away from his wife in Leatherhead and toward London. Expansion by interpolation is of course consistent with episodic structure, and later (in PR3)

Wells balanced and complemented the creation of the puling curate with that of the lawless artilleryman.

Also, the MS narrator both summarizes and disclaims the contents of Chapters XV–XVII of Book I of printed texts. A pasted-on paragraph describes the Black Smoke, which is central to Chapter XV, seemingly for the first time; and clearly the brother's story of the London exodus and the victorious demise of the ram _Thunder Child_ (Chapters XVI–XVII) did not yet exist, for the narrator mentions a London brother only to rule his testimony out, because the evacuation of greater London "northward" and "an account of the exhausting scenes along the south coast & down the mouth of the Thames, where countless ships were presently embarking the terror-stricken multitudes, at exorbitant charges, scarcely falls within the scope of my personal experiences." Moreover, tantalizingly, the MS typist is told: "Omit this in copy B and insert a blank sheet," as if Wells had other or future plans.[10] When he worked them out, he let go of the "scenes along the south coast" and an allusion to three battleships sunk in the Solent and focused on the brother's escape to the east, culminating in the set-piece of the _Thunder Child_ and Martians in the Thames estuary.

That Wells after completing MS went back and interpolated much at earlier points is further indicated by his five letters to the Authors' Syndicate and the one surviving response. The latter indicates that when negotiations for serialization began, the story was unfinished and very likely broke off somewhere near the point where MS begins. Pearson received an unfinished draft, liked it as far as it went, but wanted to see the conclusion. Wells adorned the request for his wife's amusement with a "picshua" (reproduced, with the letter, in _Experiment in Autobiography_) of a horned devil pulling an acceptable end to his "tale" from an ink pot preparatory to swapping it for a sack of money on the "serial chopping block." The sack is labeled "£200." The letter is dated March 14, 1896, and the latest date of the five letters on Wells's part is March 26.

These five reveal Wells struggling with Pearson for space, and they thereby throw light on the calendar of the Black Smoke (History of the War in Surrey), the London Exodus, and the _Thunder Child_ interpolations; and they show Wells planning on a scale he never fully realized. In 1895, he had forecast 75,000 words; he now wanted 60,000 (a length he achieved only with book publication); but a standard serial was about 40,000. In the first letter (January 2, 1896), he reports that Heinemann will do the book but that British and American serial rights are for sale. With the second letter (received January 22), he sends a "sketch," since more would "hamper me" from "doing my very best on this thing." In the third letter (received February 3), _Pearson's_ having stipulated only 42,000 words, he promises "a sufficient sample" in two weeks, but adds, "Pearson, if the story has to be cut, should pay as for 60000 say." In the fourth letter (received March 26) he writes: "If Pearson is going to mew about with demands to see all the story, & restrictions as to length, & so forth, it might be worth while to consider Jerome [K. Jerome]." With the last letter (also March 26), he sends "rest of copy in the immaturest state" and plans to

> insert a chapter after what is at present XIV describing one vivid scene of "the Exodus from London[,]" & a brief resume of the History of the Martian war after what is now XV. What is now XVII will be ruthlessly cut down & probably merged with what is now XVI. But these things cannot be definitely stated at this stage.

Also, he will be "immensely gratified" if he can have 60,000 words and nine installments, since he is "cutting out some magnificent fighting, Martian v. Ironclad & an episode of a lost child & so forth, which will be written for the book."[11]

What Wells "ruthlessly cut down" cannot be determined (apparently not "Marriott," since it does not figure in the letters). In any case, P has nine installments—Wells essentially prevailing over Pearson—yet, curiously, it has only about 50,000 words, not the 60,000 Wells spoke of, and the ninth installment shows signs of padding. Although Chapter XVII, "The *Thunder Child,*" is in P, even though Wells said it would not be, and although Chapter XVI, also in P, seems originally to have been intended for the book inasmuch as it has a slight incident of "a lost child," and although the promised history of the Martian war occupies Chapter XV, even so, the ninth installment evidently had to be expanded. The latter part of MS is an early draft of most of that installment, but after the homecoming MS ends and Wells tacked on the contents of CD. The headnote to CD tells the typist: "Type write in top corner 'Not for Pearson.' " But there it is in P, and indeed the ninth installment would be short without it.

Incidentally, even afterwards, revised as a separate chapter—as L's "The Epilogue"—CD may not have been Wells's ending of choice. Wells wrote into PR2 after the homecoming, "The End," and tore the rest off; and the Harpers edition of March 1898 (hereafter NY, for New York)—based on PR2 independent of L—duly omits "The Epilogue." But William Heinemann in effect required it. Ironically, the 50,000 words that *Pearson's* permitted Wells so grudgingly, he had grudgingly to extend for Heinemann. Only the latter's half of the correspondence survives. As early as January 3, 1897, even before P began to be serialized, a Heinemann editor started the campaign by congratulating Wells on adding five pages "because the book really is very short."[12] On October 13, Heinemann himself sent Wells two sample pages, "with either of which the book will make 288 pages," and he declared that in his experience it should be longer, although he was "in no way concerned artistically, but simply and solely from the one point of view that the plain man wants a certain amount of reading for six shillings."[13] To an obviously feeble counterproposal by Wells, Heinemann two days later responded with a specific plea for "even sixteen or twenty pages more" so as "to turn the 300,—say make the book 304 pages" (it actually contains 303 pages), adding, "I don't think under any circumstances that in a book which we are trying to make a splash of we could include a short story— the most vital of all objections on the part of the B[ritish] P[ublic]."[14] Wells capitulated and very likely cannibalized the old P ending for twelve of the fifteen pages he added. But the curious history ends with the fact that the Atlantic edition of 1924, retaining L's "The Epilogue," otherwise reflects the epilogue-less NY. In a matter of such importance, Wells of 1924 is an untrustworthy editor of 1898—assuming the decision was his; in any case, however, "The Epilogue" provides a suitable thematic coda.

By October 13, 1897, Heinemann had 288 pages worth of copy. The artilleryman episode, PR3, seems to be included, since the twenty-six pages it adds would otherwise exceed the total of 303. How much earlier it was composed is uncertain. One might conjecture that Wells wrote it when he scrapped "Marriott," then held it in reserve, since *Pearson's* wanted the story curtailed. However, a sense of Wells's timetable for revision of P emerges from a curious episode of secondary newspaper serialization. On November 8, Hearst publications remitted twenty-one guineas on behalf of the New York *Evening Journal*.[15] How the *Journal* localized events to New York and the Hudson River, and how Wells unsuspectingly authorized the Boston *Post* to proceed "as New York Journal" (whereupon the *Post* caused the Martians to enter Boston through Lexington and Concord), all that story—and how enraged Wells was when he discovered the truth about Boston (which perhaps he never learned about New York)—is told elsewhere.[16] The point here is that Wells instructed his typist: "This is wanted to send to America (where the story is now appearing in a New York paper). Send each day's work as done. N.B. It is only the stuff for America I am in a hurry for until Dec. 1st" (Illinois, 100). The "stuff" consisted of the section of PR that is most heavily revised, namely, the first seven chapters of Book II, ending with the artilleryman. The remainder of Book II was revised later. Thus, as the chief but by no means only part of the newspapers' package, the artilleryman episode looks even more like the late inspiration it appears to be on the face of it.[17]

The newspapers bear no textual authority, of course. The *Journal* ran the serial from December 15 through January 7, 1898, and the *Post* from January 9 through February 3 (and afterwards both ran Garrett P. Serviss's "Edison's Conquest of Mars"—presumably on the theory that turnabout is fair play). Following Wells's directions except for changing the locale of the story, they began by copying the American *Cosmopolitan* serial (hereafter C), which is the same as P but a somewhat less perfected text; they switched to the corrected typescripts of PR2 and PR3 up to the point (near the beginning of L's "Dead London") where Wells instructs his typist to write, " 'rest of copy follows the printed story in *Cosmopolitan*, which see' " (Illinois, 92); and they then reverted to C. Perhaps Wells directed the use of C at both ends of the story less for convenience (C being on hand in the United States) than because only in PR3 and the portion of PR2 leading up to PR3 was he offering anything really new (and maybe he had promised that much). Whatever the reason, it turns out that L—barring slight enlargement of the last three chapters—is not the first complete version of *W W*, an honor that was preempted by the New York and Boston sensationalizations.

Aside from the newspapers, C was not transmitted further. It approximates P but is continually a little closer to MS and CD. Transatlantic lag doubtless accounts for the use of a less-perfected typescript in America. Wells had dropped the Authors' Syndicate and hired J. B. Pinker as his agent. Pinker advised him on June 12, 1896, that in order to avoid any appearance of flooding the market, they should hold back the manuscript of *The Invisible Man* (then entitled "The Man at the Coach and Horses")[18] until after Pinker could close with America for serial rights to *W W*. On July 9, Pinker added that in his hurry to sell the rights and thanks to inheriting the Syndicate's muddle, he had been forced to send to America "the unrevised manuscript that I had in the office."[19] (He also reports a feeler from Harpers for book publication.) On August 25, *Cosmopolitan* cabled acceptance.[20]

The latter part of L correlates well with PR2/PR3, but, as already noted, the earlier part of L derives from some source later than PR1. It must be added that although PR1 is a paste-up of P, in actuality PR2 is a paste-up of P's proofs (hereafter PP). That is, PR2, the area of finished revision, which most nearly approaches the copy text of L, turns out to be revised from proofs—rather than from pages—of P. The anomaly is explicable assuming that Wells pasted up PR1 expecting to proceed sequentially from the beginning; that suddenly the December 1, 1897 newspaper deadline caused him instead to turn directly to the later chapters, where major revision was needed; and that he had no choice but to use PP because the requisite pages of P were not out yet. But no doubt "until Dec. 1st" explains not merely his using proofs but, notably, *uncorrected* proofs, as if the corrected ones were at the printer's. The proofs comprising PP and revised in PR are spares— not used for P—since they lack any emendations that first appear in P, save purely formal ones. Moreover, PR is based not only first on pages (through installment 6 and L's Chapter XVI) and then on proofs, but apparently first on late and then on early proofs. The proofs of installment 7 appear to be late; they match P in text and pagination. Installments 8 and 9 (the last two) seem early; they are emended in P, and the sheets of each begin numbering simply from 1. Thus, newspaper serialization appears to have dictated selection of PP as PR's textual base (aside from PR3) from "The *Thunder Child*" to the end (that is, excluding "The Epilogue," which is not part of PR).

Comparison of installments 8 and 9 of PP with the same in P and PR2 is revealing of Wells's penchants both for touch-up and for rewriting. In P, the two installments have been tinkered with lightly, presumably when Wells proofed PP's originals. In PR, besides new tinkering never overlapping significantly with P, there is wholesale revision that sometimes obliterates the tinkering of P altogether. Wells habitually made slight corrections, to the overall improvement of the given text, then was careless of their fate. Parallel texts—P and C, say, or L and NY—often vary with little to choose between them in the likes of word order and nonessential particulars—numbers, distances, colors—disparities certainly not all attributable to editors. Heinemann warned Wells of expenses for corrections in proof, and years later fussy emendations appear in the Atlantic galleys.[21]

On the other hand, PR2 is a true overhaul, variously suppressing, reordering, interpolating. The major interpolations are "The Man on Putney Hill," discussed above, and "The Days of Imprisonment" (II,3). Here, Wells greatly extends the description of the Martians and their machinery, and thereby provides a circumstantial rationale for the disintegration of civilized behavior in the two observers—the narrator and the curate. Otherwise, the following three brief examples will serve to illustrate how he transposed, deleted, and added. He slightly rearranged Book II, Chapter I to delay the narrator's immediately inferring that a Martian cylinder had landed nearly on his head. The recognition—natural after an interval of recovery and with the arrival of dawn—was improbable in darkness and amid the concussion of the cylinder's impact. In the next chapter, he excised three paragraphs from a defense of the Martians against charges of wanton cruelty, paragraphs of special pleading that sound like an anti-antivivisectionist tract. On the other hand, he inserted five memorable paragraphs earlier in the chapter, portraying a Martian handling-machine as incorporating operator into mechanism, cyborg-like. The depiction ends with a barb for Warwick Goble, whose illustrations of P Wells detested. Cosmo Rowe, his first choice, proved dilatory[22] and produced only three drawings, so the rest were Goble's. Accordingly, the narrator is now made to warn his readers that the "renderings" that illustrated "one of the first pamphlets to give a consecutive account of the war" were "no more like the Martians I saw in action than a Dutch doll is like a human being."

Ultimately, textual authority passes to NY, the Atlantic copy text for all but "The Epilogue" (as noted above). No dates have turned up for NY except the feeler of July 1896 reported by Pinker, and publication in late March 1898, two months after L. NY is essentially the L text, but it seems a more carefully corrected variant. David Lake has collated L and the Atlantic and shows that readings in the latter are generally superior,[23] and it may be added that the source of improvement is NY. Thus, the development of the text up to book publication begins in the summer of 1895 but leaves no physical trace; it moves on to the period of intense composition of the first half of 1896, of which the surviving manuscripts are MS, with its suicidal narrator; CD (the coda), suppressed in NY but retained everywhere else; and possibly (but not likely) PR3, the artilleryman episode; and the process winds up with a rush of revision in October–November 1897, the probable time of composition of PR3 and certainly of PR1 and PR2, the paste-ups of P. Finally, let it be noted that in the same period, besides volumes of essays and of short stories, Wells wrote *The Invisible Man,* which was begun later than *W W* and published earlier; and, as he said in the November 1897 letter cited above, "the rest of my time since August 1896 has been given to two still incomplete works," namely, *Love and Mr. Lewisham* and *When the Sleeper Wakes.* Only in terms of this total discourse is the interlacement of the texts of *W W* to be seen in its true proportions.

Background and Themes

The plot of *W W* is "apocalyptic" in the commonly accepted sense of unveiling a predestined future cataclysm of extrahuman proportions which destroys the world as we know it but eventuates in the triumph of good over evil. The cataclysm is predestined because the Martians are driven by what Wells elsewhere called "the Calvinism of science,"[24] that is, the inexorability of natural law, meaning the second law of thermodynamics and the degradation of solar energy. The invasion brings evil, which is death, but the invaders are overthrown and life on earth is redeemed.

To these archetypal apocalyptic events, Wells invokes three responses— the curate's Scriptural response, the narrator's moral and intellectual experimentalism,[25] and the artilleryman's survivalist-authoritarian response— reactions which in turn may usefully be examined in terms of the respective horizons of Wells's past, present, and future—while overall *W W* presents itself as an exploratory document whose readers must bridge into the world that is dawning after the invasion.[26] The Martians themselves, the most complex creations in the book, are already the victims of the forces they exert.

1

It is customary to write off the ranting curate as "no more than a conventional anti-clerical butt."[27] The characterization is apt. A page after meeting him, both narrator and reader are "beginning to take his measure" (I. 13). It is therefore all the more remarkable that it takes several chapters to kill him off. Though he is a straw man, the curate dies hard, being propped up by the bogeyman pieties of boyhood that Wells repudiated but never entirely escaped. Looking back in 1906, he wrote:

> To me in my boyhood speculation about the Future was a monstrous joke. Like most people of my generation I was launched into life with millennial assumptions. This present sort of thing . . . was going on for a time . . . and then . . . there would be trumpets and shoutings and celestial phenomena, a battle of Armageddon and the Judgment. [*The Future in America*, p. 6.]

By 1906, it was already possible for Wells to dissect the carcass of the age of Victoria with twentieth-century hindsight. The next two quotations show him rebelling while the monster still lived and he was its captive:

> One night [as a boy of eleven or twelve] I had a dream of Hell so preposterous that it blasted that undesirable resort out of my mind for ever. . . . There was Our Father in a particularly malignant phase, busy basting a poor broken sinner rotating slowly over a fire built under the wheel. I saw no Devil in the vision; my mind in its simplicity went straight to the responsible fountain head. . . . Never had I hated God so intensely. [*Experiment in Autobiography* (1934), p. 45.]

> I know now that the whole Universe is a sham, a tin simulacrum of ideals, veneered deal pretending to mahogany. If I had not been an ass, I should have understood that, when the cardboard religious structure I constructed in my kid- and calfhood caved in when I came to lean on it. [Letter to Elizabeth Healey, June 14, 1888, Wells Archive.[28]]

Wells the boy returns the onus of sin upon God, and Wells the adolescent shifts the burden from God to the "cardboard" structure of religion, a more tangible target.

In *W W*, the scapegoat is the curate, victim less of the Martians than of his suicidal delusion that they are agents of God's vengeance. "Drop that book of Revelations," the narrator tells him (in the serial version), "and be a man"; and (again in the serial version, which is generally more explicit) Wells causes the curate to certify out of his own mouth that God is a torturer and religion a futile mummery: "I have been nothing but human self-complacency in a cassock and gown," he says. "Social work! Bazaars!—Folly! The fear of the Lord is the beginning of wisdom—the *fear* of the Lord is the beginning of wisdom."[29]

Revenant as he is of the religion of Wells's childhood, the curate clings to the Scriptures. Simultaneously, the narrator's understanding is enlarged. By the eighth day of their accidental imprisonment by the Martians (II.4), the curate's ravings drive the narrator, "with one last touch of humanity," to take the butt of a meat chopper to him just before a Martian probe alerted by the yelling drags the unconscious body off. But during the days of the curate's mounting madness, the narrator closely observes the Martians. Both men watch them obsessively and fight for the one spy-hole, but the curate already "knows" them for messengers of God's wrath, whereas in the narrator fear breeds curiosity. Seen from the darkness of the ruined house in "the pitiless sunlight of that terrible June" (II.3), the vision of the Martians burns in, and he lives through it again in memory: the wonder of their appearance, anatomy, routines, processes, and functions, and of their technology. In this way, the device of the peep-hole binds the reader both to the murky struggle within and to the forbidden knowledge without, and bridges between them.

In his dealings with the curate, the narrator swings between lethargy and violence. In other situations, he is capable of acting coolly and decisively. At Weybridge, he leads the life-saving rush from the Heat-Ray into the river; and earlier, upon the first attack of the Martians, he finagles a horse and cart from an unsuspecting local innkeeper and drives to safety with his wife and servant while the innkeeper pays with his life. Yet he tolerates the curate's noisy, dangerous presence for two days before their imprisonment and for another eight days after it, until he resorts to the desperate blow that silences the clergyman and might preserve some hope of their escape; but by then, ironically, murder is his intention. Later, he blames his loss of control on mutual "incompatibility" (II.3) and calls himself "the creature of a sequence of accidents" (II.7). He forgets that an early showdown would have rid him of the troublesome tagalong before things escalated. Why the inaction, the rage, and simultaneously the cognitive daring of observing the Martians? The intensity of the fusion is beyond its components—and probably owes much to life.

Wells never forgot that at one time he capitulated to institutionalized religion. The story of his many breakouts—from family poverty, from the limitations of a meager schooling that was scheduled to end at the age of fourteen, and, later, from marriage and monogamy—is well known from his autobiographies and novels. Perhaps the most momentous in its consequences was his rebellion against slogging in the dry goods business. At age seventeen, after having been indentured by his mother to the draper's trade for three years and after earlier abortive efforts at escape, he secured a post as a student-teacher at the Midhurst Grammar School; and he was forced onto the horns of a dilemma. The school's statutes required him to accept confirmation as a member of the Church of England or lose his job. Against his conscience, he accepted confirmation. The connection of *W W* to that surrender may be noted in the narrator's dreamlike inertness and brutality in the face of the curate's deterioration and his concomitant assimilation of new, frightening, powerful knowledge as he observes the Martians. This sequence bears the psychological marks of the "choice" imposed on Wells by the educational establishment of his day as the price of admission to higher learning.

Wells's description of his confirmation in *Experiment in Autobiography* is revealing. He accepted confirmation because he felt he had to get out of the dry goods or die, and Midhurst was his only chance. "To have abandoned it now would have been like jumping from a liner in mid-Atlantic." But the stakes would turn out to be even higher. What neither he nor the headmaster could know was that enrollment at Midhurst would become a stepping-stone to the Normal School of Science in South Kensington and the classroom of T. H. Huxley. Just at this time (1884), the British Education Department in order to raise standards inaugurated cash prizes for students and their teachers, to be split fifty-fifty, for each "first" a student made on a set of standard examinations. Highly motivated by the torment of the drapery and by a genuine thirst for knowledge, Wells took "firsts" in the entire range of subjects, boning up on his own. He did it, as he says, "with such a bang that I was blown out of Midhurst altogether." As a bolt from the blue, he found himself among the first crop of scholarship students chosen for the training in biology under Huxley, which for Wells became the central formative experience of his intellectual development.[30]

In the autobiography the section on his confirmation is headed "Question of Conscience," and, although Wells deprecates his "queer little struggle between pride and practical wisdom," he records that his "private honour" was deeply wounded, so that "it was many years before I could forgive the church . . . [and] I do not think that I have forgiven her altogether even now." Moreover, he recalls in detail the scene between him and the curate who prepared him—"a fair aquiline sensitive young man," who may well be the original of the one in *W W*—as they sat by lamplight opposite each other at a table in the curate's lodgings. Wells had to accept the instruction, but not before putting the cleric through his paces:

> I asked a string of questions about the bearing of Darwinism and geology on biblical history, about the exact date of the Fall, about the nature of Hell, about Transubstantiation and the precise benefit of the communion service and so forth. After each answer I would say "So that is what I have to believe—I see." I did not attempt to argue. He was one of those people whose faces flush . . . and whose voices get higher in pitch at the slightest need for elucidation.

Wells concludes by noting that he "communicated and consumed a small cube . . . and had a lick of sweetish wine . . . [and] to please my mother repeated this performance . . . [once] and after that . . . made an end to Theophagy"; but of course in *The War of the Worlds* the blood of the God-eating curate[31] flows into the "recipient canal" of a Martian.

Such is God's passing; but like Wells and the first readers of *W W*, the narrator was born in the old time. He bridges between the Scriptural and the scientific world views. Contemptuous of the curate, all the same he prays "fetish prayers" while the curate lives and afterwards prays "steadfastly and sanely" for his wife's safety, "face to face with the darkness of God" (II.7); and when he discovers the Martians dead in their pit atop Primrose Hill, he believes for a time that "the Angel of Death had slain them in the night"—as the miracle of the plague slew Sennacherib's army. Even in retrospect it still seems to him that their fate was Providential: "slain, after all man's devices had failed, by the humblest things that God, in his wisdom, has put upon this earth." What is more, the very cause of death—the rationalization which is the book's single most striking claim to the title of hard-core science fiction—acquires a Scriptural inflection: "By the toll of a billion deaths, man has bought his birthright of the earth and it is his against all comers; it would still be his were the Martians ten times as mighty as they are. For neither do men live nor die in vain." It is a morality play. Bacteria redeem humanity as Christ redeemed the faithful from the envious Satanic hosts in the Scriptural and Miltonic accounts. On the other hand, the rationalization itself is strictly empirical and positivist, attributing earth's escape to systemic immunity. For this inconsistency, the narrator is not viewed ironically. The reader is invited to identify with his state of mind, which is muddy, yet open, watchful, and alert.

Of course, in themselves, "muddy" emotional states are no good; no good "losing our heads, and rushing off in crowds," as the artilleryman puts it; no good letting "the emotional substratum"[32] rule the roost. The very preeminence of Martian intellect is measured by nothing if not by human irrationality—for instance, by the dumb fascination of the people nosing around the strange cylinder on Horsell Common, "poised between centrifugal dread and centripetal curiosity,"[33] until they break before the Heat-Ray and bolt "as blindly as a flock of sheep" (I.6) leaving trampled bodies behind. This sequence is repeated on a large scale in the idle curiosity of London followed by the stampede on the Great North Road and the tangle of shipping in the Thames. Elements of the alarmed social organism behave with suicidal irrationality. More rational is the kamikaze bravery of the *Thunder-Child*, or the coolness of the soldiers at St. George's Hill, who "laid their guns as deliberately as if they had been on parade" (I.15), destroyed a Martian tripod, and were swept out of existence by the Heat-Ray.

Perhaps most "muddy" of all is the narrator, with his "storms of emotion" (I.11) and periods of "detachment" (I.7), and, surprisingly, the presumptive evidence from the manuscripts is that Wells deliberately intensified the narrator's errant behavior in successive major revisions. Waywardness seems to have formed no part of the original conception of the narrator, neither in circumstances nor in conduct. The surviving manuscript fragment (Appendix I) finds the narrator quite domesticated. It begins as he emerges from captivity in the ruined house. Significantly, the town is Byfleet, meaning that in this version (1) he must have been imprisoned almost as soon as he set out to return to his wife in Leatherhead; (2) upon gaining his freedom, he is physically on course for Leatherhead rather than being north of the Thames in Sheen; and (3) it seems unlikely he had traveled far enough before his imprisonment to have met the curate (nor is the latter's death ever mentioned). Accordingly, the narrator sets off immediately to rejoin his wife, with no thought other than that imperative and no distracting encounter about to occur with the artilleryman on Putney Hill. Instead, soon learning that Leatherhead has been destroyed by the Martians and that nobody could have survived, he dedicates himself to avenging his wife's presumed death. As quickly as possible, by forced march, he procures dynamite in Richmond and moves on Primrose Hill, intending himself as a human bomb. The rest is much as in other versions, ending with the reunion with his wife, the triteness of which, jarring elsewhere, here is on a level with the revenge fantasy. The actions are as predictable as they are overdetermined.

In the next stage, the *Cosmopolitan* and *Pearson's* serial (1897), the curate's role is included, the place of imprisonment has been shifted north to Sheen, and the narrator is nothing like his former self. He acts like a man well free of domesticity. Directly he escapes imprisonment, he proceeds to London, as if Leatherhead were out of the question. As will also be true in the book, he seems to be under a magic spell continually to be thinking of his wife but mysteriously unable to act on the wish. His plan had been to hurry from Woking to Leatherhead, then go south and escape with her by sea (Russell, Chapter 12; or I.12), but in fact on meeting the artilleryman (not the later Putney Hill encounter, which occurs only in the book), he volunteers to guide him to Weybridge, placing St. George's Hill between himself and his wife. From Weybridge he drifts north on the river, wanders north with the curate—whereas Leatherhead is southeast—and then, after captivity, continues north, to London. His motives are not obvious, nor are any given. Meanwhile, his brother rescues two ladies he never saw before, takes them away by sea, and wins their reciprocal aid in doing it despite danger and hardship.

In the book version, these curiously evasive actions of the narrator persist unchanged, but now he makes repeated disclaimers, such as the following: "my impotent desire to reach Leatherhead"; "I paced the rooms and cried aloud when I thought of how I was cut off from her"; "my fixed idea of reaching Leatherhead" (I.13, II.1). Indeed, it is persuasively argued by John Huntington[34] that the narrator resents marriage, as indicated by his permitting his "war fever" to separate him from his wife in the first place. Huntington points out that in the following series—which is not in the serial—the narrator simultaneously betrays anger at his wife and projects it onto the figure of the curate the moment they meet:

> For a long time I drifted, so painful and weary was I after the violence I had been through. . . . At last I landed on the Middlesex bank [not the Leatherhead side]. . . . It is a curious thing that I felt angry with my wife; I cannot account for it, but my impotent desire to reach Leatherhead worried me excessively.
> I do not clearly remember the arrival of the curate. . . . [I.13.]

Right on cue, here enters the man whom the narrator—again in the book only—later calls "as lacking in restraint as a silly woman" (II.3). Thus, the curate's obvious function of religious scapegoat is duplicated, so to speak, domestically. But this aspect of transferred homicidal rage must be unconscious on Wells's part, augmenting the curious intensity of the relationship of the narrator and the curate. To the extent that the curate's death represents a sublimated sexual breakout, one can see why the narrator later disowns contrition, claiming (in the book only) that he committed no crime because the urge was not premeditated (II.7).

It may be argued that the very muddle of the narrator's feelings enables him, by acting them out, to win for himself a psychic "space," if not at the time then later in his reflective mode as memoirist. His mood swings are legion: "anguish" in fleeing the Heat-Ray, "the strangest sense of detachment" on reaching safety, "erethism" in reciting the adventure that night at the dinner table (I.7); passivity and then the "flash of rage" against the curate (II.3); "stupid receptivity" digging with the artilleryman, "vivid delight" playing cards with him while England collapses, then "remorse," "violent revulsion of feeling," and the determination to take the bridge to London (II.7); and, once in the city, a kaleidoscope of loneliness, fear, relief, and exaltation. Some of these feelings were within his control; most were not; they were coerced, unmanageable, conflicting, and unmediated, like their grounds in the fortunes of war. But his almost clinical awareness of them, at least in retrospect, opens up an interior space for orientation and in the long run for choice.

Even more than the introspective slant of the book compared to the serial, it is the book's introduction of the Putney Hill encounter with the artilleryman that most promotes in the narrator the sense of voluntarism. The artilleryman episode replaces what in the manuscript was the narrator's suicide march on London (which Wells had simply suppressed without trace in the serial), but now the artilleryman preempts and ironizes the narrator's words and intentions of the early draft. Here is the original peroration of the narrator as he prepares to become a dynamiter, like the anarchists then much in the news, all in the name of civilization:

> [The Martians] have destroyed all that makes life worth living to me, the social order, the security & comfort of life, art will vanish, letters, all the amenities of life. Manufacture must cease, cities vanish[,] law & order must disappear. We shall soon be driven back to the woods & forests, to lairs & hiding places, to the wilderness & the incessant struggle for food & life. We shall go back to the communism of beasts from whence we arose. [See Appendix I, p. 262.]

As if in retort, the artilleryman's credo is that "cities, nations, civilisation, progress—it's all over. . . . There won't be any more blessed concerts for a million years or so; there won't be any Royal Academy of Arts, and no nice little feeds at restaurants," but "instead of our rushing about blind, on the howl, or getting dynamite on the chance of busting them up, we've got to fix ourselves up according to the new state of affairs."

Huxley himself had labeled the reign of natural selection as "the Hobbesian war of each against all,"[35] and if verbal echo means anything, in the passage from the early draft just quoted, Wells had *Leviathan*, Chapter XIII, in mind:

> In such condition [of universal war], there is no place for industry, because the fruit thereof is uncertain, and consequently no culture of the earth; . . . no knowledge of the face of the earth; no account of time; no arts; no letters; no society; and, which is worst of all, continual fear and danger of violent death; and the life of man, solitary, poor, nasty, brutish, and short.[36]

In cataclysm, the troglodytic artilleryman thrives in Hobbesian diffidence: suspicious, hoarding, fearful, wolfish, and solitary.

On the other hand, the artilleryman's plan of scientifically directing a corps of survivalists against the Martians has some merit. The artilleryman is cast in a bad light, but his plan is justified by the fact that in "the new state of affairs" only a Social Darwinian elite can survive for any length of time, and then only if its members surrender sufficient of their private freedoms to oppose themselves to their own anarchy and the Martian power in a united body. Thus, the covenant proposed by the artilleryman is itself Hobbesian, being a voluntary contract and discipline among marauders for mutual survival. As Wells said much later with reference to Hobbes's corporate state, the problem has always been that of the headship.[37] The artilleryman would nominate himself to that position, and the weakness of his idea is really only that it begins and ends in his megalomania.

Bernard Bergonzi and John Huntington have shown that both the primordialist and the eugenicist in the artilleryman appealed seriously to Wells. In reference to the artilleryman's theme that life will be real and return to basics, Bergonzi quotes from an 1897 essay on George Gissing, where Wells speaks of

> a change that is sweeping over the minds of thousands of educated men. It is the discovery of the insufficiency of the cultivated life and its necessary insincerities; it is a return to the essential, to honourable struggle as the epic factor in life, to children as the matter of morality and the sanction of the securities of civilization.[38]

Similarly, the artilleryman holds that the Martians will do humanity a service by culling it: "the useless and cumbersome and mischievous have to die. They ought to die. They ought to be willing to die. It's a sort of disloyalty, after all, to live and taint the race." Huntington points out that Wells soon set forth the same view in nonfiction in *Anticipations* (1901) and in bloody fictional action in "The Land Ironclads" (1903), a straightforward fantasy of pacifying a nonadaptive culture by means of overpowering it with the then future invention of the tank.[39] Wells's viewpoint is that of the young technicians whose weapons "Martianize" the rustics.

Wells carefully distances the artilleryman's views, to be sure, but less by his unsympathetic character of braggart and glutton than by the form of *W W* itself. The post-apocalyptic vantage of the work ensures that events and plans and possibilities that seem immediate as the narrator relates them are yet retrospective. He looks back on the world before the invasion with veritably (and salutary) "Martian" detachment, quizzical and ironic at his own expense—for example, in recalling his delusory tranquility in Ogilvy's observatory or his later dodo-like confidence that on earth a Martian can scarcely crawl since "his own body would be a cope of lead to him" (I.7). His detachment shapes his account, which is as much history as memoir. Thus, concerning the Heat-Ray, he devotes Book I, Chapter VI to retracing events he has already recounted from personal memory, voicing them now in terms of a more generalized community memory. Also, throughout the last four chapters of Book I, he interrupts the emotionally oppressive episode of himself and the curate to recount his brother's story and to report events in Surrey that neither he nor his brother saw. The brother's story is heroic by any measure, except that being told at second hand it comes across as a specimen case, an effect which is enhanced when the narrator himself interpolates into his brother's account the figure of an imaginary balloonist looking down on the frantic dots beneath (I.17).

These perspectives create a space, not an ironic or esthetic space between Wells and his narrator but a shared space, which is mutually therapeutic.[40] In the 1890s, that space would be like the unbridged space in *1984* when one wondered whether it was prophecy or fiction because 1984 had not arrived. Well's putative date of invasion lay close ahead in the early twentieth century,[41] and some of the book's original, deliberate ambiguity as between fiction and prophecy is permanent.[42] As an apocalyptic book, not literally predictive but having "the same amount of conviction as one gets in a good gripping dream,"[43] it creates a space for the imagination within the machinery of cataclysm. That it is a space for the imagination and not a commitment to the world before or after the time of change is assured by means of Wells's formal device of speaking from beyond the change but before its full significance is evident, so that, unlike *1984*, *W W* looks to a further and still unknown future, in which the balance of good and evil is doubtful but hopeful because in the nearer term it will be open to human intervention.

2

Upon this note, we may now turn to the Martians and their predicament, which is also ours in the long run. *Fin de siècle* science out-"Calvined" religion regarding both nature and human nature. Mars was the future; it presented a preview of Earth's fate much as Wells had himself envisioned it in the dying sun and shore near the end of *The Time Machine* (1895): "Astronomers . . . told us dreadful lies about the 'inevitable' freezing up of the world," he later recalled. "The whole game of life would be over in a million years or less."[44] Lord Kelvin applied the cold equations of entropy to the popular religious figure of the clock and found "nothing more of mystery or of difficulty in the automatic progress of the solar system from cold matter diffused through space, to its present manifest order and beauty. . . , than there is in the winding up of a clock and letting it go till it stops."[45] Life might be a special creation of God, but it was left captive to an unconscious mechanism slowing to a halt.[46]

In the influential view of T. H. Huxley, biological Calvinism[47] went further. Leon Stover notes that Wells rejected Huxley—however much he admired the man and teacher—in that Huxley repudiated Darwin's gladiatorial theory of existence as a proper ethical guide; whereas Wells, as Stover says, believed it was "the business of utopian planning to reduce that waste [of unbridled Darwinian elimination] by regulating the law of murder for progressive ends."[48] Exactly the artilleryman's credo: the weak must go for the sake of the race. But to dwell on the difference between Huxley's and Wells's tactics may be to overlook their mutual dilemma, namely, the fear that victory will elude us by any tactics.

Huxley died in the year of *The Time Machine*, 1895, and his pessimism had deepened in his last decade. He not only accepted Kelvin's clock, he regarded the winding up and running down as the "Sisyphæan" pattern of all systems of the cosmos, whether physical or biological[49] (though the evidence of geology and paleontology persuaded him that Kelvin had shortened the sun's probable lifespan). As to the human race, he believed the "Hobbesian war of each against all"[50] was its residual condition, inherited from animal progenitors: "I know no study which is so unutterably saddening as that of the evolution of humanity," he wrote; "man . . . is a brute, only more intelligent than the other brutes"[51]—and intelligence was powerless. Huxley held the epiphenomenalist belief that "intelligent" behavior is an automatic play of neural nets and physiological reflexes, which consciousness may accompany but cannot influence[52] (any more than Kelvin's clockmaker, if any, influences the cosmic process).

Wells's early attraction to these beliefs of Huxley was noted as far back as Mark R. Hillegas's "Cosmic Pessimism in H. G. Wells's Scientific Romances" (1961), and it is amply attested to by the biological and astrophysical decline imagined in *The Time Machine* alone. In *The Island of Dr. Moreau* (1896), the particular concern is the refractoriness of the brute in the human family tree thwarting the ideal of Dr. Moreau's "rational" science. Conversely, *W W* focuses on the limitations of rationality in itself. Extreme though the development of intelligence in the Martians is, Wells suggests that they may quite possibly be "descended from beings not unlike ourselves" (II.2). Thus, our intelligence increased to any degree would still be driven, like theirs, by the mathematics of the physical universe. Intellect is but one more trick in the Darwinian toolbox that evolved it, and it seems more fatefully programed by cosmic and biological necessity than it was by religious conviction back when speculating about the future was the "monstrous joke" of Wells's boyhood.

The Martians are at the end of history, but readers of *W W* are placed in historical time, though ostensibly on the far side of the failed invasion. Similarly, in *The Time Machine*, while the heat-death of the year 30 million is a text conceded by the literate reader that cannot be forestalled, the moribund world of 802,701 (it is implied) came about because the likes of the Time Traveller's circle of hearers (who resemble science-fiction readers) will always think that the Eloi-Morlock text is a fantasy. That is, as long as human history is still unfolding, its course has political roots and consequences. In those terms—not forgetting the cosmic connection, however—the Martians may be seen as materializations of historical forces created by the human intellect and in Wells's day increasingly uncontrollable. Thus, Mark Rose suggests that the Martian vampires are "a metaphorical projection of the capitalistic industrial system of the late nineteenth century . . . [,]

a social machine created by a ruthless economic reason that sucks the life-blood out of human beings."[53]

That the Martians may represent material forces of alienation is a suggestion worth following up in terms of Wells's allegiances in nineteenth century literature. As I. F. Clarke has exhaustively demonstrated, England dispossessed was the theme of the pulp genre known as "the imaginary war," which was immensely popular in the four decades leading up to 1914. Following the success of Sir George Chesney's cautionary tale of the collapse of Britain, *The Battle of Dorking* in 1871, the British popular press time and again portrayed the fictive invasion and conquest of the island, usually by France or Germany, involving massive engagements by land and sea, the dramatic use of advanced weapons like naval rams, and usually the depiction of the panic and massacre of civilian populations.[54] The paranoia of the genre seems to have been a reflex of guilty fears occasioned by Britain's colonial aggressions, and on one level, *W W* is quintessentially the stuff of this popular journalism, as signaled by its appearance in *Pearson's* and *Cosmopolitan* magazines and the American yellow press. With brutal poetic justice, Britain suffers an invasion of a technological sophistication and indifference to native values that reiterates what Britain visited, say, upon the Tasmanians.

But the disaffection of *W W* is of a large and existential order, and the reference systems involved are correspondingly wide. Not only are the Martians everybody's foe by definition as extraterrestrials, but they colonize Earth because they are the victims at least as much as they are the agents of forces their technological superiority will not let them or us escape. The Martian technology is a mere conditioned response to the absolute facts of biological evolution and solar entropy. In the Martians, Wells invented an analogue of what the intellectual history of the nineteenth century suggested to many as our own condition.

It happens that *W W* is one of several influential works to employ an image for alienation that had had its source in an episode near the beginning of the century in the Napoleonic wars. (Incidentally, if ever there had been a threat to England's world before 1914, Napoleon had mounted it, not Germany or its imaginary forces in *The Battle of Dorking*.) The episode was Napoleon's crossing of the Beresina River in the retreat from Moscow. It was an operation massive and daring, in some ways like the evacuation at Dunkirk in World War II but associated with ultimate defeat and uncontrollable loss of human life. In literature, it soon provided a two-edged metaphor depicting humanity as driven without recourse by historical or natural necessity, whatever its voluntary sympathies. Wells may have known little or nothing of the documentary Beresina crossing,[55] but he received and further modified the literary figure, which came to him already variously modified by more or less explicit connections with Darwinism or historical materialism in at least three major authors whom he had read and admired in his early years, namely, Heinrich Heine, Karl Marx, and T. H. Huxley.[56]

To begin with Heine—and Wells in effect boasted that he modeled his London exodus on Heine's description of the city—the young German poet recalls that on his first visit to London he was gawking along Cheapside and the Strand and was pausing at a window display picturing Napoleon's passage of the Beresina, when,

> jolted out of my gazing, I looked again on the raging street, where a parti-coloured coil of men, women, and children, horses, stage-coaches, and with them a funeral, whirled groaning and creaking along, [and] it seemed to me as though all London were such a Beresina Bridge, where every one presses on in mad haste to save his scrap of life, where the daring rider stamps down the poor pedestrian, where every one who falls is lost forever; where the best friends rush, without feeling, over each other's corpses, and where thousands, weak and bleeding, grasp in vain at the planks of the bridge, and slide down into the ice-pit of death.

A rich merchant hurries along, "busy and jingling gold," and London becomes for Heine in one instant "the pulse" or "radial artery" of the world and a "stone forest" of commerce; and above it all ambles some "lazy lord who, like a surfeited god, rides by on his high horse": "Yes, over the vulgar multitude . . . soar . . . England's nobility, who regard . . . Italy as their summer garden, Paris as their social saloon, and the whole world as their inheritance."[57]

Evidently the city's energies fascinated Heine. Wells thought the account betrayed a "quite perceptible sympathy."[58] But Heine adds: "send a philosopher to London, but no poet! . . . This machine-like . . . exaggerated London smothers the imagination and rends the heart." Beresina-London—the "raging street," the "parti-coloured coil of men, women, and children, horses, stage-coaches, and with them a funeral"—was a coupling of the people and the marketplace.[59] Heine saw it from a nonindustrial vantage: "How much more pleasant and homelike it is in our dear Germany! How . . . Sabbatically quiet all things glide along . . . !"

Twenty years later, Heine's "philosopher" visited London, but *The Communist Manifesto* (1848), written there in German, in its way is as romantic as Heine's impressions. In it, bourgeois industrialism is personified as a dying giant of still demonic energies that bestrides the world, "batters down all Chinese walls," and makes continents over in its image. Referring to the bourgeoisie, "it," say Marx and Engels (and they couple "it" with a seemingly willed, in this case deadly, action), "has drowned the most heavenly ecstacies of religious fervor, of chivalrous enthusiasm, of philistine sentimentalism, in the icy water of egotistical calculation."[60] Of course, these icy waters of calculation do not physically resemble the turbulent ice floes of the Beresina or Heine's coil of Londoners and ice-pit of death, but the common denominator is what may (clumsily) be called the inorganicizing of life. Wells had little use for Marx after his student days, yet he became capable of favoring language with similar reductionism, for example, in his autobiography, where he allowed that Marx "was the first to conceive of the contemporary social process not as a permanent system of injustice and hardship but as a changing and self-destroying order."[61]

In his student days, *Science Schools Journal* (which published the first version of *The Time Machine*) reported that Wells endorsed Marxian socialism as "a new thing based on Darwinism."[62] If so, Wells was on debatable ground, but he might have cited various utterances of T. H. Huxley in his early years of bulldogging for Darwin. To explain "natural selection" to working-class audiences, Huxley would bring the idea home by metaphorically equating the mechanism of evolution with human affairs. In an 1863 lecture, he recalled a survivor of the Beresina who spotted a giant French Cuirassier striding ahead of him, wearing a large blue cloak:

> "I caught hold of his cloak, and although he . . . cut at and struck me by turns . . . I . . . would not quit my grasp until he had at last dragged me through." Here you see was a case of selective saving . . . depending for its success on the strength of the cloth of the Cuirassier's cloak. It is the same in nature; every species has its bridge of Beresina; it has to fight its way through and struggle with other species; and when well-nigh overpowered, it may be that the smallest chance, something in its colour, perhaps—the minutest circumstance—will turn the scale one way or the other.[63]

For Darwin, "struggle" and "selection" were metaphorical,[64] but in popular understanding, they were literal. Huxley may be using metaphor as Darwin does simply to show that the cloak's accidental quality of visibility is strictly equatable with evolutionary luck or chance. On the other hand, Huxley's dramatic emotional coloring suggests the subtext that evolution is purposive, that the saving and jettisoning are no mere mechanical process. Thus, the rhetorical feeling of Huxley's Beresina is that individual action ousts chance, if it is clear-headed. But even at this early point in his career, Huxley's activism is directed toward "saving" not "eliminating," as it would be still in his late lecture on evolution and ethics cited above.[65]

In *W W*, the giant Cuirassier's function is noisily usurped by the artilleryman, who turns it into a deliberate plan of saving an elite and consciously letting the others die. As already noted, Wells was considering these ideas seriously, soon was largely adopting them, and would begin to take the (revised) role of the giant Cuirassier to himself. By 1934, Huxley's Beresina Bridge would come to look to him like this:

> [*Anticipations* (1901) is] the keystone to the main arch of my work. That
> arch rises naturally from my first creative imaginations, "The Man of the
> Year Million" (written first in 1887) and "The Chronic Argonauts" [1888]
> . . . and it leads on by a logical development to . . . the efforts I am still
> making to define and arrange for myself . . . the actual factors necessary
> . . . to rescue human society from the net of tradition in which it is en-
> tangled and to reconstruct it upon planetary lines.[66]

Wells talked like this because he had come on the literary scene during a period of rapid social change and had breached the barriers of his low social origins by means of science as vision and intended career. But he distorts by creating the impression, perhaps, that "The Chronic Argonauts" (later, *The Time Machine*) was conceived as a warning or that the anemic, Martian-like "men" of "The Man of the Year Million" were intended as an object lesson (see Appendix III).[67] Prophecies of a million years and beyond are on a scale of biological and planetary evolution—and of human nonentity, and their relation to ordinary existence is oblique.

As 1900 approached and Wells was hesitating between cosmic and mundane perspectives, in *W W* he succeeded in combining the two. To take the level of Queen Victoria's England first, Wells gives times, places, sights, sounds: the whole sensory feel of London and environs. Then he "dovetails" in the Martians (I.8) and reports "the roaring wave of fear that swept through the greatest city in the world" amid the disintegrating convulsions of the social body (Book I, Chapter XVI, "The Exodus from London"). This chapter is an adaptation of Heine; it catches and amplifies Heine's dialectic of energy and deliquescence. But the stress in the two writers differs. Heine's London may suggest an allegory of death, say a Totentanz by Bruegel. Wells paints in many more specific figures than does Heine: a blind Salvation Army man bawling "Eternity! Eternity!"; a lost child and a weeping mother; a raging man in formal dress clutching his hair; an old man with a blood-stained sock shaking out his shoe; a man trampled to death as he retrieves gold coins; and the Lord Chief Justice of England dying under a hedge. Yet the figures are less allegorical than they are samplings of the panic. The narrator's brother standing at the road's edge perceives the rush of fugitives as a "torrent," "stream," "flood"; and, from a balloon, the people would have seemed so many swarming dots, *"blotted"* in places like spilled ink, "each dot a human agony." Neither writer is really allegorical. Heine's humane heart goes out in a cry to London's disinherited: "how agonising must thy hunger be . . . !" Wells adopts the stance of a scientist observing a natural process of dissolution, though enlivening it with journalistic touches.

Technology, too, is seen in terms of process and finally becomes a way of showing how little it avails its makers, in this case the Martians. It is a technology barely conceivable to an iron and steam culture, even in principle, and it not only devastates the armies sent against it but exploits terrestrial resources previously untapped. The narrator reports the mining and smelting of the (then) refractory element, aluminum, from ore to ingots in a matter of hours while he watches (II.3).[68] From the moment the first cylinder falls, "sticking into the skin of our old planet earth like a poisoned dart" (I.8), the ecosystem itself begins to be destabilized. The red weed is "metallic" to the taste[69] and acts like industrial blight. The red growths dam the Thames and its tributaries, flooding the waters out of their courses. Like a pandemia, the Martian technology breaks up and liquidates the old local powers and creates a new, fluid superspace governed by tripod and flying machine.

Yet, through the Martians, Wells represents technology as causing or accompanying the final reduction of life into the domain of the inanimate. "We men, with our bicycles and road-skates, our Lilienthal soaring-machines, our guns and sticks and so forth," says the narrator, "are just in the beginning of the evolution that the Martians have worked out" (II.2).[70] That "evolution" has relieved them of the struggle for existence (therefore microbes kill them) and eliminated the life functions of sleep, digestion, and sexuality (they reproduce by budding).[71] Taxonomically, their nearest terrestrial analogues are primitive ("degraded") marine organisms such as polyps (to which the narrator likens them). It is possible they do not possess individual consciousness. In terrestrial experience, polypoid "individuals" are (often specialized) parts of a "colony"[72] and in "folk biology"[73] are as likely to be dubbed plant as animal. The narrator thinks them telepathic; if so, consciousness may be taken to the remove of a "hive-mind," where, again in terrestrial experience, individual self-awareness is superfluous and technology is a sort of secretion, like octagonal bee cells.

The Martians represent the last stages of time, the slide into nonexistence. With or without the heightened irony that individual self-consciousness would bestow, all their intelligence is powerless to halt Kelvin's clock. Earth, the locus of life and therefore of value, is menaced with the contagion of the Martian way.[74] A mounted Martian—outdoing Heine's lazy lord on his high horse—is a head riding a prosthetic body, a "selfish intelligence, without any of the emotional substratum of the human being" (II.2), and just as a Martian's body is lifeless, so a Martianized Earth would be dead. A planet without microbes and intelligences without entrails—these are ghosts fading into nothingness.[75] But Earth is instinct with life. The microbe, especially, is its tissue, its scavenger, and its agent of renewal and change. The narrator finally credits the invasion with fostering the idea of the "commonweal of mankind." More, it fosters the idea of the commonweal of life, a Gaea vision of Mother Earth as sentient entity,[76] warts and all (including the Huxleyan "brute" in humanity).

As Carlo Pagetti suggests in his recent and fresh discussion, *I Marziani alla Corte della Regina Vittoria*: under "the apocalyptic dominion of the Martian warriors," England's "meticulously described topography and . . . domestic space becomes 'utopia,' or 'no place,' " and, though Wells in the end seems to "restore the natural and pre-existent social order," nevertheless "the utopian universe has invaded History."[77]

Critical Reactions

W W was widely and lavishly applauded by the majority of its earliest reviewers. Their praise focused mainly on the novel's originality, on Wells's skillful writing, and on the gripping power of the narrative. Claims of originality were most frequently supported by references to the depiction of the Martians on the one hand and to the ingenious nature of their destruction on the other. An example of the former was provided by an anonymous reviewer for *The Critic*: "Mr. Wells's conception of the Martians is not only daring as a piece of imaginative work, but interesting for its deduction from biological laws." The latter claim was best exemplified by R. A. Gregory's comments in the scientific journal *Nature*. Underscoring Wells's ingenuity in manipulating scientific material, Gregory (who was a close friend of his) cited as the best instance of this skill "the manner in which the Martians are disposed of. . . . This is a distinctly clever idea. . . . Of course, outside fiction such an event is hardly worth consideration; but that the possibility of it can be convincingly stated, will be conceded after reading Mr. Wells' story."

In a letter to Wells, Joseph Conrad described the author of *W W* as a "Realist of the Fantastic." His perception of Wells's gifts was unwittingly echoed by many reviewers. They noted Wells's remarkable ability to create verisimilitude in describing the most alien conceptions and recounting the most horrific or fantastic events by his use of vivid details and precise geographical information. An anonymous critic for the *Academy* put it thus: "Mr. Wells never relaxes his hold on the commonplace, everyday life, against which his marvels stand out so luridly. A thousand deft and detailed touches create an atmosphere of actuality, bring the marvels into the realistic plane."

Sidney Brooks, who reviewed the novel for *Harper's Weekly*, reserved special praise for Wells's style. Regarding it as the novelist's major tool for preserving human interest within the context of a fantastic plot, he located the power of *W W* in a carefully articulated tension between form and content: "Much of its strength is the contrast between the tale itself and Mr. Wells's manner of telling it. He has a complete check over his imagination, and makes it effective by turning his most horrible fancies into language of the simplest, least startling denomination. . . ."

But beyond Wells's originality, beyond the remarkable effectiveness of his style, it was the suspense of the narrative that most consistently fired the imagination of his earliest reviewers. St. Loe Strachey, in an unsigned review in *The Spectator*, anticipated the reactions of millions of readers of his own generation and every subsequent one when he stated: "One reads and reads with an interest so unflagging that it is positively exhausting. *The War of the Worlds* stands, in fact, the final test of fiction. When once one has taken it up, one cannot bear to put it down without a pang. It is one of the books which it is imperatively necessary to sit up and finish."

Nevertheless, *W W* had its detractors, and even some of its most ardent admirers voiced their objections to specific aspects of the novel. Typical of the latter was an anonymous review in the *Academy* which shared Strachey's enthusiasm for the book—and also his objection to the character of the curate. Strachey regarded the curate as a figure borrowed from second-rate fiction; while the *Academy* reviewer considered him a "needlessly farcical element." By contrast to this minor objection, some of the severest criticism of *W W* seems to have been motivated by personal or political considerations, and much of it now seems quaint, irrelevant, or both. Wells's most unsympathetic reviewer was Basil Williams, writing for *The Athenaeum*, whose antipathy was an unmasked expression of his sense of "class superiority." Williams had been repelled by the "commonplace vulgarity" of the characters in Wells's short stories, and he had been at the head of the chorus in denouncing *The Island of Dr. Moreau* ("The sufferings inflicted in the course of the story have absolutely no adequate artistic reason, for it is impossible to feel the slightest interest in any one of the characters"). But Williams's snobbery rose to new heights with his (unsigned) review of *W W*, in which he discovered "too much of the young man from Clapham attitude . . . the narrator sees and hears exciting things, but he has not the gift of making them exciting to other people. . . . Mr. Wells is content with describing the cheap emotions of a few bank clerks and newspaper touts." Other, less class-conscious reviewers echoed Williams in finding Wells's style "too colloquial," but most unsympathetic critiques followed the line of the *Daily News* reviewer, who considered the novel lacking in artistic restraint. In essence, Wells had resorted to cheap effects simply to create horror, morbidity, and pessimism. Such reactions now seem quite gratuitous: it is difficult to imagine how any intelligent reader could expect a novel about global catastrophe to be uplifting or deliberately lacking in horror.

Wells himself ignored most individual reviews and seems to have remained impervious to all but one early critical tendency. He had been repeatedly irked by being labeled " 'a second'—somebody or other." St. Loe

Strachey, for example, had praised him as a second Defoe while Basil Williams had written him off as a second (and inferior) Jules Verne. Wells's irritation—even when the labeling was intended to be complimentary—rankled unspoken for many years. He eventually unburdened himself in the 1930s, starting with his Preface to *The Scientific Romances of H. G. Wells* (London, 1933), which advised his readers: "there is no literary resemblance whatever between the anticipatory inventions of the great Frenchman and these fantasies." *Experiment in Autobiography* (1934) provided a cynical follow-up. Referring directly to the original reviewers, Wells noted how

> Anybody fresh who turned up was treated as an aspirant Dalai Lama is treated, and scrutinized for evidence of his predecessor's soul. . . . A sheaf of second-hand tickets to literary distinction was thrust into our hands. These second-hand tickets were very convenient as admission tickets. It was however unwise to sit down in the vacant chairs, because if one did so, one rarely got up again. . . . I was saved . . . by the perplexing variety of my early attributions.

In *H. G. Wells and His Critics* (1962), Ingvald Raknem objected to something he considered far more consequential than mere "second-hand labels." Surveying the earliest reviews of *W W*, Raknem concluded: "It is . . . remarkable that almost every American and English critic should completely miss the implication of the fable and fail to see the significance of some [of the] more important incidents in the story." In his judgment, the (albeit hostile) reviewer for the *Daily News* was the only one who had understood the "moral" of the novel: i.e., Wells wanted "to show to what disaster intellect divorced from human sympathy tends."[78] In retrospect, however, Raknem's objection points to the limitations not only of the novel's earliest reviewers but also of his own critical approach. His notion of interpreting *W W* was to reduce its significance to a simple formula. Underlying Raknem's viewpoint was the assumption that there is nothing particularly complex about Wells's novel. It was this kind of assumption that deflected critical attention away from *W W* for more than half a century before the publication of Raknem's book—a period in which the novel had become more or less relegated to the teenage library.

Ironically, Raknem overlooked the seminal importance of Anthony West's article "The Dark World of H. G. Wells," *Harper's* 214 (May 1957):68–73. Aside from emphasizing (arguably overemphasizing) Wells's pessimism, West (Wells's illegitimate son by Rebecca West) had pointed a new direction in Wells studies by insisting that understanding his father's fiction must begin with the scientific romances. Taking his cue from West's article, Bernard Bergonzi in *The Early H. G. Wells* (1961) established the main lines along which the scholarly and critical debate has since proceeded. He demonstrated that close and serious analysis of the scientific romances meant viewing them in terms of the influences that shaped them and the period to which they belonged. And he sometimes raised, sometimes discussed, many aspects of individual novels that have since been explored, in greater depth or detail, by other commentators.

Departing from the rooted tendency to compare Wells with Verne, Bergonzi established the seriousness of his subject by analyzing the novels not as fictional illustrations of simplistic "morals" or as essays in fanciful quasiscientific speculation for bright teenagers, but as "romances in the traditional sense," whose fabric is symbolism and myth. He distinguished between major myths (which center on archetypal figures such as Prometheus and Faust) and minor myths (such as *Robinson Crusoe*, which embody "certain essential themes of modern civilization"). Categorizing Wells's scientific romances as minor myths, Bergonzi argued that "they reflect some of the dominant preoccupations of the *fin de siècle* period"—in particular a fascination with pessimistic *fin du globe* visions, reflecting widespread fears among many late Victorian intellectuals of an impending dissolution of social order. The section entitled "Fin de Siècle," in Max Nordau's heavily debated *Degeneration* (in English, 1895), had discerned "in more highly developed minds vague qualms of a Dusk of the Nations, in which all suns and all stars are gradually waning, and mankind with all its institutions and creations is perishing in the midst of a dying world." Bergonzi observed that it was from such "qualms" that *The Time Machine* and *The War of the Worlds* took their cues.

Parallel to his emphasis on reading *W W* (and the other scientific romances) in the context of the *fin de siècle*, Bergonzi indicated the need to recognize the Darwinian and Huxleyan influences on the novel: "Wells would have received the full impact of Darwin during his studies [under T. H. Huxley] at the Royal College of Science in the late eighties. . . . *The War of the Worlds* can be seen . . . as continuing the Darwinian preoccupation of *The Time Machine* and *Moreau*, even though its major stress is sociological."[79] In *W W* this preoccupation is most directly apparent in Book II, Chapter II, where Wells suggests that the Martians could be images of man's possible evolutionary future; and in Book II, Chapter VII, where the artilleryman expresses a crude "survival of the fittest" doctrine.

The strongest specific influence on the scientific romances was T. H. Huxley's Romanes lecture, "Evolution and Ethics" (1894). Huxley warned mankind to have no "millennial anticipations"; civilization and progress were not guaranteed eternals; "the time will come when . . . all forms of life will die out. . . . The most daring imagination will hardly venture upon the suggestion that the power and intelligence of man can ever arrest the procession of the great year." Huxley's teaching lay behind Wells's grim warnings about Victorian complacency in *The Time Machine* and *W W*.

And a statement by Wells's narrator in one of the final paragraphs of *W W* draws together thematically the decadent Eloi and the Martian invasion;

> We have learned now that we cannot regard this planet as being fenced in and a secure abiding-place for Man. . . . It may be that . . . this invasion from Mars is not without its ultimate benefit for men; it has robbed us of that serene confidence in the future which is the most fruitful source of decadence.

Since West and Bergonzi the most valuable commentaries on *W W* have recognized the novel's complexities and tended to explore specific aspects rather than offer simplistic general interpretations. In a wide range of books and articles scholars have focused on the novel's textual transmission and publishing history, its generic relationships, its themes, and its subtext, and on comparative studies involving fiction by other writers.

Textual History and Publication. David Y. Hughes's dissertation, "An Edition and Survey of H. G. Wells's *The War of the Worlds*" (University of Illinois, 1962), contains an extensive study of the textual transmission and publishing history of the novel. His findings are summarized in the present edition. In his "*The War of the Worlds* in the Yellow Press," (see below, Appendix II), Hughes provides detailed accounts of two little-known unauthorized American versions that were serialized in 1897 and 1898 shortly before the first book publication. These were lurid reworkings that relocated the action of the story (one version to New York City; the other to Boston). They triggered a memorable open letter from Wells, which Hughes publishes in full.

Generic Relationships. I. F. Clarke, Mark R. Hillegas, and Patrick Parrinder have all published useful work in this area. Clarke's *Voices Prophesying War 1763–1984* reveals *W W* as exploiting a late-Victorian obsession for stories about invasions of Britain, a vogue that had begun in 1872 with Sir George Chesney's *Battle of Dorking*. Hillegas's "Victorian 'Extraterrestrials,' " in Jerome H. Buckley, ed., *The Worlds of Victorian Fiction*, places *W W* in the context of the vogue of Martian romances that appeared in the last quarter of the nineteenth century. In particular, Hillegas discusses the possible influences on Wells's novel of Kurd Lasswitz's *Auf Zwei Planeten*, which was first published less than a year before *W W*. Hillegas concludes:

> the similarities are probably only coincidental and may be attributed to the fact that the two authors were acquainted with the tradition of the Martian story and knew the current theories about the habitability of the planet. . . . [*W W*] has a plot superficially similar to *Auf Zwei Planeten*, but Wells elevates his material to the level of literature.

Parrinder, in "H. G. Wells and the Fiction of Catastrophe," outlines the history of that particular subgenre (which he traces back to Defoe's *A Journal of the Plague Year*) and clarifies its influences on *W W*: "Wells did not invent the catastrophe novel, though he vastly increased its range, variety, and imaginative impact. The ingredients lay ready to hand, not only in a handful of influential earlier texts but in the mass of popular late Victorian science fiction."

Themes. Much of the commentary since Bergonzi has concentrated on elucidation of the novel's two major themes: Wells's critique of certain Victorian philosophical and political attitudes, and his visions of man's potential evolution and of Earth's inevitable fate. The distinction between these themes is made here for the purposes of clarification and summary, although some commentators treat them as overlapping concerns.

Many of the novel's later commentators view *W W* as an attack on Victorian positivism and sentimental humanism. They read it as Wells's negation of naive nineteenth-century beliefs in man's geocentric and homocentric views of the universe and in the conviction that man's moral development must necessarily parallel his technological progress. Following Bergonzi, the first critic to elaborate on this perspective was Hillegas, in his influential article "Cosmic Pessimism in H. G. Wells's Scientific Romances." After noticing that "Wells's intention to attack human complacency is evident from the very beginning [of *W W*]," Hillegas explicates the celebrated opening paragraph as the essential key to the novel's import: "Man's serene assurance of his control over the cosmic process is obviously being questioned in the world catastrophe of the invasion, when man, no longer master of his planet, becomes under the Martian heel only 'an animal among animals.' "

Robert Crossley, in a penetrating chapter in his *H. G. Wells*, reaffirms this point of view in an analysis of the same crucial passage. But he goes significantly beyond it by maintaining that "the great disillusionment," the closing words of the paragraph, not only expresses the central motif of *all* of Wells's thought but also reveals the larger ideological context of Wellsianism. As Crossley explains it, Wells recognized that the "disenchantment of *homo sapiens*" that began with the Copernican revolution and continued with Darwin and Huxley had been frustrated. Despite the astronomical and biological truths about "man's tangential place in the scheme of things," mankind still cherished many of its old illusions: positivism and sentimental humanism were the bulwarks that continued to sustain "human self-satisfaction." *W W* was Wells's counterblast, his imaginative completion of the disenchantment process. The story's Martian invasion may thus be interpreted as a rich metaphor for the ultimate destruction of mankind's illusions and self-delusions, the necessary prelude to the creation of a realistic utopia. Crossley observes that through his novel, Wells, "the great disillusioner for the post-Copernican, post-Darwinian, post-Christian, post-humanist world . . . offers his readers the bracing dose of reality and the liberated imagination necessary for building and inhabiting a viable future."

Other commentators have discerned political themes at the heart of the novel. Thus Herbert L. Sussman, in *Victorians and the Machine*, remarks that for writers of conscience such as Wells and Kipling, British imperialism was

> the social manifestation of amoral rationality. . . . The Martians use their advanced technology to destroy a civilization of which they are hardly aware; the similarity to British foreign policy in 1898 would have been clear to most readers. This anti-imperialist fable is even told from the viewpoint of the oppressed. . . .

For Darko Suvin, Wells's ironic expose of imperialism is merely an aspect of the novelist's wider onslaught on Victorian bourgeois ideologies. In his *Metamorphoses of Science Fiction*, Suvin perceives *W W* as one of a cycle of early Wells novels preoccupied with reversing

> the popular concept by which the lower social and biological classes were considered as "natural" prey in the struggle for survival. In their turn they become the predators: as laborers turn into Morlocks . . . or colonial people turn into Martians. . . . This exalting of the humble into horrible masters supplies a subversive shock to the bourgeois believer in Social Darwinism. . . .

A very different political interpretation is offered by J. Kagarlitski, who in *The Life and Thought of H. G. Wells* reads *W W* as a Wellsian testing of different approaches to collectivism.

> Through the mouth of the artilleryman Wells has proclaimed collectivism as the only hope for mankind; at the same moment he has compromised this mouthpiece of collectivism. . . . Nevertheless, at the end of the book he turns again to collectivism, but, this time, obviously to another kind of collectivism . . . a shape of society in which there will be found the just measure of expediency and humanity, of regimentation and freedom.

Other, related issues have been touched upon only briefly and invite further research: in particular Wells's complex treatment of the machine and certain less-obvious themes that his novel (possibly) carries over from mainstream Victorian thought. Sussman, in *Victorians and the Machine*, for example, states that "the main impression of . . . [W W] is the ineffectuality of ordinary men before the technological power available to the scientific mind." His observation invites us to question whether the novel was responsible for arousing a new *fin de siècle* concern for developing technology or whether Wells was merely exploiting existing fears. Roslynn D. Haynes in effect extends Sussman's perceptions of *W W* to book length in her *H. G. Wells: Discoverer of the Future*. Commenting on the finale of *W W*, she states: "Despite the final optimistic hope for a new world from the ruins, there is no effective counter-impression to that of confused, self-centred men fleeing in confusion before the advance of an efficient, amoral, technological power." Another potentially fruitful line of investigation has been introduced by Michael J. Bugeja in " 'Culture and Anarchy' in *The War of the Worlds*." Bugeja invites us to reconsider Wells's relationships with the Victorian moral and cultural high ground instead of assuming that Wells was generally reacting to it. His thesis rests on an identification of the narrator of *W W* with Arnold's description of himself as a man "tempered by experience, reflection, and renouncement . . . above all a believer in culture," and on his assertion that the character puts to the test the ideas that Arnold expounds in *Culture and Anarchy*.

> More than the Artilleryman and the Curate, the Narrator is able to maintain soundness of mind. He accomplishes this through his humanity, which Wells tests to the fullest and which ultimately prevails. . . . The Narrator through his experience has comprehended what Arnold calls "sound order and authority."

A substantial body of commentary has focused on *W W* as a vision or prophesy of what evolution portends for mankind and the planet we inhabit. Thus Samuel L. Hynes and Frank McConnell, in the latter's critical edition of *W W*, insist that "It is a tale, not simply of extraterrestrial invaders, but of apocalypse, of the end of the world . . . unlike *The Time Machine* it is an apocalypse that does not take man to his final end, but rather, more violently and dramatically, takes the final end to man *as he is now*." Other critics emphasize that Wells is exposing our age-old ignorance of or indifference to the fact that Earth cannot be habitable forever and implying that we (like the Martians) will have to reach out to the stars if we are to survive the inevitable fate of our little planet. In this regard Hillegas, in "Cosmic Pessimism," notices that "the [Martian] invaders are driven into space to seek a new home by conditions which make their world increasingly inhospitable to higher forms of life. . . . Mars is our earth after it has moved along the declining trajectory of evolution."

If *The Time Machine* envisages a parallel declining trajectory: human devolution within a perfected environment, then *W W* confronts us with a vision of highly evolved beings fleeing a deteriorating world. That the Martians are meant to be viewed as "men" of the remote future is confirmed—as many commentators note—by two facts: they are identical with the ultimately evolved human described in Wells's article "The Man of the

Year Million," and Wells ironically refers to this very article, which he describes as the prophecy of "a certain speculative writer of quasi-scientific repute," in *W W* (II.2).

Wells's objectives in using the Martians as metaphors for men have provoked considerable speculation, of which the following is merely a representative selection. Hynes and McConnell, while explaining the Martians as "possible nightmare extensions of ourselves," observe that "their invasion of the Earth is literally a time-machine story in reverse, where the future implodes upon the present. Thus it is brilliantly appropriate that the Martians are vampires: ghosts . . . of the yet-to-be-born, sucking the blood of life and joy from our own world." Kagarlitski explains the Martians as symbols of "material civilisation taken to the ultimate limit, a civilisation which has long since abandoned spiritual and moral values." Kathryn Hume, in "The Hidden Dynamics of *The War of the Worlds*," sees in them "the logical outcome of Western emphasis on technology and efficiency." Sussman identifies their physical grotesqueness as "an evolutionary extrapolation of the present effects of the machine." As noted earlier, Raknem maintains that Wells used the Martians "to show to what disaster intellect divorced from human sympathy tends." Following this interpretation, Hillegas ("Cosmic Pessimism") observes that the Martians' "cold, calculating nature . . . combined with extraordinarily great intellect" is more terrifying than their physical form: "In the inhumanity of the Martians, Wells is emphatically underlining the idea that evolution, even though it may produce creatures with superior intelligence, will not necessarily lead to a better and better."

Shifting the emphasis from man to environment, David Y. Hughes, in "The Garden in Wells's Early Science Fiction" (in Darko Suvin and Robert M. Philmus, eds., *H. G. Wells and Modern Science Fiction*, pp. 61–63), argues a Gaea theme for *W W*, i.e., that Mother Earth plays host to the "Martian" virus of a ruthless rationalized technology, but then rallies and rejects the invader—for now if not forever. Parrinder diverges still further from the foregoing commentaries by shifting the locus from men and their Earth altogether away to the Martians. He finds it too limiting to identify the Martians simply as "superior men"; they are also "non-anthropoid monsters, and . . . new and terrible gods . . . they accomplish man's dethronement. . . . Zoologically, they . . . are grotesque lower animals. . . . In mythological terms, however, their machines give them the stature of godlike giants, like Briareus or the Titans." For Parrinder *W W* climaxes not with the triumph of man but with the tragedy of these new gods represented by the solitary death throes of the last Martian (II.8): "One of the great paradoxes of *The War of the Worlds* is that . . . it is the Martians, rather than men, who finally emerge as romantic heroes. . . . This emotional transference, carefully prepared throughout the story, is Wells's most subtle effect." John Huntington, in *The Logic of Fantasy: H. G. Wells and Science Fiction*, concurs with Parrinder's judgment that the novel's tragic figures are the Martians, but his study also impinges perceptively on other approaches. Thus Huntington deploys Huxley's "Evolution and Ethics" as a thematic key to *W W* (with specific regard to Wells's use of color symbolism), and he greatly develops and ingeniously illustrates Bergonzi's remarks on the juxtaposition of exotic/mundane in Wells's science fiction.

Subtext. The groundbreaking work on nonexplicit levels of significance in Wells's fiction was Alex Eisenstein's "Very Early Wells: Origins of Some Major Physical Motifs in *The Time Machine* and *The War of the Worlds.*" Eisenstein used the revelations of *Experiment in Autobiography* as a new approach to *The Time Machine* and *W W*, tracing elements in the two novels to their author's childhood experiences. His article makes psychic connections between Wells's basement birthplace in Atlas House and the wrecked house episode in *W W* (II.2); it also ingeniously identifies "the inanimate progenitor of the Martian war machine" with the young Wells's discovery, at Up Park, of a Gregorian telescope mounted on a tripod.

So far there has been no important follow-up to Eisenstein's approach. Two different paths through the novel's imagery and symbolism have been charted by Kathryn Hume and by Tom Gibbons. After drawing attention to the incompatibility of the anonymous narrator's bourgeois existence with his vision of capitalism as exploitation, Hume (in "Hidden Dynamics") argues that Wells presents and analyzes his narrator's conflicting motifs in symbolic terms: "The narrator may appear as colorless as he is nameless, but he embellishes his story with a clear and consistent pattern of psychological images." Although the novel questions the ultimate viability of the existing social system, Hume's analysis indicates that its imagistic subtext provides a discreet justification for the narrator's acceptance of his privileged lifestyle.

In contrast to Hume's exegesis, Gibbons is concerned with the critical implications of Wells's biblical rhetoric. Norman and Jeanne Mackenzie, in their biography of Wells (p. 24), had mentioned the pervasiveness in Wells's writings of the imagery of Protestant theology he had absorbed as a child. Taking his cue from the Mackenzies, Gibbons, in "H. G. Wells's Fire Sermon: *The War of the Worlds* and The Book of Revelation," identifies the numerous biblical allusions in *W W*, then submits that Wells was possibly unaware that the rhetoric of the religion he had rejected provided "his novel's basic structure and most powerfully effective imagery." Gibbons goes on to suggest that *W W* can be read as

> a debate, no more than partly conscious, between Wells the Curate [expressing the fundamentalist beliefs he inherited from his mother], Wells

the narrator [representing his existential crisis: praising God on the one hand, yet haunted by doubts and fears on the other], and Wells the Artilleryman [anticipating the proto-fascism of *A Modern Utopia*]; as, in short, a debate between Wells's past, present, and future beliefs.

Gibbons further maintains that the religious imagery coloring that "debate" reflects the turn-of-the-century apocalypticism (to which Hynes and McConnell refer) discernible in the writings of many of Wells's contemporaries.

Comparative and Influence Studies. In practice, the distinction between comparative approaches and influence studies is often blurred. Michael J. Bugeja's aforementioned article can be viewed as both. Similarly Robert Shelton's "The Mars-Begotten Men of Olaf Stapledon and H. G. Wells" is at once a comparative analysis and a study of influences. Stapledon himself acknowledged the considerable influence of Wells but was also at pains to emphasize that *his* humanistic ideals differed significantly from Wells's. Shelton indicates that Stapledon's most direct debt was to *W W*, as is evident in the description of the Martians in *Last and First Men.* "Stapledon repeats the same scientific metaphors . . . that Wells had used in the opening paragraph of *W W* . . . [and sets up] the same thematic expectations." However, much of Shelton's commentary is concerned with detailing specific contrasts in the treatment of the Martians in the two novels and in enlarging, in general, on the differing visions of the two writers.

The comparative focus turns to Conrad and Wells in Patrick A. McCarthy's "*Heart of Darkness* and the Early Novels of H. G. Wells." Several critics have noticed important parallels between the fiction of Conrad and that of Wells, but so far McCarthy is the only one to have explored the subject in any depth. *Heart of Darkness* appeared serially a year after the first book publication of *W W*, and McCarthy supplies substantial evidence that Conrad wrote his novella under the influence of Wells's novel. He also points to various aspects of the novella that seem strikingly reminiscent of *W W*: in particular "the narrative situation, with a primary narrator whose story frames another character's description of a journey . . . [and] more importantly, several of Conrad's themes [including] . . . the disastrous effects of a colonial policy based on the assumption of evolutionary superiority. . . ." However, McCarthy disclaims interest in exploring influences. His article is concerned with countering the widely accepted view that Wells and Conrad were very different novelists, and he demonstrates their "shared vision" by making a close comparison of their treatment of Darwinian themes.

In retrospect, it is difficult to believe that there was once a time *W W* was considered a work lacking in literary sophistication. But since the early

1960s the cascade of commentary on the novel has shown no signs of abating. This brief overview has, for the most part, touched upon representative criticism and scholarship relating to general aspects. For perspectives on more-specific issues, the reader is referred to the annotations to this edition.

NOTES

1. This section is a revision of an article by David Y. Hughes in *Cahiers Victoriens et Edouardiens* 30 (October 1989):141–149.
2. A notice of this address before the Student Debating Society appeared in *Science Schools Journal.* See Bernard Bergonzi (1961), p. 36.
3. A notice of this address, delivered on October 19, appeared in *Science Schools Journal no.* 15 (November 1888). See Bergonzi (1961), p. 123.
4. *Strand Magazine* LIX (1920):154. Also, Wells dedicated the book to Frank as "this rendering of his idea."
5. *Experiment in Autobiography* (1934), p. 458.
6. Except as indicated in note 8, all correspondence cited is in the University of Illinois Wells Collection. Much of it appears, chronologically numbered, in Bernard Loing (1984). Henceforth Loing is cited thus: Loing 37: Henley to Wells.
7. Loing 38: Wells to Harpers.
8. Loing 60: Wells to unknown American recipient (original at Yale).
9. Loing 46: Wells to W.M. Colles (Authors' Syndicate).
10. See Appendix I, pp. 263 and 261, and endnote "i."
11. Loing 42, 43, 44, 45, 46: Wells to Authors' Syndicate or W.M. Colles.
12. Wells Collection: Sydney S. Pawling to Wells.
13. Wells Collection: William Heinemann to Wells.
14. Wells Collection: William Heinemann to Wells.
15. Wells Collection: Charles Watney to Wells.
16. See below, Appendix II.
17. A scene of debauch in Regent Street and Piccadilly Circus, recounted by the artilleryman, evidently echoes and satirizes a counterpart in Richard Le Gallienne's *Quest of the Golden Girl*, which Wells reviewed in March 1897, so that he presumably wrote the artilleryman chapter no earlier than that. See p. 222, note 19.
18. Loing 50: J.B. Pinker to Wells.
19. Wells Collection: J.B. Pinker to Wells.
20. Wells Collection: J.B. Pinker to Wells.
21. Wells Collection: Pawling to Wells, Dec. 22, 1897; the Atlantic proofing may be partly Dorothy Richardson's (see Anthony West, *H. G. Wells*, pp. 341, 351).
22. Wells Collection: J. B. Pinker to Wells, July 9, 1896.
23. "The Current Texts of Wells's Early SF Novels: Situation Unsatisfactory," *Wellsian* 11 (Summer 1988):3–12.
24. Wells refers to "the Calvinism of Science" ("Bio-Optimism," *Nature* [August 1895]:411) and "the Calanistic [Calvinistic?] deity of Natural Selection" ("Human Evolution, an Artificial Process," *Fortnightly Review* 60 n. s. [October 1896]:595; reprinted in Philmus and Hughes [1975]). He attributes the former phrase to "Mr. Buchanan" (untraced). T. H. Huxley spoke of "my scientific Calvinism" in

a letter of 1854, and in 1870 stated that to "introduce Calvinism into science and declare that man is nothing but a machine" is a permissible procedure, but the machine is "capable of adjusting itself within certain limits." See Leonard Huxley, ed., *Life and Letters of Thomas Henry Huxley* (1901) I, pp. 122, 352; and T. H. Huxley, *Lay Sermons* (1870), pp. 339–340.

25. See Robert P. Weeks, "Disentanglement as a Theme in H. G. Wells's Fiction," *Papers of the Michigan Academy of Science, Arts, and Letters* 39 (1954); reprinted in Bernard Bergonzi (1976). The pattern of barrier and breakthrough was first noted by Weeks.

26. Tom Gibbons proposes the same thesis in "H. G. Wells's Fire Sermon: 'The War of the Worlds' and the Book of Revelation," *Science Fiction: A Review of Speculative Literature* 6/1 (1984):5–14. Gibbons describes the narrator as "poised . . . at a moment of unresolved existential crisis" between curate and artilleryman in "a debate between Wells's past, present, and future beliefs" (p. 14). The present discussion augments the evidence brought forward by Gibbons, and the focus differs. For Gibbons, Wells is not in control of his materials because, on the one hand, the narrator can no more describe the Martian invasion without alluding to the Book of Revelation than the curate can, while, on the other hand, the reader is supposed to accept the narrator's judgment that the curate is insane. That is, Gibbons regards ironic distance between author and narrator as control. But control through irony may be preset and static. Wells's method in the 1890s is heuristic. Control lies in arranging the materials to reflect actual groping toward a future not yet crystallized. In so groping, the narrator is a representative figure not an ironic one.

27. Kenneth Young, *H. G. Wells* (1974), p. 25.

28. Quoted by David Smith (1986), p. 15.

29. Alan K. Russell, ed., *The Collector's Book of Science Fiction by H. G. Wells* (1978), pp. 48–49.

30. *Experiment in Autobiography* (1934), pp. 138, 150; hereafter EA.

31. Peter Kemp (1982), pp. 39–40, notes instances of Wells and "Godeating."

32. See below, W W II.2.9.

33. So described in the *Cosmopolitan* serial version. See below, W W I.5.1.

34. See "Problems of an Amorous Utopian," in *H. G. Wells Under Revision*, edited by Parrinder and Rolfe (1990), pp. 176–177; and in *Critical Essays on H. G. Wells*, edited by Huntington (1991), pp. 143–144.

35. Huxley, "Agnosticism," in *Some Controverted Questions* (1892), p. 289.

36. *Leviathan*, edited by Michael Oakshotte (1946 [1651]), p. 82. In "The Dark World of H. G. Wells" (in Bergonzi, as "H. G. Wells," 1976), Anthony West claims that Thomas Hobbes is basic to the early Wells. Wells mentions Hobbes only in late works (e.g., *The Holy Terror*, 1939, pp. 395, 450), but suspicion that he was thinking of Hobbes in W W deepens upon considering the giants of *The Food of the Gods* (1904). Hobbes's 1651 frontispiece shows a monarch built of the bodies of his tiny subjects crammed together. Below is the title *Leviathan, or the Matter, Forme and Power of a Commonwealth Ecclesiastical and Civil*, meaning that the state is "an artificial man; though of greater stature and strength than the natural" (p. 5). In *The Food of the Gods*, Wells intended an allegory of the crazy quilt of British municipalities transformed into scientific administrative areas (EA, p. 558). The giants "embody" the areas. The tripod colossi from Mars suggest the same idea. But, as William Bellamy remarks (in *The Novels of Wells, Bennett, and Galsworthy: 1890–1910* [1971], pp. 26, 118), "a kind of 'Icarus complex,' " or "the 'disease germs' of *fin de sièclism*," seemingly deterred Wells from consummating such flights until after 1900.

37. See *The Outlook for Homo Sapiens* (1942), p. 111.

38. Quoted by Bergonzi (1961), p. 138, from Wells's "The Novels of Mr. George Gissing," *Contemporary Review* 72 (August 1897):192–201; reprinted in Parrinder and Philmus (1980), pp. 144–155. See below, II.7.1.

39. Huntington (1982), pp. 116–119, 134–138. That weaklings will and should die for the sake of the race is also the thesis of the last pages of "A Story of the Days to Come" (1899). It turns up in "A Dream of Armageddon" (serialized 1901) and *When the Sleeper Wakes* (serialized 1898–1899) in the form of "Pleasure Cities" which exist to carry out euthanasia.

40. See n.26.

41. See Michael Draper, *H. G. Wells* (1987), p. 123, on the diminishing degree to which Wells's later novels would acknowledge "that the idea of apocalypse is itself a fiction." John Huntington makes the related point that "by means of *fiction* S[cience] F[iction] restores to the myth of science the promise of freedom and control that experience fails to give it." See "Science Fiction and the Future," in *Science Fiction: A Collection of Critical Essays*, edited by Mark Rose (1976), p. 160.

42. See below, *W W* I.1.27, I.9.5, I.12.9.

43. See Wells's Preface to *The Scientific Romances of H. G. Wells* (1933); reprinted in Parrinder and Philmus (1980).

44. See Wells's Preface to *The Time Machine* (New York: Random House, 1931).

45. William Thomson, *Popular Lectures and Addresses* (1889), I, p. 415.

46. See also Max Nordau in *W W* I.1.3.

47. See n.24.

48. Leon Stover, "Applied Natural History: Wells vs. Huxley," in *H. G. Wells Under Revision*, edited by Parrinder and Rolfe (1990), p. 130.

49. Huxley, *Evolution and Ethics* (1896), pp. 48, 204.

50. For Huxley and Darwin, the imposition of limits on the sun's age (i.e., span from beginning to end) conflicted with their belief in the slow uniform evolution of species in the past over hundreds of millions of years. The history of the dispute is laid out by Kelvin in "The Age of the Earth as an Abode Fitted for Life," *Philosophical Magazine* 47, 5th series (January 1899).

51. Huxley, "Agnosticism," in *Some Controverted Questions* (1892), p. 289.

52. Huxley, "On the Hypothesis that Animals are Automata," in *Method and Results* (1893).

53. Mark Rose, *Alien Encounters* (1981), p. 76.

54. See I. F. Clarke, *Voices Prophesying War* (1966), pp. 65, 83–85, and R. T. Stearn, "Wells and War," *Wellsian* 6 n.s. (Summer 1983):1–15.

55. Wells makes no mention of the Beresina (he refers to the burning of Moscow, I.15), and any similarities to Napoleon's crossing are what coincidence might dictate.

In November 1812, about 70,000 of Napoleon's Grand Army of 600,000 survived the retreat from Moscow to the Beresina, and half of those were stragglers. Napoleon threw up two bridges and led the main corps to safety. The stragglers stampeded. Counting camp-following women and children, 30,000 died, many drowning among the ice floes. But, curiously, when troop crossings ceased at night, panic turned to apathy; for two nights straight—ignoring efforts to get them going—the stragglers settled in and lit campfires; and at last the rear guard burned the bridges (see Richard K. Riehn [1990], p. 386). Thus, the Beresina stood for order, acumen, and courage, and equally for human and natural forces of dissolution.

Most like the Beresina in *W W* is the confluence of just these opposites. Military units die on duty while sheeplike London lies inert, then stampedes, trampling its victims in roads and bridges, or beating them off with boathooks in the Thames; Wells by naming natural disasters like the Lisbon earthquake or Pompeii buried by volcanic ash (I.13, II.1), implies a melding of humanity and natural process—just as the Beresina conjoins human and inanimate streams.

56. Admiring Huxley as he did, Wells probably knew *Darwiniana* (1894) and in it "Six Lectures to Working Men" (1863), which contains the Beresina metaphor (p. 442–44). As to Heine, on December 15, 1887, Wells sent a volume of Heine's prose writings to a friend, A. M. Davies, with a letter recommending it (letter in Illinois Wells Archive). Ten years later, in reviewing George W. Steevens's *Land of the Dollar*, Wells quoted the following description of New York City after an election: "Gunpowder flared, bands crashed, bugles rang; overhead, the late trains puffed and clattered, and above all rang volleys of cheers and the interminable discordant blare of tin trumpets, all blended in a furious jangle of jubilation. The whole place was mad. . . . And through the crowd came pushing a man with matted hair crying the morning papers." Wells commented that Steevens, "for his technique . . . may be indebted—as any sane man would probably take care to be indebted—to Heine's description of London" (*Saturday Review* 83 [March 13, 1897]:273). Since the chapter "The Exodus from London" in *W W* was composed in 1896, it appears that *Wells* was indebted to Heine and no doubt especially indebted where he thinks Steevens is, namely, to Heine's London as Beresina Bridge (see passage quoted below).

57. Heinrich Heine (1887), translated by Havelock Ellis, pp. 46–52. This was the book Wells sent to Davies.

58. The remark—in a review of Richard Le Gallienne's *Prose Fancies (Second Series)*—is aimed at Le Gallienne's lily-like "Poet in the City" in contrast to Heine's robust sensibility (*Saturday Review* 82 [August 1, 1896]:113).

59. I. A. Richards's terms for the parts of a metaphor—"vehicle" and "tenor," or "underlying idea . . . which the vehicle . . . means"—are not easy to distribute as between "London" and "Beresina Bridge," but clearly, as Richards says, "vehicle and tenor give a meaning of more varied powers than can be ascribed to either." *The Philosophy of Rhetoric* (1936), pp. 97, 100.

60. *The Communist Manifesto* (1964), pp. 61–62, 64.

61. EA, p. 200.

62. Quoted by Bergonzi (1961), p. 46, from *Science Schools Journal* of February 1889.

63. *Darwiniana* (1894), pp. 443–444.

64. *On the Origin of Species* (1859), Chapter 3.

65. See n.49.

66. EA, p. 549. 1901 was Wells's swing year: if *Anticipations* welcomes social planning, *The First Men in the Moon* hedges. The key chapter, "The Giddy Bridge," has two faces. The Selenites' rational realm is at the far side of an abyss. Mundane Bedford thinks "our resemblances [are] not going to bridge our differences," stages a massacre, and flees to earth. Scientist Cavor crosses, later radios home the news of the Selenite polity, and the Selenites surely kill him. But Wells nearly forestalled them. In drafts at Illinois, Bedford is sole narrator, Grand Lunar, and all; then both he and Cavor escape. Dissatisfied, Wells began serial publication meaning to scrap the moon-state altogether. Bedford would defect at the bridge; the rest would be silence. But then he advised Pinker early in 1901: "Happy thought. A message from Cavour sent by Marconi apparatus arriving in time to follow on to *First Men in the Moon*. Editor of Strand to announce arrival of message in number containing last instalment. Message to follow in next month. I seem to see message about 15,000 works [sic]. Will you suggest this? Terms if they catch on *at discretion*. It would be easy to write" (transcript at Illinois). The *Strand* paid extra (Pinker to Wells, May 2, 1901), Wells restored the moon-state in Cavor's postscript, and for the first time the (social) science component of his science fiction appeared in deliberate counterpoise to the romance.

67. In *W W*, the narrator is alluding to "The Man of the Year Million" when he remarks that "many a true word is written in jest" (see p. 151).

68. On aluminum, see *W W* I.12.3.

69. See II.6: the weed has a "sickly, metallic taste."

70. Having no wheel, Martian technology exploits different principles from ours, but the effects of extension and replacement of organic powers are identical.

71. Martian physiology apparently appealed to Wells's wish to be done with illness, especially repeated, dangerous hemorrhaging for years after his left kidney was crushed on a school playing field in 1887 (EA, p. 243). Wells was interested in Eli Metchnikoff's "schemes for a sort of hygienic evisceration" and thought " 'artificialisations' of the human body" might provide radical relief from organic demands on time. See, e.g., *An Englishman Looks at the World* (1914), pp. 347–351, and *The Way the World is Going* (1928), pp. 9–10.

72. Wells played with the idea of such aggregations as an evolutionary model that humans might emulate. See "Ancient Experiments in Co-operation," *Gentleman's Magazine* 273 (October 1892):418–422; reprinted in Philmus and Hughes (1975).

73. On scientific classification of species versus Wells's substitution of a "folk taxonomy" of organisms grouped according to "commonsensical" contrasts, such as that of animal versus plant, see Darko Suvin, "A Grammar of Form and a Criticism of Fact: *The Time Machine* as a Structural Model for Science Fiction," in *H. G. Wells and Modern Science Fiction*, edited by Suvin and Philmus (1977), pp. 95–96. The Martians are also "fungoid" (I.4) and, seen at a distance, "oddly suggestive . . . of a speck of blight" (I.15).

74. Ibid, pp. 94–95. Suvin's discussion is mainly of *The Time Machine*, but his general scheme of seriation levels from the highest forms of life down to nonexistence applies equally to *W W*. See below, I.1.30.

75. In "The Scepticism of the Instrument," in *A Modern Utopia* (1905), p. 346, Wells says we tend to see "such openly negative terms as the Absolute, the Infinite, as though they were real existences; and when the negative element is ever so little disguised, as it is in such a word as Omniscience, then the illusion of positive reality may be complete." The Martian puffball anatomy (see the line drawing, p. 000) may imply a metaphysical/axiological nothingness. Similarly, for Thomas Hobbes, a strong direct or indirect influence on *W W*; negative terms—for example, "incorporeal body"—are empty and literally refer to "nothing." See *Leviathan* (1651), edited by Michael Oakshotte (1946), p. 23.

76. Wells had a mystical streak, perhaps at odds with his Darwinian materialism, but it is not generally recognized that it began very early. See, for example, the 1894 essay "The Sun God and the Holy Stars" and the editors' discussion of it in Philmus and Hughes (1975), pp. 182, 200–202.

77. Carlo Pagetti (1986), pp. 32–33.

78. Cf. Geoffrey West (*H. G. Wells* [London: Gerald Howe, 1930], pp. 108–109), paraphrasing Wells: "*The Invisible Man* and *The War of the Worlds* illustrated the dangers of power without moral control, the development of the intelligence at the expense of human sympathy."

79. Bergonzi (1961), pp. 11, 134.

THE
WAR
OF THE
WORLDS

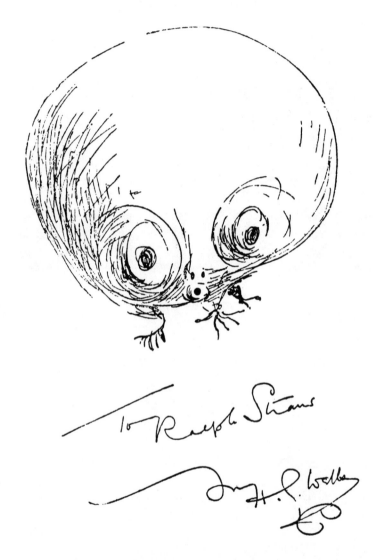

Wells's depiction of a Martian, inscribed in Ralph Straus's copy of *The War of the Worlds*. From Geoffrey West, *H. G. Wells: A Sketch for a Portrait* (1930)

Note on the Text

The copy text is the authoritative Atlantic edition (1924), slightly modified by the other texts Wells is known to have had a hand in (see below and "Gestation"). A few variants are adopted and many more are recorded. Those adopted in the text self-evidently set the Atlantic right. The others comprise all that would affect the sense of the Atlantic if adopted (as arguably some should be), as well as every variant in the Essex edition (1927): The Atlantic is the norm. Earlier (especially serial) texts may differ from it widely, but variants are recorded only when—seemingly neglected or mislaid but not purposely superseded—they "perfect" or supplement the Atlantic.

Any corrections Wells made after the Atlantic are in the Essex, which is based on a touch-up of the Atlantic galleys. The Essex is not the present copy text because it is carelessly printed and hard to find. Besides, all of the (generally slight) corrections in the Atlantic galleys are difficult to assign authorship since, according to Anthony West (*H. G. Wells: Aspects of a Life,* 1984, pp. 341, 351), Dorothy Richardson read proofs for Wells in the 1920s. Hence, both the Essex and the Atlantic may owe something to Richardson or others; but Wells supervised the Atlantic with far greater care than he did the Essex.

In the textual notes, each entry first cites the authority for the text of this edition, then records the variant(s) and the text(s) related thereto. Chronologically listed, the texts involved are as follows:

MS first half of 1896: holograph fragment. MS roughly coincides in Book II of the present edition with the last four paragraphs of Chapter V and Chapters VI, VIII, and IX.

C April–December 1897: *Cosmopolitan: A Monthly Illustrated Magazine.*

P April–December 1897: *Pearson's Magazine* (as photocopied in *The Collector's Book of Science Fiction by H. G. Wells; From Rare, Original Illustrated Magazines,* edited by Alan K. Russell, 1978).

PR late 1897: *Pearson's Magazine* paste-up. PR includes the freshly interpolated "Man on Putney Hill" (II. 7).

L 1898: Heinemann. L is based on PR and is the copy text for AG's "Epilogue."

NY 1898: Harpers. NY is based on PR independently of L and omits "The Epilogue." Otherwise it is the copy text of AG.

AG   1924: corrected galleys of A. AG was further corrected when reused
     as copy text for E.
A   1924: Atlantic edition.
E   1927: Essex edition.

CONTENTS

"But who shall dwell in these Worlds
if they be inhabited? . . . Are we or
they Lords of the World? . . . And
how are all things made for man?"[1]

—Kepler (quoted in
The Anatomy of Melancholy)

BOOK ONE

THE
COMING
OF THE
MARTIANS

I

THE EVE OF THE WAR

No one would have believed in the last years of the nineteenth century
that this world was being watched keenly and closely by intelligences greater
than man's and yet as mortal as his own; that as men busied themselves
about their various concerns they were scrutinised and studied, perhaps
almost as narrowly as a man with a microscope might scrutinise the transient
creatures that swarm and multiply in a drop of water. With infinite complacency men went to and fro over this globe about their little affairs, serene
in their assurance of their empire over matter. It is possible that the infusoria
under the microscope do the same.[1] No one gave a thought to the older
worlds[2] of space as sources of human danger,[3] or thought of them only to
dismiss the idea of life upon them as impossible or improbable.[4] It is curious
to recall some of the mental habits of those departed days. At most, terrestrial men fancied there might be other men upon Mars, perhaps inferior
to themselves and ready to welcome a missionary enterprise.[5] Yet across the
gulf of space, minds that are to our minds as ours are to those of the beasts
that perish,[6] intellects vast and cool and unsympathetic,[7] regarded this earth
with envious eyes, and slowly and surely drew their plans against us. And
early in the twentieth century came the great disillusionment.[8]

The planet Mars, I scarcely need remind the reader,[9] revolves about the
sun at a mean distance of 140,000,000 miles, and the light and heat it
receives from the sun is barely half of that received by this world. It must
be, if the nebular hypothesis has any truth, older than our world; and long
before this earth ceased to be molten, life upon its surface must have begun
its course.[10] The fact that it is scarcely one-seventh of the volume of the
earth must have accelerated its cooling to the temperature at which life
could begin. It has air and water and all that is necessary for the support
of animated existence.

Yet so vain is man and so blinded by his vanity, that no writer, up to the very end of the nineteenth century, expressed any idea that intelligent life might have developed there far, or indeed at all, beyond its earthly level.[11] Nor was it generally understood that since Mars is older than our earth, with scarcely a quarter of the superficial area and remoter from the sun, it necessarily follows that it is not only more distant from life's beginning but nearer its end.[12]

The secular cooling[13] that must some day overtake our planet has already gone far indeed with our neighbour. Its physical condition is still largely a mystery, but we know now that even in its equatorial region the mid-day temperature barely approaches that of our coldest winter. Its air is much more attenuated than ours, its oceans have shrunk until they cover but a third of its surface,[14] and as its slow seasons change huge snow caps gather and melt about either pole and periodically inundate its temperate zones. That last stage of exhaustion, which to us is still incredibly remote,[15] has become a present-day problem for the inhabitants of Mars. The immediate pressure of necessity has brightened their intellects, enlarged their powers, and hardened their hearts. And looking across space with instruments and intelligences such as we have scarcely dreamed of, they see, at its nearest distance only 35,000,000 of miles sunward of them, a morning star of hope, our own warmer planet, green with vegetation and grey with water, with a cloudy atmosphere eloquent of fertility, with glimpses through its drifting cloud-wisps of broad stretches of populous country and narrow, navy-crowded seas.

And we men, the creatures who inhabit this earth, must be to them at least as alien and lowly as are the monkeys and lemurs to us. The intellectual side of man already admits that life is an incessant struggle for existence, and it would seem that this too is the belief of the minds upon Mars. Their world is far gone in its cooling and this world is still crowded with life, but crowded only with what they regard as inferior animals. To carry warfare sunward is, indeed, their only escape from the destruction that generation after generation creeps upon them.

And before we judge of them too harshly we must remember what ruthless and utter destruction our own species has wrought, not only upon animals, such as the vanished bison and the dodo, but upon its own inferior races. The Tasmanians, in spite of their human likeness, were entirely swept out of existence in a war of extermination waged by European immigrants,[16] in the space of fifty years. Are we such apostles of mercy as to complain if the Martians warred in the same spirit?

The Martians seem to have calculated their descent with amazing subtlety—their mathematical learning is evidently far in excess of ours—and to have carried out their preparations with a well-nigh perfect unanimity. Had our instruments permitted it, we might have seen the gathering trouble far back in the nineteenth century. Men like Schiaparelli watched the red planet—it is odd, by-the-bye, that for countless centuries Mars has been the star of war—but failed to interpret the fluctuating appearances of the markings they mapped so well.[17] All that time the Martians must have been getting ready.

During the opposition[18] of 1894 a great light was seen on the illuminated part of the disc, first at the Lick Observatory,[19] then by Perrotin of Nice,[20] and then by other observers. English readers heard of it first in the issue of Nature dated August 2nd.[21] I am inclined to think that this blaze may have been the casting of the huge gun, in the vast pit[22] sunk into their planet, from which their shots were fired at us. Peculiar markings, as yet unexplained, were seen near the site of that outbreak during the next two oppositions.

The storm burst upon us six years ago now.[23] As Mars approached opposition, Lavelle of Java[24] set the wires of the astronomical exchange[25] palpitating with the amazing intelligence of a huge outbreak of incandescent gas upon the planet. It had occurred towards midnight[26] of the 12th;[27] and the spectroscope, to which he had at once resorted, indicated a mass of flaming gas, chiefly hydrogen, moving with an enormous velocity towards this earth. This jet of fire had become invisible about a quarter past twelve. He compared it to a colossal puff of flame suddenly and violently squirted out of the planet, "as flaming gases rushed out of a gun."

A singularly appropriate phrase it proved. Yet the next day there was nothing of this in the papers except a little note in the Daily Telegraph,[28] and the world went in ignorance of one of the gravest dangers that ever threatened the human race. I might not have heard of the eruption at all had I not met Ogilvy,[29] the well-known astronomer, at Ottershaw. He was immensely excited at the news, and in the excess of his feelings invited me up to take a turn with him that night in a scrutiny of the red planet.

In spite of all that has happened since, I still remember that vigil very distinctly: the black and silent observatory, the shadowed lantern throwing a feeble glow upon the floor in the corner, the steady ticking of the clockwork of the telescope, the little slit in the roof—an oblong profundity with the star-dust streaked across it. Ogilvy moved about, invisible but audible. Looking through the telescope, one saw a circle of deep blue and the little round planet swimming in the field. It seemed such a little thing, so bright and small and still, faintly marked with transverse stripes, and slightly flattened from the perfect round. But so little it was, so silvery warm—a pin's-head of light! It was as if it quivered, but really this was the telescope vibrating with the activity of the clockwork that kept the planet in view.

As I watched, the planet seemed to grow larger and smaller and to advance and recede, but that was simply that my eye was tired. Forty millions of miles it was from us—more than forty millions of miles of void. Few people realise the immensity of vacancy in which the dust of the material universe swims.

Near it in the field, I remember, were three faint points of light, three telescopic stars infinitely remote, and all around it was the unfathomable darkness of empty space. You know how that blackness looks on a frosty starlight night. In a telescope it seems far profounder.[30] And invisible to me because it was so remote and small, flying swiftly and steadily towards me across that incredible distance, drawing nearer every minute by so many thousands of miles, came the Thing they were sending us, the Thing that was to bring so much struggle and calamity and death to the earth. I never dreamed of it then as I watched; no one on earth dreamed of that unerring missile.[31]

That night, too, there was another jetting out of gas from the distant planet. I saw it. A reddish flash at the edge, the slightest projection of the outline just as the chronometer struck midnight; and at that I told Ogilvy and he took my place. The night was warm and I was thirsty, and I went, stretching my legs clumsily and feeling my way in the darkness, to the little table where the siphon stood, while Ogilvy exclaimed at the streamer of gas that came out towards us.

That night another invisible missile started on its way to the earth from Mars, just a second or so under twenty-four hours after the first one. I remember how I sat on the table there in the blackness, with patches of green and crimson swimming before my eyes. I wished I had a light to smoke by, little suspecting the meaning of the minute gleam I had seen and all that it would presently bring me. Ogilvy watched till one, and then gave it up; and we lit the lantern and walked over to his house. Down below in the darkness were Ottershaw and Chertsey and all their hundreds of people, sleeping in peace.

He was full of speculation that night about the condition of Mars, and scoffed at the vulgar idea of its having inhabitants who were signalling us.[32] His idea was that meteorites might be falling in a heavy shower upon the planet, or that a huge volcanic explosion was in progress. He pointed out to me how unlikely it was that organic evolution had taken the same direction in the two adjacent planets.

"The chances against anything man-like on Mars are a million to one," he said.[33]

Hundreds of observers saw the flame that night and the night after, about midnight, and again the night after; and so for ten nights, a flame each night. Why the shots ceased after the tenth no one on earth has attempted to explain. It may be the gases of the firing caused the Martians inconvenience. Dense clouds of smoke or dust, visible through a powerful telescope on earth as little grey, fluctuating patches, spread through the clearness of the planet's atmosphere and obscured its more familiar features.

Even the daily papers woke up to the disturbances at last, and popular notes appeared here, there, and everywhere concerning the volcanoes upon Mars. The serio-comic periodical *Punch*,[34] I remember, made a happy use of it in the political cartoon. And, all unsuspected, those missiles the Martians had fired at us drew earthward, rushing now at a pace of many miles a second through the empty gulf of space, hour by hour and day by day, nearer and nearer. It seems to me now almost incredibly wonderful that, with that swift fate hanging over us, men could go about their petty concerns as they did. I remember how jubilant Markham[35] was at securing a new photograph of the planet for the illustrated paper he edited in those days. People in these latter times scarcely realise the abundance and enterprise of our nineteenth-century papers.[36] For my own part, I was much occupied in learning to ride the bicycle,[37] and busy upon a series of papers discussing the probable developments of moral ideas as civilisation progressed.[38]

One night (the first missile then could scarcely have been 10,000,000 miles away) I went for a walk with my wife. It was starlight, and I explained the Signs of the Zodiac to her, and pointed out Mars, a bright dot of light creeping zenithward, towards which so many telescopes were pointed. It was a warm night. Coming home, a party of excursionists from Chertsey or Isleworth passed us singing and playing music. There were lights in the upper windows of the houses as the people went to bed. From the railway station in the distance came the sound of shunting trains, ringing and rumbling, softened almost into melody by the distance. My wife pointed out to me the brightness of the red, green, and yellow signal lights hanging in a framework against the sky. It seemed so safe and tranquil.[39]

THE FALLING-STAR

THEN CAME THE night of the first falling-star. It was seen early in the morning rushing over Winchester eastward,[1] a line of flame high in the atmosphere. Hundreds must have seen it, and taken it for an ordinary falling-star. Albin[2] described it as leaving a greenish streak behind it that glowed for some seconds. Denning, our greatest authority on meteorites, stated that the height of its first appearance was about ninety or one hundred miles. It seemed to him that it fell to earth about one hundred miles east of him.[3]

I was at home at that hour and writing in my study; and although my French windows face towards Ottershaw[4] and the blind was up (for I loved in those days to look up at the night sky), I saw nothing of it. Yet this strangest of all things that ever came to earth from outer space must have fallen while I was sitting there, visible to me had I only looked up as it passed. Some of those who saw its flight say it travelled with a hissing sound. I myself heard nothing of that. Many people in Berkshire, Surrey, and Middlesex must have seen the fall of it,[5] and, at most, have thought that another meteorite had descended. No one seems to have troubled to look for the fallen mass that night.

But very early in the morning poor Ogilvy,[6] who had seen the shooting-star and who was persuaded that a meteorite lay somewhere on the common between Horsell, Ottershaw, and Woking, rose early with the idea of finding it. Find it he did, soon after dawn, and not far from the sand-pits. An enormous hole had been made by the impact of the projectile, and the sand and gravel had been flung violently in every direction over the heath, forming heaps visible a mile and a half away. The heather was on fire eastward, and a thin blue smoke rose against the dawn.

The Thing itself lay almost entirely buried in sand, amidst the scattered splinters of a fir-tree it had shivered to fragments in its descent. The uncovered part had the appearance of a huge cylinder,[7] caked over and its outline softened by a thick scaly dun-coloured incrustation. It had a diameter of about thirty yards. He approached the mass, surprised at the size and more so at the shape, since most meteorites are rounded more or less completely. It was, however, still so hot from its flight through the air as to forbid his near approach. A stirring noise within its cylinder he ascribed to the unequal cooling of its surface; for at that time it had not occurred to him that it might be hollow.

He remained standing at the edge of the pit that the Thing had made for itself, staring at its strange appearance, astonished chiefly at its unusual shape and colour, and dimly perceiving even then some evidence of design in its arrival.[8] The early morning was wonderfully still, and the sun, just clearing the pine-trees towards Weybridge, was already warm. He did not remember hearing any birds that morning,[9] there was certainly no breeze stirring, and the only sounds were the faint movements from within the cindery cylinder. He was all alone on the common.

Then suddenly he noticed with a start that some of the grey clinker, the ashy incrustation that covered the meteorite, was falling off the circular edge of the end. It was dropping off in flakes and raining down upon the sand. A large piece suddenly came off and fell with a sharp noise that brought his heart into his mouth.

For a minute he scarcely realised what this meant, and, although the heat was excessive, he clambered down into the pit close to the bulk to see the Thing more clearly. He fancied even then that the cooling of the body might account for this, but what disturbed that idea was the fact that the ash was falling only from the end of the cylinder.

And then he perceived that, very slowly, the circular top of the cylinder was rotating on its body. It was such a gradual movement that he discovered it only through noticing that a black mark that had been near him five minutes ago was now at the other side of the circumference. Even then he scarcely understood what this indicated, until he heard a muffled grating sound and saw the black mark jerk forward an inch or so. Then the thing came upon him in a flash. The cylinder was artificial—hollow—with an end that screwed out! Something within the cylinder was unscrewing the top!

"Good heavens!" said Ogilvy. "There's a man in it—men in it! Half roasted to death! Trying to escape!"

At once, with a quick mental leap, he linked the Thing with the flash upon Mars.

The thought of the confined creature was so dreadful to him that he forgot the heat, and went forward to the cylinder to help turn. But luckily the dull radiation arrested him before he could burn his hands on the still glowing metal.[10] At that he stood irresolute for a moment, then turned, scrambled out of the pit, and set off running wildly into Woking. The time then must have been somewhere about six o'clock. He met a waggoner and tried to make him understand, but the tale he told and his appearance were so wild—his hat had fallen off in the pit—that the man simply drove on. He was equally unsuccessful with the potman who was just unlocking the doors of the public-house by Horsell Bridge. The fellow thought he was a lunatic at large, and made an unsuccessful attempt to shut him into the tap-room. That sobered him a little; and when he saw Henderson, the London journalist, in his garden, he called over the palings and made himself understood.

"Henderson," he called, "you saw that shooting-star last night?"

"Well?" said Henderson.

"It's out on Horsell Common now."

"Good Lord!" said Henderson. "Fallen meteorite! That's good."

"But it's something more than a meteorite. It's a cylinder—an artificial cylinder, man! And there's something inside."

Henderson stood up with his spade in his hand.

"What's that?" he said. He was deaf in one ear.

Ogilvy told him all that he had seen. Henderson was a minute or so taking it in. Then he dropped his spade, snatched up his jacket, and came out into the road. The two men hurried back at once to the common, and found the cylinder still lying in the same position. But now the sounds inside had ceased, and a thin circle of bright metal showed between the top and the body of the cylinder. Air was either entering or escaping at the rim with a thin, sizzling sound.

They listened, rapped on the scaly burnt metal with a stick, and, meeting with no response, they both concluded the man or men inside must be insensible or dead.

Of course the two were quite unable to do anything. They shouted consolation and promises, and went off back to the town again to get help. One can imagine them, covered with sand, excited and disordered, running up the little street in the bright sunlight just as the shop folks were taking down their shutters and people were opening their bedroom windows. Henderson went into the railway station at once, in order to telegraph the news to London. The newspaper articles had prepared men's minds for the reception of the idea.

By eight o'clock a number of boys and unemployed men had already started for the common to see the "dead men from Mars." That was the form the story took. I heard of it first from my newspaper boy about a quarter to nine, when I went out to get my *Daily Chronicle*.[11] I was naturally startled, and lost no time in going out and across the Ottershaw bridge to the sand-pits.

III

ON HORSELL COMMON

I FOUND A LITTLE crowd of perhaps twenty people surrounding the huge hole in which the cylinder lay. I have already described the appearance of that colossal bulk, embedded in the ground. The turf and gravel about it seemed charred as if by a sudden explosion. No doubt its impact had caused a flash of fire. Henderson and Ogilvy were not there. I think they perceived that nothing was to be done for the present, and had gone away to breakfast at Henderson's house.

There were four or five boys sitting on the edge of the pit, with their feet dangling, and amusing themselves—until I stopped them—by throwing stones at the giant mass.[1] After I had spoken to them about it, they began playing at "touch"[2] in and out of the group of bystanders.

Among these were a couple of cyclists, a jobbing gardener I employed sometimes, a girl carrying a baby, Gregg the butcher and his little boy, and two or three loafers and golf caddies who were accustomed to hang about the railway station. There was very little talking. Few of the common people in England had anything but the vaguest astronomical ideas in those days.[3] Most of them were staring quietly at the big table-like end of the cylinder, which was still as Ogilvy and Henderson had left it. I fancy the popular expectation of a heap of charred corpses was disappointed at this inanimate bulk. Some went away while I was there, and other people came. I clambered into the pit and fancied I heard a faint movement under my feet. The top had certainly ceased to rotate.

It was only when I got thus close to it that the strangeness of this object was at all evident to me. At the first glance it was really no more exciting than an overturned carriage or a tree blown across the road. Not so much so, indeed. It looked like a rusty gas-float.[4] It required a certain amount of scientific education to perceive that the grey scale of the Thing was no common oxide, that the yellowish-white metal that gleamed in the crack between the lid and the cylinder had an unfamiliar hue. "Extraterrestrial" had no meaning for most of the onlookers.

At that time it was quite clear in my own mind that the Thing had come from the planet Mars, but I judged it improbable that it contained any living creature. I thought the unscrewing might be automatic. In spite of Ogilvy, I still believed that there were men in Mars. My mind ran fancifully on the possibilities of its containing manuscript, on the difficulties in translation that might arise, whether we should find coins and models in it, and so forth.[5] Yet it was a little too large for assurance on this idea. I felt an impatience to see it opened. About eleven, as nothing seemed happening, I walked back, full of such thoughts, to my home in Maybury. But I found it difficult to get to work upon my abstract investigations.[6]

In the afternoon the appearance of the common had altered very much. The early editions of the evening papers had startled London with enormous headlines:

"A MESSAGE RECEIVED FROM MARS."[7]

"REMARKABLE STORY FROM WOKING,"[8]

and so forth. In addition, Ogilvy's wire to the Astronomical Exchange had roused every observatory in the three kingdoms.[9]

There were half a dozen flys or more from the Woking station standing in the road by the sand-pits, a basket-chaise from Chobham, and a rather lordly carriage. Besides that, there was quite a heap of bicycles. In addition, a large number of people must have walked, in spite of the heat of the day, from Woking and Chertsey,[10] so that there was altogether quite a considerable crowd—one or two gayly dressed ladies among the others.

It was glaringly hot, not a cloud in the sky nor a breath of wind, and the only shadow was that of the few scattered pine-trees. The burning heather had been extinguished, but the level ground towards Ottershaw[11] was blackened as far as one could see, and still giving off vertical streamers of smoke. An enterprising sweet-stuff dealer in the Chobham Road had sent up his son with a barrow-load of green apples and ginger-beer.

Going to the edge of the pit, I found it occupied by a group of about half a dozen men—Henderson, Ogilvy, and a tall, fair-haired man that I afterwards learned was Stent, the Astronomer Royal,[12] with several workmen wielding spades and pickaxes. Stent was giving directions in a clear, high-pitched voice. He was standing on the cylinder, which was now evidently much cooler; his face was crimson and streaming with perspiration, and something seemed to have irritated him.

A large portion of the cylinder had been uncovered, though its lower end was still embedded. As soon as Ogilvy saw me among the staring crowd on the edge of the pit he called to me to come down, and asked me if I would mind going over to see Lord Hilton, the lord of the manor.[13]

The growing crowd, he said, was becoming a serious impediment to their excavations, especially the boys. They wanted a light railing put up, and help to keep the people back. He told me that a faint stirring was occasionally still audible within the case, but that the workmen had failed to unscrew the top, as it afforded no grip to them. The case appeared to be enormously thick, and it was possible that the faint sounds we heard represented a noisy tumult in the interior.

I was very glad to do as he asked, and so become one of the privileged spectators within the contemplated enclosure. I failed to find Lord Hilton at his house, but I was told he was expected from London by the six o'clock train from Waterloo; and as it was then about a quarter past five, I went home, had some tea, and walked up to the station to waylay him.

IV

THE CYLINDER OPENS

WHEN I RETURNED to the common the sun was setting. Scattered groups were hurrying from the direction of Woking,[1] and one or two persons were returning. The crowd about the pit had increased, and stood out black against the lemon-yellow of the sky—a couple of hundred people, perhaps. There were raised voices, and some sort of struggle appeared to be going on about the pit. Strange imaginings passed through my mind. As I drew nearer I heard Stent's voice:

"Keep back! Keep back! "

A boy came running towards me.

"It's a-movin'," he said to me as he passed—"a-screwin' and a-screwin' out. I don't like it. I'm a-goin' 'ome, I am."

I went on to the crowd. There were really, I should think, two or three hundred people elbowing and jostling one another, the one or two ladies there being by no means the least active.

"He's fallen in the pit!" cried some one.

"Keep back!" said several.

The crowd swayed a little, and I elbowed my way through. Every one seemed greatly excited. I heard a peculiar humming sound from the pit.

"I say!" said Ogilvy; "help keep these idiots back. We don't know what's in the confounded thing, you know!"

I saw a young man, a shop assistant in Woking I believe he was, standing on the cylinder and trying to scramble out of the hole again. The crowd had pushed him in.

The end of the cylinder was being screwed out from within. Nearly two feet of shining screw projected. Somebody blundered against me, and I narrowly missed being pitched on to the top of the screw. I turned, and as I did so the screw must have come out, for the lid of the cylinder fell upon the gravel with a ringing concussion. I stuck my elbow into the person behind me, and turned my head towards the Thing again. For a moment that circular cavity seemed perfectly black. I had the sunset in my eyes.

I think every one expected to see a man emerge—possibly something a little unlike us terrestrial men, but in all essentials a man. I know I did. But, looking, I presently saw something stirring within the shadow: greyish billowy movements, one above another, and then two luminous discs—like eyes. Then something resembling a little grey snake, about the thickness of a walking-stick, coiled up out of the writhing middle, and wriggled in the air towards me—and then another.

A sudden chill came over me. There was a loud shriek from a woman behind. I half turned, keeping my eyes fixed upon the cylinder still, from which other tentacles were now projecting, and began pushing my way back from the edge of the pit. I saw astonishment giving place to horror on the faces of the people about me. I heard inarticulate exclamations on all sides. There was a general movement backwards. I saw the shopman struggling still on the edge of the pit. I found myself alone, and saw the people on the other side of the pit running off, Stent among them. I looked again at the cylinder, and ungovernable terror gripped me. I stood petrified and staring.

A big greyish rounded bulk, the size, perhaps, of a bear, was rising slowly and painfully out of the cylinder. As it bulged up and caught the light, it glistened like wet leather.

Two large dark-coloured eyes were regarding me steadfastly. The mass that framed them, the head of the thing, was* rounded, and had, one might say, a face. There was a mouth under the eyes, the lipless brim of which quivered and panted, and dropped saliva. The whole creature heaved and pulsated convulsively. A lank tentacular[2] appendage gripped the edge of the cylinder, another swayed in the air.

Those who have never seen a living Martian can scarcely imagine the strange horror of its appearance. The peculiar V-shaped mouth with its pointed upper lip, the absence of brow ridges, the absence of a chin beneath the wedge-like lower lip, the incessant quivering of this mouth, the Gorgon groups of tentacles,[3] the tumultuous breathing of the lungs in a strange atmosphere, the evident heaviness and painfulness of movement due to the greater gravitational energy of the earth—above all, the extraordinary intensity of the immense eyes—were at once vital, intense, inhuman, crippled and monstrous. There was something fungoid in the oily brown skin, something in the clumsy deliberation of the tedious movements unspeakably nasty. Even at this first encounter, this first glimpse, I was overcome with disgust and dread.[4]

---

* AG–A; thing, it was: E.

Suddenly the monster vanished. It had toppled over the brim of the cylinder and fallen into the pit, with a thud like the fall of a great mass of leather. I heard it give a peculiar thick cry, and forthwith another of these creatures appeared darkly in the deep shadow of the aperture.

I turned and, running madly, made for the first group of trees, perhaps a hundred yards away; but I ran slantingly and stumbling, for I could not avert my face from these things.

There, among some young pine-trees and furze-bushes, I stopped, panting, and waited further developments. The common round the sand-pits was dotted with people, standing like myself in a half-fascinated terror, staring at these creatures, or rather at the heaped gravel at the edge of the pit in which they lay. And then, with a renewed horror, I saw a round, black object bobbing up and down on the edge of the pit. It was the head of the shopman who had fallen in, but showing as a little black object against the hot western sky. Now he got his shoulder and knee up, and again he seemed to slip back until only his head was visible. Suddenly he vanished, and I could have fancied a faint shriek had reached me. I had a momentary impulse to go back and help him that my fears overruled.

Everything was then quite invisible, hidden by the deep pit and the heap of sand that the fall of the cylinder had made. Any one coming along the road from Chobham or Woking[5] would have been amazed at the sight— a dwindling multitude of perhaps a hundred people or more standing in a great irregular circle, in ditches, behind bushes, behind gates and hedges, saying little to one another and that in short, excited shouts, and staring, staring hard at a few heaps of sand. The barrow of ginger-beer stood, a queer derelict, black against the burning sky, and in the sand-pits was a row of deserted vehicles with their horses feeding out of nose-bags or pawing the ground.

V

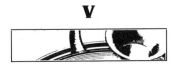

THE HEAT–RAY

AFTER THE GLIMPSE I had had of the Martians emerging from the cylinder in which they had come to the earth from their planet, a kind of fascination paralysed my actions. I remained standing knee-deep in the heather, staring at the mound that hid them. I was a battle-ground of fear and curiosity.[1]

I did not dare to go back towards the pit, but I felt a passionate longing to peer into it. I began walking, therefore, in a big curve, seeking some point of vantage and continually looking at the sand-heaps that hid these new-comers to our earth. Once a leash of thin black whips, like the arms of an octopus, flashed across the sunset and was immediately withdrawn, and afterwards a thin rod rose up, joint by joint, bearing at its apex a circular disc that spun with a wobbling motion. What could be going on there?

Most of the spectators had gathered in one or two groups—one a little crowd towards Woking, the other a knot of people in the direction of Chobham. Evidently they shared my mental conflict. There were few near me. One man I approached—he was, I perceived, a neighbour of mine, though I did not know his name—and accosted. But it was scarcely a time for articulate conversation.

"What ugly *brutes!*" he said. "Good God! what ugly brutes!" He repeated this over and over again.

"Did you see a man in the pit?" I said; but he made no answer to that. We became silent, and stood watching for a time side by side, deriving, I fancy, a certain comfort in one another's company. Then I shifted my position to a little knoll that gave me the advantage of a yard or more of elevation, and when I looked for him presently he was walking towards Woking.

The sunset faded to twilight before anything further happened. The crowd far away on the left, towards Woking, seemed to grow, and I heard now a faint murmur from it. The little knot of people towards Chobham dispersed. There was scarcely an intimation of movement from the pit.

It was this, as much as anything, that gave people courage, and I suppose the new arrivals from Woking also helped to restore confidence. At any rate, as the dusk came on a slow, intermittent movement upon the sand-pits began, a movement that seemed to gather force as the stillness of the evening about the cylinder remained unbroken. Vertical black figures in twos and threes would advance, stop, watch, and advance again, spreading out as they did so in a thin irregular crescent that promised to enclose the pit in its attenuated horns. I, too, on my side began to move towards the pit.

Then I saw some cabmen and others had walked boldly into the sand-pits, and heard the clatter of hoofs and the gride of wheels. I saw a lad trundling off the barrow of apples. And then, within thirty yards of the pit, advancing from the direction of Horsell,[2] I noted a little black knot of men, the foremost of whom was waving a white flag.

This was the Deputation. There had been a hasty consultation, and since the Martians were evidently, in spite of their repulsive forms, intelligent creatures, it had been resolved to show them, by approaching them with signals, that we too were intelligent.

Flutter, flutter, went the flag, first to the right, then to the left. It was too far for me to recognise any one there, but afterwards I learned that Ogilvy, Stent, and Henderson were with others in this attempt at communication. This little group had in its advance dragged inward, so to speak, the circumference of the now almost complete circle of people, and a number of dim black figures followed it at discreet distances.

Suddenly there was a flash of light, and a quantity of luminous greenish smoke came out of the pit[3] in three distinct puffs, which drove up, one after the other, straight into the still air.

This smoke (or flame, perhaps, would be the better word for it) was so bright that the deep blue sky overhead and the hazy stretches of brown common towards Chertsey,[4] set with black pine-trees, seemed to darken abruptly as these puffs arose, and to remain the darker after their dispersal. At the same time a faint hissing sound became audible.

Beyond the pit stood the little wedge of people with the white flag at its apex, arrested by these phenomena, a little knot of small vertical black shapes upon the black ground. As the green smoke rose, their faces flashed out pallid green, and faded again as it vanished. Then slowly the hissing passed into a humming, into a long, loud, droning noise. Slowly a humped shape rose out of the pit, and the ghost of a beam of light seemed to flicker out from it.

Forthwith flashes of actual flame, a bright glare leaping from one to another, sprang from the scattered group of men. It was as if some invisible jet impinged upon them and flashed into white flame. It was as if each man were suddenly and momentarily turned to fire.

Then, by the light of their own destruction, I saw them staggering and falling, and their supporters turning to run.

I stood staring, not as yet realising that this was death leaping from man to man in that little distant crowd. All I felt was that it was something very strange. An almost noiseless and blinding flash of light, and a man fell headlong and lay still; and as the unseen shaft of heat passed over them, pine-trees burst into fire, and every dry furze-bush became with one dull thud a mass of flames. And far away towards Knaphill[5] I saw the flashes of trees and hedges and wooden buildings suddenly set alight.

It was sweeping round swiftly and steadily, this flaming death, this invisible, inevitable sword of heat. I perceived it coming towards me by the flashing bushes it touched, and was too astounded and stupefied to stir. I heard the crackle of fire in the sand-pits and the sudden squeal of a horse that was as suddenly stilled. Then it was as if an invisible yet intensely heated finger were drawn through the heather between me and the Martians, and all along a curving line beyond the sand-pits the dark ground smoked and crackled. Something fell with a crash far away to the left where the road from Woking station[6] opens out on the common. Forthwith the hissing and humming ceased, and the black, dome-like object sank slowly out of sight into the pit.

All this had happened with such swiftness that I had stood motionless, dumbfounded and dazzled by the flashes of light. Had that death swept through a full circle, it must inevitably have slain me in my surprise. But it passed and spared me, and left the night about me suddenly dark and unfamiliar.

The undulating common seemed now dark almost to blackness, except where its roadways lay grey and pale under the deep-blue sky of the early night. It was dark, and suddenly void of men. Overhead the stars were mustering, and in the west the sky was still a pale, bright, almost greenish blue. The tops of the pine-trees and the roofs of Horsell came out sharp and black against the western afterglow. The Martians and their appliances were altogether invisible, save for that thin mast upon which their restless mirror wobbled. Patches of bush and isolated trees here and there smoked and glowed still, and the houses towards Woking station were sending up spires of flame into the stillness of the evening air.

Nothing was changed save for that and a terrible astonishment. The little[7] group of black specks with the flag of white had been swept out of existence, and the stillness of the evening, so it seemed to me, had scarcely been broken.

It came to me that I was upon this dark common, helpless, unprotected, and alone. Suddenly, like a thing falling upon me from without, came fear.*[8]

With an effort I turned and began a stumbling run through the heather.

The fear I felt was no rational fear, but a panic terror not only of the Martians but of the dusk and stillness all about me. Such an extraordinary effect in unmanning me it had that I ran weeping silently as a child might do. Once I had turned, I did not dare to look back.[9]

I remember I felt an extraordinary persuasion that I was being played with, that presently, when I was upon the very verge of safety, this mysterious death—as swift as the passage of light—would leap after me from the pit about the cylinder and strike me down.

---

*A; *came—Fear*: L–NY; *came—fear*: AG, E.

VI

THE HEAT–RAY IN THE CHOBHAM ROAD

IT IS STILL a matter of wonder how the Martians are able to slay men so swiftly and so silently. Many think that in some way they are able to generate an intense heat in a chamber of practically absolute non-conductivity. This intense heat they project in a parallel beam against any object they choose by means of a polished parabolic mirror of unknown composition,[1] much as the parabolic mirror of a light-house projects a beam of light. But no one has absolutely proved these details. However it is done, it is certain that a beam of heat is the essence of the matter. Heat, and invisible, instead of visible light. Whatever is combustible flashes into flame at its touch, lead runs like water, it softens iron, cracks and melts glass, and when it falls upon water, incontinently that explodes into steam.

That night nearly forty people lay under the starlight about the pit, charred and distorted beyond recognition, and all night long the common from Horsell to Maybury[2] was deserted and brightly ablaze.

The news of the massacre probably reached Chobham, Woking, and Ottershaw about the same time. In Woking the shops had closed when the tragedy happened, and a number of people, shop-people and so forth, attracted by the stories they had heard, were walking over the Horsell Bridge[3] and along the road between the hedges that runs out at last upon the common. You may imagine the young people brushed up after the labours of the day, and making this novelty, as they would make any novelty, the excuse for walking together and enjoying a trivial flirtation. You may figure to yourself the hum of voices along the road in the gloaming. . . .

As yet, of course, few people in Woking even knew that the cylinder had opened, though poor Henderson had sent a messenger on a bicycle to the post-office with a special wire to an evening paper.

As these folks came out by twos and threes upon the open, they found little knots of people talking excitedly and peering at the spinning mirror[4] over the sand-pits, and the new-comers were, no doubt, soon infected by the excitement of the occasion.

By half-past eight, when the Deputation was destroyed, there may have been a crowd of three hundred people or more at this place, besides those who had left the road to approach the Martians nearer. There were three policemen too, one of whom was mounted, doing their best, under instructions from Stent, to keep the people back and deter them from approaching the cylinder. There was some booing from those more thoughtless and excitable souls to whom a crowd is always an occasion for noise and horseplay.

Stent and Ogilvy, anticipating some possibilities of a collision, had telegraphed from Horsell to the barracks as soon as the Martians emerged, for the help of a company of soldiers to protect these strange creatures from violence. After that they returned to lead that ill-fated advance. The description of their death, as it was seen by the crowd, tallies very closely with my own impressions: the three puffs of green smoke, the deep humming note, and the flashes of flame.

But that crowd of people had a far narrower escape than mine. Only the fact that a hummock of heathery sand intercepted the lower part of the Heat-Ray saved them. Had the elevation of the parabolic mirror been a few yards higher, none could have lived to tell the tale. They saw the flashes and the men falling, and an invisible hand, as it were, lit the bushes as it hurried towards them through the twilight. Then, with a whistling note that rose above the droning of the pit, the beam swung close over their heads, lighting the tops of the beech-trees that line the road, and splitting the bricks, smashing the windows, firing the window-frames, and bringing down in crumbling ruin a portion of the gable of the house nearest the corner.

In the sudden thud, hiss, and glare of the igniting trees, the panic-stricken crowd seems to have swayed hesitatingly for some moments. Sparks and burning twigs began to fall into the road, and single leaves like puffs of flame. Hats and dresses caught fire. Then came a crying from the common. There were shrieks and shouts, and suddenly a mounted policeman came galloping through the confusion with his hands clasped over his head, screaming.

"They're coming!" a woman shrieked, and incontinently every one was turning and pushing at those behind, in order to clear their way to Woking again. They must have bolted as blindly as a flock of sheep. Where the road grows narrow and black between the high banks the crowd jammed, and a desperate struggle occurred. All that crowd did not escape; three persons at least, two women and a little boy, were crushed and trampled there, and left to die amid the terror and the darkness.

VII

HOW I REACHED HOME

FOR MY OWN PART, I remember nothing of my flight except the stress of blundering against trees and stumbling through the heather. All about me gathered the invisible terrors of the Martians; that pitiless sword of heat seemed whirling to and fro, flourishing overhead before it descended and smote me out of life. I came into the road between the cross-roads and Horsell, and ran along this to the cross-roads.

At last I could go no farther; I was exhausted with the violence of my emotion and of my flight, and I staggered and fell by the wayside. That was near the bridge that crosses the canal by the gas-works. I fell and lay still.

I must have remained there some time.

I sat up, strangely perplexed. For a moment, perhaps, I could not clearly understand how I came there. My terror had fallen from me like a garment. My hat had gone, and my collar had burst away from its fastener. A few minutes before there had only been three real things before me—the immensity of the night and space and nature, my own feebleness and anguish, and the near approach of death. Now it was as if something turned over, and the point of view altered abruptly. There was no sensible transition from one state of mind to the other. I was immediately the self of every day again—a decent, ordinary citizen. The silent common, the impulse of my flight, the starting flames, were as if they had been in a dream. I asked myself had these latter things indeed happened? I could not credit it.

I rose and walked unsteadily up the steep incline of the bridge. My mind was blank wonder. My muscles and nerves seemed drained of their strength. I dare say I staggered drunkenly. A head rose over the arch, and the figure of a workman carrying a basket appeared. Beside him ran a little boy. He passed me, wishing me good-night. I was minded to speak to him, but did not. I answered his greeting with a meaningless mumble and went on over the bridge.

Over the Maybury arch a train, a billowing tumult of white, firelit smoke, and a long caterpillar of lighted windows, went flying south—clatter, clatter, clap, rap, and it had gone. A dim group of people talked in the gate of one of the houses in the pretty little row of gables that was called Oriental Terrace. It was all so real and so familiar. And that behind me! It was frantic, fantastic! Such things, I told myself, could not be.

Perhaps I am a man of exceptional moods. I do not know how far my experience is common. At times I suffer from the strangest sense of detachment from myself and the world about me; I seem to watch it all from the outside, from somewhere inconceivably remote, out of time, out of space, out of the stress and tragedy of it all.[1] This feeling was very strong upon me that night. Here was another side to my dream.

But the trouble was the blank incongruity of this serenity and the swift death flying yonder, not two miles away. There was a noise of business from the gas-works, and the electric-lamps were all alight. I stopped at the group of people.

"What news from the common?" said I.

There were two men and a woman at the gate.

"Eh?" said one of the men, turning.

"What news from the common?" I said.

" 'Ain't yer just *been* there?" asked the men.

"People seem fair silly about the common," said the woman over the gate. "What's it all abart?"

"Haven't you heard of the men from Mars?" said I—"the creatures from Mars?"

"Quite enough," said the woman over the gate. "Thenks;" and all three of them laughed.

I felt foolish and angry. I tried and found I could not tell them what I had seen. They laughed again at my broken sentences.

"You'll hear more yet," I said, and went on to my home.

I startled my wife at the doorway, so haggard was I. I went into the dining-room, sat down, drank some wine, and so soon as I could collect myself sufficiently I told her the things I had seen. The dinner, which was a cold one, had already been served, and remained neglected on the table while I told my story.

"There is one thing," I said, to allay the fears I had aroused—"they are the most sluggish things[2] I ever saw crawl. They may keep the pit and kill people who come near them, but they cannot get out of it. . . . But the horror of them!"

"Don't, dear!" said my wife, knitting her brows and putting her hand on mine.

"Poor Ogilvy!" I said. "To think he may be lying dead there!"

My wife at least did not find my experience incredible. When I saw how deadly white her face was, I ceased abruptly.

"They may come here," she said again and again.

I pressed her to take wine, and tried to reassure her.

"They can scarcely move," I said.

I began to comfort her and myself by repeating all that Ogilvy had told me of the impossibility of the Martians establishing themselves on the earth. In particular I laid stress on the gravitational difficulty. On the surface of the earth the force of gravity is three times what it is on the surface of Mars. A Martian, therefore, would weigh three times more than on Mars, albeit his muscular strength would be the same. His own body would be a cope of lead to him. That, indeed, was the general opinion. Both the *Times*[3] and the *Daily Telegraph*,[4] for instance, insisted on it the next morning, and both overlooked, just as I did, two obvious modifying influences.

The atmosphere of the earth, we now know, contains far more oxygen or far less argon[5] (whichever way one likes to put it) than does Mars. The invigorating influences of this excess of oxygen upon the Martians indisputably did much to counterbalance the increased weight of their bodies. And, in the second place, we all overlooked the fact that such mechanical intelligence as the Martian possessed was quite able to dispense with muscular exertion at a pinch.

But I did not consider these points at the time, and so my reasoning was dead against the chances of the invaders. With wine and food, the confidence of my own table, and the necessity of reassuring my wife, I grew by insensible degrees courageous and secure.

"They have done a foolish thing," said I, fingering my wineglass. "They are dangerous because, no doubt, they are mad with terror. Perhaps they expected to find no living things—certainly no intelligent living things.

"A shell in the pit," said I, "if the worst comes to the worst, will kill them all."

The intense excitement of the events had no doubt left my perceptive powers in a state of erethism. I remember that dinner-table with extraordinary vividness even now. My dear wife's sweet, anxious face peering at me from under the pink lamp-shade, the white cloth with its silver and glass table furniture—for in those days even philosophical writers had many little luxuries—the crimson-purple wine in my glass, are photographically distinct. At the end of it I sat, tempering nuts with a cigarette, regretting Ogilvy's rashness, and denouncing the short-sighted timidity of the Martians.

So some respectable dodo in the Mauritius might have lorded it in his nest, and discussed the arrival of that shipful of pitiless sailors in want of animal food. "We will peck them to death to-morrow, my dear."[6]

I did not know it, but that was the last civilised dinner I was to eat for very many strange and terrible days.

VIII

FRIDAY NIGHT

THE MOST EXTRAORDINARY thing to my mind, of all the strange and wonderful things that happened upon that Friday, was the dovetailing of the
commonplace habits of our social order with the first beginnings of the
series of events that was to topple that social order headlong.[1] If on Friday
night you had taken a pair of compasses and drawn a circle with a radius
of five miles round the Woking sand-pits, I doubt if you would have had
one human being outside it, unless it were some relation of Stent or of the
three or four cyclists or London people lying dead on the common, whose
emotions or habits were at all affected by the new-comers. Many people
had heard of the cylinder, of course, and talked about it in their leisure, but
it certainly did not make the sensation that an ultimatum to Germany would
have done.

In London that night poor Henderson's telegram describing the gradual
unscrewing of the shot was judged to be a canard, and his evening paper,
after wiring for authentication from him and receiving no reply—the man
was killed—decided not to print a special edition.

Even within the five-mile circle the great* majority of people were inert.
I have already described the behaviour of the men and women to whom I
spoke. All over the district people were dining and supping; working-men
were gardening after the labours of the day, children were being put to bed,
young people were wandering through the lanes love-making, students sat
over their books.

Maybe there was a murmur in the village streets, a novel and dominant
topic in the public-houses, and here and there a messenger, or even an eye-
witness of the later occurrences, caused a whirl of excitement, a shouting,

---

*AG, E; Within the five mile circle, even the great: C; circle, even, the great: P–PR;
circle even the great: L, A.

and a running to and fro; but for the most part the daily routine of working, eating, drinking, sleeping, went on as it had done for countless years—as though no planet Mars existed in the sky. Even at Woking station and Horsell and Chobham that was the case.

In Woking junction, until a late hour, trains were stopping and going on, others were shunting on the sidings, passengers were alighting and waiting, and everything was proceeding in the most ordinary way. A boy from the town, trenching on Smith's monopoly,[2] was selling papers with the afternoon's news. The ringing impact of trucks, the sharp whistle of the engines from the junction, mingled with their shouts of "Men from Mars!" Excited men came into the station about nine o'clock with incredible tidings, and caused no more disturbance than drunkards might have done. People rattling Londonwards peered into the darkness outside the carriage windows and saw only a rare, flickering, vanishing spark dance up from the direction of Horsell, a red glow and a thin veil of smoke driving across the stars, and thought that nothing more serious than a heath fire was happening. It was only round the edge of the common that any disturbance was perceptible. There were half a dozen villas burning on the Woking border. There were lights in all the houses on the common side of the three villages, and the people there kept awake till dawn.

A curious crowd lingered restlessly, people coming and going but the crowd remaining, both on the Chobham and Horsell bridges. One or two adventurous souls, it was afterwards found, went into the darkness and crawled quite near the Martians; but they never returned, for now and again a light-ray, like the beam of a warship's searchlight, swept the common, and the Heat-Ray was ready to follow.[3] Save for such, that big area of common was silent and desolate, and the charred bodies lay about on it all night under the stars, and all the next day. A noise of hammering from the pit was heard by many people.

So you have the state of things on Friday night. In the centre, sticking into the skin of our old planet Earth like a poisoned dart, was this cylinder. But the poison was scarcely working yet. Around it was a patch of silent common, smouldering in places, and with a few dark, dimly seen objects lying in contorted attitudes here and there. Here and there was a burning bush or tree. Beyond was a fringe of excitement, and farther than that fringe the inflammation had not crept as yet. In the rest of the world the stream of life still flowed as it had flowed for immemorial years. The fever of war that would presently clog vein and artery, deaden nerve and destroy brain, had still to develop.[4]

All night long the Martians were hammering and stirring, sleepless, indefatigable, at work upon the machines they were making ready, and ever and again a puff of greenish-white smoke whirled up to the starlit sky.

About eleven a company of soldiers came through Horsell, and deployed along the edge of the common to form a cordon. Later a second company marched through Chobham to deploy on the north side of the common. Several officers from the Inkerman barracks[5] had been on the common earlier in the day, and one, Major Eden, was reported to be missing. The colonel of the regiment came to the Chobham bridge and was busy questioning the crowd at midnight. The military authorities were certainly alive to the seriousness of the business. About eleven, the next morning's papers were able to say, a squadron of hussars, two Maxims,[6] and about four hundred men of the Cardigan regiment[7] started from Aldershot.

A few seconds after midnight the crowd in the Chertsey road, Woking, saw a star fall from heaven into the pine-woods to the north-west.[8] It had a greenish colour and caused a silent brightness like summer lightning. This was the second cylinder.

IX

THE FIGHTING BEGINS

SATURDAY LIVES in my memory as a day of suspense. It was a day of lassitude too, hot and close, with, I am told, a rapidly fluctuating barometer. I had slept but little, though my wife had succeeded in sleeping, and I rose early. I went into my garden before breakfast and stood listening, but towards the common there was nothing stirring but a lark.

The milkman came as usual. I heard the rattle of his chariot, and I went round to the side-gate to ask the latest news. He told me that during the night the Martians had been surrounded by troops, and that guns were expected. Then—a familiar, reassuring note—I heard a train running towards Woking.

"They aren't to be killed," said the milkman, "if that can possibly be avoided."

I saw my neighbour gardening, chatted with him for a time, and then strolled in to breakfast. It was a most unexceptional morning. My neighbour was of opinion that the troops would be able to capture or to destroy the Martians during the day.

"It's a pity they make themselves so unapproachable," he said. "It would be curious to know how they live on another planet; we might learn a thing or two."

He came up to the fence and extended a handful of strawberries, for his gardening was as generous as it was enthusiastic. At the same time he told me of the burning of the pine-woods about the Byfleet Golf Links.

"They say," said he, "that there's another of those blessed things fallen there—number two. But one's enough, surely. This lot'll cost the insurance people a pretty penny before everything's settled."[1] He laughed with an air of the greatest good-humour as he said this. The woods, he said, were still burning, and pointed out a haze of smoke to me. "They will be hot underfoot for days, on account of the thick soil of pine-needles and turf," he said, and then grew serious over "poor Ogilvy."

After breakfast, instead of working, I decided to walk down towards the common. Under the railway bridge I found a group of soldiers—sappers, I think, men in small round caps, dirty red jackets unbuttoned, and showing their blue shirts, dark trousers, and boots coming to the calf. They told me no one was allowed over the canal, and, looking along the road towards the bridge, I saw one of the Cardigan men standing sentinel there. I talked with these soldiers for a time; I told them of my sight of the Martians on the previous evening. None of them had seen the Martians, and they had but the vaguest ideas of them, so that they plied me with questions. They said that they did not know who had authorised the movements of the troops; their idea was that a dispute had arisen at the Horse Guards.[2] The ordinary sapper is a great deal better educated than the common soldier, and they discussed the peculiar conditions of the possible fight with some acuteness. I described the Heat-Ray to them, and they began to argue among themselves.

"Crawl up under cover and rush 'em, say I," said one.

"Get aht!" said another. "What's cover against this 'ere 'eat? Sticks to cook yer! What we got to do is to go as near as the ground'll let us, and then drive a trench."

"Blow yer trenches! You always want trenches; you ought to ha' been born a rabbit, Snippy."

" 'Ain't they got any necks, then?" said a third, abruptly—a little, contemplative, dark man, smoking a pipe.

I repeated my description.

"Octopuses," said he, "that's what I calls 'em. Talk about fishers of men[3]—fighters of fish it is this time!"

"It ain't no murder killing beasts like that," said the first speaker.

"Why not shell the darned things strite off and finish 'em?" said the little dark man. "You carn tell what they might do."

"Where's your shells?" said the first speaker. "There ain't no time. Do it in a rush, that's my tip, and do it at once."

So they discussed it. After a while I left them, and went on to the railway station to get as many morning papers as I could.

But I will not weary the reader with a description of that long morning and of the longer afternoon. I did not succeed in getting a glimpse of the common, for even Horsell and Chobham church towers were in the hands of the military authorities. The soldiers I addressed didn't know anything; the officers were mysterious as well as busy. I found people in the town quite secure again in the presence of the military, and I heard for the first time from Marshall, the tobacconist, that his son was among the dead on the common. The soldiers had made the people on the outskirts of Horsell lock up and leave their houses.

I got back to lunch about two, very tired, for, as I have said, the day was extremely hot and dull; and in order to refresh myself I took a cold bath in the afternoon. About half-past four I went up to the railway station to get an evening paper, for the morning papers had contained only a very inaccurate description of the killing of Stent, Henderson, Ogilvy, and the others. But there was little I didn't know. The Martians did not show an inch of themselves. They seemed busy in their pit, and there was a sound of hammering and an almost continuous streamer of smoke. Apparently they were busy getting ready for a struggle. "Fresh attempts have been made to signal, but without success," was the stereotyped formula of the papers. A sapper told me it was done by a man in a ditch with a flag on a long pole. The Martians took as much notice of such advances as we should of the lowing of a cow.

I must confess the sight of all this armament, all this preparation, greatly excited me. My imagination became belligerent, and defeated the invaders in a dozen striking ways; something of my school-boy dreams of battle and heroism came back.[4] It hardly seemed a fair fight to me at that time. They seemed very helpless in that pit of theirs.

About three o'clock there began the thud of a gun at measured intervals from Chertsey or Addlestone. I learned that the smouldering pine-wood into which the second cylinder had fallen was being shelled, in the hope of destroying that object before it opened. It was only about five, however, that a field-gun reached Chobham for use against the first body of Martians.

About six in the evening, as I sat at tea with my wife in the summer-house talking vigorously about the battle that was lowering upon us, I heard a muffled detonation from the common, and immediately after a gust of firing. Close on the heels of that came a violent, rattling crash quite close to us, that shook the ground; and, starting out upon the lawn, I saw the tops of the trees about the Oriental College[5] burst into smoky red flame, and the tower of the little church beside it slide down into ruin. The pinnacle of the mosque had vanished, and the roof-line of the college itself looked as if a hundred-ton gun had been at work upon it. One of our chimneys cracked as if a shot had hit it, flew, and a piece of it came clattering down the tiles and made a heap of broken red fragments upon the flower-bed by my study window.

I and my wife stood amazed. Then I realised that the crest of Maybury Hill must be within range of the Martians' Heat-Ray now that the college was cleared out of the way.

At that I gripped my wife's arm, and without ceremony ran her out into the road. Then I fetched out the servant, telling her I would go upstairs myself for the box she was clamouring for.

"We can't possibly stay here," I said; and as I spoke the firing reopened for a moment upon the common.

"But where are we to go?" said my wife in terror.

I thought, perplexed. Then I remembered her cousins[6] at Leatherhead.

"Leatherhead!" I shouted above the sudden noise.

She looked away from me downhill. The people were coming out of their houses astonished.

"How are we to get to Leatherhead?" she said.

Down the hill I saw a bevy of hussars ride under the railway bridge; three galloped through the open gates of the Oriental College; two others dismounted, and began running from house to house. The sun, shining through the smoke that drove up from the tops of the trees, seemed blood-red, and threw an unfamiliar lurid light upon everything.

"Stop here," said I; "you are safe here;" and I started off at once for the Spotted Dog,[7] for I knew the landlord had a horse and dog-cart. I ran, for I perceived that in a moment every one upon this side of the hill would be moving. I found him in his bar, quite unaware of what was going on behind his house. A man stood with his back to me, talking to him.

"I must have a pound,"[8] said the landlord, "and I've no one to drive it."

"I'll give you two," said I, over the stranger's shoulder.

"What for?"

"And I'll bring it back by midnight," I said.

"Lord!" said the landlord; "what's the hurry? I'm selling my bit of a pig.[9] Two pounds, and you bring it back? What's going on now?"

I explained hastily that I had to leave my home, and so secured the dog-cart. At the time it did not seem to me nearly so urgent that the landlord should leave his.[10] I took care to have the cart there and then, drove it off down the road, and, leaving it in charge of my wife and servant, rushed into my house and packed a few valuables, such plate as we had, and so forth. The beech-trees below the house were burning while I did this, and the palings up the road glowed red. While I was occupied in this way, one of the dismounted hussars came running up. He was going from house to house, warning people to leave. He was going on as I came out of my front-door, lugging my treasures, done up in a table-cloth. I shouted after him:

"What news?"

He turned, stared, bawled something about "crawling out in a thing like a dish cover," and ran on to the gate of the house at the crest. A sudden whirl of black smoke driving across the road hid him for a moment. I ran to my neighbour's door and rapped to satisfy myself of what I already knew, that his wife had gone to London with him and had locked up their house. I went in again, according to my promise, to get my servant's box, lugged it out, clapped it beside her on the tail of the dog-cart, and then caught the reins and jumped up into the driver's seat beside my wife. In another moment we were clear of the smoke and noise, and spanking down the opposite slope of Maybury Hill towards Old Woking.[11]

In front was a quiet, sunny landscape, a wheat-field ahead on either side of the road, and the Maybury Inn with its swinging sign. I saw the doctor's cart ahead of me. At the bottom of the hill I turned my head to look at the hill-side I was leaving. Thick streamers of black smoke shot with threads of red fire were driving up into the still air, and throwing dark shadows upon the green tree-tops eastward. The smoke already extended far away to the east and west—to the Byfleet pine-woods eastward, and to Woking on the west. The road was dotted with people running towards us. And very faint now, but very distinct through the hot, quiet air, one heard the whirr of a machine-gun that was presently stilled, and an intermittent cracking of rifles. Apparently the Martians were setting fire to everything within range of their Heat-Ray.

I am not an expert driver, and I had immediately to turn my attention to the horse. When I looked back again the second hill had hidden the black smoke. I slashed the horse with the whip, and gave him a loose rein until Woking and Send lay between us and that quivering tumult. I overtook and passed the doctor between Woking and Send.[12]

IN THE STORM

LEATHERHEAD IS ABOUT twelve miles from Maybury Hill.[1] The scent of hay was in the air through the lush meadows beyond Pyrford,[2] and the hedges on either side were sweet and gay with multitudes of dog-roses. The heavy firing that had broken out while we were driving down Maybury Hill ceased as abruptly as it began, leaving the evening very peaceful and still. We got to Leatherhead without misadventure about nine o'clock, and the horse had an hour's rest while I took supper with my cousins and commended my wife to their care.

My wife was curiously silent throughout the drive, and seemed oppressed with forebodings of evil. I talked to her reassuringly, pointing out that the Martians were tied to the pit by sheer heaviness, and at the utmost could but crawl a little out of it; but she answered only in monosyllables. Had it not been for my promise to the innkeeper, she would, I think, have urged me to stay in Leatherhead that night. Would that I had! Her face, I remember, was very white as we parted.

For my own part, I had been feverishly excited all day. Something very like the war-fever that occasionally runs through a civilised community had got into my blood, and in my heart I was not so very sorry that I had to return to Maybury that night.[3] I was even afraid that that last fusillade I had heard might mean the extermination of our invaders from Mars. I can best express my state of mind by saying that I wanted to be in at the death.[4]

It was nearly eleven when I started to return. The night was unexpectedly dark; to me, walking out of the lighted passage of my cousins' house, it seemed indeed black, and it was as hot and close as the day. Overhead the clouds were driving fast, albeit not a breath stirred the shrubs about us. My cousins' man lit both lamps. Happily, I knew the road intimately. My wife stood in the light of the doorway, and watched me until

I jumped up into the dog-cart. Then abruptly she turned and went in, leaving my cousins side by side wishing me good hap.

I was a little depressed at first with the contagion of my wife's fears, but very soon my thoughts reverted to the Martians. At that time I was absolutely in the dark as to the course of the evening's fighting. I did not know even the circumstances that had precipitated the conflict. As I came through Ockham (for that was the way I returned, and not through Send and Old Woking)⁵ I saw along the western horizon a blood-red glow, which, as I drew nearer, crept slowly up the sky. The driving clouds of the gathering thunderstorm mingled there with masses of black and red smoke.

Ripley Street was deserted, and except for a lighted window or so the village showed not a sign of life; but I narrowly escaped an accident at the corner of the road to Pyrford, where a knot of people stood with their backs to me. They said nothing to me as I passed. I do not know what they knew of the things happening beyond the hill, nor do I know if the silent houses I passed on my way were sleeping securely, or deserted and empty, or harassed and watching against the terror of the night.

From Ripley until I came through Pyrford I was in the valley of the Wey, and the red glare was hidden from me. As I ascended the little hill beyond Pyrford Church the glare came into view again, and the trees about me shivered with the first intimation of the storm that was upon me. Then I heard midnight pealing out from Pyrford Church behind me, and then came the silhouette of Maybury Hill, with its tree-tops and roofs black and sharp against the red.

Even as I beheld this a lurid green glare lit the road about me and showed the distant woods towards Addlestone. I felt a tug at the reins. I saw that the driving clouds had been pierced as it were by a thread of green fire, suddenly lighting their confusion and falling into the field to my left. It was the Third Falling-Star!

Close on its apparition, and blindingly violet by contrast, danced out the first lightning of the gathering storm, and the thunder burst like a rocket overhead. The horse took the bit between his teeth and bolted.

A moderate incline runs towards the foot of Maybury Hill, and down this we clattered. Once the lightning had begun, it went on in as rapid a succession of flashes as I have ever seen. The thunder-claps, treading one on the heels of another and with a strange crackling accompaniment, sounded more like the working of a gigantic electric machine than the usual detonating reverberations. The flickering light was blinding and confusing, and a thin hail smote gustily at my face as I drove down the slope.

At first I regarded little but the road before me, and then abruptly my attention was arrested by something that was moving rapidly down the opposite slope of Maybury Hill. At first I took it for the wet roof of a house, but one flash following another showed it to be in swift rolling movement.[6] It was an elusive vision—a moment of bewildering darkness, and then, in a flash like daylight, the red masses of the Orphanage near the crest of the hill,[7] the green tops of the pine-trees, and this problematical object came out clear and sharp and bright.

And this Thing I saw! How can I describe it? A monstrous tripod, higher than many houses, striding over the young pine-trees, and smashing them aside in its career; a walking engine of glittering metal, striding now across the heather; articulate ropes of steel[8] dangling from it, and the clattering tumult of its passage mingling with the riot of the thunder. A flash, and it came out vividly, heeling over one way with two feet in the air, to vanish and reappear almost instantly as it seemed, with the next flash, a hundred yards nearer.[9] Can you imagine a milking-stool tilted and bowled violently along the ground? That was the impression those instant flashes gave. But instead of a milking-stool imagine it a great body of machinery on a tripod stand.[10]

Then suddenly the trees in the pine-wood ahead of me were parted, as brittle reeds are parted by a man thrusting through them; they were snapped off and driven headlong, and a second huge tripod appeared, rushing, as it seemed, headlong towards me. And I was galloping hard to meet it! At the sight of the second monster my nerve went altogether. Not stopping to look again, I wrenched the horse's head hard round to the right, and in another moment the dog-cart had heeled over upon the horse; the shafts smashed noisily, and I was flung sideways and fell heavily into a shallow pool of water.

I crawled out almost immediately, and crouched, my feet still in the water, under a clump of furze. The horse lay motionless (his neck was broken, poor brute!) and by the lightning flashes I saw the black bulk of the overturned dog-cart and the silhouette of the wheel still spinning slowly. In another moment the colossal mechanism went striding by me, and passed uphill towards Pyrford.

Seen nearer, the Thing was incredibly strange, for it was no mere insensate machine driving on its way. Machine it was, with a ringing metallic pace, and long, flexible, glittering tentacles (one of which gripped a young pine-tree) swinging and rattling about its strange body. It picked its road as it went striding along, and the brazen hood that surmounted it moved to and fro with the inevitable suggestion of a head looking about. Behind the main body was a huge mass of white metal like a gigantic fisherman's basket, and puffs of green smoke squirted out from the joints of the limbs as the monster swept by me. And in an instant it was gone.[11]

So much I saw then, all vaguely for the flickering of the lightning, in blinding high lights and dense black shadows.

As it passed it set up an exultant deafening howl that drowned the thunder—"Aloo! aloo!"—and in another minute it was with its companion, half a mile away, stooping over something in the field. I have no doubt this Thing in the field was the third of the ten cylinders they had fired at us from Mars.

For some minutes I lay there in the rain and darkness watching, by the intermittent light, these monstrous beings of metal moving about in the distance over the hedge-tops. A thin hail was now beginning, and as it came and went their figures grew misty and then flashed into clearness again. Now and then came a gap in the lightning, and the night swallowed them up.

I was soaked with hail[12] above and puddle-water below. It was some time before my blank astonishment would let me struggle up the bank to a drier position, or think at all of my imminent peril.

Not far from me was a little one-roomed squatter's hut of wood, surrounded by a patch of potato-garden. I struggled to my feet at last, and, crouching and making use of every chance of cover, I made a run for this. I hammered at the door, but I could not make the people hear (if there were any people inside), and after a time I desisted, and, availing myself of a ditch for the greater part of the way, succeeded in crawling, unobserved by these monstrous machines, into the pine-wood towards Maybury.

Under cover of this I pushed on, wet and shivering now, towards my own house. I walked among the trees trying to find the footpath. It was very dark indeed in the wood, for the lightning was now becoming infrequent, and the hail, which was pouring down in a torrent, fell in columns through the gaps in the heavy foliage.

If I had fully realised the meaning of all the things I had seen I should have immediately worked my way round through Byfleet to Street Cobham,* and so gone back to rejoin my wife at Leatherhead. But that night the strangeness of things about me, and my physical wretchedness, prevented me, for I was bruised, weary, wet to the skin, deafened and blinded by the storm.

I had a vague idea of going on to my own house, and that was as much motive as I had. I staggered through the trees, fell into a ditch and bruised my knees against a plank, and finally splashed out into the lane that ran down from the College Arms.[13] I say splashed, for the storm water was sweeping the sand down the hill in a muddy torrent. There in the darkness a man blundered into me and sent me reeling back.

He gave a cry of terror, sprang sideways, and rushed on before I could gather my wits sufficiently to speak to him. So heavy was the stress of the

---

*C, L; *Street Chobham*: P–PR, NY–E. See map for locations.

storm just at this place that I had the hardest task to win my way up the hill. I went close up to the fence on the left and worked my way along its palings.

Near the top I stumbled upon something soft, and, by a flash of lightning, saw between my feet a heap of black broadcloth and a pair of boots. Before I could distinguish clearly how the man lay, the flicker of light had passed. I stood over him waiting for the next flash. When it came, I saw that he was a sturdy man, cheaply but not shabbily dressed; his head was bent under his body, and he lay crumpled up close to the fence, as though he had been flung violently against it.

Overcoming the repugnance natural to one who had never before touched a dead body, I stooped and turned him over to feel for his heart. He was quite dead. Apparently his neck had been broken. The lightning flashed for a third time, and his face leaped upon me. I sprang to my feet. It was the landlord of the Spotted Dog, whose conveyance I had taken.

I stepped over him gingerly and pushed on up the hill. I made my way by the police-station and the College Arms towards my own house. Nothing was burning on the hill-side, though from the common there still came a red glare and a rolling tumult of ruddy smoke beating up against the drenching hail. So far as I could see by the flashes, the houses about me were mostly uninjured. By the College Arms a dark heap lay in the road.

Down the road towards Maybury Bridge there were voices and the sound of feet, but I had not the courage to shout or to go to them. I let myself in with my latch-key, closed, locked and bolted the door, staggered to the foot of the staircase, and sat down. My imagination was full of those striding metallic monsters, and of the dead body smashed against the fence.

I crouched at the foot of the staircase with my back to the wall, shivering violently.

XI

AT THE WINDOW

I HAVE ALREADY SAID that my storms of emotion have a trick of exhausting themselves. After a time I discovered that I was cold and wet, and with little pools of water about me on the stair-carpet. I got up almost mechanically, went into the dining-room and drank some whiskey, and then I was moved to change my clothes.

After I had done that I went upstairs to my study, but why I did so I do not know. The window of my study looks over the trees and the railway towards Horsell Common. In the hurry of our departure this window had been left open. The passage was dark, and, by contrast with the picture the window-frame enclosed, the side of the room seemed impenetrably dark. I stopped short in the doorway.

The thunderstorm had passed. The towers of the Oriental College and the pine-trees about it had gone, and very far away, lit by a vivid red glare, the common about the sand-pits was visible. Across the light, huge black shapes, grotesque and strange, moved busily to and fro.

It seemed indeed as if the whole country in that direction was on fire—a broad hill-side set with minute tongues of flame, swaying and writhing with the gusts of the dying storm, and throwing a red reflection upon the cloud-scud above. Every now and then a haze of smoke from some nearer conflagration drove across the window and hid the Martian shapes. I could not see what they were doing, nor the clear form of them, nor recognise the black objects they were busied upon. Neither could I see the nearer fire, though the reflections of it danced on the wall and ceiling of the study. A sharp, resinous tang of burning was in the air.

I closed the door noiselessly and crept towards the window. As I did so, the view opened out until, on the one hand, it reached to the houses about Woking station, and on the other to the charred and blackened pine-woods of Byfleet. There was a light down below the hill, on the railway, near the arch, and several of the houses along the Maybury road and the streets near the station were glowing ruins. The light upon the railway puzzled me at first; there were a black heap and a vivid glare, and to the right of that a row of yellow oblongs. Then I perceived this was a wrecked train, the fore-part smashed and on fire, the hinder carriages still upon the rails.

Between these three main centres of light, the houses, the train, and the burning country towards Chobham, stretched irregular patches of dark country, broken here and there by intervals of dimly glowing and smoking ground. It was the strangest spectacle, that black expanse set with fire. It reminded me, more than anything else, of the Potteries[1] at night. At first I could distinguish no people at all, though I peered intently for them. Later I saw against the light of Woking station a number of black figures hurrying one after the other across the line.

And this was the little world in which I had been living securely for years, this fiery chaos![2] What had happened in the last seven hours I still did not know; nor did I know, though I was beginning to guess, the relation between these mechanical colossi and the sluggish lumps I had seen disgorged from the cylinder. With a queer feeling of impersonal interest I turned my desk-chair to the window, sat down, and stared at the blackened country, and particularly at the three gigantic black things that were going to and fro in the glare about the sand-pits.

They seemed amazingly busy. I began to ask myself what they could be. Were they intelligent mechanisms? Such a thing I felt was impossible. Or did a Martian sit within each, ruling, directing, using, much as a man's brain sits and rules in his body?[3] I began to compare the things to human machines, to ask myself for the first time in my life how an iron-clad[4] or a steam-engine would seem to an intelligent lower animal.

The storm had left the sky clear, and over the smoke of the burning land the little fading pin-point of Mars was dropping into the west, when a soldier came into my garden. I heard a slight scraping at the fence, and rousing myself from the lethargy that had fallen upon me, I looked down and saw him dimly, clambering over the palings. At the sight of another human being my torpor passed, and I leaned out of the window eagerly.

"Hist!" said I, in a whisper.

He stopped astride of the fence in doubt. Then he came over and across the lawn to the corner of the house. He bent down and stepped softly.

"Who's there?" he said, also whispering, standing under the window and peering up.

"Where are you going?" I asked.

"God knows."

"Are you trying to hide?"

"That's it."

"Come into the house," I said.

I went down, unfastened the door, and let him in, and locked the door again. I could not see his face. He was hatless, and his coat was unbuttoned.

"My God!" he said, as I drew him in.

"What has happened?" I asked.

"What hasn't?" In the obscurity I could see he made a gesture of despair. "They wiped us out— simply wiped us out," he repeated again and again.

He followed me, almost mechanically, into the dining-room.

"Take some whiskey," I said, pouring out a stiff dose.

He drank it. Then abruptly he sat down before the table, put his head on his arms, and began to sob and weep like a little boy, in a perfect passion of emotion, while I, with a curious forgetfulness of my own recent despair, stood beside him, wondering.

It was a long time before he could steady his nerves to answer my questions, and then he answered perplexingly and brokenly. He was a driver in the artillery, and had only come into action about seven. At that time firing was going on across the common, and it was said the first party of Martians were crawling slowly towards their second cylinder under cover of a metal shield.

Later this shield staggered up on tripod legs and became the first of the fighting-machines I had seen. The gun he drove had been unlimbered near Horsell, in order to command the sand-pits, and its arrival it was that had precipitated the action. As the limber gunners went to the rear, his horse trod in a rabbit-hole and came down, throwing him into a depression of the ground. At the same moment the gun exploded behind him, the ammunition blew up, there was fire all about him, and he found himself lying under a heap of charred dead men and dead horses.

"I lay still," he said, "scared out of my wits, with the forequarter of a horse atop of me. We'd been wiped out. And the smell—good God! Like burnt meat! I was hurt across the back by the fall of the horse, and there I had to lie until I felt better. Just like parade it had been a minute before— then stumble, bang, swish!

"Wiped out!" he said.

He had hid under the dead horse for a long time, peeping out furtively across the common. The Cardigan men[5] had tried a rush, in skirmishing order, at the pit, simply to be swept out of existence. Then the monster had risen to its feet, and had begun to walk leisurely to and fro across the common among the few fugitives, with its headlike hood turning about exactly like the head of a cowled human being. A kind of arm carried a complicated metallic case, about which green flashes scintillated, and out of the funnel of this there smote the Heat-Ray.

In a few minutes there was, so far as the soldier could see, not a living thing left upon the common, and every bush and tree upon it that was not already a blackened skeleton was burning. The hussars had been on the road beyond the curvature of the ground, and he saw nothing of them. He heard the Maxims rattle for a time and then become still. The giant saved Woking station and its cluster of houses until the last; then in a moment the Heat-Ray was brought to bear, and the town became a heap of fiery ruins. Then the Thing shut off the Heat-Ray, and, turning its back upon the artilleryman, began to waddle away towards the smouldering pine-woods that sheltered the second cylinder. As it did so a second glittering Titan built itself up out of the pit.

The second monster followed the first, and at that the artilleryman began to crawl very cautiously across the hot heather ash towards Horsell. He managed to get alive into the ditch by the side of the road, and so escaped to Woking. There his story became ejaculatory. The place was impassable. It seems there were a few people alive there, frantic for the most part, and many burned and scalded. He was turned aside by the fire, and hid among some almost scorching heaps of broken wall as one of the Martian giants returned. He saw this one pursue a man, catch him up in one of its steely tentacles, and knock his head against the trunk of a pine-tree. At last, after nightfall, the artilleryman made a rush for it and got over the railway embankment.

Since then he had been skulking along towards Maybury, in the hope of getting out of danger Londonward. People were hiding in trenches and cellars, and many of the survivors had made off towards Woking village and Send. He had been consumed with thirst until he found one of the water mains near the railway arch smashed, and the water bubbling out like a spring upon the road.

That was the story I got from him, bit by bit. He grew calmer telling me and trying to make me see the things he had seen. He had eaten no food since mid-day, he told me early in his narrative, and I found some mutton and bread in the pantry and brought it into the room. We lit no lamp for fear of attracting the Martians, and ever and again our hands would touch upon bread or meat.[6] As he talked, things about us came darkly out of the darkness, and the trampled bushes and broken rose-trees outside the window grew distinct. It would seem that a number of men or animals had rushed across the lawn. I began to see his face, blackened and haggard, as no doubt mine was also.

When we had finished eating we went softly upstairs to my study, and I looked again out of the open window. In one night the valley had become a valley of ashes. The fires had dwindled now. Where flames had been there were now streamers of smoke; but the countless ruins of shattered and gutted houses and blasted and blackened trees that the night had hidden stood out now gaunt and terrible in the pitiless light of dawn. Yet here and there some object had had the luck to escape—a white railway signal here, the end of a green-house there, white and fresh amid the wreckage. Never before in the history of warfare[7] had destruction been so indiscriminate and so universal. And shining with the growing light of the east, three of the metallic giants stood about the pit, their cowls rotating as though they were surveying the desolation they had made.

It seemed to me that the pit had been enlarged, and ever and again puffs of vivid green vapour streamed up out of it towards the brightening dawn—streamed up, whirled, broke, and vanished.

Beyond were the pillars of fire[8] about Chobham. They became pillars of bloodshot smoke at the first touch of day.

XII

WHAT I SAW OF THE DESTRUCTION OF WEYBRIDGE AND SHEPPERTON

As the dawn grew brighter we withdrew from the window from which we had watched the Martians, and went very quietly downstairs.

The artilleryman agreed with me that the house was no place to stay in. He proposed, he said, to make his way Londonward, and thence rejoin his battery—No. 12, of the Horse Artillery. My plan was to return at once to Leatherhead; and so greatly had the strength of the Martians impressed me that I had determined to take my wife to Newhaven, and go with her out of the country forthwith. For I already perceived clearly that the country about London must inevitably be the scene of a disastrous struggle before such creatures as these could be destroyed.

Between us and Leatherhead, however, lay the Third Cylinder, with its guarding giants. Had I been alone, I think I should have taken my chance and struck across country. But the artilleryman dissuaded me: "It's no kindness to the right sort of wife," he said, "to make her a widow;" and in the end I agreed to go with him, under cover of the woods, northward as far as Street Cobham* before I parted with him. Thence I would make a big détour by Epsom to reach Leatherhead.[1]

I should have started at once, but my companion had been in active service and he knew better than that. He made me ransack the house for a flask, which he filled with whiskey; and we lined every available pocket with packets of biscuits and slices of meat. Then we crept out of the house, and ran as quickly as we could down the ill-made road by which I had come overnight. The houses seemed deserted. In the road lay a group of three charred bodies close together, struck dead by the Heat-Ray; and here and there were things that people had dropped—a clock, a slipper, a silver spoon,

---

*C, L; *Street Chobham*: P–PR, NY–E. See map for locations.

and the like poor valuables. At the corner turning up towards the post-office a little cart, filled with boxes and furniture, and horseless, heeled over on a broken wheel. A cash-box had been hastily smashed open and thrown under the débris.

Except the lodge at the Orphanage, which was still on fire, none of the houses had suffered very greatly here. The Heat-Ray had shaved the chimney-tops and passed. Yet, save ourselves, there did not seem to be a living soul on Maybury Hill. The majority of the inhabitants had escaped, I suppose, by way of the Old Woking road—the road I had taken when I drove to Leatherhead—or they had hidden.

We went down the lane, by the body of the man in black, sodden now from the overnight hail, and broke into the woods at the foot of the hill. We pushed through these towards the railway without meeting a soul. The woods across the line were but the scarred and blackened ruins of woods; for the most part the trees had fallen, but a certain proportion still stood, dismal grey stems, with dark-brown foliage instead of green.

On our side the fire had done no more than scorch the nearer trees; it had failed to secure its footing. In one place the woodmen had been at work on Saturday; trees, felled and freshly trimmed, lay in a clearing, with heaps of sawdust by the sawing-machine and its engine. Hard by was a temporary hut, deserted. There was not a breath of wind this morning, and everything was strangely still. Even the birds were hushed,[2] and as we hurried along I and the artilleryman talked in whispers and looked now and again over our shoulders. Once or twice we stopped to listen.

After a time we drew near the road, and as we did so we heard the clatter of hoofs and saw through the tree-stems three cavalry soldiers riding slowly towards Woking. We hailed them, and they halted while we hurried towards them. It was a lieutenant and a couple of privates of the 8th Hussars, with a stand like a theodolite, which the artilleryman told me was a heliograph.

"You are the first men I've seen coming this way this morning," said the lieutenant. "What's brewing?"

His voice and face were eager. The men behind him stared curiously. The artilleryman jumped down the bank into the road and saluted.

"Gun destroyed last night, sir. Have been hiding. Trying to rejoin battery, sir. You'll come in sight of the Martians, I expect, about half a mile along this road."

"What the dickens are they like?" asked the lieutenant.

"Giants in armour, sir. Hundred feet high. Three legs and a body like 'luminium,[3] with a mighty great head in a hood, sir."

"Get out!" said the lieutenant. "What confounded nonsense!"

"You'll see, sir. They carry a kind of box, sir, that shoots fire and strikes you dead."

"What d'ye mean—a gun?"

"No, sir," and the artilleryman began a vivid account of the Heat-Ray. Half-way through, the lieutenant* interrupted him and looked up at me. I was still standing on the bank by the side of the road.

"Did you see it?" said the lieutenant.

"It's perfectly true," I said.

"Well," said the lieutenant, "I suppose it's my business to see it too. Look here"—to the artilleryman—"we're detailed here clearing people out of their houses. You'd better go along and report yourself to Brigadier-General Marvin, and tell him all you know. He's at Weybridge. Know the way?"

"I do," I said;[4] and he turned his horse southward again.

"Half a mile, you say?" said he.

"At most," I answered, and pointed over the tree-tops southward. He thanked me and rode on, and we saw them no more.

Farther along we came upon a group of three women and two children in the road, busy clearing out a labourer's cottage. They had got hold of a little hand-truck, and were piling it up with unclean-looking bundles and shabby furniture. They were all too assiduously engaged to talk to us as we passed.

By Byfleet station we emerged from the pine-trees, and found the country calm and peaceful under the morning sunlight. We were far beyond the range of the Heat-Ray there, and had it not been for the silent desertion of some of the houses, the stirring movement of packing in others, and the knot of soldiers standing on the bridge over the railway and staring down the line towards Woking, the day would have seemed very like any other Sunday.

Several farm waggons and carts were moving creakily along the road to Addlestone, and suddenly through the gate of a field we saw, across a stretch of flat meadow, six twelve-pounders, standing neatly at equal distances pointing towards Woking. The gunners stood by the guns waiting, and the ammunition waggons were at a business-like distance. The men stood almost as if under inspection.

"That's good!" said I. "They will get one fair shot, at any rate."

The artilleryman hesitated at the gate.

"I shall go on," he said.

---

*C, A; *Half-way through the lieutenant*: P–AG, E.

Farther on towards Weybridge, just over the bridge, there were a number of men in white fatigue jackets throwing up a long rampart, and more guns behind.

"It's bows and arrows against the lightning, anyhow," said the artilleryman. "They 'aven't seen that fire-beam yet."

The officers who were not actively engaged stood and stared over the tree-tops south-westward, and the men digging would stop every now and again to stare in the same direction.

Byfleet was in a tumult; people packing, and a score of hussars, some of them dismounted, some on horseback, were hunting them about. Three or four black government waggons, with crosses in white circles, and an old omnibus, among other vehicles, were being loaded in the village street. There were scores of people, most of them sufficiently sabbatical[5] to have assumed their best clothes. The soldiers were having the greatest difficulty in making them realise the gravity of their position. We saw one shrivelled old fellow with a huge box and a score or more of flower-pots containing orchids, angrily expostulating with the corporal who would leave them behind. I stopped and gripped his arm.

"Do you know what's over there?" I said, pointing at the pine-tops that hid the Martians.

"Eh?" said he, turning. "I was explainin' these is vallyble."

"Death! " I shouted. "Death is coming! Death!"[6] and leaving him to digest that if he could, I hurried on after the artilleryman. At the corner I looked back. The soldier had left him, and he was still standing by his box, with the pots of orchids on the lid of it, and staring vaguely over the trees.

No one in Weybridge could tell us where the headquarters were established; the whole place was in such confusion as I had never seen in any town before. Carts, carriages everywhere, the most astonishing miscellany of conveyances and horseflesh. The respectable inhabitants of the place, men in golf and boating costumes, wives prettily dressed, were packing; riverside* loafers energetically helping, children excited, and, for the most part, highly delighted at this astonishing variation of their Sunday experiences. In the midst of it all the worthy vicar was very pluckily holding an early celebration, and his bell was jangling out above the excitement.

I and the artilleryman, seated on the step of the drinking-fountain,[7] made a very passable meal upon what we had brought with us. Patrols of soldiers—here no longer hussars, but grenadiers in white—were warning people to move now or to take refuge in their cellars as soon as the firing began. We saw as we crossed the railway bridge that a growing crowd of

---

*A; packing, riverside: C–AG, E.

people had assembled in and about the railway station, and the swarming platform was piled with boxes and packages. The ordinary traffic had been stopped, I believe, in order to allow of the passage of troops and guns to Chertsey, and I have heard since that a savage struggle occurred for places in the special trains that were put on at a later hour.

We remained at Weybridge until mid-day, and at that hour we found ourselves at the place near Shepperton Lock where the Wey and Thames join. Part of the time we spent helping two old women to pack a little cart. The Wey has a treble mouth, and at this point boats are to be hired, and there was a ferry across the river. On the Shepperton side[8] was an inn with a lawn, and beyond that the tower of Shepperton Church—it has been replaced by a spire[9]—rose above the trees.

Here we found an excited and noisy crowd of fugitives. As yet the flight had not grown to a panic, but there were already far more people than all the boats going to and fro could enable to cross. People came panting along under heavy burdens; one husband and wife were even carrying a small outhouse door between them, with some of their household goods piled thereon. One man told us he meant to try to get away from Shepperton station.

There was a lot of shouting, and one man was even jesting. The idea people seemed to have here was that the Martians were simply formidable human beings, who might attack and sack the town, to be certainly destroyed in the end. Every now and then people would glance nervously across the Wey, at the meadows towards Chertsey,[10] but everything over there was still.

Across the Thames, except just where the boats landed, everything was quiet, in vivid contrast to* the Surrey side.[11] The people who landed there from the boats went tramping off down the lane. The big ferry-boat had just made a journey. Three or four soldiers stood on the lawn of the inn, staring and jesting at the fugitives, without offering to help. The inn was closed, as it was now within prohibited hours.

"What's that?" cried a boatman, and "Shut up, you fool!" said a man near me to a yelping dog. Then the sound came again, this time from the direction of Chertsey, a muffled thud—the sound of a gun.

The fighting was beginning. Almost immediately unseen batteries across the river to our right, unseen because of the trees, took up the chorus, firing heavily one after the other. A woman screamed. Every one stood arrested by the sudden stir of battle, near us and yet invisible to us. Nothing was to be seen save flat meadows, cows feeding unconcernedly for the most part, and silvery pollard willows motionless in the warm sunlight.

---

*A; contrast with: C–AG ("to" is pencilled into AG with a question mark, then erased).

"The sojers'll stop 'em," said a woman beside me, doubtfully. A haziness rose over the tree-tops.

Then suddenly we saw a rush of smoke far away up the river, a puff of smoke that jerked up into the air and hung; and forthwith the ground heaved underfoot and a heavy explosion shook the air, smashing two or three windows in the houses near, and leaving us astonished.

"Here they are!" shouted a man in a blue jersey. "Yonder! D'yer see them? Yonder!"

Quickly, one after the other, one, two, three, four of the armoured Martians appeared, far away over the little trees, across the flat meadows that stretch towards Chertsey, and striding hurriedly towards the river. Little cowled figures they seemed at first, going with a rolling motion and as fast as flying birds.

Then, advancing obliquely towards us, came a fifth. Their armoured bodies glittered in the sun as they swept swiftly forward upon the guns, growing rapidly larger as they drew nearer. One on the extreme left, the remotest that is, flourished a huge case high in the air, and the ghostly, terrible Heat-Ray I had already seen on Friday night smote towards Chertsey and struck the town.

At sight of these strange, swift, and terrible creatures the crowd near the water's edge seemed to me to be for a moment horror-struck. There was no screaming or shouting, but a silence. Then a hoarse murmur and a movement of feet—a splashing from the water. A man, too frightened to drop the portmanteau he carried on his shoulder, swung round and sent me staggering with a blow from the corner of his burden. A woman thrust at me with her hand and rushed past me. I turned, with* the rush of the people, but I was not too terrified for thought. The terrible Heat-Ray was in my mind. To get under water! That was it!

"Get under water!" I shouted, unheeded.

I faced about again, and rushed towards the approaching Martian, rushed right down the gravelly beach and headlong into the water. Others did the same. A boatload of people putting back came leaping out as I rushed past. The stones under my feet were muddy and slippery, and the river was so low that I ran perhaps twenty feet scarcely waist-deep. Then, as the Martian towered overhead scarcely a couple of hundred yards away, I flung myself forward under the surface. The splashes of the people in the boats leaping into the river sounded like thunder-claps in my ears. People were landing hastily on both sides of the river.

But the Martian machine took no more notice for the moment of the people running this way and that than a man would of the confusion of

---

*AG–A; turned, too, with: C, L–NY; turned too, with: P–PR; turned with: E.

ants in a nest against which his foot has kicked. When, half suffocated, I raised my head above water, the Martian's hood pointed at the batteries that were still firing across the river, and as it advanced it swung loose what must have been the generator of the Heat-Ray.

In another moment it was on the bank, and in a stride wading half-way across. The knees of its foremost legs bent at the farther bank, and in another moment it had raised itself to its full height again, close to the village of Shepperton. Forthwith the six guns which, unknown to any one on the right bank, had been hidden behind the outskirts of that village, fired simultaneously. The sudden near concussions, the last close upon the first, made my heart jump. The monster was already raising the case generating the Heat-Ray as the first shell burst six yards above the hood.

I gave a cry of astonishment. I saw and thought nothing of the other four Martian monsters; my attention was riveted upon the nearer incident. Simultaneously two other shells burst in the air near the body as the hood twisted round in time to receive, but not in time to dodge, the fourth shell.

The shell burst clean in the face of the Thing. The hood bulged, flashed, was whirled off in a dozen tattered fragments of red flesh and glittering metal.

"Hit!" shouted I, with something between a scream and a cheer.

I heard answering shouts from the people in the water about me. I could have leaped out of the water with that momentary exultation.

The decapitated colossus reeled like a drunken giant; but it did not fall over. It recovered its balance by a miracle, and, no longer heeding its steps and with the camera that fired the Heat-Ray now rigidly upheld, it reeled swiftly upon Shepperton. The living intelligence, the Martian within the hood, was slain and splashed to the four winds of heaven,[12] and the Thing was now but a mere intricate device of metal whirling to destruction. It drove along in a straight line, incapable of guidance. It struck the tower of Shepperton Church, smashing it down as the impact of a battering-ram might have done, swerved aside, blundered on, and collapsed with tremendous force into the river out of my sight.

A violent explosion shook the air, and a spout of water, steam, mud, and shattered metal shot far up into the sky. As the camera of the Heat-Ray hit the water, the latter had immediately flashed into steam. In another moment a huge wave, like a muddy tidal bore but almost scaldingly hot, came sweeping round the bend up-stream. I saw people struggling shore-wards, and heard their screaming and shouting faintly above the seething and roar of the Martian's collapse.

For the moment* I heeded nothing of the heat, forgot the patent need of self-preservation. I splashed through the tumultuous water, pushing aside

---

*C–A; For a moment: E.

a man in black to do so, until I could see round the bend. Half a dozen deserted boats pitched aimlessly upon the confusion of the waves. The fallen Martian came into sight down-stream, lying across the river, and for the most part submerged.

Thick clouds of steam were pouring off the wreckage, and through the tumultuously whirling wisps I could see, intermittently and vaguely, the gigantic limbs churning the water and flinging a splash and spray of mud and froth into the air. The tentacles swayed and struck like living arms, and, save for the helpless purposelessness of these movements, it was as if some wounded thing were struggling for its life amid the waves. Enormous quantities of a ruddy-brown fluid were spurting up in noisy jets out of the machine.

My attention was diverted from this death flurry by a furious yelling, like that of the thing called a siren in our manufacturing towns. A man, knee-deep near the towing-path, shouted inaudibly to me and pointed. Looking back, I saw the other Martians advancing with gigantic strides down the river-bank from the direction of Chertsey. The Shepperton guns spoke this time unavailingly.

At that I ducked at once under water, and, holding my breath until movement was an agony, blundered painfully ahead under the surface as long as I could. The water was in a tumult about me, and rapidly growing hotter.

When for a moment I raised my head to take breath and throw the hair and water from my eyes, the steam was rising in a whirling white fog that at first hid the Martians altogether. The noise was deafening. Then I saw them dimly, colossal figures of grey, magnified by the mist.[13] They had passed by me, and two were stooping over the frothing, tumultuous ruins of their comrade.

The third and fourth stood beside him in the water, one perhaps two hundred yards from me, the other towards Laleham.[14] The generators of the Heat-Rays waved high, and the hissing beams smote down this way and that.

The air was full of sound, a deafening and confusing conflict of noises— the clangorous din of the Martians, the crash of falling houses, the thud of trees, fences, sheds flashing into flame, and the crackling and roaring of fire. Dense black smoke was leaping up to mingle with the steam from the river, and as the Heat-Ray went to and fro over Weybridge its impact was marked by flashes of incandescent white, that gave place at once to a smoky dance of lurid flames. The nearer houses still stood intact, awaiting their fate, shadowy, faint, and pallid in the steam, with the fire behind them going to and fro.

For a moment perhaps I stood there, breast-high in the almost boiling water, dumbfounded at my position, hopeless of escape. Through the reek

I could see the people who had been with me in the river scrambling out of the water through the reeds, like little frogs hurrying through grass from the advance of a man, or running to and fro in utter dismay on the towing-path.

Then suddenly the white flashes of the Heat-Ray came leaping towards me. The houses caved in as they dissolved at its touch, and darted out flames; the trees changed to fire with a roar. The Ray flickered up and down the towing-path, licking off the people who ran this way and that, and came down to the water's edge not fifty yards from where I stood. It swept across the river to Shepperton, and the water in its track rose in a boiling weal crested with steam. I turned shoreward.

In another moment the huge wave, well-nigh at the boiling-point, had rushed upon me. I screamed aloud, and scalded, half blinded, agonised, I staggered through the leaping, hissing water towards the shore. Had my foot stumbled, it would have been the end. I fell helplessly, in full sight of the Martians, upon the broad, bare gravelly spit that runs down to mark the angle of the Wey and Thames. I expected nothing but death.

I have a dim memory of the foot of a Martian coming down within a score of yards of my head, driving straight into the loose gravel, whirling it this way and that, and lifting again; of a long suspense, and then of the four carrying the débris of their comrade between them, now clear and then presently faint through a veil of smoke, receding interminably, as it seemed to me, across a vast space of river and meadow. And then, very slowly, I realised that by a miracle I had escaped.

XIII

HOW I FELL IN WITH THE CURATE

After getting this sudden lesson in the power of terrestrial weapons, the Martians retreated to their original position upon Horsell Common; and in their haste, and encumbered with the débris of their smashed companion, they no doubt overlooked many such a stray and negligible victim as myself. Had they left their comrade and pushed on forthwith, there was nothing at that time between them and London but batteries of twelve-pounder guns, and they would certainly have reached the capital in advance of the tidings of their approach; as sudden, dreadful, and destructive their advent would have been as the earthquake that destroyed Lisbon a century ago.[1]

But they were in no hurry. Cylinder followed cylinder on its interplanetary flight; every twenty-four hours brought them reinforcement. And meanwhile the military and naval authorities, now fully alive to the tremendous power of their antagonists, worked with furious energy. Every minute a fresh gun came into position until, before twilight, every copse, every row of suburban villas on the hilly slopes about Kingston and Richmond, masked an expectant black muzzle. And through the charred and desolated area—perhaps twenty square miles altogether—that encircled the Martian encampment on Horsell Common, through charred and ruined villages among the green trees, through the blackened and smoking arcades that had been but a day ago pine spinneys, crawled the devoted scouts with the heliographs that were presently to warn the gunners of the Martian approach. But the Martians now understood our command of artillery and the danger of human proximity, and not a man ventured within a mile of either cylinder, save at the price of his life.

It would seem that these giants spent the earlier part of the afternoon in going to and fro, transferring everything from the second and third cylinders—the second in Addlestone Golf Links and the third at Pyrford—to their original pit on Horsell Common. Over that, above the blackened heather and ruined buildings that stretched far and wide, stood one as sentinel, while the rest abandoned their vast fighting-machines and descended into the pit. They were hard at work there far into the night, and the towering pillar of dense green smoke that rose therefrom could be seen from the hills about Merrow, and even, it is said, from Banstead and Epsom Downs.

And while the Martians behind me were thus preparing for their next sally, and in front of me Humanity gathered for the battle, I made my way with infinite pains and labour from the fire and smoke of burning Weybridge towards London.

I saw an abandoned boat, very small and remote, drifting down-stream; and throwing off the most of my sodden clothes, I went after it, gained it, and so escaped out of that destruction. There were no oars in the boat, but I contrived to paddle, as well as my parboiled hands would allow, down the river towards Halliford and Walton, going very tediously and continually looking behind me, as you may well understand. I followed the river, because I considered that the water gave me my best chance of escape should these giants return.

The hot water from the Martian's overthrow drifted down-stream with me, so that for the best part of a mile I could see little of either bank. Once, however, I made out a string of black figures hurrying across the meadows from the direction of Weybridge. Halliford, it seemed, was deserted, and several of the houses facing the river were on fire. It was strange to see the place quite tranquil, quite desolate under the hot, blue sky, with the smoke and little threads of flame going straight up into the heat of the afternoon. Never before had I seen houses burning without the accompaniment of an obstructive crowd.[2] A little farther on the dry reeds up the bank were smoking and glowing, and a line of fire inland was marching steadily across a late field of hay.

For a long time I drifted, so painful and weary was I after the violence I had been through,[3] and so intense the heat upon the water. Then my fears got the better of me again, and I resumed my paddling. The sun scorched my bare back. At last, as the bridge at Walton was coming into sight round the bend, my fever and faintness overcame my fears, and I landed on the Middlesex bank[4] and lay down, deadly sick, amid the long grass. I suppose the time was then about four or five o'clock. I got up presently, walked perhaps half a mile without meeting a soul, and then lay down again in the shadow of a hedge. I seem to remember talking, wanderingly, to myself during that last spurt. I was also very thirsty, and bitterly regretful I had drunk no more water. It is a curious thing that I felt angry with my wife; I cannot account for it, but my impotent desire to reach Leatherhead worried me excessively.

I do not clearly remember the arrival of the curate,[5] so that probably I dozed. I became aware of him as a seated figure in soot-smudged shirt-sleeves, and with his upturned, clean-shaven face staring at a faint flickering that danced over the sky. The sky was what is called a mackerel sky—rows and rows of faint down-plumes of cloud, just tinted with the midsummer sunset.

I sat up, and at the rustle of my motion he looked at me quickly.

"Have you any water?" I asked abruptly.

He shook his head.

"You have been asking for water for the last hour," he said.

For a moment we were silent, taking stock of each other. I dare say he found me a strange enough figure, naked save for my water-soaked trousers and socks, scalded, and my face and shoulders blackened by the smoke. His face was a fair weakness, his chin retreated, and his hair lay in crisp, almost flaxen curls on his low forehead; his eyes were rather large, pale-blue, and blankly staring. He spoke abruptly, looking vacantly away from me.[6]

"What does it mean?" he said. "What do these things mean?"

I stared at him and made no answer.

He extended a thin white hand and spoke in almost a complaining tone.

"Why are these things permitted? What sins have we done? The morning service was over, I was walking through the roads to clear my brain for the afternoon, and then—fire, earthquake, death! As if it were Sodom and Gomorrah![7] All our work undone, all the work—What are these Martians?"

"What are we?"[8] I answered, clearing my throat.

He gripped his knees and turned to look at me again. For half a minute, perhaps, he stared silently.

"I was walking through the roads to clear my brain," he said. "And suddenly—fire, earthquake, death!"

He relapsed into silence, with his chin now sunken almost to his knees. Presently he began waving his hand.

"All the work—all the Sunday-schools— What have we done—what has Weybridge done? Everything gone—everything destroyed. The church! We rebuilt it only three years ago. Gone!—swept out of existence! Why?"

Another pause, and he broke out again like one demented.

"The smoke of her burning goeth up for ever and ever!"[9] he shouted.

His eyes flamed, and he pointed a lean finger in the direction of Weybridge.

By this time I was beginning to take his measure. The tremendous tragedy in which he had been involved—it was evident he was a fugitive from Weybridge—had driven him to the very verge of his reason.

"Are we far from Sunbury?" I said, in a matter-of-fact tone.

"What are we to do?" he asked. "Are these creatures everywhere? Has the earth been given over to them?"

"Are we far from Sunbury?"

"Only this morning I officiated at early celebration—"

"Things have changed," I said, quietly. "You must keep your head. There is still hope."

"Hope!"

"Yes. Plentiful hope—for all this destruction!"

I began to explain my view of our position. He listened at first, but as I went on the dawning interest in* his eyes gave place to their former stare, and his regard wandered from me.

"This must be the beginning of the end," he said, interrupting me. "The end! The great and terrible day of the Lord! When men shall call upon the mountains and the rocks to fall upon them and hide them—hide them from the face of Him that sitteth upon the throne!"

I began to understand the position. I ceased my laboured reasoning, struggled to my feet, and, standing over him, laid my hand on his shoulder.

"Be a man!" said I. "You are scared out of your wits! What good is religion if it collapses under calamity? Think of what earthquakes and floods, wars and volcanoes, have done before to men! Did you think God had exempted Weybridge? He is not an insurance agent."

For a time he sat in blank silence.

"But how can we escape?" he asked, suddenly. "They are invulnerable, they are pitiless."

"Neither the one nor, perhaps, the other," I answered. "And the mightier they are the more sane and wary should we be. One of them was killed yonder not three hours ago."

"Killed!" he said, staring about him. "How can God's ministers be killed?"

"I saw it happen." I proceeded to tell him. "We have chanced to come in for the thick of it," said I, "and that is all."

"What is that flicker in the sky?" he asked, abruptly.

I told him it was the heliograph signalling—that it was the sign of human help and effort in the sky.

"We are in the midst of it," I said, "quiet as it is. That flicker in the sky tells of the gathering storm. Yonder, I take it, are the Martians, and Londonward, where those hills rise about Richmond and Kingston and the trees give cover, earthworks are being thrown up and guns are being placed. Presently the Martians will be coming this way again."

And even as I spoke he sprang to his feet and stopped me by a gesture.

---

*C–NY, A; *the interest dawning in*: AG, E.

"Listen!" he said.

From beyond the low hills across the water came the dull resonance of distant guns and a remote, weird crying. Then everything was still. A cock-chafer came droning over the hedge and past us. High in the west the crescent moon hung faint and pale above the smoke of Weybridge and Shepperton and the hot, still splendour of the sunset.

"We had better follow this path," I said, "northward."[10]

XIV

IN LONDON[1]

MY YOUNGER BROTHER[2] was in London when the Martians fell at Woking. He was a medical student, working for an imminent examination, and he heard nothing of the arrival until Saturday morning. The morning papers on Saturday contained, in addition to lengthy special articles on the planet Mars, on life in the planets, and so forth, a brief and vaguely worded telegram, all the more striking for its brevity.

The Martians, alarmed by the approach of a crowd, had killed a number of people with a quick-firing gun, so the story ran. The telegram concluded with the words: "Formidable as they seem to be, the Martians have not moved from the pit into which they have fallen, and, indeed, seem incapable of doing so. Probably this is due to the relative strength of the earth's gravitational energy." On that last text their leader-writer expanded very comfortingly.

Of course all the students in the crammer's biology class,[3] to which my brother went that day, were intensely interested, but there were no signs of any unusual excitement in the streets. The afternoon papers puffed scraps of news under big headlines. They had nothing to tell beyond the movements of troops about the common, and the burning of the pine-woods between Woking and Weybridge, until eight. Then the *St. James's Gazette*,[4] in an extra special edition, announced the bare fact of the interruption of telegraphic communication. This was thought to be due to the falling of burning pine-trees across the line. Nothing more of the fighting was known that night, the night of my drive to Leatherhead and back.

My brother felt no anxiety about us, as he knew from the description in the papers that the cylinder was a good two miles from my house. He made up his mind to run down that night to me, in order, as he says, to see the Things before they were killed. He despatched a telegram, which never reached me, about four o'clock, and spent the evening at a music-hall.

In London, also, on Saturday night there was a thunderstorm, and my brother reached Waterloo in a cab. On the platform from which the midnight train usually starts he learned, after some waiting, that an accident prevented trains from reaching Woking that night. The nature of the accident he could not ascertain; indeed, the railway authorities did not clearly know at that time. There was very little excitement in the station, as the officials, failing to realise that anything further than a breakdown between Byfleet and Woking junction had occurred, were running the theatre trains which usually passed through Woking, round by Virginia Water or Guildford. They were busy making the necessary arrangements to alter the route of the Southampton and Portsmouth Sunday League[5] excursions. A nocturnal newspaper reporter, mistaking my brother for the traffic manager, to whom he bears a slight resemblance, waylaid and tried to interview him. Few people, excepting the railway officials, connected the breakdown with the Martians.

I have read, in another account of these events, that on Sunday morning "all London was electrified by the news from Woking." As a matter of fact, there was nothing to justify that very extravagant phrase. Plenty of Londoners did not hear of the Martians until the panic of Monday morning. Those who did took some time to realise all that the hastily worded telegrams in the Sunday papers conveyed. The majority of people in London do not read Sunday papers.[6]

The habit of personal security, moreover, is so deeply fixed in the Londoner's mind, and startling intelligence so much a matter of course in the papers, that they could read without any personal tremors: "About seven o'clock last night the Martians came out of the cylinder, and, moving about under an armour of metallic shields, have completely wrecked Woking station with the adjacent houses, and massacred an entire battalion of the Cardigan Regiment. No details are known. Maxims have been absolutely useless against their armour; the field-guns have been disabled by them. Flying hussars have been galloping into Chertsey. The Martians appear to be moving slowly towards Chertsey or Windsor. Great anxiety prevails in West Surrey, and earthworks are being thrown up to check the advance Londonward." That was how the Sunday *Sun*[7] put it, and a clever and remarkably prompt "hand-book" article in the *Referee*[8] compared the affair to a menagerie suddenly let loose in a village.[9]

No one in London knew positively of the nature of the armoured Martians, and there was still a fixed idea that these monsters must be sluggish: "crawling," "creeping painfully"—such expressions occurred in almost all the earlier reports. None of the telegrams could have been written by an eye-witness of their advance.[10] The Sunday papers printed separate editions as further news came to hand, some even in default of it. But there was practically nothing more to tell people until late in the afternoon, when the authorities gave the press-agencies the news in their possession. It was stated that the people of Walton and Weybridge, and all that district, were pouring along the roads Londonward, and that was all.

My brother went to church at the Foundling Hospital[11] in the morning, still in ignorance of what had happened on the previous night. There he heard allusions made to the invasion, and a special prayer for peace. Coming out, he bought a *Referee*. He became alarmed at the news in this, and went again to Waterloo station to find out if communication were restored. The omnibuses, carriages, cyclists, and innumerable people walking in their best clothes seemed scarcely affected by the strange intelligence that the news-venders were disseminating. People were interested, or, if alarmed, alarmed only on account of the local residents. At the station he heard for the first time that the Windsor and Chertsey lines were now interrupted. The porters told him that several remarkable telegrams had been received in the morning from Byfleet and Chertsey stations, but that these had abruptly ceased. My brother could get very little precise detail out of them. "There's fighting going on about Weybridge" was the extent of their information.

The train service was now very much disorganised. Quite a number of people who had been expecting friends from places on the South-Western network[12] were standing about the station. One grey-headed old gentleman came and abused the South-Western Company bitterly to my brother. "It wants showing up," he said.

One or two trains came in from Richmond, Putney, and Kingston, containing people who had gone out for a day's boating and found the locks closed and a feeling of panic in the air. A man in a blue-and-white blazer addressed my brother, full of strange tidings.

"There's hosts of people driving into Kingston in traps and carts and things, with boxes of valuables and all that," he said. "They come from Molesey and Weybridge and Walton, and they say there's been guns heard at Chertsey, heavy firing, and that mounted soldiers have told them to get off at once because the Martians are coming. We heard guns firing at Hampton Court station, but we thought it was thunder. What the dickens does it all mean? The Martians can't get out of their pit, can they?"

My brother could not tell him.

Afterwards he found that the vague feeling of alarm had spread to the clients of the underground railway, and that the Sunday excursionists began to return from all over the South-Western "lungs"[13]—Barnes, Wimbledon, Richmond Park, Kew, and so forth—at unnaturally early hours; but not a soul had anything more than vague hearsay to tell of. Every one connected with the terminus seemed ill-tempered.

About five o'clock the gathering crowd in the station was immensely excited by the opening of the line of communication, which is almost invariably closed, between the South-Eastern and the South-Western stations,[14] and the passage of carriage-trucks bearing huge guns and carriages crammed with soldiers. These were the guns that were brought up from Woolwich and Chatham to cover Kingston. There was an exchange of pleasantries: "You'll get eaten!" "We're the beast-tamers!" and so forth. A little while after that a squad of police came into the station and began to clear the public off the platforms, and my brother went out into the street again.

The church bells were ringing for evensong, and a squad of Salvation Army lasses came singing down Waterloo Road. On the bridge a number of loafers were watching a curious brown scum that came drifting down the stream in patches. The sun was just setting, and the Clock Tower and the Houses of Parliament rose against one of the most peaceful skies it is possible to imagine, a sky of gold, barred with long transverse stripes of reddish-purple cloud. There was talk of a floating body. One of the men there, a reservist he said he was, told my brother he had seen the heliograph flickering in the west.

In Wellington Street my brother met a couple of sturdy roughs who had just rushed out of Fleet Street with still wet newspapers[15] and staring placards. "Dreadful catastrophe!" they bawled one to the other down Wellington Street. "Fighting at Weybridge! Full description! Repulse of the Martians! London in Danger!" He had to give threepence for a copy[16] of that paper.

Then it was, and then only, that he realised something of the full power and terror of these monsters. He learned that they were not merely a handful of small sluggish creatures, but that they were minds swaying vast mechanical bodies; and that they could move swiftly and smite with such power that even the mightiest guns could not stand against them.

They were described as "vast spider-like machines, nearly a hundred feet high, capable of the speed of an express-train, and able to shoot out a beam of intense heat." Masked batteries, chiefly of field-guns, had been planted in the country about Horsell Common, and especially between the Woking district and London. Five of the machines had been seen moving towards the Thames, and one, by a happy chance, had been destroyed. In the other cases the shells had missed, and the batteries had been at once annihilated by the Heat-Rays. Heavy losses of soldiers were mentioned, but the tone of the despatch was optimistic.

The Martians had been repulsed; they were not invulnerable. They had retreated to their triangle of cylinders again, in the circle about Woking.

Signallers with heliographs were pushing forward upon them from all sides. Guns were in rapid transit from Windsor, Portsmouth, Aldershot, Wooi-wich—even from the north; among others, long wire-guns of ninety-five tons from Woolwich. Altogether one hundred and sixteen were in position or being hastily placed, chiefly covering London. Never before in England had there been such a vast or rapid concentration of military material.

Any further cylinders that fell, it was hoped, could be destroyed at once by high explosives, which were being rapidly manufactured and distributed. No doubt, ran the report, the situation was of the strangest and gravest description, but the public was exhorted to avoid and discourage panic. No doubt the Martians were strange and terrible in the extreme, but at the outside there could not be more than twenty of them against our millions.

The authorities had reason to suppose, from the size of the cylinders, that at the outside there could not be more than five in each cylinder— fifteen altogether. And one at least was disposed of—perhaps more. The public would be fairly warned of the approach of danger, and elaborate measures were being taken for the protection of the people in the threatened south-western suburbs. And so, with reiterated assurances of the safety of London and the ability of the authorities to cope with the difficulty, this quasi-proclamation[17] closed.

This was printed in enormous type on paper so fresh that it was still wet,[18] and there had been no time to add a word of comment. It was curious, my brother said, to see how ruthlessly the usual contents of the paper had been hacked and taken out to give this place.

All down Wellington Street people could be seen fluttering out the pink sheets and reading, and the Strand was suddenly noisy with the voices of an army of hawkers following these pioneers. Men came scrambling off buses to secure copies. Certainly this news excited people intensely, what-ever their previous apathy. The shutters of a map-shop in the Strand were being taken down, my brother said, and a man in his Sunday raiment, lemon-yellow gloves[19] even, was visible inside the window hastily fastening maps of Surrey to the glass.

Going on along the Strand to Trafalgar Square, the paper in his hand, my brother saw some of the fugitives from West Surrey. There was a man with his wife and two boys and some articles of furniture in a cart such as green-grocers use. He was driving from the direction of Westminster Bridge; and close behind him came a hay-waggon with five or six respectable-looking people in it, and some boxes and bundles. The faces of these people were haggard, and their entire appearance contrasted conspicuously with the Sab-bath-best appearance of the people on the omnibuses. People in fashionable clothing peeped at them out of cabs. They stopped at the Square as if un-decided which way to take, and finally turned eastward along the Strand.

Some way behind these came a man in work-day clothes, riding one of those old-fashioned tricycles with a small front-wheel.[20] He was dirty and white in the face.

My brother turned down towards Victoria, and met a number of such people. He had a vague idea that he might see something of me. He noticed an unusual number of police regulating the traffic. Some of the refugees were exchanging news with the people on the omnibuses. One was professing to have seen the Martians. "Boilers on stilts, I tell you, striding along like men." Most of them were excited and animated by their strange experience.

Beyond Victoria the public-houses were doing a lively trade with these arrivals. At all the street corners groups of people were reading papers, talking excitedly, or staring at these unusual Sunday visitors. They seemed to increase as night drew on, until at last the roads, my brother said, were like Epsom High Street on a Derby Day.[21] My brother addressed several of these fugitives and got unsatisfactory answers from most.

None of them could tell him any news of Woking except one man, who assured him that Woking had been entirely destroyed on the previous night.

"I come from Byfleet," he said; "a man on a bicycle came through the place in the early morning, and ran from door to door warning us to come away. Then came soldiers. We went out to look, and there were clouds of smoke to the south—nothing but smoke, and not a soul coming that way. Then we heard the guns at Chertsey, and folks coming from Weybridge. So I've locked up my house and come on."

At that time there was a strong feeling in the streets that the authorities were to blame for their incapacity to dispose of the invaders without all this inconvenience.

About eight o'clock a noise of heavy firing was distinctly audible all over the south of London. My brother could not hear it for the traffic in the main thoroughfares, but by striking through the quiet back-streets to the river he was able to distinguish it quite plainly.

He walked from Westminster to his apartments near Regent's Park, about ten.* He was now very anxious on my account, and disturbed at the evident magnitude of the trouble. His mind was inclined to run, even as mine had run on Saturday, on military details. He thought of all those silent, expectant guns, of the suddenly nomadic countryside; he tried to imagine "boilers on stilts" a hundred feet high.

---

*ten is pencilled into PR's margin with a question mark but it was never printed. Ten accords with "Sunday-night promenaders" and bed just after midnight.

There were one or two cart-loads of refugees passing along Oxford Street, and several in the Marylebone Road, but so slowly was the news spreading that Regent Street and Portland Place were full of their usual Sunday-night promenaders, albeit they talked in groups, and along the edge of Regent's Park there were as many silent couples "walking out" together under the scattered gas-lamps as ever there had been. The night was warm and still, and a little oppressive; the sound of guns continued intermittently, and after midnight there seemed to be sheet-lightning in the south.

He read and reread the paper, fearing the worst had happened to me. He was restless, and after supper prowled out again aimlessly. He returned and tried in vain to divert his attention to his examination notes. He went to bed a little after midnight, and was awakened from lurid dreams in the small hours of Monday by the sound of door-knockers, feet running in the street, distant drumming, and a clamour of bells. Red reflections danced on the ceiling. For a moment he lay astonished, wondering whether day had come or the world gone mad. Then he jumped out of bed and ran to the window.

His room was an attic; and* as he thrust his head out, up and down the street there were a dozen echoes to the noise of his window-sash, and heads in every kind of night disarray appeared. Inquiries were being shouted. "They are coming!" bawled a policeman, hammering at the door; "the Martians are coming!" and hurried to the next door.

The sound of drumming and trumpeting came from the Albany Street Barracks, and every church within earshot was hard at work killing sleep with a vehement disorderly tocsin. There was a noise of doors opening, and window after window in the houses opposite flashed from darkness into yellow illumination.

Up the street came galloping a closed carriage, bursting abruptly into noise at the corner, rising to a clattering climax under the window, and dying away slowly in the distance. Close on the rear of this came a couple of cabs, the forerunners of a long procession of flying vehicles, going for the most part to Chalk Farm station, where the North-Western special trains were loading up, instead of coming down the gradient into Euston.

For a long time my brother stared out of the window in blank astonishment, watching the policemen hammering at door after door, and delivering their incomprehensible message. Then the door behind him opened, and the man who lodged across the landing came in, dressed only in shirt, trousers, and slippers, his braces loose about his waist, his hair disordered from his pillow.

"What the devil is it?" he asked. "A fire? What a devil of a row!"

---

*A, attic, and: C–AG; attic and: F.

They both craned their heads out of the window, straining to hear what the policemen were shouting. People were coming out of the side-streets, and standing in groups at the corners talking.

"What the devil is it all about?" said my brother's fellow-lodger.

My brother answered him vaguely and began to dress, running with each garment to the window in order to miss nothing of the growing excitement. And presently men selling unnaturally early newspapers came bawling into the street:

"London in danger of suffocation! The Kingston and Richmond defences forced! Fearful massacres in the Thames Valley!"

And all about him—in the rooms below, in the houses on each side and across the road, and behind in the Park Terraces and in the hundred other streets of that part of Marylebone, and the Westbourne Park district and St. Pancras, and westward and northward in Kilburn and St. John's Wood and Hampstead, and eastward in Shoreditch and Highbury and Haggerston and Hoxton, and, indeed, through all the vastness of London from Ealing to East Ham—people were rubbing their eyes, and opening windows to stare out and ask aimless questions, and dressing hastily as the first breath of the coming storm of Fear blew through the streets. It was the dawn of the great panic. London, which had gone to bed on Sunday night oblivious and inert, was awakened in the small hours of Monday morning to a vivid sense of danger.

Unable from his window to learn what was happening, my brother went down and out into the street, just as the sky between the parapets of the houses grew pink with the early dawn. The flying people on foot and in vehicles grew more numerous every moment. "Black Smoke!" he heard people crying, and again "Black Smoke!" The contagion of such a unanimous fear was inevitable. As my brother hesitated on the door-step, he saw another news-vender approaching him, and got a paper forthwith. The man was running away with the rest, and selling his papers for a shilling each as he ran—a grotesque mingling of profit and panic.

And from this paper my brother read that catastrophic despatch of the Commander-in-Chief:

"The Martians are able to discharge enormous clouds of a black and poisonous vapour by means of rockets. They have smothered our batteries, destroyed Richmond, Kingston, and Wimbledon, and are advancing slowly towards London, destroying everything on the way. It is impossible to stop them. There is no safety from the Black Smoke but in instant flight."

That was all, but it was enough. The whole population of the great six-million city was stirring, slipping, running; presently it would be pouring *en masse* northward.[22]

"Black Smoke!" the voices cried. "Fire!"

The bells of the neighbouring church made a jangling tumult, a cart carelessly driven smashed, amid shrieks and curses, against the water-trough up the street. Sickly yellow light* went to and fro in the houses, and some of the passing cabs flaunted unextinguished lamps. And overhead the dawn was growing brighter, clear and steady and calm.

He heard footsteps running to and fro in the rooms, and up and down stairs behind him. His landlady came to the door, loosely wrapped in dressing-gown and shawl; her husband followed ejaculating.

As my brother began to realise the import of all these things, he turned hastily to his own room, put all his available money—some ten pounds altogether—into his pockets, and went out again into the streets.

---

*C–A; *lights*: E.

XV

WHAT HAD HAPPENED IN SURREY

IT WAS WHILE THE curate had sat and talked so wildly to me under the hedge in the flat meadows near Halliford, and while my brother was watching the fugitives stream over Westminster Bridge, that the Martians had resumed the offensive. So far as one can ascertain from the conflicting accounts that have been put forth, the majority of them remained busied with preparations in the Horsell pit until nine that night, hurrying on some operation that disengaged huge volumes of green smoke.

But three certainly came out about eight o'clock, and, advancing slowly and cautiously, made their way through Byfleet and Pyrford towards Ripley and Weybridge, and so came in sight of the expectant batteries against the setting sun. These Martians did not advance in a body, but in a line, each perhaps a mile and a half from his nearest fellow. They communicated with one another by means of siren-like howls, running up and down the scale from one note to another.

It was this howling and the firing* of the guns at Ripley and St. George's Hill that we had heard at Upper Halliford. The Ripley gunners, unseasoned artillery volunteers who ought never to have been placed in such a position, fired one wild, premature, ineffectual volley, and bolted on horse and foot through the deserted village, while the Martian without** using his Heat-Ray, walked serenely over their guns, stepped gingerly among them, passed in front of them, and so came unexpectedly upon the guns in Painshill Park, which he destroyed.

The St. George's Hill men, however, were better led or of a better mettle. Hidden by a pine-wood as they were, they seem to have been quite unsus-

---

*C–A; and firing: E.
**AG–A; Martian, without: E; walked over their guns serenely [, NY] without: C–NY.

pected by the Martian nearest to them. They laid their guns as deliberately as if they had been on parade, and fired at about a thousand yards range.

The shells flashed all round him, and he was seen to advance a few paces, stagger, and go down. Everybody yelled together, and the guns were reloaded in frantic haste. The overthrown Martian set up a prolonged ululation,[1] and immediately a second glittering giant, answering him, appeared over the trees to the south. It would seem that a leg of the tripod had been smashed by one of the shells. The whole of the second volley flew wide of the Martian on the ground, and, simultaneously, both his companions brought their Heat-Rays to bear on the battery. The ammunition blew up, the pine-trees all about the guns flashed into fire, and only one or two of the men who were already running over the crest of the hill escaped.

After this it would seem that the three took counsel together and halted, and the scouts who were watching them report that they remained absolutely stationary for the next half-hour. The Martian who had been overthrown crawled tediously out of his hood, a small brown figure, oddly suggestive from that distance of a speck of blight, and apparently engaged in the repair of his support. About nine he had finished, for his cowl was then seen above the trees again.

It was a few minutes past nine that night when these three sentinels were joined by four other Martians, each carrying a thick black tube. A similar tube was handed to each of the three, and the seven proceeded to distribute themselves at equal distances along a curved line between St. George's Hill, Weybridge, and the village of Send, south-west of Ripley.

A dozen rockets sprang out of the hills before them so soon as they began to move, and warned the waiting batteries about Ditton and Esher. At the same time four of their fighting-machines, similarly armed with tubes, crossed the river, and two of them, black against the western sky, came into sight of myself and the curate as we hurried wearily and painfully along the road that runs northward out of Halliford. They moved, as it seemed to us, upon a cloud, for a milky mist covered the fields and rose to a third of their height.

At this sight the curate cried faintly in his throat, and began running; but I knew it was no good running from a Martian, and I turned aside and crawled through dewy nettles and brambles into the broad ditch by the side of the road. He looked back, saw what I was doing, and turned to join me.

The two halted, the nearer to us standing and facing Sunbury, the remoter being a grey indistinctness towards the evening star, away towards Staines.

The occasional howling of the Martians had ceased; they took up their positions in the huge crescent about their cylinders in absolute silence. It was a crescent with twelve miles between its horns.[2] Never since the devising of gunpowder was the beginning of a battle so still. To us and to an observer about Ripley it would have had precisely the same effect—the Martians seemed in solitary possession of the darkling night,[3] lit only as it was by the slender moon, the stars, the after-glow of the daylight, and the ruddy glare from St. George's Hill and the woods of Painshill.

But facing that crescent everywhere—at Staines, Hounslow, Ditton, Esher, Ockham, behind hills and woods south of the river, and across the flat grass meadows to the north of it, wherever a cluster of trees or village houses gave sufficient cover—the guns were waiting. The signal rockets burst and rained their sparks through the night and vanished, and the spirit of all those watching batteries rose to a tense expectation. The Martians had but to advance into the line of fire, and instantly those motionless black forms of men, those guns glittering so darkly in the early night, would explode into a thunderous fury of battle.

No doubt the thought that was uppermost in a thousand of those vigilant minds, even as it was uppermost in mine, was the riddle—how much they understood of us. Did they grasp that we in our millions were organised, disciplined, working together? Or did they interpret our spurts of fire, the sudden stinging of our shells, our steady investment of their encampment, as we should the furious unanimity of onslaught in a disturbed hive of bees? Did they dream they might exterminate us? (At that time no one knew what food they needed.)[4] A hundred such questions struggled together in my mind as I watched that vast sentinel shape. And in the back of my mind was the sense of all the huge unknown and hidden forces Londonward. Had they prepared pitfalls? Were the powder-mills at Hounslow ready as a snare? Would the Londoners have the heart and courage to make a greater Moscow[5] of their mighty province of houses?

Then, after an interminable time, as it seemed to us, crouching and peering through the hedge, came a sound like the distant concussion of a gun. Another nearer, and then another. And then the Martian beside us raised his tube on high and discharged it, gunwise, with a heavy report that made the ground heave. The one towards Staines answered him. There was no flash, no smoke, simply that loaded detonation.

I was so excited by these heavy minute-guns following one another that I so far forgot my personal safety and my scalded hands as to clamber up into the hedge and stare towards Sunbury. As I did so a second report followed, and a big projectile hurtled overhead towards Hounslow. I expected at least to see smoke or fire, or some such evidence of its work. But all I saw was the deep-blue sky above, with one solitary star, and the white mist spreading wide and low beneath. And there had been no crash, no answering explosion. The silence was restored; the minute lengthened to three.

"What has happened?" said the curate, standing up beside me.

"Heaven knows!" said I.

A bat flickered by and vanished.[6] A distant tumult of shouting began and ceased. I looked again at the Martian, and saw he was now moving eastward along the river-bank, with a swift, rolling motion.

Every moment I expected the fire of some hidden battery to spring upon him; but the evening calm was unbroken. The figure of the Martian grew smaller as he receded, and presently the mist and the gathering night had swallowed him up. By a common impulse we clambered higher. Towards Sunbury was a dark appearance, as though a conical hill had suddenly come into being there, hiding our view of the farther country; and then, remoter across the river, over Walton, we saw another such summit. These hill-like forms grew lower and broader even as we stared.

Moved by a sudden thought, I looked northward, and there I perceived a third of these cloudy black kopjes had arisen.

Everything had suddenly become very still. Far away to the south-east, marking the quiet, we heard the Martians hooting to one another, and then the air quivered again with the distant thud of their guns. But the earthly artillery[7] made no reply.

Now at the time we could not understand these things, but later I was to learn the meaning of these ominous kopjes that gathered in the twilight. Each of the Martians, standing in the great crescent I have described, had discharged, by means of the gun-like tube he carried, a huge canister over whatever hill, copse, cluster of houses, or other possible cover for guns, chanced to be in front of him. Some fired only one of these, some two—as in the case of the one we had seen; the one at Ripley is said to have discharged no fewer than five at that time. These canisters smashed on striking the ground—they did not explode—and incontinently disengaged an enormous volume of heavy, inky vapour, coiling and pouring upward in a huge and ebony cumulus cloud, a gaseous hill that sank and spread itself slowly over the surrounding country. And the touch of that vapour, the inhaling of its pungent wisps, was death to all that breathes.

It was heavy, this vapour, heavier than the densest smoke, so that, after the first tumultuous uprush and outflow of its impact, it sank down through the air and poured over the ground in a manner rather liquid than gaseous, abandoning the hills, and streaming into the valleys and ditches and water-courses even as I have heard the carbonic-acid gas that pours from volcanic clefts[8] is wont to do. And where it came upon water some chemical action occurred, and the surface would be instantly covered with a powdery scum that sank slowly and made way for more. The scum was absolutely insoluble, and it is a strange thing, seeing the instant effect of the gas, that one could drink without hurt the water from which it had been strained. The vapour did not diffuse as a true gas would do. It hung together in banks, flowing sluggishly down the slope of the land and driving reluctantly before the wind, and very slowly it combined with the mist and moisture of the air, and sank to the earth in the form of dust. Save that an unknown element giving a group of four lines in the blue of the spectrum[9] is concerned, we are still entirely ignorant of the nature of this substance.

Once the tumultuous upheaval of its dispersion was over, the black smoke clung so closely to the ground, even before its precipitation, that fifty feet up in the air, on the roofs and upper stories of high houses and on great trees, there was a chance of escaping its poison altogether, as was proved even that night at Street Cobham* and Ditton.

The man who escaped at the former place tells a wonderful story of the strangeness of its coiling flow, and how he looked down from the church spire and saw the houses of the village rising like ghosts out of its inky nothingness. For a day and a half he remained there, weary, starving and sun-scorched, the earth under the blue sky and against the prospect of the distant hills a velvet-black expanse, with red roofs, green trees, and, later, black-veiled shrubs and gates, barns, out-houses, and walls, rising here and there into the sunlight.

But that was at Street Cobham,* where the black vapour was allowed to remain until it sank of its own accord into the ground. As a rule the Martians, when it had served its purpose, cleared the air of it again by wading into it and directing a jet of steam upon it.

This they did with the vapour-banks near us, as we saw in the starlight from the window of a deserted house at Upper Halliford, whither we had returned. From there we could see the search-lights on Richmond Hill and Kingston Hill going to and fro, and about eleven the windows rattled, and we heard the sound of the huge siege guns that had been put in position there. These continued intermittently for the space of a quarter of an hour, sending chance shots at the invisible Martians at Hampton and Ditton, and then the pale beams of the electric light vanished, and were replaced by a bright red glow.

Then the fourth cylinder[10] fell—a brilliant green meteor—as I learned afterwards, in Bushey Park. Before the guns on the Richmond and Kingston line of hills began, there was a fitful cannonade far away in the south-west, due, I believe, to guns being fired haphazard before the black vapour could overwhelm the gunners.

So, setting about it as methodically as men might smoke out a wasps' nest, the Martians spread this strange stifling vapour over the Londonward

---

*C, L–AG, E; *Street Chobham*: P–PR, A. Street Chobham is well west of the Martians' line of march.

country. The horns of the crescent slowly moved apart, until at last they formed a line from Hanwell to Coombe and Malden.[11] All night through their destructive tubes advanced. Never once, after the Martian at St. George's Hill was brought down, did they give the artillery the ghost of a chance against them. Wherever there was a possibility of guns being laid for them unseen, a fresh canister of the black vapour was discharged, and where the guns were openly displayed the Heat-Ray was brought to bear.

By midnight the blazing trees along the slopes of Richmond Park and the glare of Kingston Hill threw their light upon a network of black smoke, blotting out the whole Valley of the Thames and extending as far as the eye could reach. And through this two Martians slowly waded, and turned their hissing steam-jets this way and that.

They were sparing of the Heat-Ray that night, either because they had but a limited supply of material for its production or because they did not wish to destroy the country but only to crush and overawe the opposition they had aroused. In the latter aim they certainly succeeded. Sunday night was the end of the organised opposition to their movements. After that no body of men would stand against them, so hopeless was the enterprise. Even the crews of the torpedo-boats and destroyers that had brought their quick-firers up the Thames refused to stop, mutinied, and went down again. The only offensive operation men ventured upon after that night was the preparation of mines and pitfalls, and even in that their energies were frantic and spasmodic.

One has to imagine, as well as one may, the fate of those batteries towards Esher, waiting so tensely in the twilight. Survivors there were none. One may picture the orderly expectation, the officers alert and watchful, the gunners ready, the ammunition piled to hand, the limber gunners with their horses and waggons, the groups of civilian spectators standing as near as they were permitted, the evening stillness, the ambulances and hospital tents with the burned and wounded from Weybridge; then the dull resonance of the shots the Martians fired, and the clumsy projectile whirling over the trees and houses and smashing amid the neighbouring fields.

One may picture, too, the sudden shifting of the attention, the swiftly spreading coils and bellyings of that blackness advancing headlong, towering heavenward, turning the twilight to a palpable darkness, a strange and horrible antagonist of vapour striding upon its victims, men and horses near it seen dimly, running, shrieking, falling headlong, shouts of dismay, the guns suddenly abandoned, men choking and writhing on the ground,[12] and the swift broadening-out of the opaque cone of smoke. And then night and extinction—nothing but a silent mass of impenetrable vapour hiding its dead.

Before dawn the black vapour was pouring through the streets of Richmond, and the disintegrating organism of government was, with a last expiring effort, rousing the population of London to the necessity of flight.

XVI

THE EXODUS FROM LONDON

So you understand the roaring wave of fear that swept through the greatest city in the world just as Monday was dawning—the stream of flight rising swiftly to a torrent, lashing in a foaming tumult round the railway stations, banked up into a horrible struggle about the shipping in the Thames, and hurrying by every available channel northward and eastward. By ten o'clock the police organisation, and by mid-day even the railway organisations, were losing coherency, losing shape and efficiency, guttering, softening, running at last in that swift liquefaction of the social body.[1]

All the railway lines north of the Thames and the South-Eastern people at Cannon Street had been warned by midnight on Sunday, and trains were being filled. People were fighting savagely for standing-room in the carriages even at two o'clock. By three, people were being trampled and crushed even in Bishopsgate Street, a couple of hundred yards or more from Liverpool Street station; revolvers were fired, people stabbed, and the policemen who had been sent to direct the traffic, exhausted and infuriated, were breaking the heads of the people they were called out to protect.

And as the day advanced and the engine-drivers and stokers refused to return to London, the pressure of the flight drove the people in an ever-thickening multitude away from the stations and along the northward-running roads. By mid-day a Martian had been seen at Barnes, and a cloud of slowly sinking black vapour drove along the Thames and across the flats of Lambeth, cutting off all escape over the bridges in its sluggish advance. Another bank drove over Ealing, and surrounded a little island of survivors on Castle Hill, alive, but unable to escape.

After a fruitless struggle to get aboard a North-Western train at Chalk Farm—the engines of the trains that had loaded in the goods yard there *ploughed* through shrieking people, and a dozen stalwart men fought to keep the crowd from crushing the driver against his furnace—my brother emerged upon the Chalk Farm road, dodged across through a hurrying swarm of vehicles, and had the luck to be foremost in the sack of a cycle shop. The front tire of the machine he got was punctured in dragging it through the window, but he got up and off, notwithstanding, with no further injury than a cut wrist. The steep foot of Haverstock Hill was impassable owing to several overturned horses, and my brother struck into Belsize Road.

So he got out of the fury of the panic, and, skirting the Edgware Road, reached Edgware about seven, fasting and wearied, but well ahead of the crowd. Along the road people were standing in the roadway, curious, wondering. He was passed by a number of cyclists, some horsemen, and two motor-cars.[2] A mile from Edgware the rim of the wheel broke, and the machine became unridable. He left it by the road-side and trudged through the village. There were shops half opened in the main street of the place, and people crowded on the pavement and in the doorways and windows, staring astonished at this extraordinary procession of fugitives that was beginning. He succeeded in getting some food at an inn.

For a time he remained in Edgware not knowing what next to do. The flying people increased in number. Many of them, like my brother, seemed inclined to loiter in the place. There was no fresh news of the invaders from Mars.

At that time the road was crowded, but as yet far from congested. Most of the fugitives at that hour were mounted on cycles, but there were soon motor-cars, hansom cabs, and carriages hurrying along, and the dust hung in heavy clouds along the road to St. Albans.

It was perhaps a vague idea of making his way to Chelmsford, where some friends of his lived, that at last induced my brother to strike into a quiet lane running eastward. Presently he came upon a stile, and, crossing it, followed a foot-path north-eastward. He passed near several farm-houses and some little places whose names he did not learn. He saw few fugitives until, in a grass lane towards High Barnet, he happened upon the two ladies who became his fellow-travellers. He came upon them just in time to save them.

He heard their screams, and, hurrying round the corner, saw a couple of men struggling to drag them out of the little pony-chaise in which they had been driving, while a third with difficulty held the frightened pony's head. One of the ladies, a short woman dressed in white, was simply screaming; the other, a dark, slender figure, slashed at the man who gripped her arm with a whip she held in her disengaged hand.

My brother immediately grasped the situation, shouted, and hurried towards the struggle. One of the men desisted and turned towards him, and my brother, realising from his antagonist's face that a fight was unavoidable, and being an expert boxer, went into him forthwith and sent him down against the wheel of the chaise.

It was no time for pugilistic chivalry, and my brother laid him quiet with a kick, and gripped the collar of the man who pulled at the slender lady's arm. He heard the clatter of hoofs, the whip stung across his face, a third antagonist struck him between the eyes, and the man he held wrenched himself free and made off down the lane in the direction from which he had come.

Partly stunned, he found himself facing the man who had held the horse's head, and became aware of the chaise receding from him down the lane, swaying from side to side, and with the women in it looking back. The man before him, a burly rough, tried to close, and he stopped him with a blow in the face. Then, realising that he was deserted, he dodged round and made off down the lane after the chaise, with the sturdy man close behind him, and the fugitive, who had turned now, following remotely.

Suddenly he stumbled and fell; his immediate pursuer went headlong, and he rose to his feet to find himself with a couple of antagonists again. He would have had little chance against them had not the slender lady very pluckily pulled up and returned to his help. It seems she had had a revolver all this time, but it had been under the seat when she and her companion were attacked. She fired at six yards' distance, narrowly missing my brother. The less courageous of the robbers made off, and his companion followed him, cursing his cowardice. They both stopped in sight down the lane where the third man lay insensible.

"Take this!" said the slender lady, and she gave my brother her revolver.

"Go back to the chaise," said my brother, wiping the blood from his split lip.

She turned without a word—they were both panting—and they went back to where the lady in white struggled to hold back the frightened pony.

The robbers had evidently had enough of it. When my brother looked again they were retreating.

"I'll sit here," said my brother, "if I may;" and he got upon the empty front seat. The lady looked over her shoulder.

"Give me the reins," she said, and laid the whip along the pony's side. In another moment a bend in the road hid the three men from my brother's eyes.

So, quite unexpectedly, my brother found himself, panting, with a cut mouth, a bruised jaw, and blood-stained knuckles, driving along an unknown lane with these two women.

He learned they were the wife and the younger sister of a surgeon living at Stanmore, who had come in the small hours from a dangerous case at Pinner, and heard at some railway station on his way of the Martian advance.

He had hurried home, roused the women—their servant had left them two days before—packed some provisions, put his revolver under the seat—luckily for my brother—and told them to drive on to Edgware, with the idea of getting a train there. He stopped behind to tell the neighbours. He would overtake them, he said, at about half-past four in the morning, and now it was nearly nine and they had seen nothing of him. They could not stop in Edgware because of the growing traffic through the place, and so they had come into this side lane.

That was the story they told my brother in fragments when presently they stopped again, nearer to New Barnet. He promised to stay with them, at least until they could determine what to do, or until the missing man arrived, and professed to be an expert shot with the revolver—a weapon strange to him—in order to give them confidence.

They made a sort of encampment by the wayside, and the pony became happy in the hedge. He told them of his own escape out of London, and all that he knew of these Martians and their ways. The sun crept higher in the sky, and after a time their talk died out and gave place to an uneasy state of anticipation. Several wayfarers came along the lane, and of these my brother gathered such news as he could. Every broken answer he had deepened his impression of the great disaster that had come on humanity, deepened his persuasion of the immediate necessity for prosecuting this flight. He urged the matter upon them.

"We have money," said the slender woman, and hesitated.

Her eyes met my brother's, and her hesitation ended.

"So have I," said my brother.

She explained that they had as much as thirty pounds in gold, besides a five-pound note,[3] and suggested that with that they might get upon a train at St. Albans or New Barnet. My brother thought that was hopeless, seeing the fury of the Londoners to crowd upon the trains, and broached his own idea of striking across Essex towards Harwich and thence escaping from the country altogether.

Mrs. Elphinstone—that was the name of the woman in white—would listen to no reasoning, and kept calling upon "George"; but her sister-in-law was astonishingly quiet and deliberate, and at last agreed to my brother's suggestion. So designing* to cross the Great North Road, they went on towards Barnet, my brother leading the pony to save it as much as possible.

As the sun crept up the sky the day became excessively hot, and under foot a thick, whitish sand grew burning and blinding, so that they travelled only very slowly. The hedges were grey with dust. And as they advanced towards Barnet a tumultuous murmuring grew stronger.

---

*A; So, designing: AG, F; So they . . . Barnet, [my brother: C–P] designing: PR–NY.

They began to meet more people. For the most part these were staring before them, murmuring indistinct questions, jaded, haggard, unclean. One man in evening dress passed them on foot, his eyes on the ground. They heard his voice, and, looking back at him, saw one hand clutched in his hair and the other beating invisible things. His paroxysm of rage over, he went on his way without once looking back.

As my brother's party went on towards the cross-roads to the south of Barnet they saw a woman approaching the road across some fields on their left, carrying a child and with two other children; and then passed a man in dirty black, with a thick stick in one hand and a small portmanteau in the other. Then round the corner of the lane, from between the villas that guarded it at its confluence with the highroad, came a little cart drawn by a sweating black pony and driven by a sallow youth in a bowler hat, grey with dust. There were three girls, East End factory girls, and a couple of little children crowded in the cart.

"This'll tike us rahnd Edgware?" asked the driver, wild-eyed, white-faced; and when my brother told him it would if he turned to the left, he whipped up at once without the formality of thanks.

My brother noticed a pale grey smoke or haze rising among the houses in front of them, and veiling the white façade of a terrace beyond the road that appeared between the backs of the villas. Mrs. Elphinstone suddenly cried out at a number of tongues of smoky red flame leaping up above the houses in front of them against the hot, blue sky. The tumultuous noise resolved itself now into the disorderly mingling of many voices, the gride of many wheels, the creaking of waggons, and the staccato of hoofs. The lane came round sharply, not fifty yards from the cross-roads.

"Good heavens!" cried Mrs. Elphinstone. "What is this you are driving us into?"

My brother stopped.

For the main road was a boiling stream of people, a torrent of human beings rushing northward, one pressing on another. A great bank of dust, white and luminous in the blaze of the sun, made everything within twenty feet of the ground grey and indistinct, and* was perpetually renewed by the hurrying feet of a dense crowd of horses and of men and women on foot, and by the wheels of vehicles of every description.

"Way!" my brother heard voices crying. "Make way!"

It was like riding into the smoke of a fire to approach the meeting-point of the lane and road; the crowd roared like a fire, and the dust was hot and pungent. And, indeed, a little way up the road a villa was burning

---

*C–A; indistinct and: E.

and sending rolling masses of black smoke across the road to add to the confusion.

Two men came past them. Then a dirty* woman, carrying a heavy bundle and weeping. A lost retriever dog, with hanging tongue, circled dubiously round them, scared and wretched, and fled at my brother's threat.[4]

So much as they could see of the road Londonward between the houses to the right was a tumultuous stream of dirty, hurrying people, pent in between the villas on either side; the black heads, the crowded forms, grew into distinctness as they rushed towards the corner, hurried past, and merged their individuality again in a receding multitude that was swallowed up at last in a cloud of dust.[5]

"Go on! Go on!" cried the voices. "Way! Way!"

One man's hands pressed on the back of another. My brother stood at the pony's head. Irresistibly attracted, he advanced slowly, pace by pace, down the lane.

Edgware had been a scene of confusion, Chalk Farm a riotous tumult, but this was a whole population in movement. It is hard to imagine that host. It had no character of its own. The figures poured out past the corner, and receded with their backs to the group in the lane. Along the margin came those who were on foot, threatened by the wheels, stumbling in the ditches, blundering into one another.

The carts and carriages crowded close upon one another, making little way for those swifter and more impatient vehicles that darted forward every now and then when an opportunity showed itself of doing so, sending the people scattering against the fences and gates of the villas.

"Push on!" was the cry. "Push on! They are coming!"

In one cart stood a blind man in the uniform of the Salvation Army, gesticulating with his crooked fingers and bawling, "Eternity! eternity!" His voice was hoarse and very loud, so that my brother could hear him long after he was lost to sight in the dust. Some of the people who crowded in the carts whipped stupidly at their horses and quarrelled with other drivers; some sat motionless, staring at nothing with miserable eyes; some gnawed their hands with thirst, or lay prostrate in the bottoms of their conveyances. The horses' bits were covered with foam, their eyes bloodshot.

There were cabs, carriages, shop-carts, waggons, beyond counting; a mail-cart, a road-cleaner's cart marked "Vestry of St. Pancras,"[6] a huge timber-waggon crowded with roughs. A brewer's dray rumbled by with its two near wheels splashed with fresh blood.

"Clear the way!" cried the voices. "Clear the way!"

---

*L–E; *dusty*: PR. The paragraph is interpolated into PR; "dirty" occurs in the unaltered paragraph following.

"Eter-nity! eter-nity!" came echoing down the road.

There were sad, haggard women tramping by, well dressed, with children that cried and stumbled, their dainty clothes smothered in dust, their weary faces smeared with tears. With many of these came men, sometimes helpful, sometimes lowering and savage. Fighting side by side with them pushed some weary street outcast in faded black rags, wide-eyed, loud-voiced, and foul-mouthed. There were sturdy workmen thrusting their way along, wretched, unkempt men, clothed like clerks or shop-men, struggling spasmodically; a wounded soldier my brother noticed, men dressed in the clothes of railway porters, one wretched creature in a night-shirt with a coat thrown over it.

But varied as its composition was, certain things all that host had in common. There were fear and pain on their faces, and fear behind them. A tumult up the road, a quarrel for a place in a waggon, sent the whole host of them quickening their pace; even a man so scared and broken that his knees bent under him was galvanised for a moment into renewed activity. The heat and dust had already been at work upon this multitude. Their skins were dry, their lips black and cracked. They were all thirsty, weary, and footsore. And amid the various cries one heard disputes, reproaches, groans of weariness and fatigue; the voices of most of them were hoarse and weak. Through it all ran a refrain:

"Way! way! The Martians are coming!"

Few stopped and came aside from that flood. The lane opened slantingly into the main road with a narrow opening, and had a delusive appearance of coming from the direction of London. Yet a kind of eddy of people drove into its mouth; weaklings elbowed out of the stream, who for the most part rested but a moment before plunging into it again. A little way down the lane, with two friends bending over him, lay a man with a bare leg, wrapped about with bloody rags. He was a lucky man to have friends.

A little old man, with a grey military moustache and a filthy black frock-coat, limped out and sat down beside the trap, removed his boot—his sock was blood-stained—shook out a pebble, and hobbled on again; and then a little girl of eight or nine, all alone, threw herself under the hedge close by my brother, weeping.

"I can't go on! I can't go on!"

My brother woke from his torpor of astonishment and lifted her up, speaking gently to her, and carried her to Miss Elphinstone. So soon as my brother touched her she became quite still, as if frightened.

"Ellen!" shrieked a woman in the crowd, with tears in her voice—"Ellen!" And the child suddenly darted away from my brother, crying "Mother!"

"They are coming," said a man on horseback, riding past along the lane.

"Out of the way, there!" bawled a coachman, towering high; and my brother saw a closed carriage turning into the lane.

The people crushed back on one another to avoid the horse. My brother pushed the pony and chaise back into the hedge, and the man drove by and stopped at the turn of the way. It was a carriage, with a pole for a pair of horses, but only one was in the traces. My brother saw dimly through the dust that two men lifted out something on a white stretcher and put it gently on the grass beneath the privet hedge.

One of the men came running to my brother.

"Where is there any water?" he said. "He is dying fast, and very thirsty. It is Lord Garrick."

"Lord Garrick!" said my brother—"the Chief Justice?"[7]

"The water?" he said.

"There may be a tap," said my brother, "in some of the houses. We have no water. I dare not leave my people."

The man pushed against the crowd towards the gate of the corner house.

"Go on!" said the people, thrusting at him. "They are coming! Go on!"

Then my brother's attention was distracted by a bearded, eagle-faced[8] man lugging a small hand-bag, which split even as my brother's eyes rested on it and disgorged a mass of sovereigns that seemed to break up into separate coins as it struck the ground. They rolled hither and thither among the struggling feet of men and horses. The man stopped and looked stupidly at the heap, and the shaft of a cab struck his shoulder and sent him reeling. He gave a shriek and dodged back, and a cart-wheel shaved him narrowly.

"Way!" cried the men all about him. "Make way!"

So soon as the cab had passed, he flung himself, with both hands open, upon the heap of coins, and began thrusting handfuls in his pocket. A horse rose close upon him, and in another moment, half rising, he had been borne down under the horse's hoofs.

"Stop!" screamed my brother, and pushing a woman out of his way, tried to clutch the bit of the horse.

Before he could get to it, he heard a scream under the wheels, and saw through the dust the rim passing over the poor wretch's back. The driver of the cart slashed his whip at my brother, who ran round behind the cart. The multitudinous shouting confused his ears. The man was writhing in the dust among his scattered money, unable to rise, for the wheel had broken his back, and his lower limbs lay limp and dead. My brother stood up and yelled at the next driver, and a man on a black horse came to his assistance.

"Get him out of the road," said he; and, clutching the man's collar with his free hand, my brother lugged him sideways. But he still clutched after his money, and regarded my brother fiercely, hammering at his arm with a handful of gold. "Go on! Go on!" shouted angry voices behind. "Way! Way!"

There was a smash as the pole of a carriage crashed into the cart that the man on horseback stopped. My brother looked up, and the man with the gold twisted his head round and bit the wrist that held his collar. There was a concussion, and the black horse came staggering sideways, and the cart-horse pushed beside it. A hoof missed my brother's foot by a hair's breadth. He released his grip on the fallen man and jumped back. He saw anger change to terror on the face of the poor wretch on the ground, and in a moment he was hidden and my brother was borne backward and carried past the entrance of the lane, and had to fight hard in the torrent to recover it.

He saw Miss Elphinstone covering her eyes, and a little child, with all a child's want of sympathetic imagination, staring with dilated eyes at a dusty something that lay black and still, ground and crushed under the rolling wheels. "Let us go back!" he shouted, and began turning the pony round. "We cannot cross this—hell,"[9] he said; and they went back a hundred yards the way they had come, until the fighting crowd was hidden. As they passed the bend in the lane my brother saw the face of the dying man in the ditch under the privet, deadly white and drawn, and shining with perspiration. The two women sat silent, crouching in their seats and shivering.

Then beyond the bend my brother stopped again. Miss Elphinstone was white and pale, and her sister-in-law sat weeping, too wretched even to call upon "George." My brother was horrified and perplexed. So soon as they had retreated he realised how urgent and unavoidable it was to attempt this crossing. He turned to Miss Elphinstone, suddenly resolute.

"We must go that way," he said, and led the pony round again.

For the second time that day this girl proved her quality. To force their way into the torrent of people, my brother plunged into the traffic and held back a cab-horse, while she drove the pony across its head. A waggon locked wheels for a moment and ripped a long splinter from the chaise. In another moment they were caught and swept forward by the stream. My brother, with the cabman's whip-marks red across his face and hands, scrambled into the chaise and took the reins from her.

"Point the revolver at the man behind," he said, giving it to her, "if he presses us too hard. No!— point it at his horse."

Then he began to look out for a chance of edging to the right across the road. But once in the stream he seemed to lose volition, to become a part of that dusty rout. They swept through Chipping Barnet with the torrent; they were nearly a mile beyond the centre of the town before they had fought across to the opposite side of the way. It was din and confusion indescribable; but in and beyond the town the road forks repeatedly, and this to some extent relieved the stress.

They struck eastward through Hadley, and there on either side of the road, and at another place farther on they came upon a great multitude of people drinking at the stream, some fighting to come at the water. And farther on, from a hill near East Barnet, they saw two trains running slowly one after the other without signal or order—trains swarming with people, with men even among the coals behind the engines—going northward along the Great Northern Railway.[10] My brother supposes they must have filled outside London, for at that time the furious terror of the people had rendered the central termini impossible.

Near this place they halted for the rest of the afternoon, for the violence of the day had already utterly exhausted all three of them. They began to suffer the beginnings of hunger; the night was cold, and none of them dared to sleep. And in the evening many people came hurrying along the road near by their stopping-place, fleeing from unknown dangers before them, and going in the direction from which my brother had come.

XVII

THE "THUNDER CHILD"

HAD THE MARTIANS aimed only at destruction, they might on Monday have annihilated the entire population of London, as it spread itself slowly through the home counties.[1] Not only along the road through Barnet, but also through Edgware and Waltham Abbey, and along the roads eastward to Southend and Shoeburyness, and south of the Thames to Deal and Broadstairs, poured the same frantic rout. If one could have hung that June morning in a balloon in the blazing blue above London, every northward and eastward road running out of the tangled maze of streets would have seemed stippled black with the streaming fugitives, each dot a human agony of terror and physical distress. I have set forth at length in the last chapter my brother's account of the road through Chipping Barnet, in order that my readers may realise how that swarming of black dots appeared to one of those concerned. Never before in the history of the world had such a mass of human beings moved and suffered together. The legendary hosts of Goths and Huns, the hugest armies Asia has ever seen,[2] would have been but a drop in that current. And this was no disciplined march; it was a stampede— a stampede gigantic and terrible—without order and without a goal, six million people, unarmed and unprovisioned, driving headlong. It was the beginning of the rout of civilisation, of the massacre of mankind.

Directly below him the balloonist would have seen the network of streets far and wide, houses, churches, squares, crescents, gardens—already derelict—spread out like a huge map, and in the southward *blotted*.[3] Over Ealing, Richmond, Wimbledon, it would have seemed as if some monstrous pen had flung ink upon the chart. Steadily, incessantly, each black splash grew and spread, shooting out ramifications this way and that, now banking itself against rising ground, now pouring swiftly over a crest into a new-found valley, exactly as a gout of ink would spread itself upon blotting-paper.

And beyond, over the blue hills that rise southward of the river, the glittering Martians went to and fro, calmly and methodically spreading their poison-cloud over this patch of country and then over that, laying it again with their steam-jets when it had served its purpose, and taking possession of the conquered country. They do not seem to have aimed at extermination so much as at complete demoralisation and the destruction of any opposition. They exploded any stores of powder they came upon, cut every telegraph, and wrecked the railways here and there. They were hamstringing mankind. They seemed in no hurry to extend the field of their operations, and did not come beyond the central part of London all that day. It is possible that a very considerable number of people in London stuck to their houses through Monday morning. Certain it is that many died at home, suffocated by the Black Smoke.

Until about mid-day the Pool of London was an astonishing scene. Steamboats and shipping of all sorts lay there, tempted by the enormous sums of money offered by fugitives, and it is said that many who swam out to these vessels were thrust off with boat-hooks and drowned. About one o'clock in the afternoon the thinning remnant of a cloud of the black vapour appeared between the arches of Blackfriars Bridge. At that the Pool became a scene of mad confusion, fighting, and collision, and for some time a multitude of boats and barges jammed in the northern arch of the Tower Bridge, and the sailors and lightermen[4] had to fight savagely against the people who swarmed upon them from the river front. People were actually clambering down the piers of the bridge from above.

When, an hour later, a Martian appeared beyond the Clock Tower and waded down the river, nothing but wreckage floated above Limehouse.

Of the falling of the fifth cylinder I have presently to tell. The sixth star fell at Wimbledon. My brother, keeping watch beside the women in the chaise in a meadow, saw the green flash of it far beyond the hills. On Tuesday[5] the little party, still set upon getting across the sea, made its way through the swarming country towards Colchester. The news that the Martians were now in possession of the whole of London was confirmed. They had been seen at Highgate, and even, it was said, at Neasden. But they did not come into my brother's view until the morrow.

That day the scattered multitudes began to realise the urgent need of provisions. As they grew hungry the rights of property ceased to be regarded. Farmers were out to defend their cattlesheds, granaries, and ripening root crops with arms in their hands. A number of people now, like my brother, had their faces eastward, and there were some desperate souls even going back towards London to get food. These were chiefly people from the northern suburbs, whose knowledge of the Black Smoke came by hearsay. He heard that about half the members of the government had gathered at Bir-

mingham, and that enormous quantities of high explosives were being prepared to be used in automatic mines across the Midland counties.

He was also told that the Midland Railway Company[6] had replaced the
desertions of the first day's panic, had resumed traffic, and was running
northward trains from St. Albans to relieve the congestion of the home
counties. There was also a placard in Chipping Ongar announcing that large
stores of flour were available in the northern towns, and* that within
twenty-four hours bread would be distributed among the starving people
in the neighbourhood. But this intelligence did not deter him from the plan
of escape he had formed, and the three pressed eastward all day, and heard
no more of the bread distribution than this promise. Nor, as a matter of
fact, did any one else hear more of it. That night fell the seventh star, falling
upon Primrose Hill. It fell while Miss Elphinstone was watching, for she
took that duty alternately with my brother. She saw it.

On Wednesday the three fugitives—they had passed the night in a field
of unripe wheat—reached Chelmsford, and there a body of the inhabitants,
calling itself the Committee of Public Supply,[7] seized the pony as provisions,
and would give nothing in exchange for it but the promise of a share in it
the next day. Here there were rumours of Martians at Epping, and news of
the destruction of Waltham Abbey Powder Mills in a vain attempt to blow
up one of the invaders.

People were watching for Martians here from the church towers. My
brother, very luckily for him as it chanced, preferred to push on at once to
the coast rather than wait for food, although all three of them were very
hungry. By mid-day they passed through Tillingham, which, strangely
enough, seemed to be quite silent and deserted, save for a few furtive plunderers hunting for food. Near Tillingham they suddenly came in sight of
the sea, and the most amazing crowd of shipping of all sorts that it is possible
to imagine.

For after the sailors could no longer come up the Thames, they came
on to the Essex coast, to Harwich and Walton and Clacton, and afterwards
to Foulness and Shoebury, to bring off the people. They lay in a huge sickle-
shaped curve that vanished into mist at last towards the Naze. Close inshore
was a multitude of fishing-smacks—English, Scotch, French, Dutch, and
Swedish; steam-launches from the Thames, yachts, electric boats; and beyond were ships of large burden, a multitude of filthy colliers, trim mer-
chantmen, cattle-ships, passenger-boats, petroleum-tanks, ocean tramps, an
old white transport even, neat white and grey liners from Southampton and
Hamburg; and along the blue coast across the Blackwater my brother could

---

*C–A; towns and: E

make out dimly a dense swarm of boats chaffering with the people on the beach, a swarm which also extended up the Blackwater almost to Maldon.

About a couple of miles out lay an ironclad, very low in the water, almost, to my brother's perception, like a water-logged ship. This was the ram[8] *Thunder Child*. It was the only warship in sight, but far away to the right over the smooth surface of the sea—for that day there was a dead calm—lay a serpent of black smoke to mark the next ironclads of the Channel Fleet, which hovered in an extended line, steam up and ready for action, across the Thames estuary during the course of the Martian conquest, vigilant and yet powerless to prevent it.

At the sight of the sea, Mrs. Elphinstone, in spite of the assurances of her sister-in-law, gave way to panic. She had never been out of England before, she would rather die than trust herself friendless in a foreign country, and so forth. She seemed, poor woman, to imagine that the French and the Martians might prove very similar. She had been growing increasingly hysterical, fearful, and depressed during the two days' journeyings. Her great idea was to return to Stanmore. Things had been always well and safe at Stanmore. They would find George at Stanmore.

It was with the greatest difficulty they could get her down to the beach, where presently my brother succeeded in attracting the attention of some men on a paddle steamer from the Thames. They sent a boat and drove a bargain for thirty-six pounds[9] for the three. The steamer was going, these men said, to Ostend.

It was about two o'clock when my brother, having paid their fares at the gangway, found himself safely aboard the steamboat with his charges. There was food aboard, albeit at exorbitant prices, and the three of them contrived to eat a meal on one of the seats forward.

There were already a couple of score of passengers aboard, some of whom had expended their last money in securing a passage, but the captain lay off the Blackwater until five in the afternoon, picking up passengers until the seated decks were even dangerously crowded. He would probably have remained longer had it not been for the sound of guns that began about that hour in the south. As if in answer, the ironclad seaward fired a small gun and hoisted a string of flags. A jet of smoke sprang out of her funnels.

Some of the passengers were of opinion that this firing came from Shoeburyness, until it was noticed that it was growing louder. At the same time, far away in the south-east the masts and upper-works of three ironclads rose one after the other out of the sea, beneath clouds of black smoke. But my brother's attention speedily reverted to the distant firing in the south. He fancied he saw a column of smoke rising out of the distant grey haze.

The little steamer was already flapping her way eastward of the big crescent of shipping, and the low Essex coast was growing blue and hazy, when a Martian appeared, small and faint in the remote distance, advancing along the muddy coast from the direction of Foulness. At that the captain on the bridge swore at the top of his voice with fear and anger at his own delay, and the paddles seemed infected with his terror. Every soul aboard stood at the bulwarks or on the seats of the steamer and stared at that distant shape, higher than the trees or church towers inland, and advancing with a leisurely parody of a human stride.

It was the first Martian my brother had seen, and he stood, more amazed than terrified, watching this Titan advancing deliberately towards the shipping, wading farther and farther into the water as the coast fell away. Then, far away beyond the Crouch, came another, striding over some stunted trees, and then yet another, still farther off, wading deeply through a shiny mud-flat that seemed to hang half-way up between sea and sky. They were all stalking seaward, as if to intercept the escape of the multitudinous vessels that were crowded between Foulness and the Naze. In spite of the throbbing exertions of the engines of the little paddle-boat, and the pouring foam that her wheels flung behind her, she receded with terrifying slowness from this ominous advance.

Glancing north-westward, my brother saw the large crescent of shipping already writhing with the approaching terror; one ship passing behind another, another coming round from broadside to end on, steamships whistling and giving off volumes of steam, sails being let out, launches rushing hither and thither. He was so fascinated by this and by the creeping danger away to the left that he had no eyes for anything seaward. And then a swift movement of the steamboat (she had suddenly come round to avoid being run down) flung him headlong from the seat upon which he was standing. There was a shouting all about him, a trampling of feet, and a cheer that seemed to be answered faintly. The steamboat lurched and rolled him over upon his hands.

He sprang to his feet and saw to starboard, and not a hundred yards from their heeling, pitching boat, a vast iron bulk like the blade of a plough tearing through the water, tossing it on either side in huge waves of foam that leaped towards the steamer, flinging her paddles helplessly in the air, and then sucking her deck down almost to the water-line.

A douche of spray blinded my brother for a moment. When his eyes were clear again he saw the monster had passed and was rushing landward. Big iron upper-works rose out of this headlong structure, and from that twin funnels projected and spat a smoking blast shot with fire. It was the torpedo-ram, *Thunder Child*, steaming headlong, coming to the rescue of the threatened shipping.

Keeping his footing on the heaving deck by clutching the bulwarks, my brother looked past this charging leviathan at the Martians again, and he saw the three of them now close together, and standing so far out to sea that their tripod supports were almost entirely submerged. Thus sunken, and seen in remote perspective, they appeared far less formidable than the huge iron bulk in whose wake the steamer was pitching so helplessly. It would seem they were regarding this new antagonist with astonishment. To their intelligence, it may be, the giant was even such another as themselves. The *Thunder Child* fired no gun, but simply drove full speed towards them. It was probably her not firing that enabled her to get so near the enemy as she did. They did not know what to make of her. One shell, and they would have sent her to the bottom forthwith with the Heat-Ray.

She was steaming at such a pace that in a minute she seemed half-way between the steamboat and the Martians—a diminishing black bulk against the receding horizontal expanse of the Essex coast.

Suddenly the foremost Martian lowered his tube and discharged a canister of the black gas at the ironclad. It hit her larboard side and glanced off in an inky jet that rolled away to seaward, an unfolding torrent of Black Smoke, from which the ironclad drove clear. To the watchers from the steamer, low in the water and with the sun in their eyes, it seemed as though she were already among the Martians.

They saw the gaunt figures separating and rising out of the water as they retreated shoreward, and one of them raised the camera-like generator of the Heat-Ray. He held it pointing obliquely downward, and a bank of steam sprang from the water at its touch. It must have driven through the iron of the ship's side like a white-hot iron rod through paper.

A flicker of flame went up through the rising steam, and then the Martian reeled and staggered. In another moment he was cut down, and a great body of water and steam shot high in the air. The guns of the *Thunder Child* sounded through the reek, going off one after the other, and one shot splashed the water high close by the steamer, ricochetted towards the other flying ships to the north, and smashed a smack to match-wood.

But no one heeded that very much. At the sight of the Martian's collapse the captain on the bridge yelled inarticulately, and all the crowding passengers on the steamer's stern shouted together. And then they yelled again. For, surging out beyond the white tumult drove something long and black, the flames streaming from its middle parts, its ventilators and funnels spouting fire.

She was alive still; the steering-gear, it seems, was intact and her engines working. She headed straight for a second Martian, and was within a hundred yards of him when the Heat-Ray came to bear. Then with a violent thud, a blinding flash, her decks, her funnels, leaped upward. The Martian staggered with the violence of her explosion, and in another moment the flaming wreckage, still driving forward with the impetus of its pace, had struck him and crumpled him up like a thing of card-board. My brother shouted involuntarily. A boiling tumult of steam hid everything again.

"Two!" yelled the captain.

Every one was shouting. The whole steamer from end to end rang with frantic cheering that was taken up first by one and then by all in the crowding multitude of ships and boats that was driving out to sea.

The steam hung upon the water for many minutes, hiding the third Martian and the coast altogether. And all this time the boat was paddling steadily out to sea and away from the fight; and when at last the confusion cleared, the drifting bank of black vapour intervened, and nothing of the *Thunder Child* could be made out, nor could the third Martian be seen. But the ironclads to seaward were now quite close and standing in towards shore past the steamboat.

The little vessel continued to beat its way seaward, and the ironclads receded slowly towards the coast, which was hidden still by a marbled bank of vapour, part steam, part black gas, eddying and combining in the strangest ways. The fleet of refugees was scattering to the north-east; several smacks were sailing between the ironclads and the steamboat. After a time, and before they reached the sinking cloud-bank, the warships turned northward, and then abruptly went about and passed into the thickening haze of evening southward. The coast grew faint, and at last indistinguishable amid the low banks of clouds that were gathering about the sinking sun.

Then suddenly out of the golden haze of the sunset came the vibration of guns, and a form of black shadows moving. Every one struggled to the rail of the steamer and peered into the blinding furnace of the west, but nothing was to be distinguished clearly. A mass of smoke rose slantingly and barred the face of the sun. The steamboat throbbed on its way through an interminable suspense.

The sun sank into grey clouds, the sky flushed and darkened, the evening star trembled into sight. It was deep twilight when the captain cried out and pointed. My brother strained his eyes. Something rushed up into the sky out of the greyness—rushed slantingly upward and very swiftly into the luminous clearness above the clouds in the western sky; something flat and broad and very large, that swept round in a vast curve, grew smaller, sank slowly, and vanished again into the grey mystery of the night. And as it flew it rained down darkness upon the land.[10]

BOOK TWO

THE EARTH
UNDER
THE
MARTIANS[1]

I

UNDER FOOT

IN THE FIRST BOOK I have wandered so much from my own adventures to tell of the experiences of my brother that all through the last two chapters I and the curate have been lurking in the empty house at Halliford whither we fled to escape the Black Smoke. There I will resume. We stopped there all Sunday night and all the next day—the day of the panic—in a little island of daylight, cut off by the Black Smoke from the rest of the world. We could do nothing but wait in an aching inactivity during those two weary days.

My mind was occupied by anxiety for my wife. I figured her at Leatherhead, terrified, in danger, mourning me already as a dead man. I paced the rooms and cried aloud when I thought of how I was cut off from her, of all that might happen to her in my absence. My cousin I knew was brave enough for any emergency, but he was not the sort of man to realise danger quickly, to rise promptly. What was needed now was not bravery, but circumspection. My only consolation was to believe that the Martians were moving Londonward and away from her. Such vague anxieties keep the mind sensitive and painful. I grew very weary and irritable with the curate's perpetual ejaculations; I tired of the sight of his selfish despair. After some ineffectual remonstrance I kept away from him, staying in a room—evidently a children's schoolroom—containing globes, forms, and copy-books.[1] When he followed me thither, I went to a box-room at the top of the house and, in order to be alone with my aching miseries, locked myself in.

We were hopelessly hemmed in by the Black Smoke all that day and the morning of the next. There were signs of people in the next house on Sunday evening—a face at a window and moving lights, and later the slamming of a door. But I do not know who these people were, nor what became of them. We saw nothing of them next day. The Black Smoke drifted slowly riverward all through Monday morning, creeping nearer and nearer to us, driving at last along the roadway outside the house that hid us.

A Martian came across the fields about mid-day, laying the stuff with a jet of superheated steam that hissed against the walls, smashed all the windows it touched, and scalded the curate's hand as he fled out of the front room. When at last we crept across the sodden rooms and looked out again, the country northward was as though a black snowstorm had passed over it. Looking towards the river, we were astonished to see an unaccountable redness[2] mingling with the black of the scorched meadows.

For a time we did not see how this change affected our position, save that we were relieved of our fear of the Black Smoke. But later I perceived that we were no longer hemmed in, that now we might get away. So soon as I realised that the way of escape was open, my dream of action returned. But the curate was lethargic, unreasonable.

"We are safe here," he repeated; "safe here."

I resolved to leave him—would that I had! Wiser now for the artillery-man's teaching, I sought out food and drink. I had found oil and rags for my burns, and I also took a hat and a flannel shirt that I found in one of the bedrooms. When it was clear to him that I meant to go alone—had reconciled myself to going alone—he suddenly roused himself to come. And all being quiet throughout the afternoon, we started about five o'clock, as I should judge, along the blackened road to Sunbury.

In Sunbury, and at intervals along the road, were dead bodies lying in contorted attitudes, horses as well as men, overturned carts and luggage, all covered thickly with black dust. That pall of cindery powder made me think of what I had read of the destruction of Pompeii.[3] We got to Hampton Court without misadventure, our minds full of strange and unfamiliar appearances, and at Hampton Court our eyes were relieved to find a patch of green that had escaped the suffocating drift. We went through Bushey Park, with its deer going to and fro under the chestnuts, and some men and women hurrying in the distance towards Hampton, and so we came to Twicken-ham.[4] These were the first people we saw.

Away across the road the woods beyond Ham and Petersham were still afire. Twickenham was uninjured by either Heat-Ray or Black Smoke, and there were more people about here, though none could give us news. For the most part they were like ourselves, taking advantage of a lull to shift their quarters. I have an impression that many of the houses here were still occupied by scared inhabitants, too frightened even for flight. Here, too, the evidence of a hasty rout was abundant along the road. I remember most vividly three smashed bicycles in a heap, pounded into the road by the wheels of subsequent carts. We crossed Richmond Bridge about half-past eight. We hurried across the exposed bridge, of course, but I noticed floating down the stream a number of red masses, some many feet across. I did not know what these were—there was no time for scrutiny—and I put a more horrible interpretation on them than they deserved. Here again on the Surrey side, were* black dust that had once been smoke, and dead bodies—a heap near the approach to the station; but we had no glimpse of the Martians until we were some way towards Barnes.

We saw in the blackened distance a group of three people running down a side street towards the river, but otherwise it seemed deserted. Up the hill Richmond town was burning briskly; outside the town of Richmond there was no trace of the Black Smoke.

Then, suddenly, as we approached Kew, came a number of people running, and the upper-works of a Martian fighting-machine loomed in sight over the house-tops, not a hundred yards away from us. We stood aghast at our danger, and had the Martian looked down we must immediately have perished. We were so terrified that we dared not go on, but turned aside and hid in a shed in a garden. There the curate crouched, weeping silently, and refusing to stir again.

But my fixed idea of reaching Leatherhead would not let me rest, and in the twilight I ventured out again. I went through a shrubbery, and along a passage beside a big house standing in its own grounds, and so emerged upon the road towards Kew. The curate I left in the shed, but he came hurrying after me.

That second start was the most foolhardy thing I ever did. For it was manifest the Martians were about us. No sooner had the curate overtaken me than we saw either the fighting-machine we had seen before or another, far away across the meadows in the direction of Kew Lodge. Four or five little black figures hurried before it across the green-grey of the field, and in a moment it was evident this Martian pursued them. In three strides he was among them, and they ran radiating from his feet in all directions. He used no Heat-Ray to destroy them, but picked them up one by one. Apparently he tossed them into the great metallic carrier which projected behind him, much as a workman's basket hangs over his shoulder.

It was the first time I realised that the Martians might have any other purpose than destruction with defeated humanity. We stood for a moment petrified, then turned and fled through a gate behind us into a walled garden, fell into, rather than found, a fortunate ditch, and lay there, scarce daring to whisper to each other until the stars were out.

I suppose it was nearly eleven o'clock before we gathered courage to start again, no longer venturing into the road, but sneaking along hedgerows and through plantations, and watching keenly through the darkness, he on the right and I on the left, for the Martians, who seemed to be all

---

*NY, A; *side, was*: C, L; *side was*: P; *side were*: AG, E. In AG, the comma is deleted in pencil, not the usual ink, and the usual marginal sign of deletion is lacking.

about us. In one place we blundered upon a scorched and blackened area, now cooling and ashen, and a number of scattered dead bodies of men, burned horribly about the heads and trunks but with their legs and boots mostly intact; and of dead horses, fifty feet, perhaps, behind a line of four ripped guns and smashed gun-carriages.

Sheen, it seemed, had escaped destruction, but the place was silent and deserted. Here we happened on no dead, though the night was too dark for us to see into the side roads of the place. In Sheen my companion suddenly complained of faintness and thirst, and we decided to try one of the houses.

The first house we entered, after a little difficulty with the window, was a small semi-detached villa,[5] and I found nothing eatable left in the place but some mouldy cheese. There was, however, water to drink; and I took a hatchet, which promised to be useful in our next house-breaking.

We then crossed to a place where the road turns towards Mortlake. Here there stood a white house within a walled garden, and in the pantry of this domicile we found a store of food—two loaves of bread in a pan, an uncooked steak, and the half of a ham. I give this catalogue so precisely because, as it happened, we were destined to subsist upon this store for the next fortnight. Bottled beer stood under a shelf, and there were two bags of haricot beans and some limp lettuces. This pantry opened into a kind of wash-up kitchen, and in this was firewood; there was also a cupboard, in which we found nearly a dozen of burgundy, tinned soups and salmon, and two tins of biscuits.

We sat in the adjacent kitchen in the dark—for we dared not strike a light—and ate bread and ham, and drank beer out of the same bottle. The curate, who was still timorous and restless, was now, oddly enough, for pushing on, and I was urging him to keep up his strength by eating when the thing happened that was to imprison us.

"It can't be midnight yet," I said, and then came a blinding glare of vivid green light. Everything in the kitchen leaped out, clearly visible in green and black, and vanished again. And then followed such a concussion as I have never heard before or since. So close on the heels of this as to seem instantaneous came a thud behind me, a clash of glass, a crash and rattle of falling masonry all about us, and the plaster of the ceiling came down upon us, smashing into a multitude of fragments upon our heads. I was knocked headlong across the floor against the oven handle and stunned. I was insensible for a long time, the curate told me, and when I came to we were in darkness again, and he, with a face wet, as I found afterwards, with blood from a cut forehead, was dabbing water over me.

For some time I could not recollect what had happened. Then things came to me slowly. A bruise on my temple asserted itself.

"Are you better?" asked the curate, in a whisper.

At last I answered him. I sat up.

"Don't move," he said. "The floor is covered with smashed crockery from the dresser. You can't possibly move without making a noise, and I fancy *they* are outside."

We both sat quite silent, so that we could scarcely hear each other breathing. Everything seemed deadly still, but once something near us, some plaster or broken brick-work, slid down with a rumbling sound. Outside and very near was an intermittent, metallic rattle.

"That!" said the curate, when presently it happened again.

"Yes," I said. "But what is it?"

"A Martian!" said the curate.

I listened again.

"It was not like the Heat-Ray," I said, and for a time I was inclined to think one of the great fighting-machines had stumbled against the house, as I had seen one stumble against the tower of Shepperton Church.

Our situation was so strange and incomprehensible that for three or four hours, until the dawn came, we scarcely moved. And then the light filtered in, not through the window, which remained black, but through a triangular aperture between a beam and a heap of broken bricks in the wall behind us. The interior of the kitchen we now saw greyly for the first time.

The window had been burst in by a mass of garden mould, which flowed over the table upon which we had been sitting and lay about our feet. Outside, the soil was banked high against the house. At the top of the window-frame we could see an uprooted drain-pipe. The floor was littered with smashed hardware; the end of the kitchen towards the house was broken into, and since the daylight shone in there, it was evident the greater part of the house had collapsed. Contrasting vividly with this ruin was the neat dresser, stained in the fashion, pale green, and with a number of copper and tin vessels below it, the wall-paper imitating blue and white tiles, and a couple of coloured supplements[6] fluttering from the walls above the kitchen range.

As the dawn grew clearer, we saw through the gap in the wall the body of a Martian, standing sentinel, I suppose, over the still glowing cylinder. At the sight of that we crawled as circumspectly as possible out of the twilight of the kitchen into the darkness of the scullery.

Abruptly the right interpretation dawned upon my mind.

"The fifth cylinder,"[7] I whispered, "the fifth shot from Mars, has struck this house and buried us under the ruins!"

For a time the curate was silent, and then he whispered:

"God have mercy upon us!"

I heard him presently whimpering to himself.

Save for that sound we lay quite still in the scullery; I for my part scarce dared breathe, and sat with my eyes fixed on the faint light of the kitchen door. I could just see the curate's face, a dim, oval shape, and his collar and cuffs. Outside there began a metallic hammering, then a violent hooting, and then again, after a quiet interval, a hissing like the hissing of an engine. These noises, for the most part problematical, continued intermittently, and seemed if anything to increase in number as time wore on. Presently a measured thudding and a vibration that made everything about us quiver and the vessels in the pantry ring and shift, began and continued. Once the light was eclipsed, and the ghostly kitchen doorway became absolutely dark. For many hours we must have crouched there, silent and shivering, until our tired attention failed. . . .

At last I found myself awake and very hungry. I am inclined to believe we must have spent the greater portion of a day before that awakening. My hunger was at a stride so insistent that it moved me to action. I told the curate I was going to seek food, and felt my way towards the pantry. He made me no answer, but so soon as I began eating the faint noise I made stirred him up and I heard him crawling after me.

II

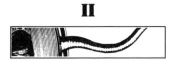

WHAT WE SAW FROM THE RUINED HOUSE

AFTER EATING we crept back to the scullery, and there I must have dozed again, for when presently I looked round I was alone. The thudding vibration continued with wearisome persistence. I whispered for the curate several times, and at last felt my way to the door of the kitchen. It was still daylight, and I perceived him across the room, lying against the triangular hole that looked out upon the Martians. His shoulders were hunched, so that his head was hidden from me.

I could hear a number of noises almost like those in an engine-shed, and the place rocked with that beating thud. Through the aperture in the wall I could see the top of a tree touched with gold, and the warm blue of a tranquil evening sky. For a minute or so I remained watching the curate, and then I advanced, crouching and stepping with extreme care amid the broken crockery that littered the floor.

I touched the curate's leg, and he started so violently that a mass of plaster went sliding down outside and fell with a loud impact. I gripped his arm, fearing he might cry out, and for a long time we crouched motionless. Then I turned to see how much of our rampart remained. The detachment of the plaster had left a vertical slit open in the débris, and by raising myself cautiously across a beam I was able to see out of this gap into what had been overnight a quiet suburban roadway. Vast, indeed, was the change that we beheld.

The fifth cylinder must have fallen right into the midst of the house we had first visited. The building had vanished, completely smashed, pulverised, and dispersed by the blow. The cylinder lay now far beneath the original foundations—deep in a hole, already vastly larger than the pit I had looked into at Woking. The earth all round it had splashed under that tremendous impact—"splashed" is the only word—and lay in heaped piles that hid the masses of the adjacent houses. It had behaved exactly like mud under the violent blow of a hammer Our house had collapsed backward; the front portion, even on the ground floor, had been destroyed completely; by a chance the kitchen and scullery had escaped, and stood buried now under soil and ruins, closed in by tons of earth on every side save towards the cylinder. Over that aspect we hung now on the very edge of the great circular pit the Martians were engaged in making. The heavy beating sound was evidently just behind us, and ever and again a bright green vapour drove up like a veil across our peep-hole.

The cylinder was already opened in the centre of the pit, and on the farther edge of the pit, amid the smashed and gravel-heaped shrubbery, one of the great fighting-machines, deserted by its occupant, stood stiff and tall against the evening sky. At first I scarcely noticed the pit and the cylinder, although it has been convenient to describe them first, on account of the extraordinary glittering mechanism I saw busy in the excavation, and on account of the strange creatures that were crawling slowly and painfully across the heaped mould near it.

The mechanism it certainly was that held my attention first. It was one of those complicated fabrics that have since been called handling-machines, and the study of which has already given such an enormous impetus to terrestrial invention. As it dawned upon me first it presented a sort of metallic spider with five jointed, agile legs, and with an extraordinary number of jointed levers, bars, and reaching and clutching tentacles about its body. Most of its arms were retracted, but with three long tentacles it was fishing out a number of rods, plates, and bars which lined the covering and apparently strengthened the walls, of the cylinder. These, as it extracted them, were lifted out and deposited upon a level surface of earth behind it.

Its motion was so swift, complex, and perfect that at first I did not see it as a machine, in spite of its metallic glitter. The fighting-machines were co-ordinated and animated to an extraordinary pitch, but nothing to compare with this. People who have never seen these structures, and have only the ill-imagined efforts of artists or the imperfect descriptions of such eye-witnesses as myself to go upon, scarcely realise that living quality.

I recall particularly the illustration of one of the first pamphlets to give a consecutive account of the war. The artist had evidently made a hasty study of one of the fighting-machines, and there his knowledge ended. He presented them as tilted, stiff tripods, without either flexibility or subtlety, and with an altogether misleading monotony of effect. The pamphlet containing these renderings had a considerable vogue, and I mention them here simply to warn the reader against the impression they may have created. They were no more like the Martians I saw in action than a Dutch doll is like a human being. To my mind, the pamphlet would have been much better without them.[1]

At first, I say, the handling-machine did not impress me as a machine, but as a crab-like creature with a glittering integument, the controlling Martian whose delicate tentacles actuated its movements seeming to be simply the equivalent of the crab's cerebral portion. But then I perceived the resemblance of its grey-brown, shiny, leathery integument to that of the other sprawling bodies beyond, and the true nature of this dexterous workman dawned upon me. With that realisation my interest shifted to those other creatures, the real Martians. Already I had had a transient impression of these, and the first nausea no longer obscured my observation. Moreover, I was concealed and motionless, and under no urgency of action.

They were, I now saw, the most unearthly creatures it is possible to conceive. They were huge round bodies—or, rather, heads—about four feet in diameter, each body having in front of it a face. This face had no nostrils—indeed, the Martians do not seem to have had any sense of smell—but* it had a pair of very large, dark-coloured eyes, and just beneath this a kind of fleshy beak. In the back of this head or body—I scarcely know how to speak of it—was the single tight tympanic surface, since known to be anatomically an ear, though it must have been almost useless in our denser air. In a group round the mouth were sixteen slender, almost whip-like tentacles, arranged in two bunches of eight each. These bunches have since been named rather aptly, by that distinguished anatomist, Professor Howes,[2] the *hands.* Even as I saw these Martians for the first time they seemed to be endeavouring to raise themselves on these hands, but of course, with the increased weight of terrestrial conditions, this was impossible. There is reason to suppose that on Mars they may have progressed upon them with some facility.

The internal anatomy, I may remark here, as dissection has since shown, was almost equally simple. The greater part of the structure was the brain, sending enormous nerves to the eyes, ear, and tactile tentacles. Besides this were the bulky lungs, into which the mouth opened, and the heart and its vessels. The pulmonary distress caused by the denser atmosphere and greater gravitational attraction was only too evident in the convulsive movements of the outer skin.

And this was the sum of the Martian organs. Strange as it may seem to a human being, all the complex apparatus of digestion, which makes up the bulk of our bodies, did not exist in the Martians. They were heads—merely heads. Entrails they had none. They did not eat, much less digest. Instead, they took the fresh, living blood of other creatures, and *injected* it into their own veins. I have myself seen this being done, as I shall mention in its place. But, squeamish as I may seem, I cannot bring myself to describe what I could not endure even to continue watching. Let it suffice to say,

---

*C, A; smell, but: P–PR, NY–AG, E.

blood obtained from a still living animal, in most cases from a human being, was run directly by means of a little pipette into the recipient canal. . . .

The bare idea of this is no doubt horribly repulsive to us, but at the same time I think that we should remember how repulsive our carnivorous habits would seem to an intelligent rabbit.[3]

The physiological advantages of the practice of injection are undeniable, if one thinks of the tremendous waste of human time and energy occasioned by eating and the digestive process. Our bodies are half made up of glands and tubes and organs, occupied in turning heterogeneous food into blood. The digestive processes and their reaction upon the nervous system sap our strength and colour our minds. Men go happy or miserable as they have healthy or unhealthy livers, or sound gastric glands. But the Martians were lifted above all these organic fluctuations of mood and emotion.

Their undeniable preference for men as their source of nourishment is partly explained by the nature of the remains of the victims they had brought with them as provisions from Mars. These creatures, to judge from the shrivelled remains that have fallen into human hands, were bipeds with flimsy, silicious skeletons (almost like those of the silicious sponges) and feeble musculature, standing about six feet high and having round, erect heads, and large eyes in flinty sockets. Two or three of these seem to have been brought in each cylinder, and all were killed before earth was reached. It was just as well for them, for the mere attempt to stand upright upon our planet would have broken every bone in their bodies.[4]

And while I am engaged in this description, I may add in this place certain further details which, although they were not all evident to us at the time, will enable the reader who is unacquainted with them to form a clearer picture of these offensive creatures.

In three other points their physiology differed strangely from ours. Their organisms did not sleep, any more than the heart of man sleeps. Since they had no extensive muscular mechanism to recuperate, that periodical extinction was unknown to them. They had little or no sense of fatigue, it would seem. On earth they could never have moved without effort, yet even to the last they kept in action. In twenty-four hours they did twenty-four hours of work, as even on earth is perhaps the case with the ants.

In the next place, wonderful as it seems in a sexual world, the Martians were absolutely without sex, and therefore without any of the tumultuous emotions that arise from that difference among men. A young Martian, there can now be no dispute, was really born upon earth during the war, and it was found attached to its parent, partially *budded* off, just as young lily-bulbs bud off, or like the young animals in the fresh-water polyp.

In man, in all the higher terrestrial animals, such a method of increase has disappeared; but even on this earth it was certainly the primitive method.

Among the lower animals, up even to those first cousins of the vertebrated animals, the Tunicates, the two processes occur side by side, but finally the sexual method superseded its competitor altogether. On Mars, however, just the reverse has apparently been the case.

It is worthy of remark that a certain speculative writer of quasi-scientific repute, writing long before the Martian invasion, did forecast for man a final structure not unlike the actual Martian condition. His prophecy, I remember, appeared in November or December, 1893, in a long-defunct publication, the *Pall Mall Budget*,[5] and I recall a caricature of it in a pre-Martian periodical called *Punch*.[6] He pointed out—writing in a foolish, facetious tone—that the perfection of mechanical appliances must ultimately supersede limbs; the perfection of chemical devices, digestion; that such organs as hair, external nose, teeth, ears, and chin were no longer essential parts of the human being, and that the tendency of natural selection would lie in the direction of their steady diminution through the coming ages. The brain alone remained a cardinal necessity. Only one other part of the body had a strong case for survival, and that was the hand, "teacher and agent of the brain."[7] While the rest of the body dwindled, the hands would grow larger.

There is many a true word written in jest, and here in the Martians we have beyond dispute the actual accomplishment of such a suppression of the animal side of the organism by the intelligence. To me it is quite credible that the Martians may be descended from beings not unlike ourselves,[8] by a gradual development of brain and hands (the latter giving rise to the two bunches of delicate tentacles at last) at the expense of the rest of the body. Without the body the brain would, of course, become a mere selfish intelligence, without any of the emotional substratum[9] of the human being.[10]

The last salient point in which the systems of these creatures differed from ours was in what one might have thought a very trivial particular. Micro-organisms, which cause so much disease and pain on earth, have either never appeared upon Mars or Martian sanitary science eliminated them ages ago. A hundred diseases, all the fevers and contagions of human life, consumption, cancers, tumours and such morbidities, never enter the scheme of their life.[11] And speaking of the differences between the life on Mars and terrestrial life, I may allude here to the curious suggestions of the red weed.

Apparently the vegetable kingdom in Mars, instead of having green for a dominant colour, is of a vivid blood-red tint. At any rate, the seeds which the Martians (intentionally or accidentally) brought with them gave rise in all cases to red-coloured growths. Only that known popularly as the red weed, however, gained any footing in competition with terrestrial forms. The red creeper was quite a transitory growth, and few people have seen it growing. For a time, however, the red weed grew with astonishing vigour and luxuriance. It spread up the sides of the pit by the third or fourth day of our imprisonment, and its cactus-like branches formed a carmine fringe to the edges of our triangular window. And afterwards I found it broadcast throughout the country, and especially wherever there was a stream of water.[12]

The Martians had what appears to have been an auditory organ, a single round drum at the back of the head-body, and eyes with a visual range not very different from ours except that, according to Philips,[13] blue and violet were as black to them. It is commonly supposed that they communicated by sounds and tentacular gesticulations; this is asserted, for instance, in the able but hastily compiled pamphlet (written evidently by some one not an eye-witness of Martian actions) to which I have already alluded,[14] and which, so far, has been the chief source of information concerning them. Now no surviving human being saw so much of the Martians in action as I did. I take no credit to myself for an accident, but the fact is so. And I assert that I watched them closely time after time, and that I have seen four, five, and (once) six of them sluggishly performing the most elaborately complicated operations together without either sound or gesture. Their peculiar hooting invariably preceded feeding; it had no modulation, and was, I believe, in no sense a signal, but merely the expiration of air preparatory to the suctional operation. I have a certain claim to at least an elementary knowledge of psychology, and in this matter I am convinced—as firmly as I am convinced of anything—that the Martians interchanged thoughts without any physical intermediation. And I have been convinced of this in spite of strong preconceptions. Before the Martian invasion, as an occasional reader here or there may remember, I had written with some little vehemence against the telepathic theory.[15]

The Martians wore no clothing. Their conceptions of ornament and decorum were necessarily different from ours; and not only were they evidently much less sensible of changes of temperature than we are, but changes of pressure do not seem to have affected their health at all seriously. Yet though they wore no clothing, it was in the other artificial additions to their bodily resources, that* their great superiority over man lay. We men, with our bicycles and road-skates, our Lilienthal soaring-machines,[16] our guns and sticks[17] and so forth, are just in the beginning of the evolution that the Martians have worked out. They have become practically mere brains, wearing different bodies according to their needs just as men wear suits of clothes and take a bicycle in a hurry or an umbrella in the wet.[18] And of their appliances, perhaps nothing is more wonderful to a man than

---

*AG–A; resources certainly that: C; resources, certainly, that: P–NY; resources that: E.

the curious fact that what is the dominant feature of almost all human devices in mechanism is absent—the *wheel* is absent; among all the things they brought to earth there is no trace or suggestion of their use of wheels. One would have at least expected it in locomotion. And in this connection it is curious to remark that even on this earth Nature has never hit upon the wheel, or has preferred other expedients to its development. And not only did the Martians either not know of (which is incredible), or abstain from, the wheel, but in their apparatus singularly little use is made of the fixed pivot, or relatively fixed pivot, with circular motions thereabout confined to one plane. Almost all the joints of the machinery present a complicated system of sliding parts moving over small but beautifully curved friction bearings.[19] And while upon this matter of detail, it is remarkable that the long leverages of their machines are in most cases actuated by a sort of sham musculature of discs in an elastic sheath; these discs become polarised and drawn closely and powerfully together when traversed by a current of electricity. In this way the curious parallelism to animal motions, which was so striking and disturbing to the human beholder, was attained. Such quasi-muscles abounded in the crab-like handling-machine which, on my first peeping out of the slit, I watched unpacking the cylinder. It seemed infinitely more alive than the actual Martians lying beyond it in the sunset light, panting, stirring ineffectual tentacles, and moving feebly after their vast journey across space.

While I was still watching their sluggish motions in the sunlight, and noting each strange detail of their form, the curate reminded me of his presence by pulling violently at my arm. I turned to a scowling face, and silent, eloquent lips. He wanted the slit, which permitted only one of us to peep through; and so I had to forego watching them for a time while he enjoyed that privilege.

When I looked again, the busy handling-machine had already put together several of the pieces of apparatus it had taken out of the cylinder into a shape having an unmistakable likeness to its own; and down on the left a busy little digging mechanism had come into view, emitting jets of green vapour and working its way round the pit, excavating and embanking in a methodical and discriminating manner. This it was which had caused the regular beating noise, and the rhythmic shocks that had kept our ruinous refuge quivering. It piped and whistled as it worked. So far as I could see, the thing was without a directing Martian at all.[20]

III

THE DAYS OF IMPRISONMENT

THE ARRIVAL OF a second fighting-machine drove us from our peep-hole into the scullery, for we feared that from his elevation the Martian might see down upon us behind our barrier. At a later date we began to feel less in danger of their eyes, for to an eye in the dazzle of the sunlight outside our refuge must have been blank blackness, but at first the slightest suggestion of approach drove us into the scullery in heart-throbbing retreat. Yet terrible as was the danger we incurred, the attraction of peeping was for both of us irresistible. And I recall now with a sort of wonder that, in spite of the infinite danger in which we were between starvation and a still more terrible death, we could yet struggle bitterly for that horrible privilege of sight. We would race across the kitchen in a grotesque way between eagerness and the dread of making a noise, and strike each other, and thrust and kick, within a few inches of exposure.

The fact is that we had absolutely incompatible dispositions and habits of thought and action, and our danger and isolation only accentuated the incompatibility. At Halliford I had already come to hate the curate's trick of helpless exclamation, his stupid rigidity of mind. His endless muttering monologue vitiated every effort I made to think out a line of action, and drove me at times, thus pent up and intensified, almost to the verge of craziness. He was as lacking in restraint as a silly woman. He would weep for hours together, and I verily believe that to the very end this spoiled child of life thought his weak tears in some way efficacious. And I would sit in the darkness unable to keep my mind off him by reason of his importunities. He ate more than I did, and it was in vain I pointed out that our only chance of life was to stop in the house until the Martians had done with their pit, that in that long patience a time might presently come when we should need food. He ate and drank impulsively in heavy meals at long intervals. He slept little.

As the days wore on, his utter carelessness of any consideration so intensified our distress and danger that I had, much as I loathed doing it, to resort to threats, and at last to blows. That brought him to reason for a time. But he was one of those weak creatures, void of pride, timorous, anæmic, hateful souls, full of shifty cunning who face neither God nor man, who face not even themselves.

It is disagreeable for me to recall and write these things, but I set them down that my story may lack nothing. Those who have escaped the dark and terrible aspects of life will find my brutality, my flash of rage in our final tragedy, easy enough to blame; for they know what is wrong as well as any, but not what is possible to tortured men. But those who have been under the shadow, who have gone down at last to elemental things, will have a wider charity.

And while within we fought out our dark, dim contest of whispers, snatched food and drink, and gripping hands and blows, without, in the pitiless sunlight of that terrible June, was the strange wonder, the unfamiliar routine of the Martians in the pit. Let me return to those first new experiences of mine. After a long time I ventured back to the peep-hole, to find that the new-comers had been reinforced by the occupants of no fewer than three of the fighting-machines. These last had brought with them certain fresh appliances that stood in an orderly manner about the cylinder. The second handling-machine was now completed, and was busied in serving one of the novel contrivances the big machine had brought. This was a body resembling a milk-can in its general form, above which oscillated a pear-shaped receptacle, and from which a stream of white powder flowed into a circular basin below.

The oscillatory motion was imparted to this by one tentacle of the handling-machine. With two spatulate hands the handling-machine was digging out and flinging masses of clay into the pear-shaped receptacle above, while with another arm it periodically opened a door and removed rusty and blackened clinkers from the middle part of the machine. Another steely tentacle directed the powder from the basin along a ribbed channel towards some receiver that was hidden from me by the mound of bluish dust. From this unseen receiver a little thread of green smoke rose vertically into the quiet air. As I looked, the handling-machine, with a faint and musical clinking, extended, telescopic fashion, a tentacle that had been a moment before a mere blunt projection, until its end was hidden behind the mound of clay. In another second it had lifted a bar of white aluminium into sight, untarnished as yet and shining dazzlingly, and deposited it in a growing stack of bars that stood at the side of the pit. Between sunset and starlight this dexterous machine must have made more than a hundred such bars out of the crude clay, and the mound of bluish dust rose steadily until it topped the side of the pit.

The contrast between the swift and complex movements of these contrivances and the inert, panting clumsiness of their masters was acute, and for days I had to tell myself repeatedly that these latter were indeed the living of the two things.

The curate had possession of the slit when the first men were brought to the pit. I was sitting below, huddled up, listening with all my ears. He made a sudden movement backward, and I, fearful that we were observed, crouched in a spasm of terror. He came sliding down the rubbish and crept beside me in the darkness, inarticulate, gesticulating, and for a moment I shared his panic. His gesture suggested a resignation of the slit, and after a little while my curiosity gave me courage, and I rose up, stepped across him, and clambered up to it. At first I could see no reason for his frantic behaviour. The twilight had now come, the stars were little and faint, but the pit was illuminated by the flickering green fire that came from the aluminium-making. The whole picture was a flickering scheme of green gleams and shifting rusty black shadows, strangely trying to the eyes. Over and through it all went the bats, heeding it not at all. The sprawling Martians were no longer to be seen, the mound of blue-green powder had risen to cover them from sight, and a fighting-machine, with its legs contracted, crumpled, and abbreviated, stood across the corner of the pit. And then, amid the clangour of the machinery, came a drifting suspicion of human voices, that I entertained at first only to dismiss.

I crouched, watching this fighting-machine closely, satisfying myself now for the first time that the hood did indeed contain a Martian. As the green flames lifted I could see the oily gleam of his integument and the brightness of his eyes. And suddenly I heard a yell, and saw a long tentacle reaching over the shoulder of the machine to the little cage that hunched upon its back. Then something—something struggling violently—was lifted high against the sky, a black, vague enigma against the starlight; and as this black object came down again, I saw by the green brightness that it was a man. For an instant he was clearly visible. He was a stout, ruddy, middle-aged man, well dressed; three days before he must have been walking the world, a man of considerable consequence. I could see his staring eyes and gleams of light on his studs and watch-chain. He vanished behind the mound, and for a moment there was silence. And then began a shrieking and a sustained and cheerful hooting from the Martians.

I slid down the rubbish, struggled to my feet, clapped my hands over my ears, and bolted into the scullery. The curate, who had been crouching silently with his arms over his head, looked up as I passed, cried out quite loudly at my desertion of him, and came running after me.

That night, as we lurked in the scullery balanced between our horror and the terrible fascination this peeping had, although I felt an urgent need of action I tried in vain to conceive some plan of escape; but afterwards, during the second day, I was able to consider our position with great clearness. The curate, I found, was quite incapable of discussion; this new and culminating atrocity had robbed him of all vestiges of reason or forethought. Practically he had already sunk to the level of an animal. But, as the saying goes, I gripped myself with both hands. It grew upon my mind, once I could face the facts, that, terrible as our position was, there was as yet no justification for absolute despair. Our chief chance lay in the possibility of the Martians making the pit nothing more than a temporary encampment. Or even if they kept it permanently, they might not consider it necessary to guard it, and a chance of escape might be afforded us. I also weighed very carefully the possibility of our digging a way out in a direction away from the pit, but the chances of our emerging within sight of some sentinel fighting-machine seemed at first too great. And I should have had to do all the digging myself. The curate would certainly have failed me.

It was on the third day, if my memory serves me right, that I saw the lad killed. It was the only occasion on which I actually saw the Martians feed. After that experience I avoided the hole in the wall for the better part of a day. I went into the scullery, removed the door, and spent some hours digging with my hatchet as silently as possible; but when I had made a hole about a couple of feet deep the loose earth collapsed noisily, and I did not dare continue. I lost heart, and lay down on the scullery floor for a long time, having no spirit even to move. And after that I abandoned altogether the idea of escaping by excavation.

It says much for the impression the Martians had made upon me that at first I entertained little or no hope of our escape being brought about by their overthrow through any human effort. But on the fourth or fifth night I heard a sound like heavy guns.

It was very late in the night, and the moon was shining brightly. The Martians had taken away the excavating-machine, and, save for a fighting-machine that stood on the remoter bank of the pit and a handling-machine that was busied out of my sight in a corner of the pit immediately beneath my peephole, the place was deserted by them. Except for the pale glow from the handling-machine and the bars and patches of white moonlight, the pit was in darkness, and, except for the clinking of the handling-machine, quite still. That night was a beautiful serenity; save for one planet, the moon seemed to have the sky to herself. I heard a dog howling, and that familiar sound it was that made me listen. Then I heard quite distinctly a booming exactly like the sound of great guns. Six distinct reports I counted, and after a long interval six again. And that was all.

IV

THE DEATH OF THE CURATE

IT WAS ON THE sixth day of our imprisonment that I peeped for the last time, and presently found myself alone. Instead of keeping close to me and trying to oust me from the slit, the curate had gone back into the scullery. I was struck by a sudden thought. I went back quickly and quietly into the scullery. In the darkness I heard the curate drinking. I snatched in the darkness, and my fingers caught a bottle of burgundy.

For a few minutes there was a tussle. The bottle struck the floor and broke, and I desisted and rose. We stood panting, threatening each other. In the end I planted myself between him and the food, and told him of my determination to begin a discipline. I divided the food in the pantry into rations to last us ten days. I would not let him eat any more that day.[1] In the afternoon he made a feeble effort to get at the food. I had been dozing, but in an instant I was awake. All day and all night we sat face to face, I weary but resolute, and he weeping and complaining of his immediate* hunger. It was, I know, a night and a day, but to me it seemed—it seems now—an interminable length of time.

And so our widened incompatibility ended at last in open conflict. For two vast days we struggled in undertones and wrestling contests. There were times when I beat and kicked him madly, times when I cajoled and persuaded him, and once I tried to bribe him with the last bottle of burgundy, for there was a rain-water pump from which I could get water. But neither force nor kindness availed; he was indeed beyond reason. He would neither desist from his attacks on the food nor from his noisy babbling to himself. The rudimentary precautions to keep our imprisonment endurable he would not observe. Slowly I began to realise the complete overthrow of his intel-

---

*L E; immoderate: PR.

ligence, to perceive that my sole companion in this close and sickly darkness was a man insane.

From certain vague memories I am inclined to think my own mind wandered at times. I had strange and hideous dreams whenever I slept. It sounds paradoxical, but I am inclined to think that the weakness and insanity of the curate warned me, braced me, and kept me a sane man.

On the eighth day he began to talk aloud instead of whispering, and nothing I could do would moderate his speech.

"It is just, O God!" he would say, over and over again. "It is just. On me and mine be the punishment laid. We have sinned, we have fallen short. There was poverty, sorrow; the poor were trodden in the dust, and I held my peace. I preached acceptable folly—my God, what folly!—when I should have stood up, though I died for it, and called upon them to repent—repent! . . . Oppressors of the poor and needy! . . . The wine-press of God!"

Then he would suddenly revert to the matter of the food I withheld from him, praying, begging, weeping, at last threatening. He began to raise his voice—I prayed him not to. He perceived a hold on me—he threatened he would shout and bring the Martians upon us. For a time that scared me; but any concession would have shortened our chance of escape beyond estimating. I defied him, although I felt no assurance that he might not do this thing. But that day, at any rate, he did not. He talked, with* his voice rising slowly, through the greater part of the eighth and ninth days—threats, entreaties, mingled with a torrent of half-sane and always frothy repentance for his vacant sham of God's service, such as made me pity him. Then he slept awhile, and began again with renewed strength, so loudly that I must needs make him desist.

"Be still!" I implored.

He rose to his knees, for he had been sitting in the darkness near the copper.

"I have been still too long," he said, in a tone that must have reached the pit, "and now I must bear my witness. Woe unto this unfaithful city! Woe! woe! Woe! woe! woe! to the inhabitants of the earth by reason of the other voices of the trumpet—"[2]

"Shut up!" I said, rising to my feet, and in a terror lest the Martians should hear us. "For God's sake—"

"Nay!" shouted the curate, at the top of his voice, standing likewise and extending his arms. "Speak! The word of the Lord is upon me!"

In three strides he was at the door leading into the kitchen.

"I must bear my witness! I go! It has already been too long delayed."

---

*NY–A; *talked with*: PR–L, E; *would talk* [, C] *with*: P.

I put out my hand and felt the meat-chopper hanging to the wall. In a flash I was after him. I was fierce with fear. Before he was half-way across the kitchen I had overtaken him. With one last touch of humanity I turned the blade back and struck him with the butt. He went headlong forward and lay stretched on the ground. I stumbled over him and stood panting. He lay still.

Suddenly I heard a noise without, the run and smash of slipping plaster, and the triangular aperture in the wall was darkened. I looked up and saw the lower surface of a handling-machine coming slowly across the hole. One of its gripping limbs curled amid the débris; another limb appeared, feeling its way over the fallen beams. I stood petrified, staring. Then I saw through a sort of glass plate near the edge of the body the face, as we may call it, and the large dark eyes of a Martian, peering, and then a long metallic snake of tentacle came feeling slowly through the hole.

I turned by an effort, stumbled over the curate, and stopped at the scullery door. The tentacle was now some way, two yards or more, in the room, and twisting and turning, with queer sudden movements, this way and that. For a while I stood fascinated by that slow, fitful advance. Then, with a faint, hoarse cry, I forced myself across the scullery. I trembled violently; I could scarcely stand upright. I opened the door of the coal-cellar, and stood there in the darkness staring at the faintly lit door-way into the kitchen, and listening. Had the Martian seen me? What was it doing now?

Something was moving to and fro there, very quietly; every now and then it tapped against the wall, or started on its movements with a faint metallic ringing, like the movement of keys on a split-ring. Then a heavy body—I knew too well what—was dragged across the floor of the kitchen towards the opening. Irresistibly attracted, I crept to the door and peeped into the kitchen. In the triangle of bright outer sunlight I saw the Martian, in its Briareus[3] of a handling-machine, scrutinising the curate's head. I thought at once that it would infer my presence from the mark of the blow I had given him.

I crept back to the coal-cellar, shut the door, and began to cover myself up as much as I could, and as noiselessly as possible in the darkness, among the firewood and coal therein. Every now and then I paused, rigid, to hear if the Martian had thrust its tentacle through the opening again.

Then the faint metallic jingle returned. I traced it slowly feeling over the kitchen. Presently I heard it nearer—in the scullery, as I judged. I thought that its length might be insufficient to reach me. I prayed copiously. It passed, scraping faintly across the cellar door. An age of almost intolerable suspense intervened; then I heard it fumbling at the latch. It* had found the door! The Martians understood doors!

---

*C–A; *latch!* It: E.

It worried at the catch for a minute, perhaps, and then the door opened.

In the darkness I could just see the thing—like an elephant's trunk more than anything else—waving towards me and touching and examining the wall, coals, wood, and ceiling. It was like a black worm swaying its blind head to and fro.

Once, even, it touched the heel of my boot. I was on the verge of screaming; I bit my hand. For a time the tentacle was silent. I could have fancied it had been withdrawn. Presently, with an abrupt click, it gripped something—I thought it had me!—and seemed to go out of the cellar again. For a minute I was not sure. Apparently it had taken a lump of coal to examine.

I seized the opportunity of slightly shifting my position, which had become cramped, and then listened. I whispered passionate prayers for safety.

Then I heard the slow, deliberate sound creeping towards me again. Slowly, slowly it drew near, scratching against the walls and tapping the furniture.

While I was still doubtful, it rapped smartly against the cellar door and closed it. I heard it go into the pantry, and the biscuit-tins rattled and a bottle smashed, and then came a heavy bump against the cellar door. Then silence, that passed into an infinity of suspense.

Had it gone?

At last I decided that it had.

It came into the scullery no more; but I lay all the tenth day in the close darkness, buried among coals and firewood, not daring even to crawl out for the drink for which I craved. It was the eleventh day before I ventured so far from my security.

V

THE STILLNESS

MY FIRST ACT before I went into the pantry was to fasten the door between the kitchen and the scullery. But the pantry was empty; every scrap of food had gone. Apparently, the Martian had taken it all on the previous day. At that discovery I despaired for the first time. I took no food, or no drink either, on the eleventh or the twelfth day.

At first my mouth and throat were parched, and my strength ebbed sensibly. I sat about in the darkness of the scullery, in a state of despondent wretchedness. My mind ran on eating. I thought I had become deaf, for the noises of movement I had been accustomed to hear from the pit had ceased absolutely. I did not feel strong enough to crawl noiselessly to the peep-hole, or I would have gone there.

On the twelfth day my throat was so painful that, taking the chance of alarming the Martians, I attacked the creaking rain-water pump that stood by the sink, and got a couple of glassfuls of blackened and tainted rain-water. I was greatly refreshed by this, and emboldened by the fact that no inquiring tentacle followed the noise of my pumping.

During these days, in a rambling, inconclusive way, I thought much of the curate and of the manner of his death.

On the thirteenth day I drank some more water, and dozed and thought disjointedly of eating and of vague impossible plans of escape. Whenever I dozed I dreamt of horrible phantasms, of the death of the curate, or of sumptuous dinners; but, asleep or awake, I felt a keen pain that urged me to drink again and again. The light that came into the scullery was no longer grey, but red. To my disordered imagination it seemed the colour of blood.

On the fourteenth day I went into the kitchen, and I was surprised to find that the fronds of the red weed had grown right across the hole in the wall, turning the half-light of the place into a crimson-coloured obscurity.

It was early on the fifteenth day that I heard a curious, familiar sequence of sounds in the kitchen, and, listening, identified it as the snuffing and scratching of a dog. Going into the kitchen, I saw a dog's nose peering in through a break among the ruddy fronds. This greatly surprised me. At the scent of me he barked shortly.

I thought if I could induce him to come into the place quietly I should be able, perhaps, to kill and eat him; and, in any case, it would be advisable to kill him, lest his actions attracted the attention of the Martians.

I crept forward, saying "Good dog!" very softly; but he suddenly withdrew his head and disappeared.

I listened—I was not deaf—but certainly the pit was still. I heard a sound like the flutter of a bird's wings, and a hoarse croaking, but that was all.

For a long while I lay close to the peep-hole, but not daring to move aside the red plants that obscured it. Once or twice I heard a faint pitter-patter like the feet of the dog going hither and thither on the sand far below me, and there were more birdlike sounds, but that was all. At length, encouraged by the silence, I looked out.

Except in the corner, where a multitude of crows hopped and fought over the skeletons of the dead the Martians had consumed, there was not a living thing in the pit.

I stared about me, scarcely believing my eyes. All the machinery had gone. Save for the big mound of greyish-blue powder in one corner, certain bars of aluminium in another, the black birds, and the skeletons of the killed, the place was merely an empty circular pit in the sand.

Slowly I thrust myself out through the red weed, and stood upon the mound of rubble. I could see in any direction save behind me, to the north, and neither Martians nor sign of Martians were to be seen. The pit dropped sheerly from my feet, but a little way along the rubbish afforded a practicable slope to the summit of the ruins. My chance of escape had come. I began to tremble.

I hesitated for some time, and then, in a gust of desperate resolution, and with a heart that throbbed violently, I scrambled to the top of the mound in which I had been buried so long.

I looked about again. To the northward, too, no Martian was visible.

When I had last seen this part of Sheen in the daylight it had been a straggling street of comfortable white and red houses, interspersed with abundant shady trees. Now I stood on a mound of smashed brickwork, clay, and gravel, over which spread a multitude of red cactus-shaped plants, knee-high, without a solitary terrestrial growth to dispute their footing. The trees near me were dead and brown, but further a* network of red threads scaled the still living stems.

The neighbouring houses had all been wrecked, but none had been burned; their walls stood, sometimes to the second story, with smashed windows and shattered doors. The red weed grew tumultuously in their roofless rooms. Below me was the great pit, with the crows struggling for its refuse. A number of other birds hopped about among the ruins. Far away I saw a gaunt cat slink crouchingly along a wall, but traces of men there were none.

The day seemed, by contrast with my recent confinement, dazzlingly bright, the sky a glowing blue. A gentle breeze kept the red weed that covered every scrap of unoccupied ground gently swaying. And oh! the sweetness of the air!

---

*NY–E; *further,* a: MS–L.

VI

THE WORK OF FIFTEEN DAYS

For some time I stood tottering on the mound regardless of my safety. Within that noisome den from which I had emerged I had thought with a narrow intensity only of our immediate security. I had not realised what had been happening to the world, had not anticipated this startling vision of unfamiliar things. I had expected to see Sheen in ruins—I found about me the landscape, weird and lurid, of another planet.

For that moment I touched an emotion beyond the common range of men, yet one that the poor brutes we dominate know only too well. I felt as a rabbit might feel returning to his burrow and suddenly confronted by the work of a dozen busy navvies digging the foundations of a house.[1] I felt the first inkling of a thing that presently grew quite clear in my mind, that oppressed me for many days, a sense of dethronement, a persuasion that I was no longer a master, but an animal among the animals, under the Martian heel. With us it would be as with them, to lurk and watch, to run and hide; the fear and empire of man had passed away.

But so soon as this strangeness had been realised it passed, and my dominant motive became the hunger of my long and dismal fast. In the direction away from the pit I saw, beyond a red-covered wall, a patch of garden ground unburied. This gave me a hint, and I went knee-deep, and sometimes neck-deep, in the red weed. The density of the weed gave me a reassuring sense of hiding. The wall was some six feet high, and when I attempted to clamber it I found I could not lift my feet to the crest. So I went along by the side of it, and came to a corner and a rockwork that enabled me to get to the top and* tumble into the garden I coveted. Here I found some young onions, a couple of gladiolus bulbs, and a quantity of

---

*PR–A; top, and: E.

immature carrots, all of which I secured, and, scrambling over a ruined wall, went on my way through scarlet and crimson trees towards Kew—it was like walking through an avenue of gigantic blood-drops[2]—possessed with two ideas: to get more food, and to limp, as soon and as far as my strength permitted,[3] out of this accursed unearthly region of the pit.

Some way farther, in a grassy place, was a group of mushrooms which also I devoured, and then I came upon a broad* sheet of flowing shallow water, where meadows used to be. These fragments of nourishment served only to whet my hunger. At first I was surprised at this flood in a hot, dry summer, but afterwards I discovered that it was caused by the tropical exuberance of the red weed. Directly this extraordinary growth encountered water it straightway became gigantic and of unparalleled fecundity. Its seeds were simply poured down into the waters** of the Wey and Thames, and its swiftly growing and Titanic water-fronds speedily choked both those rivers.

At Putney, as I afterwards saw, the bridge was almost lost in a tangle of this weed, and at Richmond, too, the Thames waters** poured in a broad and shallow stream across the meadows of Hampton and Twickenham. As the waters spread the weed followed them, until the ruined villas of the Thames Valley were for a time lost in this red swamp, whose margin I explored, and much of the desolation the Martians had caused was concealed.

In the end the red weed succumbed almost as quickly as it had spread. A cankering[4] disease, due, it is believed, to the action of certain bacteria, presently seized upon it. Now by the action of natural selection, all terrestrial plants have acquired a resisting power against bacterial diseases—they never succumb without a severe struggle, but the red weed rotted like a thing already dead. The fronds became bleached, and then shrivelled and brittle. They broke off at the least touch, and the waters that had stimulated their early growth carried their last vestiges out to sea.

My first act on coming to this water was, of course, to slake my thirst. I drank a great deal of it, and, moved[†] by an impulse, gnawed some fronds of red weed; but they were watery, and had a sickly, metallic taste. I found the water was sufficiently shallow for me to wade securely, although the red weed impeded my feet a little; but the flood evidently got deeper towards the river, and I turned back to Mortlake. I managed to make out the road by means of occasional ruins of its villas and fences and lamps, and so

---

*MS; brown: C–E.
**MS; water: C–E.
†NY–A; it and, moved: E; great bulk of water, and, moved: PR–L.

presently I got out of this spate and made my way to the hill going up towards Roehampton and came out on Putney Common.

Here the scenery changed from the strange and unfamiliar to the wreckage of the familiar: patches of ground exhibited the devastation of a cyclone, and in a few score yards I would come upon perfectly undisturbed spaces, houses with their blinds trimly drawn and doors closed, as if they had been left for a day by the owners, or as if their inhabitants slept within. The red weed was less abundant; the tall trees along the lane were free from the red creeper. I hunted for food among the trees, finding nothing, and I also raided a couple of silent houses, but they had already been broken into and ransacked. I rested for the remainder of the daylight in a shrubbery, being, in my enfeebled condition, too fatigued to push on.

All this time I saw no human beings, and no signs of the Martians. I encountered a couple of hungry-looking dogs, but both hurried circuitously away from the advances I made them. Near Roehampton I had seen two human skeletons—not bodies, but skeletons, picked clean—and in the wood by me I found the crushed and scattered bones of several cats and rabbits and the skull of a sheep. But though I gnawed parts of these in my mouth, there was nothing to be got from them.

After sunset I struggled on along the road towards Putney, where I think the Heat-Ray must have been used for some reason. And in a garden beyond Roehampton I got a quantity of immature potatoes, sufficient to stay my hunger. From this garden one looked down upon Putney and the river. The aspect of the place in the dusk was singularly desolate: blackened trees, blackened, desolate ruins, and down the hill the sheets of the flooded river, red-tinged with the weed. And over all—silence. It filled me with indescribable terror to think how swiftly that desolating change had come.

For a time I believed that mankind had been swept out of existence, and that I stood there alone, the last man left alive.[5] Hard by the top of Putney Hill I came upon another skeleton, with the arms dislocated and removed several yards from the rest of the body. As I proceeded I became more and more convinced that the extermination of mankind was, save for such stragglers as myself, already accomplished in this part of the world. The Martians, I thought, had gone on and left the country desolated, seeking food elsewhere. Perhaps even now they were destroying Berlin or Paris, or it might be they had gone northward.

VII

THE MAN ON PUTNEY HILL[1]

I SPENT THAT NIGHT in the inn that stands at the top of Putney Hill, sleeping in a made bed for the first time since my flight to Leatherhead. I will not tell the needless trouble I had breaking into that house—afterwards I found the front door was on the latch—nor how I ransacked every room for food, until, just on the verge of despair, in what seemed to me to be a servant's bedroom, I found a rat-gnawed crust and two tins of pineapple. The place had been already searched and emptied. In the bar I afterwards found some biscuits and sandwiches that had been overlooked. The latter I could not eat, they were too rotten, but the former not only stayed my hunger, but filled my pockets. I lit no lamps, fearing some Martian might come beating that part of London for food in the night. Before I went to bed I had an interval of restlessness, and prowled from window to window, peering out for some sign of these monsters. I slept little. As I lay in bed I found myself thinking consecutively—a thing I do not remember to have done since my last argument with the curate. During all the intervening time my mental condition had been a hurrying succession of vague emotional states or a sort of stupid receptivity. But in the night my brain, reinforced, I suppose, by the food I had eaten, grew clear again, and I thought.

Three things struggled for possession of my mind: the killing of the curate, the whereabouts of the Martians, and the possible fate of my wife. The former gave me no sensation of horror or remorse to recall; I saw it simply as a thing done, a memory infinitely disagreeable but quite without the quality of remorse. I saw myself then as I see myself now, driven step by step towards that hasty blow, the creature of a sequence of accidents leading inevitably to that. I felt no condemnation; yet the memory, static, unprogressive, haunted me. In the silence of the night, with that sense of the nearness of God that sometimes comes into the stillness and the darkness, I stood my trial, my only trial, for that moment of wrath and fear. I retraced every step of our conversation* from the moment when I had found him crouching beside me, heedless of my thirst, and pointing to the fire and smoke that streamed up from the ruins of Weybridge. We had been incapable of co-operation—grim chance had taken no heed of that. Had I foreseen, I should have left him at Halliford. But I did not foresee; and crime is to foresee and do.[2] And I set this down as I have set all this story down, as it was. There were no witnesses—all these things I might have concealed. But I set it down, and the reader must form his judgment as he will.

And when, by an effort, I had set aside that picture of a prostrate body, I faced the problem of the Martians and the fate of my wife. For the former I had no data; I could imagine a hundred things, and so, unhappily, I could for the latter. And suddenly that night became terrible. I found myself sitting up in bed, staring at the dark. I found myself praying that the Heat-Ray might have suddenly and painlessly struck her out of being. Since the night of my return from Leatherhead I had not prayed. I had uttered prayers, fetish prayers, had prayed as heathens mutter charms when I was in extremity; but now I prayed indeed, pleading steadfastly and sanely, face to face with the darkness of God. Strange night! strangest in this, that so soon as dawn had come, I, who had talked with God, crept out of the house like a rat leaving its hiding-place—a creature scarcely larger, an inferior animal, a thing that for any passing whim of our masters might be hunted and killed. Perhaps they also prayed confidently to God. Surely, if we have learned nothing else, this war has taught us pity—pity for those witless souls that suffer our dominion.[3]

The morning was bright and fine, and the eastern sky glowed pink, and was fretted with little golden clouds. In the road that runs from the top of Putney Hill to Wimbledon was a number of poor vestiges of the panic torrent that must have poured Londonward on the Sunday night after the fighting began. There was a little two-wheeled cart inscribed with the name of Thomas Lobb, Green-grocer, New Malden, with a smashed wheel and an abandoned tin trunk; there was a straw hat trampled into the now hardened mud, and at the top of West Hill a lot of blood-stained glass about the overturned water-trough. My movements were languid, my plans of the vaguest. I had an idea of going to Leatherhead, though I knew that there I had the poorest chance of finding my wife. Certainly, unless death had overtaken them suddenly, my cousins and she would have fled thence; but it seemed to me I might find or learn there whither the Surrey people had fled. I knew I wanted to find my wife, that my heart ached for her and the world of men, but I had no clear idea how the finding might be done. I was also sharply aware now of my intense loneliness. From the corner I

---

*L–E; connexion: PR.

went, under cover of a thicket of trees and bushes, to the edge of Wimbledon Common, stretching wide and far.

That dark expanse was lit in patches by yellow gorse and broom; there was no red weed to be seen, and as I prowled, hesitating, on the verge of the open, the sun rose, flooding it all with light and vitality. I came upon a busy swarm of little frogs in a swampy place among the trees. I stopped to look at them, drawing a lesson from their stout resolve to live.[4] And presently, turning suddenly, with an odd feeling of being watched, I beheld something crouching amid a clump of bushes. I stood regarding this. I made a step towards it, and it rose up and became a man armed with a cutlass. I approached him slowly. He stood silent and motionless, regarding me.

As I drew nearer I perceived he was dressed in clothes as dusty and filthy as my own; he looked, indeed, as though he had been dragged through a culvert. Nearer, I distinguished the green slime of ditches mixing with the pale drab of dried clay and shiny, coaly patches. His black hair fell over his eyes, and his face was dark and dirty and sunken, so that at first I did not recognise him. There was a red cut across the lower part of his face.

"Stop!" he cried, when I was within ten yards of him, and I stopped. His voice was hoarse. "Where do you come from?" he said.

I thought, surveying him.

"I come from Mortlake," I said. "I was buried near the pit the Martians made about their cylinder. I have worked my way out and escaped."

"There is no food about here," he said. "This is my country. All this hill down to the river, and back to Clapham, and up to the edge of the common. There is only food for one. Which way are you going?"

I answered slowly.

"I don't know," I said. "I have been buried in the ruins of a house thirteen or fourteen days. I don't know what has happened."

He looked at me doubtfully, then started, and looked with a changed expression.

"I've no wish to stop about here," said I. "I think I shall go to Leatherhead, for my wife was there."

He shot out a pointing finger.

"It is you," said he—"the man from Woking. And you weren't killed at Weybridge?"

I recognised him at the same moment.

"You are the artilleryman[5] who came into my garden."

"Good-luck!" he said. "We are lucky ones! Fancy *you*!" He put out a hand, and I took it. "I crawled up a drain," he said. "But they didn't kill every one. And after they went away I got off towards Walton across the fields. But— It's not sixteen days altogether—and your hair is grey." He looked over his shoulder suddenly. "Only a rook," he said. "One gets to know that birds have shadows these days. This *is* a bit open. Let us crawl under those bushes and talk."

"Have you seen any Martians?" I said. "Since I crawled out—"

"They've gone away across London," he said. "I guess they've got a bigger camp there. Of a night, all over there, Hampstead way, the sky is alive with their lights. It's like a great city, and in the glare you can just see them moving. By daylight you can't. But nearer—I haven't seen them—" (he counted on his fingers) "five days. Then I saw a couple across Hammersmith way carrying something big. And the night before last"—he stopped and spoke impressively—"it was just a matter of lights, but it was something up in the air. I believe they've built a flying-machine, and are learning to fly."

I stopped, on hands and knees, for we had come to the bushes.

"Fly!"

"Yes," he said, "fly."

I went on into a little bower, and sat down.

"It is all over with humanity," I said. "If they can do that they will simply go round the world."

He nodded.

"They will. But— It will relieve things over here a bit. And besides—" He looked at me. "Aren't you satisfied it *is* up with humanity? I am. We're down;* we're beat."

I stared. Strange as it may seem, I had not arrived at this fact—a fact perfectly obvious so soon as he spoke. I had still held a vague hope; rather, I had kept a lifelong habit of mind. He repeated his words, "We're beat." They carried absolute conviction.

"It's all over," he said. "They've lost one—just *one.*[6] And they've made their footing good and crippled the greatest power in the world. They've walked over us. The death of that one at Weybridge was an accident. And these are only pioneers. They keep** on coming. These green stars—I've seen none these five or six days, but I've no doubt they're falling somewhere every night. Nothing's to be done. We're under! We're beat!"

I made him no answer. I sat staring before me, trying in vain to devise some countervailing thought.

"This isn't a war," said the artilleryman. "It never was a war, any more than there's war between men and ants."

Suddenly I recalled the night in the observatory.

"After the tenth shot they fired no more—at least, until the first cylinder came."

---

*L–E; done: PR.
**PR–A; kept: E.

"How do you know?" said the artilleryman. I explained. He thought. "Something wrong with the gun," he said. "But what if there is? They'll get it right again. And even if there's a delay, how can it alter the end? It's just men and ants. There's the ants build* their cities, live their lives, have wars, revolutions, until the men want them out of the way, and then they go out of the way.[7] That's what we are now—just ants. Only—"

"Yes," I said.

"We're eatable ants."

We sat looking at each other.

"And what will they do with us?" I said.

"That's what I've been thinking," he said—"that's what I've been thinking. After Weybridge I went south—thinking. I saw what was up. Most of the people were hard at it squealing and exciting themselves. But I'm not so fond of squealing. I've been in sight of death once or twice; I'm not an ornamental soldier, and at the best and worst, death—it's just death. And it's the man that keeps on thinking comes through. I saw every one tracking away south. Says I, 'Food won't last this way,' and I turned right back. I went for the Martians like a sparrow goes for man. All round"—he waved a hand to the horizon—"they're starving in heaps, bolting, treading on each other." . . .

He saw my face, and halted awkwardly.

"No doubt lots who had money have gone** away to France," he said. He seemed to hesitate whether to apologise, met my eyes, and went on: "There's food all about here. Canned things in shops; wines, spirits, mineral waters; and the water mains and drains are empty. Well, I was telling you what I was thinking. 'Here's intelligent things,' I said, 'and it seems they want us for food. First, they'll smash us up—ships, machines, guns, cities, all the order and organisation. All that will go. If we were the size of ants we might pull through. But we're not. It's all too bulky to stop. That's the first certainty.' Eh?"

I assented.

"It is; I've thought it out. Very well, then—next; at present we're caught as we're wanted. A Martian has only to go a few miles to get a crowd on the run. And I saw one, one day, out by Wandsworth, picking houses to pieces and routing among the wreckage. But they won't keep on doing that. So soon as they've settled all our guns and ships, and smashed our railways, and done all the things they are doing over there, they will begin catching us systematic, picking the best and storing us in cages and things. That's

---

*PR, A; builds: L–AG, E.
**L–E; got: PR.

what they will start doing in a bit. Lord! they haven't begun on us yet. Don't you see that?"

"Not begun!" I exclaimed.

"Not begun. All that's happened so far is through our not having the sense to keep quiet—worrying them with guns and such foolery. And losing our heads, and rushing off in crowds to where there wasn't any more safety than where we were. They don't want to bother us yet. They're making their things—making all the things they couldn't bring with them, getting things ready for the rest of their people. Very likely that's why the cylinders have stopped for a bit, for fear of hitting those who are here. And instead of our rushing about blind, on the howl, or getting dynamite on the chance of busting them up, we've got to fix ourselves up according to the new state of affairs. That's how I figure it out. It isn't quite according to what a man wants for his species, but it's about what the facts point to. And that's the principle I acted upon. Cities, nations, civilisation, progress—it's all over.[8] That game's up. We're beat."

"But if that is so, what is there to live for?"

The artilleryman looked at me for a moment.

"There won't be any more blessed concerts for a million years or so; there won't be any Royal Academy of Arts, and no nice little feeds at restaurants. If it's amusement you're after, I reckon the game is up. If you've got any drawing-room manners or a dislike to eating peas with a knife or dropping aitches, you'd better chuck 'em away. They ain't no further use."

"You mean—"

"I mean that men like me are going on living—for the sake of the breed. I tell you, I'm grim set on living. And if I'm not mistaken, you'll show what insides you've got, too, before long. We aren't going to be exterminated. And I don't mean to be caught, either, and tamed and fattened and bred like a thundering ox. Ugh! Fancy those brown creepers!"

"You don't mean to say—"

"I do. I'm going on. Under their feet. I've got it planned; I've thought it out. We men are beat. We don't know enough. We've got to learn before we've got a chance. And we've got to live and keep independent while we learn. See! That's what has to be done."

I stared, astonished, and stirred profoundly by the man's resolution.

"Great God!" cried I. "But you are a man, indeed!" And* suddenly I gripped his hand.

"Eh!" he said, with his eyes shining. "I've thought it out, eh?"

"Go on," I said.

---

*PR–A; *man indeed!*": E.

"Well, those who mean to escape their catching must get ready. I'm getting ready. Mind you, it isn't all of us that are made for wild beasts; and that's what it's got to be. That's why I watched you. I had my doubts. You're slender. I didn't know that it was you, you see, or just how you'd been buried. All these—the sort of people that lived in these houses, and all those damn little clerks that used to live down that way—they'd be no good. They haven't any spirit in them—no proud dreams and no proud lusts; and a man who hasn't one or the other—Lord! what is he but funk and precautions? They just used to skedaddle off to work—I've seen hundreds of 'em, bit of breakfast in hand, running wild and shining to catch their little season-ticket train, for fear they'd get dismissed if they didn't; working at businesses they were afraid to take the trouble to understand; skedaddling back for fear they wouldn't be in time for dinner; keeping indoors after dinner for fear of the black* streets, and sleeping with the wives they married, not because they wanted them, but because they had a bit of money that would make for safety in their one little miserable skedaddle through the world. Lives insured and a bit invested for fear of accidents. And on Sundays—fear of the hereafter. As if hell was built for rabbits! Well, the Martians will just be a godsend to these. Nice roomy cages, fattening food, careful breeding, no worry. After a week or so chasing about the fields and lands on empty stomachs, they'll come and be caught cheerful. They'll be quite glad after a bit. They'll wonder what people did before there were Martians to take care of them. And the bar-loafers, and mashers, and singers—I can imagine them. I can imagine them," he said, with a sort of sombre gratification. "There'll be any amount of sentiment and religion loose among them. There's hundreds of things I saw with my eyes** that I've only begun to see clearly these last few days. There's lots will take things as they are—fat and stupid; and lots will be worried by a sort of feeling that it's all wrong, and that they ought to be doing something. Now whenever things are so that a lot of people feel they ought to be doing something, the weak, and those who go weak with a lot of complicated thinking, always make for a sort of do-nothing religion, very pious and superior, and submit to persecution and the will of the Lord. Very likely you've seen the same thing. It's energy in a gale of funk, and turned clean inside out. These cages will be full of psalms and hymns and piety.⁹ And those of a less simple sort will work in a bit of—what is it?—eroticism."¹⁰

He paused.

---

*PR; *back*: L–E.
**L–E; *my own eyes*: PR.

"Very likely these Martians will make pets of some of them; train them to do tricks—who knows?—get sentimental over the pet boy who grew up and had to be killed. And some, maybe, they will train to hunt us."

"No," I cried, "that's impossible! No human being—"

"What's the good of going on with such lies?" said the artilleryman. "There's men who'd do it cheerful. What nonsense to pretend there isn't!"

And I succumbed to his conviction.

"If they come after me," he said—"Lord! if they come after me!" and subsided into a grim meditation.

I sat contemplating these things. I could find nothing to bring against this man's reasoning. In the days before the invasion no one would have questioned my intellectual superiority to his—I, a professed and recognised writer on philosophical themes, and he, a common soldier; and yet he had already formulated a situation that I had scarcely realised.

"What are you doing?" I said, presently. "What plans have you made?"

He hesitated.

"Well, it's like this," he said. "What have we to do? We have to invent a sort of life where men can live and breed, and be sufficiently secure to bring the children up. Yes—wait a bit, and I'll make it clearer what I think ought to be done. The tame ones will go like all tame beasts; in a few generations they'll be big, beautiful, rich-blooded, stupid—rubbish! The risk is that we who keep wild will go savage—degenerate into a sort of big, savage rat. . . . You see, how I mean to live is underground. I've been thinking about the drains. Of course, those* who don't know drains think horrible things; but under this London are miles and miles—hundreds of miles—and a few days' rain and London empty will leave them sweet and clean. The main drains are big enough and airy enough for any one. Then there's cellars, vaults, stores, from which bolting passages may be made to the drains. And the railway tunnels and subways. Eh? You begin to see? And we form a band—able-bodied, clean-minded men. We're not going to pick up any rubbish that drifts in. Weaklings go out again."

"As you meant me to go?"

"Well—I parleyed, didn't I?"

"We won't quarrel about that. Go on."

"Those who stop obey orders. Able-bodied, clean-minded women we want also—mothers and teachers. No lackadaisical ladies—no blasted rolling eyes. We can't have any weak or silly. Life is real again, and the useless and cumbersome and mischievous have to die. They ought to die. They ought to be willing to die. It's a sort of disloyalty, after all, to live and taint the

---

*PR–A; *course those*: E.

race. And they can't be happy. Moreover, dying's none so dreadful; it's the funking makes it bad.[11] And in all those places we shall gather. Our district will be London. And we may even be able to keep a watch, and run about in the open when the Martians keep away. Play cricket, perhaps. That's how we shall save the race.[12] Eh? It's a possible thing? But saving the race is nothing in itself. As I say, that's only being rats. It's saving our knowledge and adding to it is the thing. There men like you come in. There's books, there's models. We must make great safe places down deep, and get all the books we can; not novels and poetry swipes,[13] but ideas, science books. That's where men like you come in. We must go to the British Museum and pick all those books through.[14] Especially we must keep up our science— learn more. We must watch these Martians. Some of us must go as spies. When it's all working, perhaps I will. Get caught, I mean. And the great thing is, we must leave the Martians alone. We mustn't even steal. If we get in their way, we clear out. We must show them we mean no harm. Yes, I know. But they're intelligent things, and they won't hunt us down if they have all they want, and think we're just harmless vermin."

The artilleryman paused and laid a brown hand upon my arm.

"After all, it may not be so much we may have to learn before— Just imagine this: Four or five of their fighting-machines suddenly starting off— Heat-Rays right and left, and not a Martian in 'em. Not a Martian in 'em, but men—men who have learned the way how. It may be in my time, even— those men. Fancy having one of them lovely things, with its Heat-Ray wide and free! Fancy having it in control![15] What would it matter if you smashed to smithereens at the end of the run, after a bust like that? I reckon the Martians'll open their beautiful eyes! Can't you see them, man? Can't you see them hurrying, hurrying—puffing and blowing and hooting to their other mechanical affairs? Something out of gear in every case. And swish, bang, rattle, swish! just as they are fumbling over it, *swish* comes the Heat-Ray, and, behold! man has come back to his own."

For a while the imaginative daring of the artilleryman, and the tone of assurance and courage he assumed, completely dominated my mind. I be- lieved unhesitatingly both in his forecast of human destiny and in the prac- ticability of his astonishing scheme, and the reader who thinks me suscep- tible and foolish must contrast his position, reading steadily with all his thoughts about his subject, and mine, crouching fearfully in the bushes and listening, distracted by apprehension. We talked in this manner through the early morning time, and later crept out of the bushes, and, after scanning the sky for Martians, hurried precipitately to the house on Putney Hill where he had made his lair.[16] It was the coal-cellar of the place, and when I saw the work he had spent a week upon—it was a burrow scarcely ten yards long, which he designed to reach to the main drain on Putney Hill—I had my first inkling of the gulf between his dreams and his powers. Such a hole I could have dug in a day. But I believed in him sufficiently to work with him all that morning until past mid-day at his digging. We had a garden-barrow and shot the earth we removed against the kitchen range. We refreshed ourselves with a tin of mock-turtle soup and wine from the neighbouring pantry. I found a curious relief from the aching strangeness of the world in this steady labour. As we worked, I turned his project over in my mind, and presently objections and doubts began to arise; but I worked there all the morning, so glad was I to find myself with a purpose again. After working an hour I began to speculate on the distance one had to go before the cloaca was reached, the chances we had of missing it altogether. My immediate trouble was why we should dig this long tunnel, when it was possible to get into the drain at once down one of the manholes, and work back to the house. It seemed to me, too, that the house was inconveniently chosen, and required a needless length of tunnel. And just as I was beginning to face these things, the artilleryman stopped digging, and looked at me.

"We're working well," he said. He put down his spade. "Let us knock off a bit," he said. "I think it's time we reconnoitred from the roof of the house."

I was for going on, and after a little hesitation he resumed his spade; and then suddenly I was struck by a thought. I stopped, and so did he at once.

"Why were you walking about the Common,"* I said, "instead of being here?"

"Taking the air," he said. "I was coming back. It's safer by night."

"But the work?"

"Oh, one can't always work," he said, and in a flash I saw the man plain. He hesitated, holding his spade. "We ought to reconnoitre now," he said, "because if any come near they may hear the spades and drop upon us unawares."

I was no longer disposed to object. We went together to the roof and stood on a ladder peeping out of the roof door. No Martians were to be seen, and we ventured out on the tiles, and slipped down under shelter of the parapet.

From this position a shrubbery hid the greater portion of Putney, but we could see the river below, a bubbly mass of red weed, and the low parts of Lambeth flooded and red. The red creeper swarmed up the trees about the old palace,[17] and their branches stretched gaunt and dead, and set with shrivelled leaves, from amid its clusters. It was strange how entirely depen-

---

*PR–NY, E; common: A.

dent both these things[18] were upon flowing water for their propagation. About us neither had gained a footing; laburnums, pink mays, snowballs, and trees of arborvitæ, rose out of laurels and hydrangeas, green and brilliant into the sunlight. Beyond Kensington dense smoke was rising, and that and a blue haze hid the northward hills.

The artilleryman began to tell me of the sort of people who still remained in London.

"One night last week," he said, "some fools got the electric light in order, and there was all Regent's Street* and the Circus ablaze, crowded with painted and ragged drunkards, men and women, dancing and shouting till dawn. A man who was there told me. And as the day came they became aware of a fighting-machine standing near by the Langham and looking down at them. Heaven knows how long he had been there. It must have given some of them a nasty turn. He came down the road towards them, and picked up nearly a hundred too drunk or frightened to run away."[19]

Grotesque gleam of a time no history will ever fully describe!

From that, in answer to my questions, he came round to his grandiose plans again. He grew enthusiastic. He talked so eloquently of the possibility of capturing a fighting-machine that I more than half believed in him again. But now that I was beginning to understand something of his quality, I could divine the stress he laid on doing nothing precipitately. And I noted that now there was no question that he personally was to capture and fight the great machine.

After a time we went down to the cellar. Neither of us seemed disposed to resume digging, and when he suggested a meal, I was nothing loath. He became suddenly very generous, and when we had eaten he went away and returned with some excellent cigars. We lit these, and his optimism glowed. He was inclined to regard my coming as a great occasion.

"There's some champagne in the cellar," he said.

"We can dig better on this Thames-side burgundy,"[20] said I.

"No," said he; "I am host to-day. Champagne! Great God! we've a heavy enough task before us! Let us take a rest and gather strength while we may. Look at these blistered hands!"

And pursuant to this idea of a holiday, he insisted upon playing cards after we had eaten. He taught me euchre, and after dividing London between us, I taking the northern side and he the southern, we played for parish points.[21] Grotesque and foolish as this will seem to the sober reader, it is absolutely true, and, what is more remarkable, I found the** card game and several others we played extremely interesting.

---

*PR–A; *Regent Street*: E.
**L–E; *this*: PR.

Strange mind of man! that, with our species upon the edge of extermination or appalling degradation, with no clear prospect before us but the
chance of a horrible death, we could sit following the chance of this painted
pasteboard, and playing the "joker" with vivid delight.[22] Afterwards he
taught me poker, and I beat him at three tough chess games. When dark
came we decided to take the risk, and lit a lamp.

After an interminable string of games, we supped, and the artilleryman
finished the champagne. We went on smoking the cigars. He was no longer
the energetic regenerator of his species I had encountered in the morning.[23]
He was still optimistic, but it was a less kinetic, a more thoughtful optimism.
I remember he wound up with my health, proposed in a speech of small
variety and considerable intermittence. I took a cigar, and went upstairs to
look at the lights of which he had spoken, that blazed so greenly along the
Highgate hills.

At first I stared unintelligently across the London valley. The northern
hills were shrouded in darkness; the fires near Kensington glowed redly, and
now and then an orange-red tongue of flame flashed up* and vanished in
the deep blue night. All the rest of London was black. Then, nearer, I
perceived a strange light, a pale, violet-purple fluorescent glow, quivering
under the night breeze. For a space I could not understand it, and then I
knew that it must be the red weed from which this faint irradiation proceeded. With that realisation my dormant sense of wonder, my sense of the
proportion of things, awoke again. I glanced from that to Mars, red and
clear, glowing high in the west, and then gazed long and earnestly at the
darkness of Hampstead and Highgate.

I remained a very long time upon the roof, wondering at the grotesque
changes of the day. I recalled my mental states from the midnight prayer
to the foolish card-playing. I had a violent revulsion of feeling. I remember
I flung away the cigar with a certain wasteful symbolism. My folly came
to me with glaring exaggeration. I seemed a traitor to my wife and to my
kind; I was filled with remorse. I resolved to leave this strange undisciplined
dreamer of great things to his drink and gluttony, and to go on into London.[24] There, it seemed to me, I had the best chance of learning what the
Martians and my fellow-men were doing. I was still upon the roof when
the late moon rose.

---

*L–E; *flickered*: PR.

VIII

DEAD LONDON

AFTER I HAD PARTED from the artilleryman, I went down the hill, and by the High Street across the bridge to Fulham.* The red weed was tumultuous at that time, and nearly choked the bridge roadway; but** its fronds were already whitened in patches by the spreading disease that presently removed it so swiftly.

At the corner of the lane that runs to Putney Bridge station I found a man lying. He was as black as a sweep with the black dust, alive, but helplessly and speechlessly drunk. I could get nothing from him but curses and furious lunges at my head. I think I should have stayed by him but for the brutal expression of his face.

There was black dust along the roadway from the bridge onwards, and it grew thicker in Fulham. The streets were horribly quiet. I got food—sour, hard, and mouldy, but quite eatable—in a baker's shop here. Some way towards Walham Green the streets became clear of powder, and I passed a white† terrace of houses on fire; the noise of the burning was an absolute relief. Going on towards Brompton, the streets were quiet again.

Here I came once more upon the black powder in the streets and upon dead bodies. I saw altogether about a dozen in the length of the Fulham Road. They had been dead many days, so that I hurried quickly past them. The black powder covered them over, and softened their outlines. One or two had been disturbed by dogs.

Where there was no black powder, it was curiously like a Sunday in the City,[1] with the closed shops, the houses locked up and the blinds drawn, the desertion, and the stillness. In some places plunderers had been at work,

---

*E; *Lambeth*: PR–A. Lambeth is some miles east of the narrator's position.
**AG, E; *roadway, but*: PR–NY; *roadway: but*: A.
†C–E; *whole*: MS.

but rarely at other than the provision and wine shops. A jeweller's window had been broken open in one place, but apparently the thief had been disturbed, and a number of gold chains and a watch were* scattered on the pavement. I did not trouble to touch them. Farther on was a tattered woman in a heap on a doorstep; the hand that hung over her knee was gashed and bled down her rusty brown dress, and a smashed magnum of champagne formed a pool across the pavement. She seemed asleep, but she was dead.

The farther I penetrated into London, the profounder grew the stillness. But it was not so much the stillness of death—it was the stillness of suspense, of expectation. At any time the destruction that had already singed the north-western borders of the metropolis, and had annihilated Ealing and Kilburn, might strike among these houses and leave them smoking ruins. It was a city condemned and derelict. . . .

In South Kensington the streets were clear of dead and of black powder. It was near South Kensington that I first heard the howling. It crept almost imperceptibly upon my senses. It was a sobbing alternation of two notes, "Ulla, ulla, ulla, ulla," keeping on perpetually. When I passed streets that ran northward it grew in volume, and houses and buildings seemed to deaden and cut it off again. It came in a full tide down Exhibition Road. I stopped, staring towards Kensington Gardens, wondering at this strange, remote wailing. It was as if that mighty desert of houses had found a voice for its fear and solitude.

"Ulla, ulla, ulla, ulla," wailed that superhuman note—great waves of sound sweeping down the broad, sunlit roadway, between the tall buildings on each side. I turned northward, marvelling, towards the iron gates of Hyde Park. I had half a mind to break into the Natural History Museum[2] and find my way up to the summits of the towers, in order to see across the park. But I decided to keep to the ground, where quick hiding was possible, and so went on up the Exhibition Road. All the large mansions on each side of the road were empty and still, and my footsteps echoed against the sides of the houses. At the top, near the park gate, I came upon a strange sight—a bus overturned, and the skeleton of a horse picked clean. I puzzled over this for a time, and then went on to the bridge over the Serpentine. The voice grew stronger and stronger, though I could see nothing above the house-tops on the north side of the park, save a haze of smoke to the north-west.

"Ulla, ulla, ulla, ulla," cried the voice, coming, as it seemed to me, from the district about Regent's Park. The desolating cry worked upon my mind. The mood that had sustained me passed. The wailing took possession

---

*MS–NY, A; *lay*: AG, E.

of me. I found I was intensely weary, footsore, and now again hungry and thirsty.

It was already past noon. Why was I wandering alone in this city of the dead? Why was I alone when all London was lying in state, and in its black shroud? I felt intolerably lonely. My mind ran on old friends that I had forgotten for years. I thought of the poisons in the chemists' shops, of the liquors the wine-merchants stored; I recalled the two sodden creatures[3] of despair who, so far as I knew, shared the city with myself. . . .

I came into Oxford Street by the Marble Arch, and here again were black powder and several bodies, and an evil, ominous smell from the gratings of the cellars of some of the houses. I grew very thirsty after the heat of my long walk. With infinite trouble I managed to break into a public-house and get food and drink. I was weary after eating, and went into the parlour behind the bar, and slept on a black horse-hair sofa I found there.

I awoke to find that dismal howling still in my ears, "Ulla, ulla, ulla, ulla." It was now dusk, and after I had routed out some biscuits and a cheese in the bar—there was a meat-safe, but it contained nothing but maggots—I wandered on through the silent residential squares to Baker Street—Portman Square is the only one I can name—and so came out at last upon Regent's Park. And as I emerged from the top of Baker Street, I saw far away over the trees in the clearness of the sunset the hood of the Martian giant from which this howling proceeded. I was not terrified. I came upon him as if it were a matter of course. I watched him for some time, but he did not move. He appeared to be standing and yelling, for no reason that I could discover.

I tried to formulate a plan of action. That perpetual sound of "Ulla, ulla, ulla, ulla," confused my mind. Perhaps I was too tired to be very fearful. Certainly I was more curious to know the reason of this monotonous crying than afraid. I turned back away from the park and struck into Park Road, intending to skirt the park, went along under shelter of the terraces, and got a view of this stationary, howling Martian from the direction of St. John's Wood. A couple of hundred yards out of Baker Street I heard a yelping chorus, and saw, first a dog with a piece of putrescent red meat in his jaws coming headlong towards me, and then a pack of starving mongrels in pursuit of him. He made a wide curve to avoid me, as though he feared I might prove a fresh competitor. As the yelping died away down the silent road, the wailing sound of "Ulla, ulla, ulla, ulla," reasserted itself.[4]

I came upon the wrecked handling-machine halfway to St. John's Wood station. At first I thought a house had fallen across the road. It was only as I clambered among the ruins that I saw, with a start, this mechanical Samson[5] lying, with its tentacles bent and smashed and twisted, among the ruins it had made. The forepart was shattered. It seemed as if it had driven blindly straight at the house, and had been overwhelmed in its overthrow. It seemed to me then that this might have happened by a handling-machine escaping from the guidance of its Martian. I could not clamber among the ruins to see it, and the twilight was now so far advanced that the blood with which its seat was smeared, and the gnawed gristle of the Martian that the dogs had left, were invisible to me.

Wondering still more at all that I had seen, I pushed on towards Primrose Hill. Far away, through a gap in the trees, I saw a second Martian, as motionless as the first, standing in the park towards the Zoological Gardens, and silent. A little beyond the ruins about the smashed handling-machine I came upon the red weed again, and found the Regent's Canal a spongy mass of dark-red vegetation.

As I crossed the bridge, the sound of "Ulla, ulla, ulla, ulla," ceased. It was, as it were, cut off. The silence came like a thunder-clap.

The dusky houses about me stood faint and tall and dim; the trees towards the park were growing black. All about me the red weed clambered among the ruins, writhing to get above me in the dimness. Night, the mother of fear and mystery,[6] was coming upon me. But while that voice sounded, the solitude, the desolation, had* been endurable; by virtue of it London had still seemed alive, and the sense of life about me had upheld me. Then suddenly a change, the passing of something—I knew not what—and then a stillness that could be felt. Nothing but this gaunt quiet.

London about me gazed at me spectrally. The windows in the white houses were like the eye-sockets of skulls.[7] About me my imagination found a thousand noiseless enemies moving. Terror seized me, a horror of my temerity. In front of me the road became pitchy black as though it was tarred, and I saw a contorted shape lying across the pathway. I could not bring myself to go on. I turned down St. John's Wood Road, and ran headlong from this unendurable stillness towards Kilburn. I hid from the night and the silence, until long after midnight, in a cabmen's shelter in Harrow Road. But before the dawn my courage returned, and while the stars were still in the sky I turned once more towards Regent's Park. I missed my way among the streets, and presently saw down a long avenue, in the half-light of the early dawn, the curve of Primrose Hill. On the summit, towering up to the fading stars, was a third Martian, erect and motionless like the others.[8]

An insane resolve possessed me. I would die and end it. And I would save myself even the trouble of killing myself. I marched on recklessly towards this Titan, and then, as I drew nearer and the light grew, I saw

---

*L; *sounded the solitude, & the desolation had:* MS; *sounded the solitude, the desolation, had:* C, NY–E; *sounded the solitude, the desolation had:* P–PR.

that a multitude of black birds was circling and clustering about the hood. At that my heart gave a bound, and I began running along the road.

I hurried through the red weed that choked St. Edmund's Terrace (I waded breast-high across a torrent of water that was rushing down from the water-works towards the Albert Road), and emerged upon the grass before the rising of the sun. Great mounds had been heaped about the crest of the hill, making a huge redoubt of it—it was the final and largest place the Martians had made—and from behind these heaps there rose a thin smoke against the sky. Against the sky-line an eager dog ran and disappeared. The thought that had flashed into my mind grew real, grew credible. I felt no fear, only a wild, trembling exultation, as I ran up the hill towards the motionless monster. Out of the hood hung lank shreds of brown, at which the hungry birds pecked and tore.[9]

In another moment I had scrambled up the earthen rampart and stood upon its crest, and the interior of the redoubt was below me. A mighty space it was, with gigantic machines here and there within it, huge mounds of material and strange shelter-places. And scattered about it, some in their overturned war-machines, some in the now rigid handling-machines, and a dozen of them stark and silent and laid in a row, were the Martians—*dead!*— slain by the putrefactive and disease bacteria against which their systems were unprepared; slain as the red weed was being slain; slain, after all man's devices had failed, by the humblest things that God, in his wisdom, has put upon this earth.[10]

For so it had come about, as indeed I and many men might have foreseen had not terror and disaster blinded our minds. These germs of disease have taken toll of humanity since the beginning of things—taken toll of our prehuman ancestors since life began here. But by virtue of this natural selection of our kind we have developed resisting power; to no germs do we succumb without a struggle, and to many—those that cause putrefaction in dead matter, for instance—our living frames are altogether immune. But there are no bacteria in Mars, and directly these invaders arrived, directly they drank and fed, our microscopic allies began to work their overthrow. Already when I watched them they were irrevocably doomed, dying and rotting even as they went to and fro. It was inevitable. By the toll of a billion deaths man has bought his birthright of the earth, and it is his against all comers; it would still be his were the Martians ten times as mighty as they are. For neither do men live nor die in vain.[11]

Here and there they were scattered, nearly fifty altogether, in that great gulf they had made, overtaken by a death that must have seemed to them as incomprehensible as any death could be. To me also at that time this death was incomprehensible. All I knew was that these things that had been alive and so terrible to men were dead. For a moment I believed that the destruction of Sennacherib[12] had been repeated, that God had repented, that the Angel of Death had slain them in the night.

I stood staring into the pit, and my heart lightened gloriously, even as the rising sun struck the world to fire about me with his rays. The pit was still in darkness; the mighty engines, so great and wonderful in their power and complexity, so unearthly in their tortuous forms, rose weird and vague and strange out of the shadows towards the light. A multitude of dogs, I could hear, fought over the bodies that lay darkly in the depth of the pit, far below me. Across the pit on its farther lip, flat and vast and strange, lay the great flying-machine with which they had been experimenting upon our denser atmosphere when decay and death arrested them. Death had come not a day too soon. At the sound of a cawing overhead I looked up at the huge fighting-machine that would fight no more forever,[13] at the tattered red shreds of flesh that dripped down upon the overturned seats on the summit of Primrose Hill.

I turned and looked down the slope of the hill to where, enhaloed now in birds, stood those other two Martians that I had seen overnight, just as death had overtaken them. The one had died, even as it had been crying to its companions; perhaps it was the last to die, and its voice had gone on perpetually until the force of its machinery was exhausted. They glittered now, harmless tripod towers of shining metal, in the brightness of the rising sun.

All about the pit, and saved as by a miracle from everlasting destruction, stretched the great Mother of Cities. Those who have only seen London veiled in her sombre robes of smoke can scarcely imagine the naked clearness and beauty of the silent wilderness of houses.

Eastward, over the blackened ruins of the Albert Terrace and the splintered spire of the church, the sun blazed dazzling in a clear sky, and here and there some facet in the great wilderness of roofs caught the light and glared with a white intensity.

Northward were Kilburn and Hampstead, blue and crowded with houses; westward the great city was dimmed; and southward, beyond the Martians, the green wash* of Regent's Park, the Langham Hotel, the dome of the Albert Hall, the Imperial Institute, and the giant mansions of the Brompton Road came out clear and little in the sunrise, the jagged ruins of Westminster rising hazily beyond. Far away and blue were the Surrey hills, and the towers of the Crystal Palace glittered like two silver rods. The dome of St. Paul's was dark against the sunrise, and injured, I saw for the first time, by a huge gaping cavity on its western side.

---

*MS; water: C; waves: P–E.

And as I looked at this wide expanse of houses and factories and churches, silent and abandoned; as I thought of the multitudinous hopes and efforts, the innumerable hosts of lives that had gone to build this human reef, and of the swift and ruthless destruction that had hung over it all; when I realised that the shadow had been rolled back, and that men might still live in the streets, and this dear vast dead city of mine be once more alive and powerful, I felt a wave of emotion that was near akin to tears.

The torment was over. Even that day the healing would begin. The survivors of the people scattered over the country—leaderless, lawless, food-less, like sheep without a shepherd—the thousands who had fled by sea, would begin to return; the pulse of life, growing stronger and stronger, would beat again in the empty streets and pour across the vacant squares. Whatever destruction was done, the hand of the destroyer was stayed. All the gaunt wrecks, the blackened skeletons of houses that stared so dismally at the sunlit grass of the hill, would presently be echoing with the hammers of the restorers and ringing with the tapping of their trowels. At the thought I extended my hands towards the sky and began thanking God.[14] In a year, thought I—in a year . . .

With overwhelming force, came the thought of myself, of my wife, and the old life of hope and tender helpfulness that had ceased forever.

IX

WRECKAGE

AND NOW COMES the strangest thing in my story. Yet, perhaps, it is not altogether strange. I remember, clearly and coldly and vividly, all that I did that day until the time that I stood weeping and praising God upon the summit of Primrose Hill. And then I forget.

Of the next three days I know nothing. I have learned since that, so far from my being the first discoverer of the Martian overthrow, several such wanderers as myself had already discovered this on the previous night. One man—the first—had gone to St. Martin's-le-Grand, and, while I sheltered in the cabmen's hut, had contrived to telegraph to Paris. Thence the joyful news had flashed all over the world; a thousand cities, chilled by ghastly apprehensions, suddenly flashed into frantic illuminations; they knew of it in Dublin, Edinburgh, Manchester, Birmingham, at the time when I stood upon the verge of the pit. Already men, weeping with joy, as I have heard, shouting and staying their work to shake hands and shout, were making up trains, even as near as Crewe, to descend upon London. The church bells that had ceased a fortnight since suddenly caught the news, until all England was bell-ringing. Men on cycles, lean-faced, unkempt, scorched along every country lane shouting of unhoped deliverance, shouting to gaunt, staring figures of despair. And for the food! Across the Channel, across the Irish Sea, across the Atlantic, corn, bread, and meat were tearing to our relief. All the shipping in the world seemed going Londonward in those days. But of all this I have no memory. I drifted—a demented man. I found myself in a house of kindly people, who had found me on the third day wandering, weeping, and raving through the streets of St. John's Wood. They have told me since that I was singing some inane doggerel about "The Last Man Left Alive! Hurrah! The Last Man Left Alive!"[1] Troubled as they were with their own affairs, these people, whose name, much as I would like to express my gratitude to them, I may not even give here, nevertheless cumbered themselves with me, sheltered me, and protected me from myself. Apparently they had learned something of my story from me during the days of my lapse.

Very gently, when my mind was assured again, did they break to me what they had learned of the fate of Leatherhead. Two days after I was imprisoned it had been destroyed, with every soul in it, by a Martian. He had swept it out of existence, as it seemed, without any provocation, as a boy might crush an ant-hill, in the mere wantonness of power.

I was a lonely man, and they were very kind to me. I was a lonely man and a sad one, and they bore with me. I remained with them four days after my recovery. All that time I felt a vague, a growing craving to look once more on whatever remained of the little life that seemed so happy and bright in my past. It was a mere hopeless desire to feast upon my misery. They dissuaded me. They did all they could to divert me from this morbidity. But at last I could resist the impulse no longer, and, promising faithfully to return to them, and parting, as I will confess, from these four-day friends with tears, I went out again into the streets that had lately been so dark and strange and empty.

Already they were busy with returning people; in places even there were shops open, and I saw a drinking-fountain running water.

I remember how mockingly bright the day seemed as I went back on my melancholy pilgrimage to the little house at Woking, how busy the streets and vivid the moving life about me. So many people were abroad everywhere, busied in a thousand activities, that it seemed incredible that any great proportion of the population could have been slain. But then I noticed how yellow were the skins of the people I met, how shaggy the hair of the men, how large and bright their eyes, and that every other man still wore his dirty rags. Their faces seemed all with one of two expressions— a leaping exultation and energy or a grim resolution. Save for the expression of the faces, London seemed a city of tramps. The vestries were indiscriminately distributing bread sent us by the French government. The ribs of the few horses showed dismally. Haggard special constables with white badges stood at the corners of every street. I saw little of the mischief wrought by the Martians until I reached Wellington Street, and there I saw the red weed clambering over the buttresses of Waterloo Bridge.

At the corner of the bridge, too, I saw one of the common contrasts of that grotesque time—a sheet of paper flaunting against a thicket of the red weed, transfixed by a stick that kept it in place. It was the placard of the first newspaper to resume publication—the *Daily Mail*.[2] I bought a copy for a blackened shilling I found in my pocket. Most of it was in blank, but the solitary compositor who did the thing had amused himself by making a grotesque scheme of advertisement stereo[3] on the back page. The matter he printed was emotional; the news organisation had not as yet found its way back. I learned nothing fresh except that already in one week the examination of the Martian mechanisms had yielded astonishing results. Among other things, the article assured me what I did not believe at the time, that the "Secret of Flying" was discovered. At Waterloo I found the free trains that were taking people to their homes. The first rush was already over. There were few people in the train, and I was in no mood for casual conversation. I got a compartment to myself, and sat with folded arms, looking greyly at the sunlit devastation that flowed past the windows. And just outside the terminus the train jolted over temporary rails, and on either side of the railway the houses were blackened ruins. To Clapham Junction the face of London was grimy with powder of the Black Smoke, in spite of two days of thunderstorms and rain, and at Clapham Junction the line had been wrecked again; there were hundreds of out-of-work clerks and shop-men working side by side with the customary navvies, and we were jolted over a hasty relaying.

All down the line from there the aspect of the country was gaunt and unfamiliar; Wimbledon particularly had suffered. Walton, by virtue of its unburned pine-woods, seemed the least hurt of any place along the line. The Wandle, the Mole, every little stream, was a heaped mass of red weed, in appearance between butcher's meat and pickled cabbage. The Surrey pine-woods were too dry, however, for the festoons of the red climber. Beyond Wimbledon, within sight of the line, in certain nursery grounds, were the heaped masses of earth about the sixth cylinder. A number of people were standing about it, and some sappers were busy in the midst of it. Over it flaunted a Union Jack, flapping cheerfully in the morning breeze. The nursery grounds were everywhere crimson with the weed, a wide expanse of livid colour cut with purple shadows, and very painful to the eye. One's gaze went with infinite relief from the scorched greys and sullen reds of the foreground to the blue-green softness of the eastward hills.

The line on the London side of Woking station[4] was still undergoing repair, so I descended at Byfleet station and took the road to Maybury, past the place where I and the artilleryman had talked to the hussars, and on by the spot where the Martian had appeared to me in the thunderstorm. Here, moved by curiosity, I turned aside to find, among a tangle of red fronds, the warped and broken dog-cart with the whitened bones of the horse, scattered and gnawed. For a time I stood regarding these vestiges. . . .

Then I returned through the pine-wood, neck-high with red weed here and there, to find the landlord of the Spotted Dog had already found burial, and so came home past the College Arms. A man standing at an open cottage door greeted me by name as I passed.

I looked at my house with a quick flash of hope that faded immediately. The door had been forced; it was unfastened, and was opening slowly as I approached.

It slammed again. The curtains of my study fluttered out of the open window from which I and the artilleryman had watched the dawn. No one had closed it since. The smashed bushes were just as I had left them nearly four weeks ago. I stumbled into the hall, and the house felt empty. The stair-carpet was ruffled and discoloured where I had crouched, soaked to the skin from the thunderstorm the night of the catastrophe. Our muddy footsteps I saw still went up the stairs.

I followed them to my study, and found lying on my writing-table still, with the selenite paper-weight upon it, the sheet of work I had left on the afternoon of the opening of the cylinder. For a space I stood reading over my abandoned arguments. It was a paper on the probable development of Moral Ideas with the development of the civilising process; and the last sentence was the opening of a prophecy: "In about two hundred years," I had written, "we may expect—" The sentence ended abruptly.[5] I remembered my inability to fix my mind that morning, scarcely a month gone by, and how I had broken off to get my *Daily Chronicle*[6] from the newsboy. I remembered how I went down to the garden gate as he came along, and how I had listened to his odd story of "Men from Mars."

I came down and went into the dining-room. There were the mutton and the bread, both far gone now in decay, and a beer bottle overturned, just as I and the artilleryman had left them. My home was desolate. I perceived the folly of the faint hope I had cherished so long. And then a strange thing occurred. "It is no use," said a voice. "The house is deserted. No one has been here these ten days. Do not stay here to torment yourself. No one escaped but you."

I was startled. Had I spoken my thought aloud? I turned, and the French window was open behind me. I made a step to it, and stood looking out.

And there, amazed and afraid, even as I stood amazed and afraid, were my cousin and my wife—my wife white and tearless. She gave a faint cry.

"I came," she said. "I knew—knew—"

She put her hand to her throat—swayed. I made a step forward, and caught her in my arms.[7]

X

THE EPILOGUE

I CANNOT BUT REGRET, now that I am concluding my story, how little I am able to contribute to the discussion of the many debatable questions which are still unsettled. In one respect I shall certainly provoke criticism. My particular province is speculative philosophy. My knowledge of comparative physiology is confined to a book or two, but it seems to me that Carver's[1] suggestions as to the reason of the rapid death of the Martians is so probable as to be regarded almost as a proven conclusion. I have assumed that in the body of my narrative.

At any rate, in all the bodies of the Martians that were examined after the war, no bacteria except those already known as terrestrial species were found. That they did not bury any of their dead, and the reckless slaughter they perpetrated, point also to an entire ignorance of the putrefactive process. But probable as this seems, it is by no means a proven conclusion.

Neither is the composition of the Black Smoke known, which the Martians used with such deadly effect, and the generator of the Heat-Ray remains a puzzle. The terrible disasters at the Ealing and South Kensington laboratories have disinclined analysts for further investigations upon the latter. Spectrum analysis of the black powder points unmistakably to the presence of an unknown element with a brilliant group of three lines in the green, and it is possible that it combines with argon[2] to form a compound which acts at once with deadly effect upon some constituent in the blood. But such unproven speculations will scarcely be of interest to the general reader, to whom this story is addressed. None of the brown scum that drifted down the Thames after the destruction of Shepperton was examined at the time, and now none is forthcoming.

The results of an anatomical examination of the Martians, so far as the prowling dogs had left such an examination possible, I have already given. But everyone is familiar with the magnificent and almost complete specimen in spirits at the Natural History Museum, and the countless drawings that have been made from it; and beyond that the interest of their physiology and structure is purely scientific.

A question of graver and universal interest is the possibility of another attack from the Martians.[3] I do not think that nearly enough attention is being given to this aspect of the matter. At present the planet Mars is in conjunction, but with every return to opposition[4] I, for one, anticipate a renewal of their adventure. In any case, we should be prepared. It seems to me that it should be possible to define the position of the gun from which the shots are discharged, to keep a sustained watch upon this part of the planet, and to anticipate the arrival of the next attack.

In that case the cylinder might be destroyed with dynamite or artillery before it was sufficiently cool for the Martians to emerge, or they might be butchered by means of guns so soon as the screw opened. It seems to me that they have lost a vast advantage in the failure of their first surprise. Possibly they see it in the same light.

Lessing[5] has advanced excellent reasons for supposing that the Martians have actually succeeded in effecting a landing on the planet Venus. Seven months ago now, Venus and Mars were in alignment with the sun; that is to say, Mars was in opposition from the point of view of an observer on Venus. Subsequently a peculiar luminous and sinuous marking appeared on the unillumined half of the inner planet, and almost simultaneously a faint dark mark of a similar sinuous character was detected upon a photograph of the Martian disc. One needs to see the drawings of these appearances in order to appreciate fully their remarkable resemblance in character.[6]

At any rate, whether we expect another invasion or not, our views of the human future must be greatly modified by these events. We have learned now that we cannot regard this planet as being fenced in and a secure abiding-place for Man; we can never anticipate the unseen good or evil that may come upon us suddenly out of space. It may be that in the larger design of the universe this invasion from Mars is not without its ultimate benefit for men; it has robbed us of that serene confidence in the future which is the most fruitful source of decadence, the gifts to human science it has brought are enormous, and it has done much to promote the conception of the commonweal of mankind. It may be that across the immensity of space the Martians have watched the fate of these pioneers of theirs and learned their lesson, and that on the planet Venus they have found a securer settlement. Be that as it may, for many years yet there will certainly be no relaxation of the eager scrutiny of the Martian disc, and those fiery darts of the sky, the shooting stars, will bring with them as they fall an unavoidable apprehension to all the sons of men.

The broadening of men's views that has resulted can scarcely be exaggerated. Before the cylinder fell there was a general persuasion that through all the deep of space no life existed beyond the petty surface of our minute sphere. Now we see further. If the Martians can reach Venus, there is no reason to suppose that the thing is impossible for men, and when the slow cooling of the sun makes this earth uninhabitable, as at last it must do, it may be that the thread of life that has begun here will have streamed out and caught our sister planet within its toils.

Dim and wonderful is the vision I have conjured up in my mind of life spreading slowly from this little seed-bed of the solar system throughout the inanimate vastness of sidereal space. But that is a remote dream. It may be, on the other hand, that the destruction of the Martians is only a reprieve. To them, and not to us, perhaps, is the future ordained.

I must confess the stress and danger of the time have left an abiding sense of doubt and insecurity in my mind. I sit in my study writing by lamplight, and suddenly I see again the healing valley below set with writhing flames, and feel the house behind and about me empty and desolate. I go out into the Byfleet Road, and vehicles pass me, a butcher-boy in a cart, a cabful of visitors, a workman on a bicycle, children going to school, and suddenly they become vague and unreal, and I hurry again with the artilleryman through the hot, brooding silence. Of a night I see the black powder darkening the silent streets, and the contorted bodies shrouded in that layer; they rise upon me tattered and dog-bitten. They gibber and grow fiercer, paler, uglier, mad distortions of humanity at last, and I wake, cold and wretched, in the darkness of the night.

I go to London and see the busy multitudes in Fleet Street and the Strand, and it comes across my mind that they are but the ghosts of the past, haunting the streets that I have seen silent and wretched, going to and fro, phantasms in a dead city, the mockery of life in a galvanised body.[7] And strange, too, it is to stand on Primrose Hill, as I did but a day before writing this last chapter, to see the great province of houses, dim and blue through the haze of the smoke and mist, vanishing at last into the vague lower sky, to see the people walking to and fro among the flower-beds on the hill, to see the sightseers about the Martian machine that stands there still, to hear the tumult of playing children, and to recall the time when I saw it all bright and clear-cut, hard and silent, under the dawn of that last great day. . . .[8]

And strangest of all is it to hold my wife's hand again, and to think that I have counted her, and that she has counted me, among the dead.

NOTES ON *THE WAR OF THE WORLDS*

"Russell" signifies the *Pearson's* serial *W W* photocopied in *The Collector's Book of Science Fiction by H. G. Wells*, edited by Alan K. Russell (Secaucus, NJ: Castle Books Division, 1978), pp.3–103.

EA signifies Wells's *Experiment in Autobiography* (1934).

Cross-references are by book, chapter, and note (e.g., I.1.1 = Book I, Chapter I, note 1).

Epigraph

1. The German astronomer Johannes Kepler (1571–1630) contributed to the foundations of modern astronomy with his studies in planetary motions. *The Anatomy of Melancholy* (1621) was the major work of English churchman Robert Burton (1577–1640). Wells has slightly abridged Burton's quotation from Kepler. The passage from *The Anatomy of Melancholy* (part 2, sect. 2, memb. 3) reads in full:

> But who shall dwell in these vast bodies; Earths, Worlds, "if they be inhabited? rational creatures?" as Kepler demands, "or have they souls to be saved? Or do they inhabit a better part of the World than we do? Or are we or they Lords of the World? And how are all things made for man?"

A 1931 insurance inventory of Wells's library lists a copy of Burton's work edited by Arthur Richard Shilleto (London, 1893). (Illinois Wells Archive.)

Book I: The Coming of the Martians

I.1. THE EVE OF THE WAR

1. Michael Draper (1987), p.50, comments:

> Science may enable the narrator to loftily contemplate the stars through a telescope, but the extension of awareness opens up a disorientating, relativistic view of the universe. The narrator's inspection of Mars through a telescope is preceded by the complementary image of the Martians looking down at us as through a microscope, locking us in an uncomfortable position somewhere between the Martians above and microscopic organisms below. Among those organisms are the bacteria which will destroy the apparently invincible Martians after our own defences have humiliatingly failed.

See also I.5.7, I.16.5, and Wells's earlier, similar perspective in "Through a Microscope":

> And all the time these creatures are living their vigorous, fussy little lives in this drop of water they are being watched by a creature of whose presence they do not dream, who can wipe them all out of existence with a stroke of his thumb, and who is withal as finite, and sometimes as fussy and unreasonably energetic, as themselves. He sees them, and they do not see him, because he has senses they do not possess, because he is too incredibly vast and strange to come, save as an overwhelming catastrophe, into their lives. Even so, it may be, the dabbler himself is being curiously observed.... [*Pall Mall Gazette* 59 (December 31, 1894): 244–245; reprinted in *Certain Personal Matters* (1898).]

For a different Martian perspective on the Earth, see the concluding paragraph of Wells's short story "The Star," *Graphic* (Christmas number, 1897), reprinted in *Tales of Space and Time* (1898).

2. See Percival Lowell, *Mars* (1895), p.122: Mars "is older in age, if not in years; for whether his birth as a separate world antedated ours or not, his smaller size, by causing him to cool more quickly, would necessarily age him faster." See also I.1.12, I.1.13.

3. Wells immediately introduces three of the novel's major themes: a perspective on human destiny that transcends the anthropocentric; a revelation of the perils of human complacency; and a critique of the conviction that progress is inevitable. These are essentially the same themes that echo throughout *The Time Machine*. But there is one notable difference. In *The Time Machine* neither of the two narrators subscribes to the complacency of their Victorian contemporaries. But at the outset of *W W* there are no such exceptions—not even among scientists. Ogilvy, "the well-known astronomer," pours scorn on the notion that there might be other intelligent life forms in the solar system. (Ironically, he is one of the first to be killed by the Martians.) At the same time, the story's unnamed narrator tells us that at the very time that the first Martian cylinder landed and the Earth was about to be devastated, he was "busy upon a series of papers discussing the probable developments of moral ideas as civilisation progressed."

In fact, the nineteenth-century *fin de siècle* was a period when many writers and artists—besides numerous scientists (including Wells's mentor, Thomas Henry Huxley)—entertained grave doubts about man's future. In his influential book *Degeneration* (1895), Max Nordau attacked (and provided some justification for) the deep-seated pessimism of many of his contemporaries:

> The disposition of the times is curiously confused, a compound of feverish restlessness and blunted discouragement, of fearful presage and hang-dog renunciation. The prevalent feeling is that of imminent perdition and extinction. *Fin de siècle* is at once a confession and a complaint. The old Northern faith contained the fearsome doctrine of the Dusk of the Gods. In our days there have arisen in more highly developed minds vague qualms of a Dusk of the Nations, in which all suns and all stars are gradually waning, and mankind with all its institutions and creations is perishing in the midst of a dying world. [Quoted by Bernard Bergonzi (1961), p.5.]

By carefully avoiding any suggestion of such a pessimistic disposition among his contemporaries, Wells underscores the shock of the Martian attack: it becomes a totally unanticipated onslaught on a planet blindly preoccupied with its own "little affairs." There are no warnings, no prophecies, no doomsayers. However, the general thrust of the fiction is that human complacency has been at least temporarily eradicated by the events of six years previous; for the narrator, "the mental habits of those departed days" are a curiosity. But the significance of his words will not be fully understood by the reader until the concluding paragraphs of the novel:

> We have learned now that we cannot regard this planet as being fenced in and a secure abiding-place for Man . . . this invasion from Mars . . . has robbed us of that serene confidence in the future which is the most fruitful source of decadence. . . . The broadening of men's views that has resulted can scarcely be exaggerated.

4. During the 1890s there was widespread popular interest in the possibility of life on other planets. Much of it was generated by the writings and lectures of Camille Flammarion and Percival Lowell. C. A. Young, writing in the Boston *Herald*, October 18, 1896, noted: "There seems to be an extremely popular interest in the question of the habitability of 'other worlds,' and of late it has been greatly intensified by the rather sensational speculations and deliverances of Flammarion, Lowell and others."

In a review of Lowell's *Mars*, W. W. Campbell spoke for many astronomers who were critical of the sensational interest in the subject: "The world at large is anxious for the discovery of intelligent life on *Mars*, and every advocate gets an instant and large audience." (*Publications of the Astronomical Society of the Pacific* 51 [1896]:207. Quoted by William Graves Hoyt [1976], pp.91, 94.)

5. Wells is mocking the nineteenth century's most "adventurous" form of religious activity. In Kipling's famous lines:

> Take up the White Man's burden—
> Send forth the best ye breed—
> Go bind your sons to exile
> To serve your captives' need.

See also II.7.9 for the artilleryman's parody of early Christian martyrs.

6. See Psalm 49: 12: "Nevertheless man being in honour abideth not: he is like the beasts that perish." In *W W*, biblical echoes abound in theme and language, although they are amplified, with intentional irony, by what Wells called "the Calvinism of science." See "Bio-Optimism," *Nature* 52 (August 29, 1895):410–411; reprinted in *H. G. Wells: Early Writings in Science and Science Fiction*, edited by Robert M. Philmus and David Y. Hughes (1975), pp.206–210, with commentary, pp.179–186. On Wells's evangelical upbringing, see EA, pp.29–30, 139; and Norman and Jeanne Mackenzie, *H. G. Wells* (1973), pp.4–5, 8–9, 23–24. For biblical echoes, see Tom Gibbons's exhaustive "H. G. Wells's Fire Sermon: *The War of the Worlds* and the Book of Revelation," *Science Fiction: A Review of Speculative Literature* 6/1 (1984):5–14, which is cited repeatedly in these notes (despite the naiveté of Gibbons's conclusions).

7. Patrick A. McCarthy (1986), p.47, notes that the phrase "intellects vast and cool and unsympathetic"

> relates the Martians to a possible future human race envisioned in *The Time Machine* [Chapter 3], where the Time Traveller worries about what he will encounter in the future: "What if cruelty had grown into a common passion? What if in this interval the race had lost its manliness, and had developed into something inhuman, unsympathetic, and overwhelmingly powerful?"

8. Robert Crossley (1986), pp.17–18, comments:

> The famous opening paragraph of *The War of the Worlds* is the definitive instance of fictional reportage, of the documentary imagination in Wells's fiction. He does not abjure style, effect, or design, but he seeks appropriate strategies of narration for improbable events—in this case, a post-catastrophic reconstruction of a war between Earth and Mars. With its declarative, cumulative weight, the paragraph steadily drives a wedge between reality, things as they are, and man's "realistic" conception of human hegemony. . . . The paragraph is carefully orchestrated to build toward the elaborate proportional measurement of Martian, human, and animal minds and to yield up the "disillusionment" of the closing periodic sentence. Like the microscopic bacteria and the beasts that perish, human dignity and durability appear ephemeral when measured against a larger scale. Scrutinized and studied by envious Martian eyes, humanity becomes a zoological specimen.

9. Wells never identifies his narrator by name—not even a label name comparable to the Time Traveller. And in other respects he remains a shadowy figure. He recounts his experiences and reveals his reactions, but we learn little about his circumstances other than that he is a writer on philosophical subjects, lives in Maybury, is married, has a younger brother, and appears to be a comfortable member of the middle class.

The phrase "I scarcely need remind the reader" is Wells's flattering equivalent of Macaulay's erudite schoolboy ("Every schoolboy knows who imprisoned Montezuma and who strangled Atahualpa").

10. Wells has in mind the claim, as Lowell put it (he was hotly supported and disputed by other astronomers), that:

> If the nebular hypothesis is correct, and there is good reason at present for believing
> in its general truth, then to develop life more or less distinctly resembling our own
> must be the destiny of every member of the solar family which is not prevented
> by purely physical conditions, size and so forth, from doing so. [Quoted by Hoyt
> (1976), pp.57–58, from the Boston *Commonwealth*, May 26, 1894.]

In the nebular hypothesis of Kant, refined in Laplace's *Exposition du système du monde* (1786), as the sun formed from a rotating gaseous mass, it threw off rings that successively condensed into the planets—the older the planet, the farther from the sun—and since the orbit of Mars is farther from the sun than Earth's is, Mars is older.

11. In the 1890s, the idea of Darwinian evolution on other worlds was in the air, but only recently. As late as 1865, Camille Flammarion's *Lumen* upheld Giordano Bruno's sixteenth-century idea of a plurality of worlds and a hierarchy of intelligences. Once evolutionary speculation was initiated, however, life on Mars was assumed to be in advance of Earth's because of the greater age of Mars. For example, Percy Gregg's *Across the Zodiac* (1880) depicts humanoid Martians evolved beyond their terrestrial counterparts.

12. Cf. Lowell (1895), pp.207–209:

> Now, in the special case of Mars, we have before us the spectacle of a world relatively
> well on in years, a world much older than the Earth. . . . Mars being thus old himself,
> we know that evolution on his surface must be similarly advanced. . . . Certainly
> what we see hints at the existence of beings who are in advance of, not behind us,
> in the journey of life.

See also I.1.2, I.1.13.

13. Cooling over a long period of time. Wells's now obsolete usage of *secular* is actually closer to the original Latin *saecularis* (= an age) than the current significance (i.e., not sacred or spiritual). McCarthy (1986), p.56, comments:

> Just as plague once seemed to threaten the immediate extinction of all human life,
> so entropy promises the eventual death of the world. . . . The connection between
> plague and entropy is perhaps made clearest by the opening chapter of *The War
> of the Worlds*, where the narrator traces the Martian invasion to the "secular
> cooling" of the planet Mars. . . : here, entropy at an advanced stage in one part of
> the solar system produces a plague elsewhere in the system.

See I.1.2 and 12.

14. On Mars's water and air loss, see Lowell (1895), pp.50–51, 122–128. As late as 1965, the question of water and oxygen on Mars was open, and the evidence pro and con was marshalled by Francis Jackson and Patrick Moore in *Life on Mars*. But later that year, the first Russian and American Mars probes settled matters in the negative. For a study written after the probes, see Arthur E. Smith, *Mars: The Next Step* (1989). See also II.2.12.

15. For the same fate on earth in 30 million years, see *The Time Machine*; in a 1931 introduction, Wells added that the scientists' "dreadful lies" had actually set the end at barely a million years. Camille Flammarion's story "The Last Days of the Earth" gives humanity about 2.2 million years (*Contemporary Review* 59 [April 1891]:558–569). Ley (1957), p.44, puts it well: "Mars [in the 1890s] was a replica of the earth as it was to be later; looking at Mars one looked, actually and almost literally, into the future."

16. See I.7.6 on the dodo. In *The Outline of History* (1920) I, p.138; II, p.189, Wells tells how British settlers shot the "Palaeolithic" Tasmanians on sight and set out poisoned meat for them to find. The last one died in 1877.

17. During the opposition of 1877, Giovanni Virginio Schiaparelli (1835–1910) made the first systematic observations of Mars's *canali*; the Italian term may mean "grooves" or "canals"—an ambiguity that fostered belief in intelligence on Mars.

Wells is referring to the mysterious phenomenon of "gemination," or doubling of the "canals," which Schiaparelli describes as follows:

> A given canal changes its appearance, and is found transformed through all its length, into two lines or uniform stripes, more or less parallel to one another, and which run straight and equal with the exact geometrical precision of the two rails of a railroad. ["The Planet Mars," *Astronomy and Astrophysics* 13 (1894):720.]

Lowell continued Schiaparelli's work and produced the most diligent mapping of Mars. Schiaparelli was never sure whether the "canals" were made by intelligent beings, but Lowell was positive they were the work of Martians.

18. See II.10.4.

19. Lick Observatory is located on Mount Hamilton, California, 4,250 feet above sea level. In the late nineteenth century Lick was the main observatory of the University of California. It was funded by the bequest of James Lick (1796–1876) and opened in 1888. It boasted a 36″ refracting telescope with a 33″ photographic lens. In the 1890s, Lick astronomers spearheaded scientific attacks on Lowell's theories about Mars. See Hoyt (1976), p.57.

20. France's most important nineteenth-century observatory was constructed in 1880 at the summit of Mt. Gros, northeast of Nice, the resort town on the French Riviera. Endowed by R. L. Bischoffsheim for the French Bureau of Longitude, it utilized a 30″ refracting telescope.

21. See Appendix VI. Lick Observatory is not cited in *Nature* (still Britain's premier science journal). At first, it was not cited in *WW* either: not, that is, in *Cosmopolitan*, where Wells apologized in a later installment for omitting it:

> In the first instalment of this story it was stated (the grain of fact from which the story grew) that a light had been seen on the unilluminated part of Mars "first" by Pereoten [sic], of Nice, in 1894. This statement involved a slight to the Lick Observatory, whereat similar lights were observed as early as 1890—a fact of which I was unaware at the time of writing the story. I trust any American astronomer who may read this story will acquit me of intentional discourtesy.—Author. [*Cosmopolitan* 23 (August 1897):391.]

But Wells did not "slight" Lick Observatory—not in *Cosmopolitan* or in "Intelligence on Mars" (see Appendix IV)—in both of which 1894 is singled out precisely because that sighting was of unusual brilliance. It was newsworthy, being discussed, for example, in *Athenaeum* 3485 (August 11, 1894):199; and in *Black and White* 8 (August 25, 1894):244. The latter wondered whether Mars might be signaling (see also I.1.32).

22. Wells's conviction that some prodigious development of the gun would be the eventual means of interplanetary travel persisted—in the face of mounting evidence of the superiority of rocket propulsion—even into the 1930s. A space gun is used to send two people around the Moon in Wells's film *Things to Come* (1936). However, Leon Stover (1987), pp.86–87, asserts:

> We need not suppose, as have some critics, that Wells was ignorant of rocket power.... Wells chose to ignore rocketships [in *Things to Come*] for the sake of a vehicle more in keeping with Saint-Simonian symbolism . . . the Space Gun is not for the conquest of space, but for "the conquest of the social order." With its gun sight and military bearing, it is in fact a weapon of civil war between state and society, party and people.

Nevertheless, it is difficult to see how Stover's argument could also apply to Wells's Martian gun, which seems no more than a nod to Jules Verne. Technically, Willy Ley (1957, pp.298–300) shows that even on Mars no gun like Verne's could achieve escape velocity; but a radical earth-to-moon gun, using hydrogen, as did Wells's, is now under development (*New York Times*, September 29, 1992).

23. According to John Batchelor (1985), p.26; "A double perspective is at work since with his six years' retrospect he [the narrator] 'now' knows—and [he later] indicates to the reader—that he had underestimated the Martians."

24. This seems a conscious or unconscious echo of "Javelle of Nice." See Appendix VI and II.10.5.

25. During the nineteenth century the Royal Astronomical Society (established 1820) acted as an astronomical exchange for observatories within Great Britain. It was not until the establishment of the International Astronomical Union, in 1919, that various national astronomical societies (including the Royal Astronomical Society, the Astronomische Gesellschaft of Germany, and the Société Astronomique de France) were coordinated, thereby providing an international exchange for astronomical information.

26. Though the arrival times of some cylinders are unspecified, they all depart and they generally land at about midnight (pp.54, 76, 83, 144). This may be a salute to Jules Verne. Chapter 4 of _De la Terre à la Lune, trajet direct en 97 heures 20 minutes_ (1865) concludes by announcing that the moonshot will hit at midnight exactly. But midnight is also the witching hour—probably why Wells chose it; in reality Mars would not be on Greenwich Time.

27. By dating the firing of the first cylinder to the day, but not the month or year, Wells creates a sense of historicity without recourse to calendar time. The relation of "the 12th" to "real" dating is tied up, first of all, with the question of the travel time required from Mars to Earth. Incredibly, the evidence is that following "June 12th," one month suffices for the trip, the invasion, and the death of the Martians. The night after the first cylinder is launched, i.e., the 13th, "was warm and I was thirsty" (p.54); when the first cylinder is 10 million miles off, the night again is warm (p.55); just before the first cylinder lands, the tenth one is launched (p.171); and the fifth cylinder falls in "the pitiless sunlight of that terrible June" (p.155). It looks like just one month, June, all through.

What June? Mars invades Earth when the planets are in close opposition early in the twentieth century (p.53). If Wells were Verne, he would have noticed that the astronomical charts predicted only one opposition in the summer of any year through 1910, and that was on July 6, 1907. This might do. But the first cylinder landed on a Thursday midnight (p.74), and if the year is 1907 (the cylinder takes ten days, starting on the 12th), the only possible Thursday is June 27, and the fifth cylinder, which traps the narrator for fifteen days, cannot fall until July. The conclusion is that Wells is careless of such calculations. "That terrible June" impends— but not by the calendar. See I.12.9.

28. To this day the _Daily Telegraph_ is one of Great Britain's foremost national newspapers, the influential organ of the Conservative middle and upper-middle class. Established in 1855, it was the first modern British newspaper to sell for only one penny (then the equivalent of two cents). In the 1890s its daily circulation was around 300,000 copies.

29. Ogilvy is no doubt a fictive name. An astronomer of the same name first observes the approaching cataclysm in Wells's short story "The Star."

30. Mark Rose (1981), p.70, notes:

> The contrast drawn here between light and darkness, warmth and cold, quivering movement and vacancy, is ultimately a contrast between life and death: the "unfathomable darkness" of space is also the mystery of non-being, and the passage as a whole suggests the preciousness and fragility of life in a universe that is mostly empty.

31. An unveiling of the skies is frequent in the early Wells. Besides "The Star" (see I.1.1), examples are provided by "In the Avu Observatory," _Pall Mall Budget_ 9 (August 1894), reprinted in _Stolen Baccillus_, 1895); and "From an Observatory,"

Saturday Review 78 (December 1, 1894), reprinted in *Certain Personal Matters* (1897), slightly altered. In the first, an astronomer in Borneo, absorbed in the stars, is attacked in the darkness by a "Thing" that drops through the slit of the dome (perhaps a bat or a flying lemur). In the second, Wells anticipates Isaac Asimov's "Nightfall." Noting that the stars would be invisible if the moon were brighter, he then imagines the swift, painful conceptual breakthrough of humanity if the stars suddenly appeared; and he asks, "what then if *our* heavens were to open?" In *W W*, indeed, *our* heavens open. Cited by Bergonzi (1961), p.17.

32. A signaling mania struck in the 1890s. See Willy Ley (1957), pp.31–45, who notes that the *Prix Guzman* of 100,000 francs, offered in 1900 for achieving extraterrestrial communication, expressly excluded messages involving Mars "because communication with Mars would be too easy to deserve a prize." See further, Mark R. Hillegas, "The First Invasions from Mars," *Michigan Alumnus Quarterly Review* 66 (Winter 1960):107–112.

33. Lowell (1895), p.211, cautioned: "To talk of Martian beings is not to mean Martian men. Just as the probabilities point to the one, so do they point away from the other." Wells of course agreed: see Appendixes IV and V.

34. *Punch*, the British weekly magazine famous for its political and social cartoons, was established in 1841 and is still flourishing. It provided the original model for *The New Yorker*.

35. The name Markham has not been traced. See II.10.5.

36. In the 1890s London boasted at least eight morning newspapers and seven evening newspapers. All of them had nationwide circulation; some (like the *Daily Graphic*) proudly advertised themselves as "illustrated papers," and others (like the *Daily Mail* and the *Evening News*) sold for as little as a halfpenny a copy.

37. In EA, pp.457–458, Wells recounts how, in 1895, he and his (second) wife settled in Woking:

> We borrowed a hundred pounds . . . and . . . furnished a small resolute semi-detached villa with a minute greenhouse in the Maybury Road. . . . There I planned and wrote *The War of the Worlds*. . . . I learnt to ride my bicycle upon sandy tracks with none but God to help me; he chastened me considerably in the process. . . . I wheeled about the district marking down suitable places and people for destruction by my Martians. The bicycle in those days was still very primitive. The diamond frame had appeared but there was no free-wheel. You could only stop and jump off when the treadle was at its lowest point, and the brake was an uncertain plunger upon the front wheel. Consequently you were often carried on beyond your intentions.

Holbrook Jackson (1927), p.32, notes the novelty, popularity, and social impact of the bicycle during the *fin de siècle*:

> The "safety" bicycle was invented, and it took its place as an instrument of the "new" freedom as we glided forth in our thousands into the country, accompanied by our sisters and sweethearts and wives, who sometimes abandoned skirts for neat knickerbocker suits. "The world is divided into two classes," said a wit of the period, "those who ride bicycles and those who don't."

Amusingly, in the unauthorized *Boston Post* version (January 9, 1898), the narrator learns to ride what the *Post* was just then trumpeting as the latest thing: "the chainless bicycle."

38. See I.3.6, II.9.5.

39. The machinery in the yards and, earlier, the clockwork of the observatory, are "safe and tranquil," domesticated to human use. Wells is setting the stage for estrangement and terror caused by Martian machinery.

I.2. THE FALLING-STAR

1. In the direction of Salisbury and Bristol. See I.2.3.
2. The name has not been traced. See II.10.5.
3. William Frederick Denning (1848–1931) was the chief authority on cometary systems and meteorites (see II.10.5). He worked from his home in Bristol, and the cylinder would have appeared to fall one hundred miles east of him. See his *Telescopic Work for Starlight Evenings* (1891), p.81; as the title suggests, it conveys just the sense of absolute security that the narrator feels in the observatory with "poor Ogilvy."
4. Facing the first cylinder's fiery trail: northwest. Higher up Maybury Hill than Wells's home, the narrator's home is more affluent. See Iain Wakeford, "Wells, Woking and 'The War of the Worlds,' " *Woking History Journal* 2 (Spring 1990):4, 12; reprinted in *Wellsian* 14 (Summer 1991):18–29.
5. It was visible not only in the county of Surrey (where the narrator lives) but also in at least two and perhaps as many as four surrounding counties: an area of several hundred square miles.
6. The adjective "poor" is an economic device foreshadowing Ogilvy's impending fate: the narrator (by hindsight) anticipates his death. But cf. I.2.10. Gibbons (1984), p.12, comments:

> Wells's use of the first-person narrator is . . . far from being rigorously controlled or even consistent. It is impossible, for example, for the narrator to have been acquainted with the detailed thoughts and experiences of "poor Ogilvy" the astronomer, which make up most of Book One, chapter 2.

7. The cylinder would doubtless remind the novel's earliest readers of the man-made projectile in Jules Verne, *From the Earth to the Moon* (1865).
8. Some indication that it had not landed on Earth by chance or naturally; that there was an intelligent purpose behind its journey.
9. See I.12.2, and cf. Chapter 11 of *The Time Machine*: "All the sounds of man, the bleating of sheep, the cries of birds, the hum of insects, the stir that makes the background of our lives—all that was over."
10. His luck is short-lived: he avoids burning his hands but gets incinerated a few hours later. The narrator's references to him are somewhat inconsistent. A few paragraphs earlier he had described him as "poor Ogilvy."
11. See the end of II.9, where the narrator "rounds off" this episode of buying his newspaper. The *Daily Chronicle*, established in 1877, was the most popular pro-Liberal Party newspaper among the British bourgeoisie.

I.3. ON HORSELL COMMON

1. The first of Wells's meddlesome boys. Another, in *The First Men in the Moon* (Chapter XX in the Atlantic edition; Chapter XXI in some other editions), gets himself shot into outer space.
2. The name for game of "tag" in Britain.
3. That is, six years earlier: see Chapter I, paragraph 9.
4. Cf. the "homely" description of the tripods in I.14: "Boilers on stilts." The *OED* quotes the *Daily News* of May 26, 1897: "A gas float is a species of beacon, shaped at the bottom like a ship, and carrying on a lofty pyramid the light, which is fed from a gas cylinder placed in the hull."
5. Until about 1800, science rejected evidence of "rocks falling from the sky" (as flying saucers are now rejected). Later, in the "Unparalleled Adventures of One Hans Pfall" (1835), Poe speculated that "meteoric stones" were volcanic ejecta of the moon. See I.1.31 and Ley (1957), pp.40–43. By Wells's day, the origin of meteorites was known; but a meteorite's fall may well seem extranatural; and if so, why not artificial? The idea of messages in "meteorites" became a common literary

device. For example, Percy Gregg's *Across the Zodiac* (1880) purports to be deciphered from a manuscript found in a "meteorite" that came from Mars.

6. The narrator is writing "a paper on the probable development of Moral Ideas with the development of the civilising process." See I.1.38, II.9.5.

7. This headline probably inspired one of the most popular British plays of the late nineteenth century. Richard Ganthony's *A Message from Mars* (1899), which ran for many months at the Avenue Theatre, London, was a melodrama about a Martian who is not permitted to return to his own planet until he has cured a human being of selfishness.

8. Cf. *The Time Machine*, Chapter 2: " 'Remarkable Behaviour of an Eminent Scientist,' I heard the Editor say, thinking (after his wont) in head-lines."

9. England, Ireland, and Scotland.

10. They had walked just over a mile from Woking and about two miles from Chertsey.

11. A northerly direction.

12. The name has not been traced; see II.10.5. The Astronomer Royal was director of the Royal Greenwich Observatory (founded by King Charles II in 1675) until the two posts were separated in 1971.

13. In the *Cosmopolitan* and *Pearson's* serial versions, this is "Lord Hilton, the Lord of Horsell Manor" (Russell, p.10), but no Horsell Manor or Lord Hilton has been traced, and the local lord was Lord Onslow of Clandon (see Wakeford, p.6).

I.4. THE CYLINDER OPENS

1. From the south.

2. Wells repeatedly associated the imagery of tentacles (octopus) and antennae (crab) with the terrifyingly inhuman or simply with dehumanization. Cf. *W W*, II.4: "In the darkness I could just see the thing. . . . It was like a black worm swaying its blind head to and fro. . . . Once, even, it touched the heel of my boot. I was on the verge of screaming . . . "; and *The Time Machine*, Chapter 11: "I felt a tickling on my cheek. . . . With a frightful qualm, I turned, and saw that I had grasped the antenna of another monster crab that stood just behind me."

Stover (1987), p.53, notices an application of this imagery to the politics of Wells's film *Things to Come* (1936): "So it is with John Cabal [the film's hero]. His octopus-headed helmet is a symbol . . . of the organic state-monster. . . . The tentacles of the Modern State octopus . . . are the extensions of his dictatorial will. . . . "

3. The Gorgons were monsters of Greek myth. They had brass claws and golden wings, and their hair was a tangle of writhing snakes. Humans who came near them were irresistibly tempted to look at them, but their gaze was so terrible that anyone who did was turned to stone. The associations of the image are picked up two paragraphs later, when the narrator observes: "I ran slantingly and stumbling, for I could not avert my face from these things."

4. For Martian anatomy and physiology, see II.2. An early reviewer likened them to the beings Aeneas saw in the courtyard of hell: hundred-handed Briareus, Gorgons, Harpies, and Chimaeras armed with flame. These are the original "bug-eyed monsters" of science fiction; Wells fathered them. See *Saturday Review* 85 (January 29, 1898):146–147; see also I.5.9, II.4.3. On all of this, however, Wells himself provided both visual and verbal last words: a half-humorous, bulbous sketch of a Martian which originally appeared in Geoffrey West (1930), p.107, and which is reproduced on p.42 in this edition; and a passage in his late novel *Star Begotten* (1937), p.96, in which he parodied the description of the Martians in *W W* by recounting the fanciful imaginings of his *angst*-driven bourgeois hero, Joseph Davis:

"he pictured a Martian as something hunched together, like an octopus, tentacular, saturated with evil poisons, oozing unpleasant juices, a gigantic leathery bladder of hate. The smell he thought would be terrible."

5. This would be southeast from Chobham and north from Woking. See Glossary of Places.

I.5. THE HEAT-RAY

1. In the earliest surviving text only (*Cosmopolitan*, April 1897, pp.624–625), the following additional sentence concludes this paragraph:

> When I was a boy I used to amuse myself by frightening the deer in Siddermorton Park, crawling on all fours toward them, with a coat stuck upon a stick, so as to make a strange grotesque shape. The stupid animals would stop feeding and begin to watch me, neither retreating nor approaching, but circling about me, poised between centrifugal dread and centripetal curiosity. I can imagine now that their feelings were not unlike those that the strangeness of the Martians aroused in me.

Whatever Wells's reason for deleting this overt analogy, it applies to the behavior of the narrator and the crowd throughout the chapter.

2. From the southwest.

3. Cf. Revelation 9:2: "and there arose a smoke out of the pit. . . ."

4. To the north.

5. Knaphill is only about three miles from Horsell Common. The narrator's scale is a pedestrian's; distances seem exaggerated to us, who in effect have the mobility of the Martians themselves. See I.15 on the narrator's sense of the great size of the Martian "crescent" attack on London, when in fact the horns are twelve miles apart.

6. The Chertsey and the Chobham roads start at Woking station, then divide. The "Something" that "fell with a crash far away to the left" fell presumably to the west. So the road referred to here is presumably the Chobham Road.

7. "Little" occurs nine times in this short chapter, eight times applied to groups of people. Wells uses lenses of varying magnitudes, depending on his desired perspective. Thus, for example, in a remote perspective a Martian (they are about the size of a bear, p.63) is said to be "oddly suggestive . . . of a speck of blight" (p.116); and in a deleted passage, it is said of the dead Martians that "these little creatures that had been so active intelligent & malignant were now no more than dead vermin putrefying upon the hill slopes" (p.271). See also I.1.1, I.16.5.

8. Terror objectified as outside—like the "meteorites" and heat rays from Mars—is common in Wells. To the Time Traveller, the possibility of being stranded in time is "like a lash across the face" (*The Time Machine*, Chapter 5), and to Prendick in *The Island of Dr. Moreau* the sound of his own laughter comes "suddenly like a thing from without" (Chapter 1). The world is phenomenologically instinct with emotion.

9. Cf. the petrifying gaze of a Gorgon (see I.4.3); Coleridge, *The Ancient Mariner* VI:

> Like one that on a lonesome road
> Doth walk in fear and dread,
> And having once turned round, walks on,
> And turns no more his head;
> Because he knows a frightful fiend
> Doth close behind him tread.

and "The Giant Rats" episode, I.3, of Wells's *The Food of the Gods* (1904), in which the Podbourn doctor is pursued along a dark and lonely road.

I.6. THE HEAT-RAY IN THE CHOBHAM ROAD

1. Frank McConnell (1977), p.145, notes: "Though the details of the heat-ray are vague, they do anticipate in some remarkable ways the development of the laser beam in the 1950s."

2. A distance of about a mile.

3. Gibbons (1984), p.12, finds that this passage provides evidence of Wells's "narrative confusion": the Woking villagers are led to Horsell Common by the news of a massacre having already taken place, and shortly afterwards they witness the identical massacre taking place themselves. But the villagers are attracted to the Common "by the stories they had heard." Who said they heard of a massacre? Ogilvy found the cylinder "very early in the morning" (I.2), and rumors have been flying. Flashing back after the narrator's personal account of the massacre, Wells describes it again (but now at second hand), as witnessed from a different vantage on the Common. The device lends perspective and verisimilitude (like the one McConnell defends in I.14.2).

4. The Martians later trade the periscopic mirror and the protection of the pit for the superior aim, firepower, and mobility of the tripods.

I.7. HOW I REACHED HOME

1. J. D. Beresford (1915), p.29, notes:

> The War of the Worlds (1898), although written in the first person, is in some ways the most detached of all . . . [of Wells's] fantasies; and it is in this book that Mr. Wells frankly confesses his own occasional sense of separation. [Beresford then quotes this passage from the novel.] That sense must have remained with him as he wrote the account of the invading Martians, so little passion does the book contain.

See further, on Wells's recurrent sense of detachment, Draper (1987), p.58.

2. Cf. II.2, where the narrator speaks of six Martians "sluggishly performing the most elaborately complicated operations together." Yet he refers contemptuously to the "fixed idea that these monsters must be sluggish" (I.14). That is, dismounted they are contemptible, mounted, invincible.

3. Established in 1788, the Times was Britain's most prestigious daily newspaper. In the 1890s its political slant was predominantly Liberal Unionist.

4. See I.1.28.

5. Argon is a chemically inactive, odorless, colorless, gaseous element, no. 18 on the Periodic Table of the Elements. It had just been discovered and was in the news. Wells had written it up in "The Newly Discovered Element" and "The Protean Gas," Saturday Review 79 (February 9 and May 4, 1895):183–184, 576–577. See I. 15.8, II.10.2.

6. Hundreds of sailors came before the last dodo died about the year 1680. See also I.1.16. Later, the very idea of such a bird was ridiculed—like the idea of "rocks falling from the sky"—until skeletal remains came to light in 1863 and 1889. See Ley (1959), pp.334–354.

I.8. FRIDAY NIGHT

1. McConnell (1977), p.151, notes: "This introduces another 'Darwinian' theme of the story: the transformation of an established, normal-seeming social order by extreme stress from outside."

2. Cutting into or "poaching on" W. H. Smith's monopoly of selling newspapers inside the station. The chain of W. H. Smith to this day has the exclusive rights to selling newspapers, magazines, and books in many British railroad stations.

3. For the passage "now and again a light-ray . . . was ready to follow" the Cosmopolitan text (May 1897), p.9, substitutes: "from the eyes of the Martians

darkness was no concealment." Indeed, at least one astronomer had theorized that Martians,

> if actually existent, would probably be of a considerably larger build than those who people the Earth, and might, therefore, in their larger bodies maintain a higher temperature than ourselves, and for their larger eyes need less light. [Edmund Ledger, *The Sun: Its Planets and their Satellites* (1882), p.247.]

But if so, the darkness of the ruined house (p.154) would have been no shield for the narrator and the curate.

4. For a key gloss on the passage "In the centre, sticking into the skin . . . still to develop," see David Y. Hughes, "The Garden in Wells's Early Science Fiction," in Suvin and Philmus (1977), pp.62–63. Note also a remarkable analogue to Wells's image of the poisoned dart sticking into the skin of the planet Earth: Conan Doyle's short story "When the World Screamed," originally published in the *Strand Magazine*, April–May 1928, and subsequently in book form in the same author's *The Maracot Deep and Other Stories* (1929).

5. The Inkerman barracks was located about two and a half miles southwest of the Horsell sand pits and about two miles west of Woking Station. The barracks was named for the British and French victory over the Prussians at the Battle of Inkerman in 1854. According to *The Victoria History of Surrey* IV (1912), p.453, for many years some 1,200 men had been stationed there.

6. The Maxim Gun, patented in 1884 by Sir Hiram Stevens Maxim, was an early form of machine gun. After some modification it was adopted by the British Army in 1889. In the field, Maxims were usually mounted on wheeled carriages. See further the detailed description (with drawings) in *Encyclopedia Britannica*, 13th ed. (1926), vol.17, p.242; and the account of the gun's development in H. C. Engelbrecht and F. C. Hanighen, *Merchants of Death* (1934), pp.85–94; also John Ellis, *The Social History of the Machine Gun* (1975), *passim*.

7. The Cardigan regiment was named for Cardiganshire, a western county of Wales located between Fishguard and Aberystwyth.

8. This is a slip. The second cylinder falls to the northeast (pp.77, 101) in or near the "Byfleet" or "Addlestsone" Golf Links (really the New Zealand Golf Course, then the only course thereabouts and the one Wells must mean). See Wakeford, p.6.

I.9. THE FIGHTING BEGINS

1. Among other belittling references to insured "safety" and the smug, fearful insurance mentality, the narrator tells the curate, " 'Did you think God had exempted Weybridge? He is not an insurance agent' " (p.104), and the artilleryman sneers at the little clerks with " 'lives insured and a bit invested for fear of accidents. And on Sundays—fear of the hereafter. As if hell was built for rabbits!' " (p.174). See also I.13.1.

2. Their notion is that there was an operational or tactical dispute—about how to deal with the situation—among the officers of the elite Horse Guards at the Horse Guard barracks (a building in central London opposite Whitehall). The Horse Guards are the cavalry brigade of the English Household troops (the third regiment of Horse Guards is known as the Royal Horse Guards).

3. See Matthew 4: 19: "And he saith unto them, Follow me, and I will make you fishers of men."

4. Wells's dreams recurred continually, from boyhood war games and the illustrated campaigns of his first literary endeavor, about 1878, the *Desert Daisy* (edited by Gordon Ray, 1957), at least up until *The Shape of Things to Come* (1933). Also, Wells agitated for a tank corps in story and essay, beginning in 1903 with "The Land Ironclads." During World War I he designed an aerial telpherage system to ferry supplies over the seas of mud to the trenches. It functioned well and had

the backing of Winston Churchill but was not deployed. See EA, pp.584–591; and R. T. Stearn, "Wells and War," *The Wellsian* 6 (Summer 1983):1–15.

5. See Glossary of Places. Wells picks landmarks for destruction that will presumably endure—and by enduring will keep up the illusion that the Martians will soon be coming. See also I.1.9.

6. McConnell (1977), p.158, notes an apparent slip: "Everywhere else these cousins are the narrator's cousins, not his wife's (see Book I, Chapter Ten, first paragraph, for instance)."

7. The pub on the site described was and is the Princess of Wales; see Wakeford, p.11. Wells disguises its identity with a common British pub name.

8. At that period a British pound was equivalent to five U.S. dollars (about fifty of today's dollars).

9. As McConnell (1977), p.159, dubiously explains, "The landlord fears he may be selling (not buying) a 'pig in a poke.'" But there are more reasonable interpretations. One nineteenth-century slang meaning of "pig" was *goods* or *property.* Hence the sentence might simply mean: "I'm selling my bit of property." Another slang meaning of "pig" was *nag, donkey,* or *moke;* while "bit of" was an adjectival term that could be used variously to express affection for the subject it preceded. See Eric Partridge, *A Dictionary of Slang and Unconventional English* (1961), entries for "bit of," "pig," and "donkey." Hence the sentence might mean the "modern" equivalent of "I'm selling my trusty nag." Another possibility is a real pig, i.e., the landlord is surprised—after asking a pig buyer to pay a pound and drive the pig home himself—to be offered two pounds with a promise moreover to return the pig. According to this, people are simply talking at cross-purposes, and the narrator then explains he wants a dogcart, not a pig.

10. See p.86 for the fate of the innkeeper.

11. Heading due south.

12. The narrator continues due south. When he passes the doctor, he is about two miles south of the sand pits on Horsell Common, and Send is another mile south. See Glossary of Places.

I.10. In the Storm

1. In an easterly direction.

2. That is, south of Pyrford; but the narrator actually enters the town only upon returning from Leatherhead to Maybury by a northerly swing through Ockham–Ripley–Pyrford. See map.

3. The narrator is a warhawk and sightseer. To save his wife, he hires the unsuspecting innkeeper's cart, promising to return it that day. But his return—leaving his wife at risk in Leatherhead—is really prompted by "war-fever," and the reader has already guessed that he will be too late to save the innkeeper. In a parody, Charles Graves and Edward Lucas save time by killing the innkeeper before stealing his automobile, in *The War of the Wenuses* (1898), pp.81–82. See also I.12.4, I.13.3, II.1.4.

4. Likewise, this same night the narrator's brother was thinking of going down to Woking from London "to see the Things before they were killed" (p.106).

5. He went to Leatherhead by a southerly route, through Send, but returns by a northerly route. See map.

6. Cf., in *The Time Machine,* Chapter 3, the sphinx-statue glimpsed in lightning and thunder, looming through hail that "drove along the ground like smoke." But unlike the sphinx, the tripod acts as if animated, perhaps by the storm, reminding the narrator of "a gigantic electric machine" (and perhaps anticipating the lightning bringing the Bride of Frankenstein to life in James Whale's 1935 film). In the 1890s, electric machines had been familiar for a century. Most spectacular was the Wims-

hurst, "bristling with electricity . . . comparable in loudness to a pistol shot." A seven-foot Wimshurst was permanently installed in 1884 in the Science Museum at South Kensington, the year Wells began classes there under Huxley. See John Gray, *Electrical Influence Machines* (1890), pp.159, 167; and Dayton C. Miller, *Sparks, Lightning, Cosmic Rays* (1939), p.41.

7. "This short paragraph has fooled many. The Orphanage that used to be in Oriental Road is nowhere near the crest of Maybury Hill and . . . was not built until 1909! The building Wells described was . . . the old St. Peter's Memorial Home" (Wakeford, p.13).

8. Steel ropes with joints.

9. McConnell (1977), p.164, notes: "This is a remarkable anticipation of the 'strobe effect' of rapid flashes of light, which we have come to associate (through films as much as through real experience of warfare) with modern battle scenes."

10. Alex Eisenstein (1972), p.124, finds the origin of the Martian war machine in fourteen-year-old Wells's discovery of a Gregorian telescope in the attic storeroom at Up Park (described in EA, p.106):

> Here [says Eisenstein] is the inanimate progenitor of the Martian war machine—both are tripodal devices assembled from cylinders. The parts of the telescope screw together, whereas the cylinders from Mars *unscrew* to open. Both the telescope and the war machine involve optical systems—the first for concentrating distant radiation, the other for projecting concentrated radiation over considerable distance (the narrator repeatedly calls the heat-ray mechanism a "camera" or "projector"). The war machines are variously described, but most often as metallic and "glittering." Nothing glitters like gold, of course—except, perhaps, the highly polished tube of a brass telescope; the cowled head of one of these monster machines is termed a "brazen hood" soon after their initial appearance in the story.

On the other hand, Wells ridiculed Warwick Goble and his stiff, inflexible illustrations of the tripods in the serial version. See p.148 and II.2.1.

11. Wells encourages speculation about the tripods and handling-machines. Do Martians ride tripods, or are Martians and tripods cyborgs (p.88)? Are tripods mechanical or organic? After being hit, a tripod is said to reel along blindly (in the serial version, it "staggered pitifully like a wounded man" [Russell, p.43]), discharging "enormous quantities of a ruddy-brown fluid" (p.99). Handling-machines are even more mysterious; they mimic the tentaculate Martian form, and once at least one functions "so far as I could see . . . without a directing Martian at all" (p.153). See I.11.3.

12. Likewise when the Time Traveller stops in the year 802,701 (*The Time Machine*, Chapter 3), "a pitiless hail was hissing round me, and I was sitting on soft turf in front of the overset [Time] machine." See also I.10.6.

13. Licensed in the 1890s to one Chas. A. Hibbert, this pub is still standing.

I.11. AT THE WINDOW

1. The famous pottery-making region of Staffordshire, England. They are also known as "The Five Towns," i.e., Stoke-on-Trent, Hanley, Burslem, Tunstall, and Longton. Arnold Bennett was born and raised in Hanley; his novels deal extensively with the Five Towns. Wells noted rather whimsically:

> Arnold Bennett . . . wrote to me first, in September 1897 . . . to ask how I came to know about the Potteries, which I had mentioned in [the first chapter of] the *Time Machine* . . . and after that we corresponded. In a second letter he says he is "glad to find the Potteries made such an impression" on me, so I suppose I had enlarged upon their scenic interest. [EA, p.533.]

Wells spent three months in the Potteries region in 1888, and in his letters—moved as always by the sight of machinery—he spoke of the furnace glare and the smoke "streaming by under the white clouds" (Harris Wilson, *Arnold Bennett and H. G. Wells* [1960], p.35). Thus, the Potteries later came to figure prominently in "The Cone" (1895; reprinted in *Plattner Story*, 1897), the early chapters of *In the Days of the Comet* (1906), and the ending of *The Food of the Gods* (1904), with the giants firing up their battle-forges.

2. Gibbons (1984), p.7, comments:

> Well's "fiery chaos" seems perhaps familiar, and if we try to remember where we have previously encountered such nightmarish visions . . . we might very well call to mind such paintings as *The Last Judgement* of Hieronymus Bosch, or the "Hell" panel of his *The Garden of Earthly Delights*. The prime source of such visions in Wells . . . is of course the Book of Revelation, and in particular such characteristic sentences as "and fire came down from God out of heaven, and devoured them" (Rev. 20: 9).

3. McConnell (1977), p.169, comments: "One of Wells's most resonant prophecies. The Martians, hyper-evolved brains dependent upon mechanical bodies, are an early version of that mind-machine symbiosis which recent thinkers (and science-fiction writers) call the *cyborg*, or 'cybernetic organism.' " See I.10.11.

4. A warship. In his short story "The Land Ironclads" (first published in *The Strand Magazine*, December 1903), Wells extended the term to signify what later (in 1916) became known as a Tank.

5. See I.8.7.

6. The narrator and the curate likewise in a secret fellowship of fear "dared not strike a light—and ate bread and ham, and drank beer out of the same bottle" (p.144).

7. McConnell (1977), p.173, notes:

> In many ways, *The War of the Worlds* is a startling anticipation of the grim and unprecedented realities of World Wars I and II. But the novel itself arises from a long tradition of speculations on the future "history of warfare." . . . The first and most famous of these was *The Battle of Dorking* (1871) by Sir George Tomkyns Chesney.

See further: I. F. Clarke, *Voices Prophesying War, 1763–1984* (1966), pp.94–99.

8. See Exodus 13: 21: "And the Lord went before them [to guide the Israelites through the Sinai] . . . by night in a pillar of fire."

I.12. WHAT I SAW OF THE DESTRUCTION OF WEYBRIDGE AND SHEPPERTON

1. He intends to make a northerly bypass of Leatherhead then circle back to it from the east.

2. See I.2.9.

3. Aluminum was first produced in 1825 by the Danish physician Hans Christian Oersted, but the cheap method of electrolysis was invented only in 1886. See Charles Singer et al., *A History of Technology* V (1958), p.91.

4. The narrator acts on impulse. While his resolute brother rescues two ladies, reaches the coast, and leaves the country (I.16–17), the narrator drives his wife to Leatherhead, returns the rented cart to Maybury, starts on a northerly way back to Leatherhead to avoid newly landed Martians at Pyrford, volunteers a further detour to guide the artilleryman to Weybridge, and then, amid general confusion, continues north toward London, dropping the plan of escaping with his wife south to Newhaven and away by sea. See I.10.3, I.13.3, II.1.4.

5. Appropriately enough, it is Sunday. McConnell (1977), p.177, comments that it is "ironically, the day of rest and peace."

6. Gibbons (1984), pp.7–8, observes that the narrator "echoes the description of Death in Revelation 6: 8: 'And I looked, and behold a pale horse: and his name that sat on him was Death.' "

7. Gibbons (1984), p.9, notes:

> On his first appearance in Book One, the Artilleryman seems no more than a short-lived authorial device for varying the narrative point of view. . . . It is noticeable that when he becomes separated from the narrator in the confusion of the Martian attack upon Weybridge (Book One, chapter 12), this fact is not even thought worthy of mention. It is therefore something of a surprise to be re-introduced to the Artilleryman as "The Man on Putney Hill" in Book Two, chapter 7, and to find this entire chapter devoted to a presentation of his views upon the future of the human race which is of the greatest thematic importance.

In the *Pearson's* serial (Russell, p.42) the narrator says: "In my convulsive excitement I took no heed of the artilleryman behind me, and to this day . . . I never set eyes on him again." The artilleryman's reappearance is evidently a late interpolation. See above, "Gestation," in the Introduction.

8. On the north bank of the Thames.

9. Pictured in *An Inventory of the Historical Monuments in Middlesex* (1937), p.110, this tower (to the Church of St. Nicholas) is "of stock bricks with an embattled parapet." It is soon smashed by the Martians (see p.98). By selecting durable landmarks for destruction, Wells enlists their aid, so long as they stand, to sustain the illusion for future readers that invasion is impending. See I.9.5.

10. Chertsey is about one mile northwest of Weybridge.

11. The southern side of the Thames.

12. Cf. Daniel 7: 2: "and, behold, the four winds of the heaven strove upon the great sea."

13. The tripods are powerfully visualized. They are also seen "receding interminably . . . across a vast space of river and meadow" (p.100), or apparently moving "upon a cloud, for a milky mist covered the fields and rose to a third of their height" (p.116), or looming over the Black Smoke and clearing it with jets of steam (p.119), or wading "deeply through a shiny mud-flat that seemed to hang half-way up between sea and sky" (p.135).

14. Laleham is about two miles north of Weybridge.

I.13. How I Fell In with the Curate

1. The great earthquake of Lisbon, Portugal, occurred November 1 (All Saints Day), 1755, when many people were at church. About 50,000 died, and 90 percent of the city was destroyed. Shock waves were felt as far away as Scotland and Finland. "A century ago" is rough. *W W*'s putative date (about 1905) would mark a century and a half, but the book does recall the actual Lisbon streams of refugees and open camps and fear of the plague. See Sir Thomas Downing Kendrick, *The Lisbon Earthquake* (1957).

With the quake as ammunition, Voltaire's *Poème sur le désastre de Lisbonne* (1755) expressed moral outrage at the "optimistic" Deism of the times, which had lately professed to find, with Pope, that:

> All nature is but art, unknown to thee;
> All chance, direction, which thou canst not see;
> All discord, harmony not understood;
> All partial evil, universal good:
> And, spite of pride, in erring reason's spite,
> One truth is clear, Whatever is, is right.
>   —"An Essay on Man" (1733), Epistle I.x.

Like Voltaire, Wells is no believer in a hidden harmony, but unlike Voltaire (and like his own artilleryman), he relishes the destruction of that illusion and of such bearers of it as the weak-kneed curate, whining because he thought his service to

God was an insurance policy against catastrophe. On the subject of insurance, see I.9.1; for another view of the curate, see I.13.5.

2. McConnell (1977), p.187, notes: "Another grim prophecy of the First World War."

3. After a sample of Martian warfare, the narrator not surprisingly wants out. But he comes ashore on the north bank—apparently by chance—and continues Londonward, away from Leatherhead. See I.10.3, I.12.4, II.1.4.

4. The north shore of the Thames.

5. John Huntington comments:

> The claim to be anxious about reaching Leatherhead has all the earmarks of a rationalization to prevent further inquiry into the sources of anger that [the narrator] has just declared to be unaccountable. At this moment of explicit but inexplicable anger at the narrator's wife, the curate appears. For the middle part of the novel the curate replaces the wife as the narrator's housemate. Now the "anxiety" for the *absent* companion converts to a declared anger at the *present* one. [Patrick Parrinder and Christopher Rolfe, eds., *H. G. Wells under Revision* (1990), p.177; reprinted in Huntington, ed., *Critical Essays on H. G. Wells* (1991), p.144.]

On the curate, see also I.13.1 and 6; and on the narrator's general disaffection, see I.10.3.

6. The curate resembles the Eloi of *The Time Machine*. Like them, fair, curly-haired, large-eyed, and childlike or effeminate, he is a sort of calf for the slaughter. On human cattle, see the artilleryman, pp.172–175.

7. See Genesis 19.

8. See the Kepler epigraph, p.47.

9. To the curate, the Book of Revelation is coming true (Rev. 14: 2, 19: 3). Other examples: " 'The end! The great and terrible day of the Lord! When men shall call upon the mountains and the rocks to fall upon them and hide them—hide them from the face of Him that sitteth upon the throne!' " (p.104; Rev. 6: 16–17); " 'What is that flicker in the sky?' " (p.104; Rev. 15: 1); " 'The wine-press of God!' " (p.394; Rev. 14: 19); " 'I must bear my witness. Woe unto this unfaithful city! Woe! woe! woe! woe! woe! to the inhabitants of the earth by reason of the other voices of the trumpet' " (p.395; Rev. 8: 13).

10. McConnell (1977), p.190, notes: " 'Northward' is the movement of the whole book. . . . Uttered here, the word is a cue—almost a stage direction—for the radical shift in point of view in the following chapter." However, the narrator's brother, already in London, heads east.

I.14. IN LONDON

1. Various descriptions relayed to the narrator by his brother in Book I, Chapters XIV, XVI, and XVII may call to mind Dante or Shelley's "Triumph of Life" (see I.16.9). A more specific influence is Heinrich Heine; see Introduction, above, p.21.

2. McConnell (1977), p.191, considers the shift of viewpoint from the narrator to the narrator's brother in this chapter to be "a technical feat of some brilliance."

> [B]y doing this Wells enhances the verisimilitude of his most violent scenes . . . being presented at second hand, they gain rather than lose conviction. And also, by suspending most of the narrator's own story till the beginning of Book II, he increases the suspense of the whole novel.

By contrast, Gibbons (1984), p.12, regards this shift of viewpoint as an indication of Wells's inadequate control of the narrative:

> [T]he younger brother's account of events given in the last four chapters of Book One removes us so far from the first-person narrator himself that Wells is obliged

to begin Book Two with a virtual (and inaccurate) apology to the reader. . . . Neither the prose style of the brother's narrative, nor even that of the Artilleryman's conversation, differs in any significant respect from that of the first-person narrator.

In partial objection to Gibbons, it must be noted that he overlooks the fact (which absolves Wells of being "inaccurate") that the brother's story is not told in Chapter XV but in Chapter XIV and resumed in Chapters XVI and XVII; the fact that the brother's story is *recounted by the narrator*; and the fact that many quoted remarks of the artilleryman in no way resemble the language of the narrator: e.g., "dying's none so dreadful; it's the funking makes it bad"; or "what would it matter if you smashed to smithereens at the end of the run, after a bust like that?"

   3. In 1890–1893, Wells "prepped" students like the narrator's brother for a University of London biology examination always held on the third Monday in July. "We drew away a swarm of medical students from the rather otiose hospital teaching in biology," Wells recalled. See the University of London Calendar for 1898, p.vi, and EA, pp.283–285. This seems consistent with a June invasion. See I.1.27.

   4. Established in 1880, *St. James's Gazette* was a pro-Tory paper with features that also appealed to readers with intellectual and literary interests. Wells's "Temptation of Harringay" appeared there on February 9, 1895 (and in *The Stolen Bacillus* [1895]).

   5. The Southampton and Portsmouth Sunday League was an organization that campaigned for temperance and strict Sabbath Day observance.

   6. In the 1890s, Sunday papers far outsold dailies, until the Harmsworth influence set in (see I.1.28, II.9.2), notably with the *Daily Mail* (1896); see Richard D. Altick, *The English Common Reader* (1957), pp.342–355. But the Harmsworth biography states that only in 1899 did the *Daily Mail* and the *Daily Telegraph* introduce Sunday editions, and even then soon dropped them because of public outcry over desecration of the Sabbath. See Reginald Pound and Geoffrey Harmsworth (1959), pp.241–242. The two accounts seem to conflict, but soon the Sunday editions indeed far outstripped the dailies. Wells did not foresee the change and unwittingly "dated" his narrative for future readers.

   7. The *Sun*, London's first popular halfpenny evening newspaper, was established in 1893 by T. P. O'Connor.

   8. A former London weekly, the *Referee* (founded 1877), was popular for its focus on humor, satire, sports, and theater. Perhaps it puffed the *W W* serial. Wells had appreciated its puffing *The Time Machine* (Bergonzi [1960], p.24).

   9. Though *W W* is sometimes as farcical as a menagerie let loose in a village (or "Epsom High Street on a Derby Day," p.111), the tone is prevailingly settled and historical; high spirits are much more the mark of the opening chapters of *The Invisible Man: A Grotesque Romance*, written concurrently.

   10. But the narrator himself *was* an eyewitness and had used the same vocabulary to describe the Martians to his wife: see I.7.2.

   11. The Foundling Hospital, in Bloomsbury, London, near the British Museum, was established in 1739 by Thomas Coram. Despite its name, it was not a home for foundlings but a shelter for illegitimate children whose mothers were known.

   12. The various routes and stations of the (now defunct) South-Western Railway Company. Its terminus was Waterloo Station, London. The network had three main branches: the Northern, serving locations in the direction of Staines and Reading; the Central, serving locations in the direction of Bournemouth and Southampton; and the Southern, serving locations in the direction of Guildford, Epsom, and Leatherhead.

   13. The *OED* notes "lungs of London" as referring in the nineteenth century to surrounding open spaces. Here "lungs" may signify the area served by one branch

of the South-Western Railway. McConnell (1977), p.195, comments: "the authorities are blocking off the area from which the Martian invasion comes."

14. Adjoining the Waterloo Station terminus of the South-Western Railway was another station belonging to the South-Eastern Railway (a separate company providing service to locations in the direction of Margate, Dover, Folkestone, and Hastings), whose terminus was Charing Cross. Normally there were barriers preventing passengers from moving directly from one railroad to the other. These barriers had been lifted because of the emergency situation.

15. See I.14.18.

16. Threepence a copy was three to six times the normal price. Later the narrator's brother encounters a man selling papers for a shilling (at least twelve times the normal price), and the narrator himself pays this amount for the first copy of the *Daily Mail* he sees after the demise of the Martians.

17. McConnell (1977), p.197, explains this as "an official statement which does not quite claim to *be* an official statement."

18. This is a slip. Until about 1870, paper was dampened to ensure a good printing impression and was then dried, but by the 1890s dry paper was used (Singer [1958], V, p.712) The anachronism disappears in the Heinemann edition (p.127), which reads: "type, so fresh that the paper was still wet."

19. See also "lemon-yellow" sunset (p.62), another sign of the *fin de siècle*. On Wells and the *fin de siècle*, see Bergonzi (1960), Chapter 1.

20. These tricycles, which were obsolete by the early 1890s, were sometimes nicknamed "Tuppence-farthing bikes" on account of their appearance. The cycle-saddle was located between two large wheels (the "pence" of the nickname), and a third, much smaller wheel (the "farthing") was at the front of the vehicle. See the illustration of the Columbia Tricycle in Robert A. Smith. *A Social History of the Bicycle* (1972), p.43.

21. Teeming with people: see Frith's famous painting "Derby Day." Epsom, in Surrey, is the town nearest the racetrack where the most celebrated British horse-race, the Derby (pronounced "Darby"), is held annually.

22. The metaphor of liquefaction briefly stated here is carried through in I.16 and I.17.

I.15. WHAT HAD HAPPENED IN SURREY

1. Perhaps like the "ulla, ulla" in dead London, in II.8.

2. The bow of the crescent points northeast toward London, and its two horns trail behind it to the southwest, covering the flanks of the Martian advance.

3. One of Wells's last novels was titled *Babes in the Darkling Wood* (1940).

4. Wells drops a hint of the Martian dietary here, furnishes a clinical description (II.2), and then ironically alludes to the "cheerful hooting" of the Martian consuming the blood of a "stout, ruddy" Englishman (II.3).

5. To frustrate the Martians by destroying their major objective, London, as the Russians did to Napoleon in 1812 by setting fire to Moscow.

6. A diabolical omen (see also p.156), like no birds singing. See I.2.9, I.12.2.

7. The implied inverse in the context is not "celestial artillery" but "infernal artillery." See John Milton, *Paradise Lost* (1674), Book VI, ll.472ff., on Satan's infernal artillery.

8. Carbonic acid gas is carbon dioxide. This passage recalls the smoke issuing from the infernal regions in *The Island of Dr. Moreau* (1896), "pungent in whiffs to nose and eyes" (Chapter 11). Wells later observes that something in the Black Smoke may combine with atmospheric argon, a newly isolated element about which Wells had written (see I.7.5), which is spewed out during volcanic eruptions.

9. Wells inserted this passage in revising *Pearson's* for book publication, forgetting that in "The Epilogue" he had stipulated "a brilliant group of three lines in the green" (p.191). He had intended to scrap "The Epilogue" but at some point changed his mind—a fact that probably explains the inconsistency. See above, Introduction, pp.5–6.

10. Starting Thursday, a cylinder falls each night. This fourth cylinder must fall on Sunday. See further, II.1.7.

11. See I.15.2.

12. Wells recaptured these images forty years later in the opening air raid and gas attack sequence of his film *Things to Come* (1936).

I.16. THE EXODUS FROM LONDON

1. Draper (1987) compares this image to Wells's account of the degeneration of Moreau's Beast People and to the view from the Time Machine:

> "Can you imagine language, once clear-cut and exact, softening and guttering, losing shape and import, becoming mere lumps of sound again?" *Moreau*, ch.21.
> "the whole surface of the earth seemed changed—melting and flowing under my eyes." *Time Machine*, ch.3.

Draper comments: "Seen in a moment of crisis, or from a sufficient conceptual distance, human existence is revealed as an aimless flux" (p.53).

Aimless: perhaps; repetitive: not necessarily. Wells speculated in "The Cyclic Delusion" (*Saturday Review*, November 10, 1894; reprinted in Philmus and Hughes [1975], pp.110–113) that in the course of time all that we know may be swept away in "the great stream of the universe . . . from the things that are past and done with for ever to things that are altogether new." Most famously, the image of "liquefaction" powers the destroyer at the end of *Tono-Bungay* (1909), as it cuts down the River Thames and out to sea while "the traditional and ostensible England falls from you altogether."

2. In 1895 bicycles were "the swiftest thing upon the roads" (EA, p.458), and if automobiles constituted a real presence in *W W*, they would muddy the Martians' technological supremacy; yet the parody *The War of the Wenuses* (1898) includes the automobile. See I.5.5, I.10.3.

3. "Gold" refers to sovereigns: gold coins worth one English pound each. Later in the chapter, "a bearded eagle-faced man" has his back broken by a cart as he attempts to recover a quantity of sovereigns he has dropped in the road.

4. Wells disliked sentimentality over dogs (also pp.163, 167). See, in *A Modern Utopia* (1905), pp.230–231, the botanist's stupid inability to comprehend utopian sanitary views on pets. On the related issue of vivisection, see II.2.3.

5. Cf. "Up the street came galloping a closed carriage, bursting abruptly into noise at the corner, rising to a clattering climax under the window, and dying away slowly in the distance" (p.112). Wells foreshadows cinematic effects. As if in the eye of a camera, the focus scans the length and pans the segments of the road to St. Albans—both the ruck and flow and the vignettes like that of the man with gold coins—and then the next chapter starts with the same scene as seen by a balloonist. See I.1.1, I.5.7.

6. Vestry here is not used in its usual ecclesiastical sense but refers to a committee of citizens "vested" with the task of arranging for such basic local services as health and food inspection and garbage disposal. St. Pancras (then a London borough) is located northwest of the City of London. Bernard Shaw was for a time a Vestryman of St. Pancras. See Harry M. Geduld, "Bernard Shaw, Vestryman and Borough Councillor," *The California Shavian* (Los Angeles) IV/i (Summer 1962):1–15.

7. The name Garrick has not been traced; see II.10.5. The Lord Chief Justice of England is the Judge who presides over the Court of the King's Bench and the Court of Common Pleas. The nearest American equivalent (although there are many differences in the two offices) would be the Chief Justice of the Supreme Court.

8. This episode involving a regrettable anti-semitic caricature is even more explicit in the serial version (Russell, pp.70–71). See further Sam Moskowitz, "The Jew in Science Fiction," *Worlds of Tomorrow* 4 (November 1966):109–122.

9. Parrinder (1981), p.28, comments:

> The fury and violence of this "exodus from London" are in some ways reminiscent of medieval visions of Hell ... and some of the incidents ... seem designed to illustrate the traditional "Deadly Sins" of greed and rage. The tumultuous procession described in Percy Bysshe Shelley's poem "The Triumph of Life" (1822) may also have been in Wells's mind.

But the immediate influence is Heinrich Heine. See above, Introduction, p.21.

10. The now-defunct system provided communications from London to the north and northeast parts of Britain: e.g., Manchester, Liverpool, Sheffield, and Edinburgh. The London terminus of the Great Northern Railway was King's Cross Station.

I.17. The "Thunder Child"

1. See Glossary of Places.

2. The Goths, a Germanic tribe, invaded Rome's Eastern and Western Empires during the third through the fifth century. The Huns, a nomadic Asian people, under their leader Atilla, invaded and ravaged much of Europe during the fifth century. In his *Short History of the World* (1922) p.245, Wells described the Huns as "the least kindred and most redoubtable of ... devastators ... a yellow people active and able, such as the western world had never before encountered."

3. Wells varied and recycled this metaphor in his review of *Land of the Dollar* (see above, Introduction, n.56): "After all, the entire American civilisation, in relation to its scenery, is very like a penny bottle of ink spilt over a half-acre lawn."

4. Sailors on or owners of lighters or barges (boats used in the "lightening," or unloading, of large ships).

5. This is a slip. The sixth and seventh cylinders must fall on Tuesday and Wednesday nights.

6. The Midland Railway Company provided public transportation to such Midlands cities as Nottingham, Leicester, Manchester, and Leeds. Its London terminus was St. Pancras Station.

7. An unofficial "vigilante" group whose name Wells intended to echo the notorious Committee of Public Safety of the French Revolution. (In MS the counterpart is "Vigilance Committee." See Appendix I, p.262.)

8. R. T. Stearns comments, in "Wells and War" [*Wellsian* 6 [Summer 1983]:14]: "Ramming, so dramatic and decisive, was a recurring theme in future-war fiction, e.g., H. O. Arnold-Forster, *In a Conning Tower* (1888) and the Earl of Mayo, *The War Cruise of the 'Aries'* (1894)." See also Clarke (1966), pp.65, 83–85.

9. This was at least ten times the usual amount.

10. The artilleryman says in II.7: "I believe they've built a flying machine, and are learning to fly." The craft seems to have wings; it is not a dirigible. The Wright brothers flew in December 1903, but powered flight might have been achieved first in Europe—by Lilienthal (d. 1896) or Pilcher (d. 1899)—had they not died in crashes. See Singer (1958) V, p.406.

Wells is an uneven prophet as regards aircraft. In *When the Sleeper Wakes* (1899), he pictures flapping ornithopters in the year 2100; in *Anticipations* (1901) he doubts if "aeronautics will ever come into play as a serious modification of transport and communication" but concedes that "long before the year A.D. 2000 and very probably before 1950, a successful aeroplane will have soared" (pp.29, 168). Nevertheless, this paragraph of *W W* embodies one of Wells's most extraordinary prophecies: warplanes dropping poison gas. The same vision reappears in his novel *The War in the Air* (1908) and in his film *Things to Come* (1936). While the film was being made Mussolini carried out the prophecy in earnest by gas-bombing helpless Ethiopians.

Wells's last sentence echoes several biblical passages: "The Lord rained upon Sodom and upon Gomorrah brimstone and fire" (Genesis 19: 24); "and there was a thick darkness in all the land of Egypt" (Exodus 10: 22); and "Now from the sixth hour there was darkness over all the land" (Matthew 27: 45).

Book II: The Earth under the Martians

1. Batchelor (1985), p.27, describes the title of Book II as a "somewhat misleading heading, since the Martians never get further than the South of England."

II.1. UNDER FOOT

1. Benches and workbooks.

2. This redness and the "red masses" (p.142) are Red Weed (not bloody corpses, as the narrator implies he mistook them for).

3. The eruption of Mount Vesuvius near Naples on August 24, A.D. 79 buried the towns of Pompeii and Herculaneum under thousands of tons of volcanic ash and lava, killing some 20,000 inhabitants.

4. The narrator claims he wants to help his wife in Leatherhead, to the south, but he goes north. Yet turning south would not be impossible since he is now east of the dangers of Horsell, Pyrford, and Weybridge. See I.10.3, I.12.4, I.13.3.

5. A fashionable name for a kind of small suburban house—in this case a two-family structure—popularly considered to be a "better class" of dwelling.

6. Reproductions of works of art or scenes of history, included in late nineteenth-century British newspapers (usually the Sunday issues) as so-called free gifts, were a popular house decoration among people who could not afford to buy framed pictures.

7. McConnell (1977), p.240, states:

> The fourth star had fallen late Sunday night, north of where the narrator and the curate are hiding (Book I, Chapter Sixteen [actually Fifteen]), and the narrator only hears of it later, from his brother. So it is impossible for him to know, at the time, that this is the *fifth* star; he should think it the fourth.

But the first three cylinders fell one after the other late on the nights of Thursday, Friday, and Saturday. Doubtless the narrator simply assumes that the fourth fell "late Sunday night" and that this one (late Monday night) is the fifth. See I.1.26. The real trouble is that—far from being unaware of the fourth cylinder—the narrator should be only too well acquainted with it. It fell the previous night, into Bushey Park, which he and the curate have just traversed. But Wells has forgetfully caused the park to contain nothing more remarkable than "the deer going to and fro under the chestnuts." See I.15.10.

II.2. WHAT WE SAW FROM THE RUINED HOUSE

1. Harris Wilson (1960), p.42, quotes Arnold Bennett to Wells, September 1899: "I gathered from a passage in *The War of the Worlds* that you were not exactly enchanted with Warwick Goble's efforts." (Goble did most of the *Pearson's/Cosmopolitan* illustrations.) Wilson continues:

Fifteen of his illustrations were reproduced in the American edition of the book in 1898. Wells and his agent Pinker had tried to get illustrations in 1896 from Cosmo Rowe, a follower of William Morris and later a Fabian and rationalist. Only two of his illustrations, however, were used in *Pearson's* . . . ; [but] one of these appeared as the frontispiece of the American edition.

Wells replied to Bennett: "Goble's a good chap no doubt but he made people think my tale was a wearisome repetition of kettles on camera stands. I really don't think he put a fair quantity of brain into that enterprise or I wouldn't have slanged him in the book." Yet Wells had actually moderated his vexation. Where the book speaks of "tilted, stiff tripods, without either flexibility or subtlety, and with an altogether misleading monotony of effect," the holograph revision of *Pearson's* contains a more caustic sally (though canceled without any substitution in the manuscript):

> His sole method of conveying its movement was to tilt the thing either to left, or to the right, & of suggesting its detailed gesture, to dangle gigantic nutcrackers & tweezers & the like primitive contrivances in awkward curves about its body. . . . And that the artist never saw a Handling Machine & drew on an exhausted imagination for his one picture of these structures is beyond dispute. [Illinois *W W* 109.]

Wells was not easy to please. At about this date, he complained to his friend Elizabeth Healey concerning *The Wheels of Chance* (1896): "I've got a serial in 'To-Day'— illustrated with incredible violence and vulgarity" (undated, transcript in Illinois Wells Archive). By 1920, however, he felt that over the years illustrators had done *W W* proud, and he said so in introducing a condensation he did for the *Strand Magazine* LIX (February 1920):154–163.

2. George Bond Howes, T. H. Huxley's assistant, taught Huxley's biology class when the master fell ill shortly after Wells enrolled (EA, p.161). Howes contributed the introduction to Wells's first book, *Text-Book of Biology* (1893).

3. For book publication, Wells here suppressed three paragraphs of the *Pearson's* serial that allege that the Martians took no special pleasure in cruelty, since in target practice they killed humans without the maiming that we do in pigeon-shoots; and in the case of the "still living body of an eminent physician" transfixed and "horribly mutilated," they exercised scientific curiosity: "man who vivisects the lower animals certainly has no claim to exemption when in his turn he becomes a lower animal" (Russell, pp.84–85).

A similar irony occurs in *The First Men in the Moon* (Chapter 23 in the Atlantic edition; Chapter 24 in some other editions) when Cavor defends the Selenite practice of drugging surplus workers for later use rather than letting them starve as we do. In *W W*, however, Wells avoids irony that may be construed as directed at the Martians and not at us. As to his feelings on vivisection, he expressed himself plainly in *The Way the World is Going* (1928), p.228, where he mocks the rhapsodizing of the anti-vivisectionists in the cause of the "noble" dog and their silence when it comes to "the curious, materialistic, shameless, and intelligent monkey." See also I.16.4.

In his introduction to his forthcoming edition of *The Island of Dr. Moreau*, Robert M. Philmus notes that the theory that man has evolved from lower animals offered rationales both for and against vivisection, causing heated debate, and that by 1875 the first anti-vivisectionist society was formed.

4. When Wells seriously considered the question of silicon-based life on Mars, he rejected it because only an un-Marslike "environment some 1000 degrees above that of a blast furnace" could cause silicon to act as carbon does in terrestrial organisms ("Another Basis for Life," *Saturday Review* 78 [December 22, 1894]:676–677). But the idea of silicon-based life on Mars was not unusual. See, e.g., Camille Flammarion, *North American Review* 162 (May 1896):546–557.

5. A weekly offshoot of the daily *Pall Mall Gazette* (to which Wells was a notable contributor) established in 1889 by W. T. Stead. Much of the material in the *Budget* consisted of reprints from the *Gazette*.

6. For *Punch*, see I.1.34. Wells refers to his own illustrated essay "The Man of the Year Million" (Appendix III), which had a certain vogue. It appeared in the *Pall Mall Gazette* (November 9, 1893), *Pall Mall Budget* (November 16, 1893), and *English Illustrated Magazine* (January 1902); and *Punch* parodied it in illustrated verses (November 25, 1893). Wells included it in *Certain Personal Matters* (1897) as "Of a Book Unwritten," and Warren Wagar anthologized it in *H. G. Wells: Journalism and Prophecy* (1964). Moreover, Wells had substantially anticipated "The Man of the Year Million" as early as 1885 in an address before the Science Schools Debating Society, "The Past and Future of the Human Race." See Bergonzi (1961), p.36.

7. "Teacher and agent of the brain" was a popular maxim; its author has not been traced. In "The Man of the Year Million" (1893), Wells renders it as "teacher and interpreter of the brain."

8. Anne B. Simpson comments: "The romance schema of hero versus villain is complicated by an indefinite stance regarding the nature of good and evil: when . . . the Martians are posited as evolved humanoids, the assumed radical difference [between 'them' and 'us'] is perceived to be founded in identity." (*Extrapolation* 31/2 [Summer 1990]:145).

9. McConnell (1977), p.247, defines "emotional substratum" as the "underlying quality or essence." In biology (appropriate to the context here), the substratum is the base in which a structure is rooted. In "Under the Knife" the narrator remarks:

> It has been proven, I take it, as thoroughly as anything can be proven in this world, that the higher emotions, the moral feelings, even the subtle tenderness of love, are evolved from the elemental desires and fears of the simple animal: they are the harness in which man's mental freedom goes. [*New Review* (January 1896); reprinted in *Plattner Story and Others* (1897).]

10. Mark R. Hillegas (1961), p.661, observes: "In the humanity of the Martians, Wells is emphatically underlining the idea that evolution, even though it may produce creatures with superior intelligence, will not necessarily lead to better and better." Parrinder (1970), p.31, comments: "this is both a statement of the 'ideological basis' of the story, and a verbal comment upon it."

11. Similarly, the Time Traveller concludes that probably the environment of the Eloi is germ-free (*Time Machine*, Chapter 4). Beyond that, the idea of outer space acting as a barrier or bubble that preserves a pasteurized existence—and the breaching of the barrier by pathenogens of another world—goes back (at least) to Percy Gregg's *Across the Zodiac* (1880). Here and in commenting on the red weed (p.166), Wells foreshadows the fate of the Martians.

12. The dark areas of Mars were often regarded as oceans and the red areas as vegetation; see, e.g., Camille Flammarion (1892), pp.216–217; Edmund Ledger (1882), p.243. Thus, in the novel *Across the Zodiac*, it follows from the reddish tints of Mars that yellows and oranges "must be as much the predominant colour of the vegetation as green upon Earth" (Percy Gregg [1880], Chapter 3). Wells apparently modifies the formula of red = vegetation and green = oceans by associating the reddish tints with vegetation in abundant shallow waters on Mars, while ascribing the dark areas to true oceans (see I.1 and I.1.14) and to green vegetation. At any rate, those are the conditions which are directly observed on Mars in an offshoot of *WW*, "The Crystal Egg" (first published in *New Review* 16 [May 1897]:556). There, tentacled, winged Martians inhabit a land of green vegetation bordering "a broad and mirror-like expanse of water" full of "dense *red* weeds." Accordingly, *WW*'s red weed is some sort of water lily.

13. The name has not been traced. See II.10.5.

14. Wells may mean the pamphlet with "stiff" illustrations, the serial version of *W W* (see p.148 and II.2.1). But the serial has no "tentacular gesticulations" or anything about Martian communication save some hooting by tripods. The subject does not come up in the serial, and this paragraph bestowing extrasensory powers on the aliens, is one that Wells interpolated as he revised for book publication (Illinois archive contains the revision).

15. Reviewing Frank Podmore's *Apparitions and Thought Transference* (1894), Wells had roasted psychic investigators as unscientific and gullible, and added:

> The public mind is incapable of the suspended judgment; it will not stop at telepathy. Any general recognition of the evidence of "psychical" research will be taken by the outside public to mean the recognition of ghosts, witchcraft, miracles, and the pretensions of many a shabby-genteel Cagliostro, now pining in a desert of incredulity, as undeniable facts. Were Mr. Podmore's case strong—and it is singularly weak—the undeniable possibility of a recrudescence of superstition remains as a consideration against the unqualified recognition of his evidence. [A rejoinder by (Sir) Oliver Lodge and a retort by Wells followed. *Nature* 51 (December 6, 1894 and January 10 and 17, 1895):121–122, 247, 274.]

Wells's hostility to spiritualism and telepathy also marks the Chaffery chapters of *Love and Mr. Lewisham* (1900).

16. German engineer Otto Lilienthal (1848–1896) was one of the pioneers of man-bearing gliders.

17. "Sticks" was a common abbreviation for "shooting-sticks": pistols.

18. Samuel Butler, in *Erewhon* (1872) and elsewhere, in part anticipated Wells's Martian evolution. He theorized as a mental exercise that machines may evolve as competitors that surpass and subjugate humans. More seriously, he also proposed that machines are external limbs. See Basil Willey, *Darwin and Butler: Two Versions of Evolution* (1960), pp.67–70. But since Wells's ideas in part go back at least to 1885 (see II.2.6) and since Butler's work was little regarded until George Bernard Shaw rediscovered it after 1900, Wells most likely worked independently.

19. McConnell (1977), p.250, notes:

> A friction bearing is any device interposed between two moving surfaces to reduce the friction they generate. Wells's description of Martian technology is a subtle reinforcement of his previous allusion to "natural selection." Since the Martians do not use the principle of the wheel—the great originating principle of all human machinery—they have been forced to develop a technology that imitates the muscular activity of the body. But in doing this, they have rendered the activity of the *real* body superfluous: they have been trapped, by their own engineering genius, into becoming the physically pathetic monsters, dependent upon a kind of absolute prosthetics, which the narrator sees.

20. As McConnell (1977), p.251, observes, Wells is here describing a robot before the term was coined (in 1921) by Karel Capek. However, functional robots were by no means first conceived by Wells. See further "Genesis II," in Harry M. Geduld and Ronald Gottesman, *Robots, Robots, Robots* (1978), pp.3–37.

II.4. THE DEATH OF THE CURATE

1. Darko Suvin (1977), p.24, discussing a favorite Wellsian narrative device—"The loss of the narrator's vehicle and the ensuing panic of being a castaway under alien rule"—maintains that "in *The War of the Worlds* this is inverted as hiding in a trap with dwindling supplies."

2. Most of the passage is merely biblical-sounding rhetoric. "I have been still too long" apparently echoes Isaiah 42: 14: "I have been still, and refrained myself."

3. In Greek mythology Briareus was a giant with fifty heads and a hundred hands. Lord Byron figuratively called master-linguist Cardinal Mezzofanti (who knew 58 languages) "the Briareus of languages." Really, the Cardinal of course did not have 58 heads but Wells's machines "really" have many "hands." On literalization of metaphor in science fiction, see Samuel R. Delany, "About Five Thousand One Hundred and Seventy Five Words," in Thomas D. Clareson, ed., *SF: the Other Side of Realism* (1971), pp.130–146. See also I.4.4, I.5.9.

II.6. THE WORK OF FIFTEEN DAYS
1. Crossley (1986), p.47, observes:

> Under the terror of the Martian occupation in Book II, *Homo sapiens* is often likened to rabbits, ants, and rats. All are animals we often think of in social terms, in dense throngs breeding and multiplying, panicky and confused when their community is violated. But each species also has its distinctive resonance for us: rabbits are timid, ants are puny, rats are nasty. The associations are not flattering to their human analogues in Book II.

Crossley is right except that the narrator takes heart from the little frogs' "stout resolve to live" (p.170). Humanity and lower organisms are compared throughout *W W*: to dodos (p.73), microbes (p.51), deer (p.64: see I.5.1), sheep (p.70), cattle (p.79), frogs (p.100), bees (p.117) wasps (p.119), rabbits (pp.150, 165, 174), rats (pp.169, 175), ants (pp.172, 188), sparrows (p.172), and oxen (p.173). The Martians may represent our future, but lower organisms represent our Darwinian heritage. As regards herd psychology, see I.5.1.

2. Gibbons (1984), p.6, suggests that this is a possible echo of Luke 22: 44: "and his sweat was as it were great drops of blood falling down to the ground."

3. Recalling the Time Traveller's limp. See further Harry M. Geduld, ed., *The Definitive Time Machine* (1987), p.111, n.13.

4. Festering, corrupting. McConnell (1977), p.265, notes: "This is an instance of 'foreshadowing' in the classic tradition of the Victorian novel. The death of the red Martian weed is our first hint that the invasion of the Martians themselves may be doomed to failure through the same 'natural' processes." But see II.2.11.

5. See p.187 and II.9.1.

II.7. THE MAN ON PUTNEY HILL
1. Bergonzi (1961), p.138, observes:

> It is significant that the chapter in which the Artilleryman appears is lacking in the serialized version of the novel [i.e., *Pearson's* lacks Book II, Chapter VII, and Chapter VIII, para.1–5], and so presumably was deliberately inserted by Wells before the novel appeared in permanent form. [See above, "Gestation," in the Introduction.] Nor can there be any doubt that the Artilleryman's views are those of Wells himself, or at least that they are based on ideas which Wells was prepared to consider very seriously, if in a speculative fashion. For evidence, one can turn to some passages in an essay on Gissing that Wells published in August 1897, when *The War of the Worlds* was being serialized. There he speaks of "a change that is sweeping over the minds of thousands of educated men. It is the discovery of the insufficiency of the cultivated life and its necessary insincerities; it is a return to the essential, to honourable struggle as the epic factor in life, to children as the matter of morality and the sanction of the securities of civilization." The deliberate introduction of these ideas in *The War of the Worlds* is, as it were, the thin end of the didactic wedge that within a few years was to transform Wells from an artist into a prophet. But in the context of the narrative Wells ironically redresses the balance by making his narrator perceive, within a few pages, that the Artilleryman is a complete idler who has neither the intention nor the ability to put his plans into effect.

See also II.7.10,11, and 19.

2. An allusion to the concept associated with *mens rea* (the guilty mind): that crime is defined not as any illegal action but as illegal action based on premeditation.

3. Crossley (1986), pp.47–48, comments on this passage: "*The War of the Worlds* is too complex a text to be reduced to a . . . 'message,' but one lesson that impresses itself on the philosophic narrator is his new conviction that man is not lord of creation but 'an inferior animal.' "

4. McConnell (1977), p.269, maintains that this sentence has autobiographical significance: i.e., it relates to Wells's sudden determination to recover from what was diagnosed as tuberculosis, which afflicted him during 1888: "It was after this resolution to live that . . . he began his career as a writer."

5. McCarthy (1986), p.48, takes issue with McConnell's description of the artilleryman as "a clownish version of the Nietzschean superman" (see McConnell [1981], p.140). McCarthy states: "although *Thus Spake Zarathustra* appeared in English translation in 1896, there is no clear evidence that . . . Wells . . . read Nietzsche at the time. In any case . . . [he] could have derived the same ideas from other sources." In support of his position, McCarthy cites David S. Thatcher, *Nietzsche in England, 1890–1914* (Toronto: University of Toronto Press, 1970), p.82: "Nietzschean motifs appear in Wells's work long before Nietzsche was available in English—certainly before his ideas began to make themselves felt." Bergonzi (1961), p.134, regards Dr. Moreau in *The Island of Dr. Moreau* (1896), Griffin in *The Invisible Man* (1897), and the Martians in *W W* as protagonists manifesting a Nietzschean rebellion against conventional science and morality.

6. McConnell (1977), p.271, notes that by this time the Martians have lost *more* than one tripod (see I.17) although neither the narrator nor the artilleryman is aware of that fact.

7. Lucian's *Icaromennipus* (the source of the epigraph of *The First Men in the Moon*), provides an analogue here:

> I suppose you have often seen a swarm of ants, in which some are huddling together about the mouth of the hole and transacting affairs of state . . . some are going out and others are going back again into the city; one is carrying out the dung, and another has caught up the skin of a bean . . . and no doubt there are among them . . . builders, politicians, aldermen, musicians, and philosophers. But however that may be, the cities with their population resembled nothing so much as anthills. [*Lucian*, edited by Austin M. Harmon (1929), II, p.301.]

8. Thomas Hobbes seems to be echoed. See above, Introduction, p.161.

9. The scene is reminiscent of early Christians awaiting martyrdom in the Roman arena. See I.1.5.

10. Glossing an exclamation of Dr. Moreau—"Bah! What is your theologian's ecstacy but Mahomet's houri in the dark?" (Chapter 14)—Robert Philmus says in his forthcoming edition of *The Island of Dr. Moreau*:

> [B]y Moreau's sentence, Wells seems to be suggesting that the only difference between this Muslim vision of heaven [the promised garden of sensual delights for true believers] and its Christian counterpart ("the theologian's ecstacy") is that the latter obscures or disguises the kind of pleasurable satisfaction involved (hence "in the dark").

The artilleryman agrees—in clearer terms than Moreau's. Both speak for Wells regarding religio-eroticism. See II.7.1 and 19.

11. The artilleryman's idea that weaklings will and should die to purify the race is prominent in "A Story of the Days to Come," where Bindon, man of pleasure, elects a sybaritic death to end bodily pain brought on by his debauchery: he telephones the Euthanasia Company (see *Tales of Space and Time* [1899]). Here and in *When the Sleeper Wakes* (1899), Wells views (sexual) pleasure pursued for its own sake as a biological vent that eliminates unfit stock. Likewise, in *Anticipations*

(1901), p.149, he predicts a time when "the pleasure-seeker will be seeking such pleasure as he pleases, no longer debased by furtiveness and innuendo, going his primrose path to a congenial, picturesque, happy, and highly desirable extinction." See II.7.1 and 19.

12. Wells's father, Joseph, had been a skillful professional cricketer. See EA, p.41.

13. Nineteenth-century Cockney slang for bad or watery beer. In the context of the novel the word is used figuratively—so that the expression "poetry swipes" signifies something like "drippy poetry."

14. This sentence was possibly the inspiration for Ray Bradbury's novel *Fahrenheit 451* (1950), in which people living in a future when all books are destroyed by government decree manage to preserve the culture of the past by memorizing the most important works.

15. The script of the Orson Welles broadcast aptly interpolates, " 'We'd turn it on Martians, we'd turn it on men.' " See Hadley Cantril, *The Invasion from Mars* (1940), p.40.

16. Wells considered calling the chapter "The Lair of the Man on Putney Hill," but canceled and replaced it with the present title in manuscript (Illinois *W W* 47).

17. Parrinder (1981), p.35, identifies this as Lambeth Palace, London, official residence of the Archbishop of Canterbury.

18. The "red creeper" and the "red weed" are different growths (see p.151).

19. Piccadilly Circus in London is like Times Square in New York. Some months before composing the artilleryman episode, Wells reviewed Richard Le Gallienne's *Quest of the Golden Girl* (1896), quoting the phrase "the Venusberg of Piccadilly" (*Saturday Review* 83 [6 March 1897]:249–250; reprinted in Parrinder and Philmus [1983]). The passage Wells had in mind is: "The Venusberg of Piccadilly looked white as a nun with snow and moonlight, but the melancholy music of pleasure, and the sad daughters of joy, seemed not to heed the cold. For another hour death and pleasure would dance there beneath the electric lights" (*Golden Girl*, p.294). Wells disliked Le Gallienne's worship of sexual interludes and ignoring of "the manifest fact that sexual affairs primarily concern children"—concern the future of the species. The apocalyptic tripod makes the point simply by standing over Piccadilly's heedless dance.

Similarly, in *The Food of the Gods* (1904), p.256, a giant whose race will inherit the earth walks into London, city of little folk, and stands staring at Piccadilly, but "none . . . seemed to feel the shadow of that giant's need, that shadow of the future, that lay athwart their paths."

In the world of *When the Sleeper Wakes* (1899), pp.242, 396, 418, "Venusberg" and Le Gallienne are linked to the customary end of lives of pleasure, namely, a self-selected pleasure-death. Of course, Wells himself soon launched into love-making, with and without offspring (see his *H. G. Wells in Love* [1987]). The sin of Le Gallienne was being an aesthete. In an earlier review, Wells had likened him (very much as the artilleryman might) to "that instructive type of civilised security, the tame rabbit. . . . If I am sold, what of it? The lettuce grows in France" (a country Le Gallienne wished might conquer and civilize the English). *Saturday Review* 82 (August 1, 1896):113–114. See II.7.1, 10, and 11.

20. British wine, regarded as inferior to French burgundy.

21. Gambled for the parishes (or districts) of London instead of using money.

22. In euchre the joker may be used as the highest-ranking card. The player who gets the joker is thus able to take any trick.

23. Parrinder (1970), p.30, comments: "The Artilleryman is . . . shown up as a braggart and drunkard, but he clearly points to the values which Wells himself invests in the Martians."

24. Anne B. Simpson argues that the narrator and the artilleryman are much alike. The narrator—a consenting partner in the artilleryman's "fascist fantasy"—leaves only because of the artilleryman's inaction: because of "the Other's failure to act out the narrator's desires" (*Extrapolation* 31/2 [Summer 1990]:142).

II.8. DEAD LONDON

1. On Sundays stores and businesses in the City of London (see Glossary) are closed, and as the area is largely nonresidential, few people are to be seen.

2. The Time Traveller actually *does* break into the Palace of Green Porcelain (*The Time Machine*, Chapter 8), described as a kind of Natural History Museum of the year 802,701.

3. The drunken man who is black as a sweep and the dead woman with the magnum of champagne. Wells added the statement that she is dead in revising the serial (Illinois *W W* 91) and evidently forgot to drop the mention of her here.

4. Crossley (1986), p.49, remarks:

[O]ne of the ironies of the ending of *The War of the Worlds* is that the dying ululation of the last Martian on Earth is far more moving than the narrator's return to Woking and reunion with his lost wife. (It would be convenient to believe Wells intended this irony, but the effect more likely has something to do with his usual inability to create female characters or to represent marital love convincingly.) The haunting, thoroughly alien death-wail the narrator repeatedly hears piercing the silence of London . . . has the conviction of truth, signaling tragic overreaching on the Martians' part.

Huntington (1982), p.63, similarly concludes: "the machinery of decline and fall that has been set up and which we have been led to anticipate to be designed for humanity, comes down on the Martians; the tragedy of the novel is theirs."

5. See Judges 13–16.

6. This allusive-sounding, pietistic phrase is apparently Wells's coinage.

7. Gibbons (1984), p.6, notes: "London has become, perhaps, 'Golgotha, that is to say, a place of a skull' (Matthew 27: 33)."

8. Kathryn Hume (1983), pp.288–89, comments:

The sexual symbolism of the story's end is . . . striking. As the narrator achieves a view of London by climbing Primrose Hill, he sees "the great Mother of Cities," whose "naked clearness and beauty" are revealed, now that she is not "veiled in her sombre robes of smoke" [II.8]. In an impact crater on that hill are the Martians, struck dead as if in the very act of violation. And on that same hill, the narrator experiences his epiphanic moment of ecstasy in a high place, and so great is his emotion that his conscious and rational faculties blank out for three days thereafter. Psychologically, the narrator achieves an interesting victory. The threatening father-monsters are killed off, and since he is not responsible for their destruction, he need not feel direct guilt. Furthermore, he regains the mother.

Freudian interpretations of *W W* are scarce. Another Freudian essay is cited in I.13.5.

9. Cf. "Great birds that fought and tore," the final sentence of Wells's short story "A Dream of Armageddon" (1901).

10. Draper (1987), p.51, comments that the narrator's

pronouncements recall similar remarks on the will of God in Defoe's *Journal of the Plague Year*, one of Wells's models, but in Wells's book pious observations have a hollow sound. After all, the explanation of the Martians' failure is persuasive because it deals solely with material causation, while his assumption that God takes an active interest in the survival of the human race carries little weight in the light of God's apparent indifference to individual human suffering and to the survival of the Martians, who must also be His creations. The effective world view of the book is of a universe in which good and evil are relative, depending on your ecological position.

J. O. Bailey, in *Pilgrims Through Space and Time* (1972), p.246, credits Percy Gregg's *Across the Zodiac* (1880) as "the first book to suggest that an invasion may be repelled through the use of bacteria," adding that "apparently Wells made use of this suggestion" in *W W* and *Men Like Gods*. However, there is no evidence that Wells read Gregg.

11. Cf. Abraham Lincoln's Gettysburg Address (1863): "We here highly resolve that these dead shall not have died in vain."

12. In a single night, in answer to the prayers of the Israelites, God destroyed the Assyrian army led by King Sennacherib (II Kings 19: 35–37). This is the subject of Byron's celebrated poem "The Destruction of Sennacherib." Gibbons (1984) rather simplistically suggests that, like his narrator, Wells by implication takes the Book of Revelation for text (see, e.g., I.11.2, I.12.6). Similarly, W. M. S. Russell calls the adversary of the diabolical Martians "an old god of earth, namely Jehova [sic], who sends the bacteria to destroy them" ("Folktales and H. G. Wells," *Wellsian* 5 [Summer 1982]:9). Such interpretations, taken alone, seem to deny Darwinian evolution as primary.

13. On surrendering to the U.S. cavalry in 1877, Chief Joseph of the Nez Perce Indians, said: "I am tired of fighting. Our chiefs are killed. . . . From where the sun now stands I will fight no more forever." McConnell (1977), p.290, comments:

> Wells, by associating the tragic dignity of Chief Joseph's language with the now-defeated Martian invader, achieves a striking reversal of emotion. For we now understand that it is the Martians . . . who are the truly pitiable, foredoomed losers of this war of worlds. . . .

This is farfetched. In McConnell's "schools" text, the sentence ends with "for ever," but even on that basis, McConnell's "reversal" belongs to the Vietnam era, when "I Will Fight No More Forever" became a catchword (even a book and film title). But the Nez Perce in Wells's day were unsung, and he would not deal in such an obscure allusion.

14. Crossley (1986), p.49 comments:

> Perhaps we are to see the spirituality of [Book II] chapters 8 and 9 as a momentary lapse into primitive feelings under stress. Or, perhaps, that episode demonstrates the viability of the Judeo-Christian tradition in providing myths to explain the inexplicable and a language for coming to terms with events so massive or overwhelming or horrible that they are otherwise unspeakable.

II.9. WRECKAGE

1. In "On Extinction," Wells wrote:

> Hood, who sometimes rose abruptly out of the most mechanical punning to sublime heights, wrote a travesty, grotesquely fearful, of Campbell's "The Last Man." In this he probably hit upon the most terrible thing that man can conceive as happening to man: the earth desert through a pestilence, and two men, and then one man, looking extinction in the face. [*Chambers's Journal of Popular Literature, Science and Art* X, 5th series (September 1893):624; reprinted in Philmus and Hughes (1975).]

Hood writes in "The Last Man," in *Selected Poems of Thomas Hood*, edited by John Clubbe (1970), p.139:

> So there he hung and there I stood
> The LAST MAN left alive,
> To have my own will of all the earth:
> Quoth I, now shall I thrive!
> But when was ever honey made
> With one bee in a hive!

Wells evidently relished Hood's blustering, humorous parody of Thomas Campbell's solemn quasi-religious verses of the same title.

2. London's first popular halfpenny morning newspaper, established by Alfred Harmsworth (Lord Northcliffe) in 1896. Its circulation in the 1890s was over a million copies a day. The paper introduced yellow-press journalism to Britain.

3. Repeated stereotype advertising. Newspaper advertising in the late nineteenth century frequently took the form of patterned repetitions of the same slogans.

4. The north side, i.e., the side nearer Horsell Common.

5. The narrator says he is "a professed and recognised writer on philosophical themes" (p.175) and has already mentioned his interrupted paper on civilization and morality (p.55). Ironically, his chronicle of the invasion replaces or nullifies his paper, and Wells evidently thought best to let the irony speak for itself. In revising the serial version, he added, but then cancelled: "Morals and civilization indeed! I had some new lights now—" (see Illinois *W W*, 99). For Wells, the joke no doubt included his just having made a serious forecast of morals and civilization along the optimistic lines for which he would soon be famous, starting with *Anticipations* (1901). The article "Morals and Civilisation" was accepted by *Fortnightly Review* on December 9, 1896 (see EA, 473) and published in February 1897; it was reprinted in Philmus and Hughes (1975).

6. See I.2., final paragraph.

7. Crossley (1986), p.49, calls the scene "stale with banality.... A made-for-TV movie could have done no worse."

II.10. THE EPILOGUE

1. The name Carver has not been traced. See II.10.5.

2. This contradicts the earlier statement (see I.15.8) that the Black Smoke contained "an unknown element giving a group of four lines in the blue of the spectrum." A certain carelessness in this final chapter probably reflects Wells's changing intentions regarding its publication (see above, Introduction, pp.5–6). For argon, see I.7.5 and I.15.8. Actually, argon, as an inert gas, cannot combine with another element to form a compound.

3. McCarthy (1986), p.55, comments:

> [T]he invasion from Mars is remarkably like the process of a disease: the narrator tells us that another invasion is always possible, even though the microbes on our planet have destroyed the invaders. The process here, however, is that of successful resistance to disease (the microbes are our planet's antibodies) and the development of immunity: we are now on guard against the Martians.

See also David Y. Hughes, "The Garden in Wells's Early Science Fiction," in Suvin and Philmus (1977), pp.60–63.

4. Mars and Earth are in (superior) conjunction, and farthest from each other, when they are lined up with the sun between them; they are in opposition, and closest to each other, when they are lined up with Earth between Mars and the sun.

5. The name Lessing has not been traced. Wells shrewdly mixes real names, like Denning (I.2.3), with fictitious ones; and the latter may be well known—hence subliminally more believable—as with "Lessing" here, "Garrick" (p.128), and "Markham" (p.55)—names displaced from their actual fields.

6. These sinuous markings are evidently signals. The first occurs on Venus and signals Mars that the Martian invasion of Venus is under way, and the response, occurring on Mars, appears immediately after ("dark" presumably because the signal flare makes a dark mark on a photographic plate).

7. Cf. Prendick's new perceptions of his fellow-Londoners in *The Island of Dr. Moreau* (1896), Chapter 22.

8. Crossley (1986), p.50, comments that the narrator

ominously . . . observes sightseers on Primrose Hill come to gawk at the tripod that still stands there. . . . Human beings resume their lives, as before. . . . History slides toward the museum; horror becomes a tourist attraction. The descendants of the survivors are in peril of losing the indispensable lesson of the Martian invasion announced in the book's first sentence.

Crossley's words seem particularly topical to one of the present editors, a survivor of the London Blitz, who recently stood in line with his wife and young son in order to experience a simulated air raid, created at great expense and presented as a "show" (with paid admission) in London's Imperial War Museum.

GLOSSARY OF PLACES
MENTIONED IN THE TEXT

> Wells . . . explicitly linked his destructive fantasies
> with his keen topographical sense—a link that he
> made repeatedly in his scientific romances.
> —Norman and Jeanne Mackenzie

All distances relating to central London are measured from Charing Cross.

ADDLESTONE. A village in Surrey, about four miles north of Woking.

ALBANY STREET BARRACKS. Army barracks on the east side of Regent's Park in central London.

ALBERT HALL. In full: The Royal Albert Hall. A huge enclosed amphitheater in the Italian Renaissance style in South Kensington, London. It was constructed in 1867–71, mainly as a concert hall and is still regularly used for that purpose.

ALBERT ROAD. A large thoroughfare north of Regent's Park in central London. Also known as Prince Albert Road.

ALBERT TERRACE. A street linking Regent's Park Road and Albert Road, north of Regent's Park in central London.

ALDERSHOT. Since 1855 an important garrison town in Hampshire, thirty miles southwest of London and about ten miles west of Woking, Surrey.

BAKER STREET. An important thoroughfare in London's West End area. The (fictitious) home of Sherlock Holmes was at 221B Baker Street.

BANSTEAD. A town in Surrey three miles east of Epsom and eighteen miles east of Woking. It is the possible location of the Palace of Green Porcelain in *The Time Machine* (see Chapter 6 of that novel).

BARNES. A district of greater London south of the Thames, between Putney (on the east) and Mortlake (on the west), and about six miles west-southwest of central London.

BARNET (Chipping Barnet, East Barnet, High Barnet, New Barnet). Towns in South Hertford, all about eight to ten miles north-northwest of central London.

BERKSHIRE. A county of southern England bordered by Oxford and Buckingham (on the north), Gloucester (on the northwest), Hampshire (on the south), Surrey (on the southeast), and Wiltshire (on the west).

BIRMINGHAM. England's second largest city, in northwest Warwick, about 110 miles northwest of London.

BLACKFRIARS BRIDGE. A bridge in central London between Waterloo Bridge and Southwark Bridge. It spans the Thames from Queen Victoria Street (on the north) to Southwark Street (on the south).

BLACKWATER. A river about forty miles long in the south of England. It flows from Saffron Walden to Mersea Island, where it enters the North Sea.

BROADSTAIRS. A coastal town in northeast Kent, on the English Channel, about seventy miles east-southeast of central London.

BROMPTON ROAD. A thoroughfare in South Kensington (West London), linking Fulham Road with Knightsbridge.

BYFLEET. A village in Surrey, about three miles east-northeast of Woking.

BYFLEET GOLF LINKS. Located about three-quarters of a mile east of central Woking. Now known as West Byfleet Golf Course.

BYFLEET STATION. Located about two and a half miles northeast of central Woking and about one mile east of Horsell Common.

CHALK FARM STATION. In the 1890s this was a busy station on the London and North-Western Railway (terminus Euston), at the junction of Adelaide Road and Haverstock Hill, immediately north of Primrose Hill in central London.

CHATHAM. A town in north Kent and the site of an important naval base. It is on the river Medway, about thirty miles east-southeast of London.

CHELMSFORD. A small town in central Essex, about twenty-five miles east-northeast of London.

CHERTSEY. A small town about three miles north of Woking, Surrey.

CHIPPING ONGAR. A small town in west Essex about sixteen miles north-northeast of London.

CHOBHAM. A village about three and a half miles northwest of Woking, Surrey. To the southeast it borders on Horsell Common, where the first cylinder landed.

CHOBHAM BRIDGE. A river bridge about three miles northwest of Woking Station, Woking, Surrey.

CHOBHAM ROAD. A thoroughfare bordering the north side of Horsell Common, located about a mile and a half north of Woking, Surrey.

CHURCH COBHAM. Part of Cobham, see below.

CITY, THE. London's commercial and financial center, north of the Thames between the Temple (on the west) and Aldgate Pump (on the east). The Bank of England and the Royal Exchange are situated in The City.

CLACTON. Correct: Clacton-on-Sea. A resort town on the North Sea, about eighty miles northeast of London.

CLAPHAM. A working-class district of south London, about a mile and a half south of the city center.

CLAPHAM JUNCTION. South London's major railroad intersection, southeast of Wandsworth Bridge. In the 1890s Clapham Junction was the key exchange point for the South-Western Railway.

CLOCK TOWER. St. Stephen's Tower, which contains the great clock of the Houses of Parliament. The clock's great bell is popularly known as Big Ben, after Sir Benjamin Hall, Commissioner of Works at the time of the Tower's erection.

COBHAM. A small town about five miles east of Woking, Surrey.

COLCHESTER. A town in northeast Sussex, on the river Colne, about seventy miles northeast of central London.

COOMBE. Now mainly a golf course, the area is just to the south of Richmond Park, about eleven miles south of central London. In the 1890s Coombe was a rural area with a farm belonging to Lord Archibald Campbell. Wells refers to Coombe (as Combe Wood) in Chapter 6 of *The Time Machine*.

CREWE. A major railroad center in the Midlands of England, in south-central Cheshire, about twenty-six miles south-southwest of Manchester.

CROUCH. A river in Essex about twenty-four miles long. It flows from Brentwood to Foulness Point, where it enters the North Sea.

CRYSTAL PALACE. A Victorian exhibition center constructed (in 1854 by Sir John Paxton) of glass and iron. It was originally used to showcase materials from the Great Exhibition of 1851. The Palace, which burned in the 1930s, was in Sydenham in southeast London, about eight miles from the city center.

DEAL. A resort town in Eastern Kent, about seven miles from Dover and sixty-eight miles east-southeast of central London.

DITTON. A small town in central Kent, about four miles northwest of Maidstone.

EALING. A London borough in the county of Middlesex, some eight miles west of the city center.

EAST HAM. London district in the county of Essex, about seven miles east of the city center.

EDGWARE. A suburban area of greater London, in Middlesex, about seven miles north-west of the city center.

EPPING. A small town in west Essex, at the edge of Epping Forest, about twelve miles north-northeast of central London.

EPSOM. A small town in north-central Surrey, about thirteen miles east of Woking and fourteen miles southwest of central London.

EPSOM DOWNS. On the edge of Epsom; the Derby (horse race) is held here each year.

ESHER. A small town in northeast Surrey, fifteen miles southwest of London.

ESSEX. A county of southeast England bordered by Cambridge and Suffolk (on the north), the river Thames (on the south), London (on the southwest), and the North Sea, Middlesex, and Hertford (on the east).

ESSEX COAST. The North Sea coastline of the county of Essex, northeast of London.

EUSTON. Euston Square (railroad) Station. In the 1890s this was the terminus of the (now defunct) London and North-Western Railway, serving the Midlands and Wales.

EXHIBITION ROAD. A spacious thoroughfare in South Kensington, London. Location of the Imperial College of Science, formerly the Normal School of Science (part of the University of London), where Wells studied under Thomas Henry Huxley.

FLEET STREET. A famous central London thoroughfare linking Ludgate Circus and The Strand. Until 1988 it was the home of many of London's most important newspapers. During Wells's lifetime "Fleet Street" was a term synonymous with the British press.

FOULNESS. An island at the mouth of the river Crouch in southeast Essex, about six miles northeast of Shoeburyness and forty-five miles east of London. The island is about five miles long and three miles wide.

FOUNDLING HOSPITAL. Popular misnomer for a home (since 1760) for illegitimate children. Sunday services in the chapel were attractive to the public because of the Hospital's children's choir.

FULHAM. A district of West London, located just north of the Thames and south of Hammersmith, about four miles from the city center.

GREAT NORTH ROAD. A major highway leading from London to the north of England.

GUILDFORD. A town in west-central Surrey, on the river Wey, about twenty-five miles southwest of central London.

HADLEY. A town in South Hertford, about ten miles north of central London.

HAGGERSTON. A tough, working-class district in north London, north of Bethnal Green and east of Shoreditch.

HALLIFORD. See Upper Halliford.

HAM. A district in north Surrey, about two miles northwest of Kingston-on-Thames.

HAMMERSMITH. A west London borough just north of the Thames between Kensington (on the east) and Chiswick (on the west) about four miles from the city center.

HAMPSTEAD. A hilly northwest London suburb, about five miles from the city center. From its highest point, on Hampstead Heath, it offers a magnificent vista of London.

HAMPTON COURT. A district in Middlesex, on the Thames, eleven miles southwest of London. Hampton Court Palace was built in 1515 by Cardinal Wolsey.

HANWELL. A suburban area in Middlesex, about seven miles west of central London.

HARROW ROAD. A main thoroughfare of northwest London, north of Hammersmith and south of Willesden.

HARWICH. A North Sea port in northeast Essex, at the confluence of the rivers Stour and Orwell, about seventy miles northeast of London.

HIGHGATE. A district of north London, on a hill below Hampstead Heath (see Hampstead). One of the most picturesque parts of London, it was (in the 1890s) and still is an area of many fine houses.

HOME COUNTIES. The counties nearest London: Middlesex, Surrey, Kent, and Essex. Sussex and Hertford are sometimes included.

HORSELL. Northern sector of Woking, Surrey.

HORSELL BRIDGE. A canal bridge near the center of Woking.

HORSELL COMMON. Recreational area immediately north of Woking, Surrey, where the first cylinder landed.

HOUNSLOW. A suburban area of Middlesex, about ten miles west of central London.

HOXTON. A tough, working-class district in north London, between Shoreditch and Haggerston, about two miles northeast of Charing Cross in central London.

HYDE PARK. London's most famous park, about a mile north of the Thames at Chelsea Bridge.

IMPERIAL INSTITUTE. On Exhibition Road, South Kensington, London. It was opened in 1893 as an exhibition center displaying raw materials and manufactured products that represented the commercial, industrial, and agricultural progress of the British Empire.

ISLEWORTH. Residential district of greater London, just east of Kew Gardens, about eight miles west-southwest of the center of the city.

KENSINGTON GARDENS. A celebrated park in central London, an extension of Hyde Park, about a mile north of the Thames.

KEW. Residential district in Richmond, northeast Surrey, on the Thames, about eight miles west of central London. It is the site of Kew Gardens (the Royal Botanical Gardens), with its famous Pagoda.

KILBURN. A northwest London district between Hampstead (on the north) and Paddington (on the south), about three and a half miles northwest of central London.

KINGSTON. Usually called Kingston-on-Thames. A municipal borough in northeast Surrey, about nine miles southwest of central London.

KNAPHILL. A village about three miles due west of Woking, Surrey.

LALEHAM. A small town in Middlesex, near Staines, about seventeen miles west-southwest of central London.

LAMBETH. A metropolitan borough of London, on the south bank of the Thames. Waterloo Station, key exit point for southwest England, is located in this borough.

LANGHAM HOTEL. A large, modern (in the 1890s) hotel on Portland Place, in central London, between Marylebone Road and Langham Place.

LEATHERHEAD. A town in central Surrey, about twelve miles due east of Woking (see opening sentence of I.10). It is sixteen miles southwest of central London, on the river Mole.

LIMEHOUSE. A tough, working-class district in London's East End. It is north of Commercial Road and East India Dock Road, about five miles east of Charing Cross.

MALDEN. A suburban district in north Surrey, about nine miles southwest of central London.

MALDON. A town in east-central Essex, on the river Blackwater, about thirty-three miles east of central London. At Maldon the river Chelmer flows into the Blackwater.

MARBLE ARCH. A triumphal stone arch (designed in 1828 by John Nash) in central London, at the northeast corner of Hyde Park.

MARYLEBONE ROAD. A busy central-London thoroughfare, south of Regent's Park, between Lisson Grove (on the west) and Baker Street (on the east).

MAYBURY. Eastern sector of the town of Woking, Surrey. The location of the narrator's house and also of Wells's home at the time of the writing of *WW*. In *Experiment in Autobiography* Wells describes that home as "a small resolute semi-detached villa with a minute greenhouse in the Maybury Road facing the railway line." Maybury Road extends northeast from Woking Station and runs parallel to the railroad track. Although it is greatly altered, Wells's house still stands, located on low ground and facing a high railroad embankment—so that (unlike the narrator's house) no views are possible from it. Horsell Common is approximately half a mile north of Maybury Road.

MAYBURY ARCH. A railroad bridge about three-quarters of a mile northeast of Woking Station.

MAYBURY HILL. A street that extends south, at almost a right angle, from the northeast end of Maybury Road. (See Maybury.)

MERROW. A small town in central Surrey, two miles east-northeast of Guildford and about five miles south of Woking.

MIDDLESEX. A major residential district that forms a sizeable part of London's metropolitan area. It borders Essex and London (on the east), Surrey (on the south), Hertford (on the north), and Buckingham (on the west).

MIDLAND COUNTIES. An area of central England embracing the counties of Bedford, Buckingham, Derby, Leicester, Northampton, Nottingham, Rutland, and Warwick.

MOLE. A river in Surrey that flows northwest from the boundaries of Kent and Sussex to the Thames near Thames Ditton. It is about ten miles from Woking at its nearest point.

MORTLAKE. Now part of greater London; in the 1890s it was a small rural parish in north Surrey, about six miles west-southwest of central London.

NATURAL HISTORY MUSEUM. Britain's major museum of natural history. It is south of the Imperial Institute and the Imperial College of Science (formerly the Normal School of Science), at the Corner of Exhibition Road and Cromwell Road, South Kensington.

NAZE, THE. A promontory on the North Sea coast of Essex, about four miles south of the seaport of Harwich.

NEASDEN. A northwest suburb of greater London, about six miles from the city center. It is now heavily residential but it was quite rural in the 1890s.

NEW MALDEN. A district in north Surrey, about three miles southeast of Kingston-on-Thames and about twelve miles southeast of central London.

OCKHAM. A village in Surrey, about two and a half miles southeast of Woking and five miles northwest of Guildford.

OLD WOKING. Southeast sector of Woking, about a mile from the center of the town.

ORIENTAL COLLEGE. Also known as the Oriental Institute, it was located about half a mile east of Woking Station. The Oriental College comprised the former buildings of the Royal Dramatic College. They were taken over by Gottleib Leitner during the second half of the nineteenth century and converted into a center for distinguished visitors from India. Leitner also built a mosque for Muslim visitors to the College, and this still survives. However, the buildings and land that had formed the Oriental College were sold in 1899 and used for industrial development. A few buildings of the Oriental College still survive as part of a factory complex (the Lion Works) on Oriental Road.

ORIENTAL TERRACE. Not traced. In the 1890s there were an Oriental Place and an Oriental Parade along Maybury Hill, in Woking. Oriental Road now runs parallel to the railroad line and extends about three-quarters of a mile from Woking Station east-northeast to Maybury Hill.

ORPHANAGE. A home for orphaned children alongside the Mosque on Oriental Road, Woking, Surrey. But see *WW*, I.10.7.

OTTERSHAW. A small village about two miles north-northwest of Woking, Surrey, and about three miles from the narrator's home in Maybury. It is the location of Ogilvy's observatory (see Chapter I).

OXFORD STREET. A major shopping thoroughfare in central London, northeast of Hyde Park. It extends east from Marble Arch to Tottenham Court Road.

PAINSHILL PARK. A recreation area in Surrey about six and a half miles east of Woking Station.

PETERSHAM. A suburb of Richmond in north Surrey, about nine miles west-southwest of central London.

POOL OF LONDON. Strictly speaking this refers to the stretch of the river Thames between London Bridge (on the west) and Cuckold's Point (on the east), near West India Dock. But more popularly it has come to signify the area of London below (i.e., east of) London Bridge. Fairly large sea-going vessels have access to the port of London up to this part of the Thames.

PORTLAND PLACE. A wide London thoroughfare, south of Regent's Park, extending south from Park Crescent to Langham Place. Many fashionable homes are located here.

PORTMAN SQUARE. An upper-class area about a quarter of a mile south of Regent's Park. It is adjacent to Baker Street in London's fashionable West End area.

PORTSMOUTH. A town and major naval base on Portsea Island, southeast Hampshire, sixty-three miles southwest of central London.

POTTERIES. A district in the upper Trent Valley, Staffordshire. It embraces the five towns of Hanley, Burslem, Tunstall, Longton, and Stoke-on-Trent. Wells refers to Burslem in the first chapter of *The Time Machine*. Popularly known as the "Five Towns," the Potteries district, in which many of Arnold Bennett's novels are located, has been a center for the manufacture of china and earthenware since the sixteenth century.

PRIMROSE HILL. An eminence north of Regent's Park, with the London Zoo below. It commands an extensive view of London. The seventh cylinder lands there, and the narrator finds the dead Martians there.

PUTNEY. A district of London located immediately south of the Thames, about seven miles west of the city center.

PUTNEY BRIDGE. A Thames bridge linking the districts of Putney (south of the river) and Fulham (north of the river), about three and a half miles from the city center.

PUTNEY HILL. A hilly main road in the district of Wandsworth, about four miles from the center of London.

PYRFORD. A village in Surrey, about three-quarters of a mile east of Woking.

PYRFORD CHURCH. Located at a bend of the River Wey, about two miles east of Woking Station.

REGENT STREET. A major central London thoroughfare renowned for its department stores and fashionable shops. It links Oxford Street and Piccadilly Circus.

REGENT'S CANAL. One of London's key commercial waterways. It begins at the Commercial Docks, Limehouse (east London), runs north to Victoria Park, traverses much of north London, and then links up with the Paddington Canal, which belongs to a network of canals that extend as far north as Liverpool.

REGENT'S PARK. Central London's largest park, containing the London Zoo and the Botanical Gardens. It extends north from Marylebone Road to Primrose Hill; and west from Albany to Grand Union Canal.

RICHMOND. A borough of greater London, on the Thames in north Surrey, about eight miles west-southwest of central London. The home of Wells's Time Traveller was placed here.

RICHMOND PARK. A large recreation area in Richmond.

RIPLEY. A village in Surrey adjoining Send, two and a half miles southeast of Woking and five miles north-northeast of Guildford.

RIPLEY STREET. The High Street or main thoroughfare of Ripley, Surrey.

ROEHAMPTON. A suburb of London, about five miles southwest of the city center.

ROYAL ACADEMY OF ARTS. Located in Burlington House, Piccadilly, in central London. It is famous for its annual exhibitions of new works of art.

ST. ALBANS. A town in south-central Hertford, about twenty miles north-northwest of central London.

ST. EDMUND'S TERRACE. A street in central London, between Regent's Park (on the south) and Primrose Hill (on the north).

ST. GEORGE'S HILL. Located about five miles north-northeast of Woking Station.

ST. JOHN'S WOOD. A middle-to-upper-class residential district northwest of Regent's Park, in north London.

ST. JOHN'S WOOD ROAD. A London thoroughfare west of Regent's Park.

ST. MARTIN'S-LE-GRAND. A street in central London extending north of St. Paul's Cathedral. Its name commemorates a church that was demolished in 1548. In the 1890s, London's General Post Office stood at the southeast corner of St. Martin's-le-Grand.

ST. PANCRAS. A London borough north of the Thames, two miles from the city center. It is the site of Euston and St. Pancras stations, main transit points for northern England and Scotland.

ST. PAUL'S. Sir Christopher Wren's great cathedral. In London, east of Ludgate Hill, one-eighth of a mile north of the Thames at Blackfriars.

SAND PITS. On the east side of Horsell Common, about a mile and a half north of Woking. Ogilvy finds the first Martian cylinder "not far from the sand pits" (I.2.para.3).

SEND. A village about two miles southeast of Woking, Surrey.

SERPENTINE. An artificial lake in Kensington Gardens (see above), used for boating.

SHEEN. A district of greater London south of the Thames, between Richmond (on the west) and Roehampton (on the east), about eight miles west of central London.

SHEPPERTON. A small town in Middlesex, on the Thames near Sunbury, about fourteen miles west-southwest of central London.

SHOEBURY or SHOEBURYNESS. Coastal town at the mouth of the Thames, just east of Southend and thirty-eight miles east of London.

SHOREDITCH. A working-class district in east London, about a mile from the city center.

SOUTHAMPTON. A major seaport in south Hampshire, about seventy miles southwest of London.

SOUTHEND. Fully named Southend-on-Sea. A resort town in southeast Essex at the mouth of the Thames, thirty-three miles east of central London.

SOUTH KENSINGTON. The sector of the west London borough of Kensington due south of Kensington Gardens and Hyde Park. It is the home of many of London's great museums.

STAINES. A town in Middlesex, at the junction of the rivers Colne and Thames, eighteen miles west-southwest of central London.

STANMORE. A small town in Middlesex, about nine miles northwest of the city center. It is now part of greater London but was a rural area in the 1890s.

STRAND, THE. An important thoroughfare in central London. It runs parallel with the Thames (a very short distance away) and extends west from the Aldwych to Trafalgar Square. It is the location of fashionable stores, hotels, theatres, and office buildings.

STREET COBHAM. Part of Cobham. See above.

SUNBURY. A town in Middlesex, known fully as Sunbury-on-Thames, thirteen miles west-southwest of London.

SURREY. A county of southern England bordered by Buckingham, Middlesex, and London (on the north), Berkshire (on the northwest), Kent (on the east), Hampshire (on the west), and Sussex (on the southwest). It is drained by the rivers Thames, Wey, and Mole.

THAMES. England's principal river and London's major waterway. It is about 200 miles long.

THAMES ESTUARY. The tidal mouth of the river Thames, where the fresh river water meets the North Sea; the stretch of the Thames between Tilbury and Gravesend (on the west) and Shoeburyness (on the east).

TILLINGHAM. A small town in Essex, about four miles west of the North Sea and sixty-five miles northeast of central London.

TOWER BRIDGE. London's most famous bridge. It opens periodically to admit the passage of shipping. It spans the Thames between the Tower of London (on the north) and the district of Bermondsey (on the south).

TRAFALGAR SQUARE. Central London's most famous concourse, dedicated to England's naval hero, Lord Nelson (and his victory at Trafalgar in 1805). In the center of the Square there is a granite column, 145 feet tall, crowned with a statue of Nelson.

TWICKENHAM. A London borough in Middlesex, about ten miles west-southwest of the city center.

UPPER HALLIFORD. A district southwest of greater London, between Sunbury and Shepperton, thirteen miles west-southwest of the city center.

VICTORIA. Victoria (Railroad) Station, on Victoria Street, near Buckingham Palace. In the 1890s, the terminus of the London, Chatham, and Dover Railway.

VIRGINIA WATER. A small town in northwest Surrey, eighteen miles west-southwest of central London. It is the site of an artificial lake from which the town takes its name.

WALHAM GREEN. An area of Fulham, just north of the river Thames, about three miles southwest of central London.

WALTHAM ABBEY. A small town on the river Lea, in southwest Essex, bordering Epping Forest. In the 1890s there was an old gunpowder factory in the area; in *WW* Wells refers to it as Waltham Abbey Powder Mills.

WALTON (on the Naze). A town on the North Sea, about seventy-five miles northeast of London.

WALTON (upon Thames). A town in north Surrey, about seven miles northeast of Woking and fourteen miles southwest of central London. It is more generally known as Walton-on-Thames.

WANDLE. A short tributary of the river Thames. It rises south of Merstham and flows through south London into the Thames between Putney Bridge and Wandsworth Bridge.

WATERLOO. Waterloo (railroad) Station, in Waterloo Road, Lambeth. In the 1890s this station was the terminus of the South-Western Railway, which served points in southern England.

WATERLOO BRIDGE. One of central London's major bridges. It spans the Thames from Wellington Street (on the north) to Waterloo Road (on the south).

WATERLOO ROAD. A major thoroughfare in south London, extending south from Waterloo Bridge to St. George's Circus.

WELLINGTON STREET. A road in central London, north of the Thames. It leads from Bow Street to Waterloo Bridge.

WEST HILL. The area immediately south of Epsom railroad station, about two and a half miles south of New Malden and about eleven miles southwest of central London.

WESTBOURNE PARK. A district in the London borough of Kensington, about two and a half miles from the city center.

WESTMINSTER. A central London district bounded on the north by Bayswater Road, on the south by the Thames, and on the west by Chelsea, Kensington, and Brompton. It is the location of the Houses of Parliament.

WESTMINSTER BRIDGE. One of central London's major bridges. It spans the Thames just north of the Houses of Parliament and south of County Hall.

WEY. A river in southern England, about thirty-five miles long. It flows from Hampshire into Surrey at Farnham, then southeast to Godalming, and then north to reach the Thames at Weybridge.

WEYBRIDGE. A north Surrey town about four miles northeast of Woking and seventeen miles southwest of central London.

WIMBLEDON. A district in greater London, in north Surrey, about eight miles southwest of central London. Famous as the home of the All England Lawn Tennis Club—where international tennis tournaments are held annually. The sixth cylinder lands here.

WINCHESTER. A city in southern England, in Hampshire, about sixty miles southwest of London. Famous for its great Cathedral (founded in 1079) and its public school (Britain's oldest).

WINDSOR. A town in east Berkshire, on the Thames about twenty miles west of London. It is the site of Windsor Castle and Eton College.

WOKING. A town in Surrey, about four miles north of Guildford and twenty-three miles southwest of central London.

WOKING STATION. Located in the center of Woking, Surrey.

WOOLWICH. A suburb of greater London, on the south bank of the Thames, about ten miles from central London. It is the site of the Royal Arsenal, Royal Military Academy, and Royal Artillery Barracks.

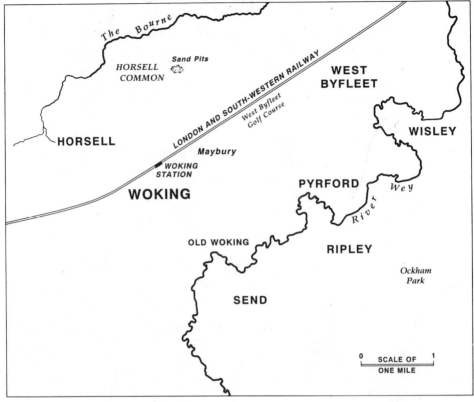

Woking and environs

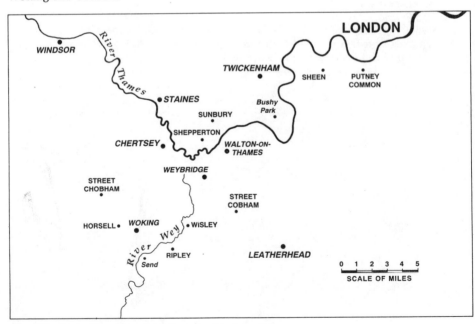

The Thames Valley—focus of the Martian invasion

RADIO AND FILM ADAPTATIONS

The most sensational of all adaptations from literature, Orson Welles's Mercury Theatre radio version of *The War of the Worlds*, was broadcast over CBS on the evening of October 30, 1938. The program has generated volumes of commentary, most notably Hadley Cantril's *The Invasion from Mars* and Howard Koch's *The Panic Broadcast*, both of which contain the script.

The celebrity of this adaptation has far less to do with its source than with the panic it created (and that panic's reflection of the *angst* of the Munich era), with its extraordinary demonstration of the power of radio, with the international fame (notoriety?) it brought to Orson Welles, and with its significance as the major stepping-stone to his Hollywood career and the making of *Citizen Kane*. These extraliterary matters are beyond our present concern. It is the specific nature of Welles's broadcast version that interests us here.

In *Citizen Welles*, Frank Brady provides a succinct account of Welles's working methods with particular relevance to *The War of the Worlds* production. He reveals the fact that although Howard Koch was responsible for the original rough draft of the script, the adaptation in its final form was essentially a collaborative effort supervised by Welles:

> Welles maintained completed control and authority over the content of all his [Mercury Theatre] shows. He alone selected, sometimes after consultation with [John] Houseman and others, the story to be dramatized. Often he had clear ideas of what approach was to be taken, what scenes were to be developed or deleted, which characters were to be highlighted or excised. This was conveyed, usually by direct discussion, sometimes by memorandum, to whoever was responsible for putting the first rough-draft script together . . . . Once the first draft was written, Welles went over it to see how well the story flowed and to see how it *sounded*. . . . Welles gathered his actors around him, passed around copies . . . they read it aloud, changing lines as they went, revising and refining the words until the dialogue sounded like real dialogue. . . . Everyone made suggestions . . . after the first run-through, a second script was prepared, and Welles would work on it, still changing dialogue, shifting scenes, and adding action as he deemed it necessary. It was at this point that he would begin conferring with Paul Deitz, the sound engineer, using the script as guide. . . . Musical bridges and cues had to be added. . . . A preliminary "dress" rehearsal was then held. . . . This rehearsal was meticulously timed, and further paring and honing of the script was done to make it fit into the scheduled time, approximately sixty pages for an hour-long show.

Orson Welles giving a Mercury Theater broadcast. Manuscripts
Department, Lilly Library, Indiana University

A selection of phonograph record jacket illustrations

Cover illustration for *Amazing Stories* serialization of *The War of the Worlds*

In the wake of Wells—the enduring popularity of fiction about Mars and Martians

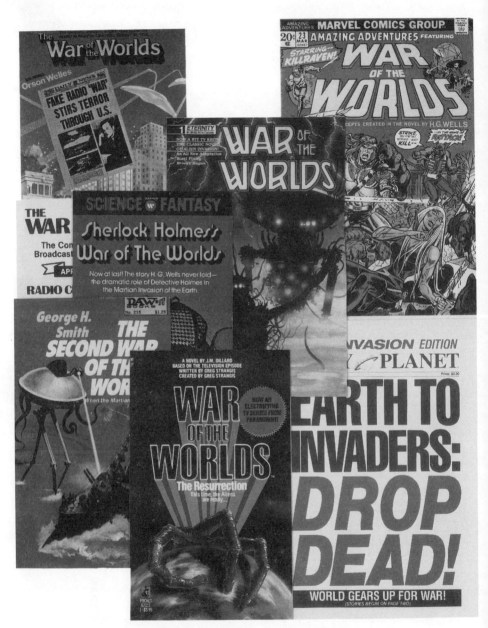

Various spin-offs of *The War of the Worlds*

In *The Panic Broadcast*, Koch claims that he used "practically nothing" from the novel other than Wells's "idea of a Martian invasion and his description of their appearance and their machines." However, while this statement may well have been true of Koch's (unavailable) rough draft, it is clear both from published versions of the scripts (including the one in Koch's book) and from extant sound recordings that the adaptation as originally broadcast was far more indebted to the novel than Koch would have us believe. It is undoubtedly true that the broadcast version was a very free adaptation. The setting was updated to 1938 and relocated to New Jersey and New York City, and with those changes the adaptation inevitably abandoned Wells's satirical onslaughts on Victorian imperialism. At the same time, much of the dialogue and language were modernized and a substantial amount of the narrative was presented in the form of newscasts, interviews, and special bulletins. There are also major plot omissions: neither the brother's narrative nor the main narrator's experiences with the curate are represented in the script, and Wells's anonymous narrator is replaced by an American scientist, a Princeton astronomer named Professor Pierson (Orson Welles). Notwithstanding these differences, the script retained numerous Wellsian "elements," which may be summarized as follows:

1. Direct quotation or paraphrase of the text of the novel, most notably in the script's prologue, in a sequence adapted from Book II, Chapter VII ("The Man on Putney Hill") and in the finale.
2. Details of Mars and astronomical observations of mysterious phenomena on the red planet prior to the invasion.
3. The arrival of the first cylinder and the initial Martian attack.
4. Descriptions of the Martians, their fighting machines, the Heat-Ray, and the Black Smoke.
5. The rapid Martian liquidation of all military resistance.
6. The rout of the civilian population.
7. The isolation of the main narrator, who believes that he is the last man on Earth.
8. His wanderings through a desolate and ruined landscape.
9. His description of a deserted and ruined city.
10. His discovery of the dead Martians.
11. His explanation of their deaths.

These derivative "elements" failed to impress the author of the novel. Wells was deeply incensed by the extensive changes. They must have reminded him of other "liberties" that had aroused his ire forty years earlier: in 1897 and 1898 two American yellow-press journals had published unauthorized versions of the novel, one relocating the action to New York City, the other to Boston (see Appendix II).

In a press conference after the broadcast reporters asked Welles why he substituted the names of American cities and government officers. He justified the changes as the editors of their journals might have done: "H. G. Wells used real cities in Europe, and to make the play more acceptable to American listeners we used real cities in America." If Wells ever heard this explanation, it failed to pacify him. When details of the adaptation and the ensuing panic reached him, he ordered his New York representative, Jacques Chambrun (who had granted permission for the novel to be adapted), to voice his protests to CBS. Chambrun told the network representatives,

> It was not explained to me that this dramatization would be made with a liberty that amounts to a complete rewriting of *The War of the Worlds* and renders it into an entirely different story. Mr. Wells and I consider that by so doing the Columbia Broadcasting System should make a full retraction. Mr. H. G. Wells is personally deeply concerned that any work of his should be used in a way, and with totally unwarranted liberty, to cause deep distress and alarm throughout the United States.

Orson Welles reacted to this statement by praising the novel on the one hand and insisting on the other that the broadcast "constituted a legitimate dramatization of a published work." Wells received an apology and financial compensation from CBS. In his biography of H. G. Wells, David C. Smith comments:

> The use of the book's title (and the transposed plot) was probably simply a misunderstanding. Wells was concerned that the radio show would hurt his message of the period (he had just been lecturing in America, and was on the way to Australia within a month) but in the event his stock was raised by the show, which traded on beginning fears in the US of the German and Japanese menace.

His wrath soon subsided, and H. G. harbored no resentment toward Orson. The two had an unexpected, cordial encounter in Texas in 1940 shortly before Wells published *Babes in the Darkling Wood;* and about a year later, when Welles had become Hollywood's *wunderkind*, H. G. sent him a telegram congratulating him on his masterly new film, *Citizen Kane.*

Hollywood made no immediate attempt to follow Welles's radio version with an adaptation of its own. *The War of the Worlds* was not adapted to the screen until 1954. In retrospect, it is difficult to comprehend Hollywood's prolonged indifference to such an obvious best-seller.

The expense of production and the limitations of film technology have sometimes been given as explanations of this long delay. (They have also, incidentally, been cited as reasons why none of Edgar Rice Burroughs's Martian novels have ever been filmed.) Both explanations are spurious. Expense has seldom been a serious obstacle to production of a "hot" film property. Indeed, it has often been used to advertise the opulence or epic qualities of a production. Similarly, technological difficulties have frequently acted as a spur to movie creativity. The limitations of film technology did not prevent pioneer film-maker Georges Méliès from making *Le Voyage dans la Lune* (France, 1901), a conflation of Verne's *From the Earth to the Moon* (1865) and Wells's *The First Men in the Moon* (1901). Nor did they prevent British film-makers from attempting another version of *The First Men in the Moon* in 1918. Rather the subjects presented challenges which often resulted in developing new film techniques. Méliès, as is widely known, was intrigued with science fiction and fantasy themes, and he made many films that belong to these genres; it is curious that he never turned his talents to an adaptation of *The War of the Worlds*.

Nevertheless, almost from the inception of cinema Mars fascinated film-makers. Although they sidetracked Wells's novel, they kept the red planet in the public eye with one film after another. Perhaps the first was Lubin's *A Trip to Mars* (U.S., 1903), which, despite its title, was merely a pirated version of the Méliès 1901 film. De Chomon's melodramatic *Mars* (France, 1909) also avoided Wells. It was followed by three adaptations of Richard Ganthony's popular play *A Message from Mars* (New Zealand, 1909; Britain, 1913; U.S., 1921) about a benign Martian visiting our planet. From 1909 to the onset of World War II British film-makers tried to warn or terrify the public with movies about invasion scares. The many examples ranged from *England Invaded* (1909) to *Went the Day Well?* (1942). However, the imaginary invaders were usually Germans, never Martians. Whenever their focus actually was on Mars and Martians, the makers of silent films focused not on invasions of Earth but on human voyages to the red planet, on radio communications with aliens, and on Martian civilizations as a satirical commentary on our own. Thus *Heaven Ship* (Denmark, 1917) featured a rocket trip to Mars. *Mars Calling* (U.S., 1923) concentrated on radio, and also pioneered the use of 3-D. *Aelita: The Revolt of the Robots* (U.S.S.R., 1924), based on a story by Alexei Tolstoy, dealt with a Martian uprising that strikingly paralleled another, more-familiar Red Revolution. It is evident that Mars and Martians fascinated movie audiences throughout the silent period; however, by the end of the 1920s there was still no sign that film-makers were interested in adapting the most famous novel on the subject.

However, in the early 1930s Hollywood became seriously interested in the movie potential of H. G. Wells's science fiction. Universal secured rights to *The Invisible Man* and released a highly successful—in terms of the box office—adaptation (directed by James Whale, 1933), which spawned a host of sequels. Paramount took options on *The Island of Dr. Moreau* and *The War of the Worlds*. The first was adapted as *Island of Lost Souls* (directed by Erle C. Kenton, 1932). The second was offered (by Jesse L. Lasky) to the great Soviet director Sergei M. Eisenstein, when he came under contract to the studio in April 1930, but he soon dropped the project and turned to an adaptation of Dreiser's *An American Tragedy*. There is no evidence that Eisenstein scripted any of the Wells novel, but he did complete a brilliant screenplay of Dreiser's book. When Paramount terminated Eisenstein's contract, the Dreiser film was reassigned to director Josef Von Sternberg, who completed it in 1931. The adaptation of *The War of the Worlds* was not passed on to another director, but was shelved. Jay Leyda, in an appendix to Eisenstein's *The Film Sense*, states that the Wells project was abandoned because it was "too costly." If so, this was probably an assessment by Eisenstein rather than by the studio. It may have been an honest opinion, or he may simply have offered Lasky what sounded like a plausible reason for turning down a project that did not interest him. Surely if Paramount considered an adaptation impossibly expensive there was no reason for the studio to continue retaining the rights to the novel.

In the event, the only notable "Martian" film of the 1930s was Universal's low-budget, fifteen-episode serial, *Flash Gordon's Trip to Mars* (U.S., 1937), based on Alex Raymond's comic strip. It ranked among the most popular of the 1930s serials, and through its depiction of hostile Martians was probably a factor in making the American public overly receptive to Orson Welles's 1938 radio adaptation of *The War of the Worlds*. Curiously, Paramount did not capitalize on the sensational broadcast by luring Welles to Hollywood to direct the film adaptation. Sixteen more years would elapse before the studio released a movie version. In the interim, another serial, Republic's fifteen-episode *The Purple Monster Strikes* (U.S., 1945), depicted an invasion from Mars; however, it resembled other serials of the period more than it did Wells's novel.

Thus far, interest in Mars had been sporadic. But in the 1950s Hollywood rediscovered the planet in a big way. The studios responded not to some pre-Sputnik upsurge of interest in astronomy but to McCarthy-era Cold War paranoia. (The terror of Welles's broadcast had stemmed in part from jitters attending the approach of World War II.) Mars and the Martians became obvious metaphors for the U.S.S.R. and foreign and home-grown Communists. It was during this period, in 1954, that the first, and to date only, film adaptation of *The War of the Worlds* appeared, amid a wave of other movies about alien invasions and journeys to the red planet. These included: *Rocketship X-M* (1951), *Flight to Mars* (1951), *Flying Disc Man from Mars* (1951), *Red Planet Mars* (1952), *Abbott and Costello Go to Mars* (1953), *Invaders from Mars* (1953), *The Killers from Space* (1953), *Devil Girl from Mars* (1954), *The Conquest of Space* (1955), *Invasion of the Saucermen* (1957), *It! The Terror from Beyond Space* (1958), *Angry*

Red Planet (1959), *A Martian in Paris* (France, 1960), *The Day Mars Invaded the Earth* (1962), *Mars Needs Women* (1964), *Robinson Crusoe on Mars* (1964), *Mission Mars* (1968), and *Five Million Years to Earth* (Britain, 1968)—the last-mentioned film being by far the most intelligent treatment of the Martian invasion theme, although it owes virtually nothing to Wells's novel.

Like the curate's egg, Paramount's *The War of the Worlds* (directed by Byron Haskin) is good in parts. Unfortunately, those parts have little or nothing to do with Wells's novel. They have to do with the film's technology. The movie's special effects—most notably sequences depicting the Martian fighting machines—seemed masterly in 1954 and are still admirable compared to the state-of-the-art effects in such films of the 1970s and 1980s as *Close Encounters* and *Alien*. It is necessary to add, however, that the film version is a travesty of the novel, not simply because it is blatantly unfaithful to its source. Fidelity is not a *sine qua non* in adaptation. Some of the most creative adaptations take liberties with their source (consider *West Side Story* and *Throne of Blood*), while some of the dullest attempt to be slavishly faithful. If it is to be creative, a free adaptation must either treat the original in a vital, meaningful way or provide a new perspective on the original work. In either case it must not violate the essence of the original or trivialize its themes. Haskin's film does both. It uses the bare bones of Wells's narrative to make a naive pietistic statement about the power of collective faith and prayer. Wells would doubtless have recoiled with horror at this perversion of his work. He would, assuredly, have been even more aghast at the *War of the Worlds* television series—still being broadcast as this edition goes to press—which is a crude spin-off from Haskin's travesty.

Haskin's adaptation updates and relocates the story from late Victorian England to 1950s United States, and Wells's narrator and his brother are replaced by an eager-beaver scientist rather improbably in love with a simple-minded religious librarian who hero-worships him. A brief prologue before the credits contrasts the "crude weapons" of World War I, the "new devices of warfare" in World War II, and the "weapons of super-science" in *The War of the Worlds*. What follows is, of course, a vision of World War III (for *Martians* read *Russians*) in which American super-weaponry (the atom bomb) is tested against the fire power of another superpower and found to be totally inadequate. Equally inadequate is the ingenuity of America's leading scientists (represented by the hero and his colleagues) in their efforts to find the enemy's Achilles heel. Significantly, when they reach the conclusion that it will take the Martians six days to destroy Earth, the heroine responds, "That's exactly how long it took God to create it." Such simple, fundamentalist belief, expressed communally rather than individually, is ultimately revealed to be the only salvation for mankind in the face of the red menace.

Two key scenes underscore this message. In the first the red enemy is shown to be militantly anti-Christian. The army is about to use the Bomb on the invaders when the heroine's uncle intervenes with a plea for conciliation. A benign cleric, he argues that since the Martians are more advanced than man, they must be nearer the Creator. But when he courageously approaches them with a Bible and an upraised crucifix, uttering the words of the 23rd Psalm, they blast him to Kingdom Come. Their violent reaction to his lone missionary appeal—at this point even his religious niece lacks his fearless faith—triggers the maximum fire-power of the U.S. Army. But the Martians prove to be invulnerable to the Bomb. By implication, if America (and the rest of the world) is to be saved it must be through some even greater (i.e., "Higher") power. The second scene occurs at the end of the film. As the Martians converge on Los Angeles, the last city on Earth to be destroyed, the scientist-hero staggers through Armageddon (the enemy's intense bombardment) from one overcrowded church to another in search of the heroine. As he finds her, the film cuts away from the inevitable clinch to shots of stained-glass windows and burning candles, of tranquil families singing hymns and listening to the comforting words of a Billy Graham lookalike. Having witnessed the inefficacy of American strength and ingenuity, the masses have at last turned to God to provide a miraculous salvation. And now, in answer to their prayers, a Martian fighting machine crashes to destruction outside the church. Examining its dead occupant, the scientist declares, "We were all praying for a miracle," and he and the rest of the congregation look heavenwards. Church bells peal. Now a voice-over commentator (the voice of Cedric Hardwicke) utters a paraphrase of Wells's words from "Dead London" (II.8): "After all that men could do had failed, the Martians were destroyed and humanity was saved by the littlest things which God, in his wisdom, had put upon this Earth." A shot of a cathedral towering over the city and the sounds of a choir chanting "Amen" bring to an end the perversion of Wells's story into one of Hollywood's major Cold War sermons.

APPENDIXES

The six appendixes that follow deal with various aspects of *The War of the Worlds*. The first two concern pre-publication and post-publication treatments of the text. Appendix I offers a transcript of the oldest surviving fragment of *The War of the Worlds* manuscript and traces its textual descent by collating it with ten other texts. A previously unpublished segment of the novel is embodied in this transcript. Appendix II describes the "yellow press" piracies of the novel in 1897 and 1898—prior to its publication in book form—which in certain respects anticipated Orson Welles's sensational 1938 radio adaptation. Appendixes III and VI illuminate specific passages in the novel. Appendix III, "Of a Book Unwritten," provides the text of the "prophecy" about man's ultimate physical structure to which the narrator refers in Book II, Chapter II (see II.2.6). The author of this "prophecy," described by the narrator as "a certain speculative writer of quasi-scientific repute," was, of course, Wells. The piece is excerpted from Wells's *Certain Personal Matters* (1898) and is, essentially, the text of his essay "The Man of the Year Million," originally published in the *Pall Mall Gazette* 57 (November 9, 1893). Appendix VI, "A Strange Light on Mars," provides the text of the article in *Nature* mentioned in the first chapter of the novel (see I.1.21). Finally, Appendixes IV and V reveal Wells's thoughts on the possibility of life on Mars in two speculative articles, one written before, the other after the publication of the novel. The first, "Intelligence on Mars," was published in *Saturday Review* 81 (April 4, 1896):345–346, while Wells was writing *The War of the Worlds*. The second, "The Things that Live on Mars," appeared in *Cosmopolitan Magazine* XLIV, n.s. (March 1908):335–342.

APPENDIX I

Transcript and Collation of MS (University of Illinois)

MS, the earliest known fragment of *The War of the Worlds*, is about a sixth the length of the book. As noted in the Introduction, the unique "Marriott" episode is of interest by itself, by contrast to its book replacement, "The Man on Putney Hill," and by the fact that the serial version (now photo-reproduced)[a] does not contain either episode. But MS is of interest also because it corresponds to, and collates readily with, three of the four chapters before "The Epilogue" of the present edition, "Putney Hill" alone excepted. MS was appreciably altered when it was first printed in *Cosmopolitan*, once again in *Pearson's*, sweepingly as part of a complete *Pearson's* paste-up for book publication (with a draft of "Putney Hill," not transcribed here), and slightly in various later editions. But in the big *Pearson's* fix-up, Wells revised the MS chapters no more than he did all the last half of the narrative (hardly altering the first half). Thus, this collation is no substitute for a variorum *The War of the Worlds*, yet, quite aside from "Marriott," it offers the deepest possible core sampling of the growth of the text, as well as illustrating the methods used to produce this edition.

Wells composed in longhand and habitually corrected, canceled, and inserted as he went along, though he might also return to make later alterations. In the "Marriott" portion, the transcription as far as possible records these (instant) changes. The same holds for the rest of MS and the corresponding portion of the *Pearson's* paste-up, but, in addition, the two are collated with the printed texts deriving from them. Among the latter, certain texts encompass revisions that Wells bypassed because they were out of reach when he next revised. All this entails extensive use of diacritical marks (explained below); but "Marriott," the episode doubtless of greatest interest to most readers, is easily readable, free as it is of revision once Wells suppressed it.

The following are the texts used in collating MS. A variorum edition would add only two more, since no text survives of which MS is not partially the basis except "Putney Hill" and a draft of the narrator's brief philosophical speculations on coming home. Since MS is a relatively short segment, the dating, descriptions, and sequence of this list do not always apply to the book as a whole (for which see "Gestation," in the Introduction).

MS Oldest known fragment of *WW*; holograph; c. spring 1896. Chapter I corresponds in the present edition to the last four paragraphs of "The Stillness" and all of "After the Fifteen Days" and ends with the suppressed "Marriott" segment; Chapter II corresponds to "Dead London"; and Chapter III corresponds to "Wreckage." Wells evidently corrected MS in a lost triplicate typescript (requested at the head of MS) first for C, then independently and more fully for P.

C   *Cosmopolitan: A Monthly Illustrated Magazine*, November-December, 1897. Evidently based on a corrected copy of MS's lost typescript. It is not in line of direct evolution of later texts in this collation.

P   *Pearson's Magazine*, November-December, 1897. Evidently based on a corrected copy of MS's lost typescript, like C, but separately, more fully, and departing further from MS.

PP   Proofs of P of October-December 1897, pasted up as the basis of PR. Seemingly Wells finished PR when he had only uncorrected proofs of the last two installments at hand (earlier—before the MS portion—PR is a paste-up of P's pages, not the proofs).

PR   Paste-up of PP, c. fall 1897. The basis of a part of J and all of L and NY, in that order, each evidently corrected separately from a lost typescript requested in triplicate in PR. The text includes the draft of "Putney" (virtually as it is in this edition, which is therefore omitted from the transcript).

J   New York *Evening Journal*, January 3–4, 1898. Evidently based on a copy of PR's lost typescript, but with unauthorized use of New York names. (After "Putney" the *Journal* drops from the collation because it is not based on PR, but on C.)

L   Heinemann, London, late January, 1898. Evidently based on a copy of PR's lost typescript corrected after J and probably independently of it, though differences are few (barring J's New York names).

NY   Harpers, New York, March 1898. Evidently based on the third copy of PR's lost typescript, corrected later than, and probably independently of, L.

AG   A's proofs, c. 1924. Based on NY. (Overall, the Atlantic proofs are based on NY—except for "The Epilogue," which is based on L—and were emended again for the Essex edition. In both cases, changes are generally minor and to an indeterminate extent were made by others, perhaps including Dorothy Richardson.[b]

A   Atlantic edition, 1924. Authorized by Wells. (In general, the Atlantic reflects most of the emendations written into its proofs; only a few were added for the Essex.)

E   Essex edition, 1927. The last text Wells supervised. (The collation records one emendation in AG reflected in E and not in A, and one change in E that is not in AG or anywhere else.)

The following diacritical marks appear in MS, in the textual annotations, or in both:

{ }   Curved brackets in MS enclose text interpolated at any time into MS itself, from single words to pasted-on sheets. Within an annotation,

curved brackets enclose an interpolation made after MS, whether written into PR or AG or simply appearing in print in C, PP, P, J, L, NY,
A, or E. Interpolations within interpolations are further signaled by
italics.

< > Angle brackets in MS enclose text altered after MS; the stage and
alteration are supplied by annotation, but the annotation itself is not
normally bracketed; bracketing, if it occurs, indicates and encloses continuing variation at later stages.

¥ A yen sign in MS signals that text was interpolated there at a later stage;
the stage and interpolation are supplied by annotation.

~~Strike-throughs~~ indicate deletion; deletion within deletion is further signaled
by italics.

<u>Underlining</u> represents absence at a later stage, which is designated paren-
thetically: the underlined is not there or is canceled there (as denoted
by a small "x" after the stage designation).

/ Single slashes / set off doubtful or illegible words, and, in the notes, within
angle brackets, also set off discrete textual variants.

• An end stop after a designated textual span (e.g., C• or P–AG•) signals
that a given deletion, interpolation, or alteration ceases after that span.
Lack of an end stop after a stage of origin signals a permanent change,
reaching through E.

φ A nil sign marks a deleted period in a sentence not itself canceled.

+ A plus sign marks a deleted comma in a sentence not itself canceled.

¶ A paragraph sign marks a canceled paragraph cut. (Wells made paragraph signs as he wrote, occasionally canceling one.)

The use of these marks may be illustrated by examining the heading
of MS, the first two sentences, and the first two textual notes. "After the
Fifteen Days" is underlined, meaning it vanishes at a stage after MS, and
"PR" designates the stage, with a small "x" meaning a cancel. The first
sentence, "Very cautiously I crawled out of my prison," is struck through,
meaning it was deleted in MS. The second sentence, "I looked about me,"
has curved brackets around "me," meaning it is interpolated in MS. But
change continues after MS. In J only, the sentence disappears; hence, it is
underlined, with a "J" and end stop following. Otherwise, the sentence
survives but changes. The angle brackets around "me" (within the curved
brackets) signal the change, and the note stipulates "again," not "me," from
L on (no end stop). Finally, the " ¥ " in the transcript signals and sites—
and the note supplies—three post-MS interpolations: "Martians there were
none in sight"; "But the change and strangeness of things!"; and, "To the
northward, too, no Martian was visible." It happens that these discrete
variants occur in the same place. A set of angle brackets in the note encloses
all three, the textual stage of each is labeled, and end stops or lack thereof
indicate duration. Thus, the first sentence is in PR–J only, the second is

added in J only, and the third—set off by a slash—supplants both from L on (no end stop).

Variant spelling, capitalization, punctuation, and paragraphing are ignored unless the sense is appreciably affected. In general, Wells and British texts, but not American texts, tend to capitalize initial letters of the likes of "black smoke," "red weed," and "fighting machine," and do not distinguish "farther" from "further"; but the Essex and Atlantic editions in effect are American (British orthography excepted) since their copy text is Harper's. Among such variants, whether in transcript or notes, the form preferred is always the earliest, British or American, and any later ones are ignored— though of course the final state is preserved in the main text of this edition.

~~Write up~~   (Three Copies)   Sixth instalment   Wanted immediately

~~VIII~~

XVII

After the Fifteen Days (PRx)ᶜ

~~Very cautiously I crawled out of my prison.~~ I looked about {<me>¹}. (J•) ¥² When I had last seen ¥³ <Byfleet>⁴ in the daylight, it had been a straggling street of comfortable white & red houses, interspersed with {abundant ~~green~~ <shady>⁵} trees. Now I stood ¥⁶ on a mound of ¥⁷ clay & gravel over which spread a multitude of red cactus shaped plants, knee high, ~~& with only thistles & willow herb~~ without a solitary terrestrial ~~plant~~ growth to dispute their ~~poss~~ footing. ~~About me~~ The trees near me were all (C) dead & brown, but <further, a>⁸ network of red threads scaled the still living stems. The neighbouring houses had all been wrecked but none had been burnt, their walls, [sic] stood, sometimes to the second story with ~~vacant~~ smashed windows & shattered doors. ¥⁹ Below me was the {great} pit, with its {sloping side & (C) the crows struggling ~~for~~ <over>¹⁰ its} refuse. A number of {other} birds hopped about among the ruins. Far away I saw

---

1. L: again.
2. <PR–J•: Martians there were none in sight. J•: But the change and strangeness of things! /L: To the northward, too, no Martian was visible.>
3. C: this part of {J•: the outskirts of}
4. <C: Sheen /J•: Yonkers>
5. C•: shade
6. C–PRx: by this cage
7. PR: smashed brickwork[,]
8. J•, NY: further a
9. C: The red weed grew tumultuously in their roofless rooms.
10. C: for

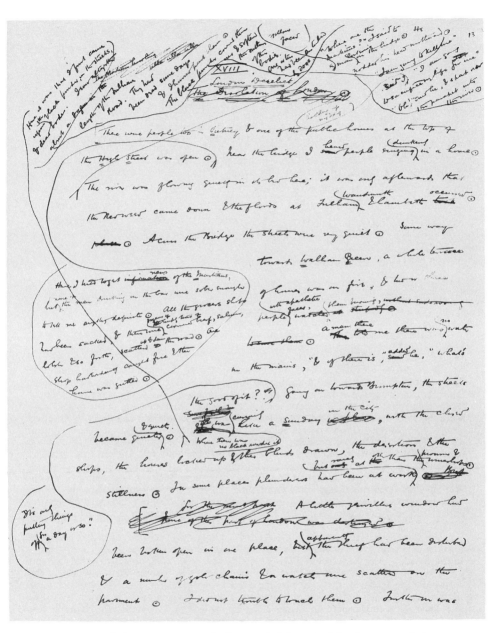

A page of the manuscript of *The War of the Worlds*. Courtesy of the
University of Illinois at Urbana-Champaign

a gaunt cat+ ~~far away~~+ ~~craw~~ slink crouchingly along a wall, but traces of men <there were>[11] none. The day ~~was gloriously fine~~ {seemed, by contrast with my ¥[12] confinement, dazzlingly bright} the sky ~~bright~~ a glowing <blue, & a>[13] gentle breeze kept the red /~~her~~/<weeds>[14] ¥[15] <that had covered>[16] every scrap of unoccupied ground, gently swaying. ¥[17] /~~Cla~~/ [123]d

For a time I stood marvelling at the change that had come over the world. ¥[18] Then the ~~thought~~ fact of my insecurity came to mind, & clambering past the empty cage, I crossed the ~~top~~ summit of the ~~heap~~ mound, & descended on the other side ¥[19]. I ~~found~~ was of course alert for food, & here was a patch of garden unburied. (PRx) ¥[20] I found some young onions, a couple of ~~crocus~~ gladiolus bulbs, (J•) & a quantity of immature carrots, all of which I secured, & scrambling over a ruined wall, went on my way through the (J) ¥[21] trees towards <Weybridge>,[22] ¥[23] possessed

---

11. PP•: were were [corrected in proof]
12. PP: recent
13. J: blue. A
14. L: weed
15. J•: the seeds of which had been scattered by the Martians and
16. <J•: which had covered /L: that covered>
17. PR: And {L: oh!} the sweetness of the air! "VI. The Work of Fifteen Days"
18. PR: ~~VI. On Putney Common~~
19. PP–P•: , away from the pit
20. <PR: VI. /J• Chapter XXIX> The Work of Fifteen Days [see note c]. For some time I stood tottering on the mound, regardless of my safety. Within that ~~dark~~ noisome den from which I {had} emerged, I had thought {with a narrow intensity} only of ~~my safety~~ our ~~personal escape~~ immediate security. I had not realised what had been happening ~~in~~ <to /J• in>the world, had not anticipated this startling vision of unfamiliar things. I had {J•: only} expected ~~Kew~~ to see <Sheen /J•: Yonkers> in ruins.—I found about me the landscape, weird & lurid, of another planet. For that moment I touched an emotion beyond the {common} range of men,—{yet} one that the poor brutes we dominate know only too well. I felt, as a rabbit might feel, returning to his burrow & suddenly confronted by the work of a dozen busy <navvies /J•: laborers> ~~who design~~ digging the foundations of a house. I felt the first inkling of a thing that {presently grew quite clear in my mind, that} oppressed me for {J•}many days, ~~the~~ a sense of dethronement, a persuasion that I was no longer ~~the~~ a master, but an animal among the animals, under the Martian heel. With us it would be as with them, to lurk & watch, to run & hide—{L} & the fear {& empire} of man ~~would pass~~ had passed away.
But <so /J•: as> soon as ~~my~~ <the /L: this> strangeness had been realised, it passed, & my dominant motive ~~was no longer~~ became the hunger of my long & dismal <fast /J•: past>. In the direction away from the pit, I saw beyond a red covered wall, a patch of garden ground ~~unburied~~ unburied. This gave me a hint & I went knee deep, & sometimes neck deep in the red weed. {The density of the weed gave me a reassuring sense of hiding.} The wall was some six feet high & when I attempted to clamber it I found <I could not /J•: myself too weak to> lift my feet to the crest. So I went along by the side of it, & came to a <corner, & a rockwork /J•: stile>, that enabled me to get to the ~~crest~~ top & tumble into the garden I coveted. Here
21. PR: scarlet & crimson
22. <C: Kew /J•: New York>
23. PR: —it was like walking through an avenue <of /J•: hung with> gigantic blood drops—

with two ideas,—to get {more} food & to limp ~~as far & as soon~~ as soon &
as far as my strength permitted, out of <the>[24] /radius/ ¥[25] region of <
this>[26] pit. <u>For I did not know when the Martians might return.</u> (PRx)

Some way further in a grassy place was a group of mushrooms which
<I also>[27] devoured, & then I came upon a ~~broad expanse of water, where~~
<broad>[28] sheet of flowing shallow water, where ~~we~~ meadows ~~had w~~ used
to be. ¥[29] At first I was surprised at this flood in a hot, dry summer, but
afterwards I discovered that <this>[30] was [124] caused by the <extraor-
dinary>[31] exuberance of the Red Weed. Directly this extraordinary growth
~~touched~~ encountered water, it {straightway} became gigantic & of ~~extraor-
dinary~~ unparalleled fecundity. Its seeds were simply poured down into the
<waters>[32] of the <Wey & Thames>[33], ~~& its gigantic fr~~ its swiftly grow-
ing & Titanic {water-}fronds, speedily choked <both these rivers>[34]. At
<Richmond>[35] as I afterwards saw, the bridge ¥[36] was almost lost in a
tangle of this <weed, & ¥ the {Thames} waters>[37] poured in a broad <u>&
shallow</u> (J•) stream across the <meadows of {Hampton &} Twickenham>[38].
As the waters spread ~~they~~ the weed followed them, until the {ruined <villas
of the} Thames & valley>[39] ~~became smothered in its~~ were for a time ~~embed-
ded in~~ lost in <a {red} swamp ¥>[40] & much of the desolation the Martians
had (C•) caused was concealed. In the end the Red Weed ~~in the end~~ succumbed {almost} as quickly as it ¥[41] spread. A cankering disease, due {it is
believed} to the action of ¥[42] bacteria, presently seized upon it. ¥[43] The
fronds became bleached & then shrivelled & brittle. They broke off at the
least touch, & the waters that had stimulated their {early} growth, carried

---

24. PR: this
25. PR: accursed unearthly
26. C: the
27. AG: also I
28. C: brown
29. PR: These fragments of nourishment served only to whet my hunger.
30. AG: it
31. C: tropical
32. C: water
33. J•: Hudson
34. <AG: both those rivers /J•: this river>
35. <C: Putney /J•: Marble Hill>
36. J•: over the canal
37. <C: weed, and at Richmond, too, the Thames water /J•: weed. The water>
38. J•: Harlem River meadows
39. J•: cottages of the valley
40. PR: this red swamp, whose margin I explored
41. NY: had
42. C: certain
43. PR: Now, by the action of natural selection all terrestrial plants have ~~a certain~~ acquired
a resisting power against bacterial diseases, they never succumb without a severe struggle, but
the Red Weed rotted like a thing already dead.

their {last} vestiges out to sea. But I am wandering again from my story—
—. this is <a digression from my story.>[44] [125]

{My first act on coming to this water was of course to slake my thirst.}
¥[45] I found the water was sufficiently shallow for me to wade {securely,
although the red weed impeded my feet a little,} ¥[46] & (C) I managed to
make out the road by means of its hedges(C) ¥[47] & presently to get so
¥[48] <to get across>[49] <this spate>[50] ¥[51] <to the hill towards Wey-
bridge{—St. George's Hill it is used to be called}.>[52e] Here ¥[53] I rested
hunted for food {among the trees and I also} finding but little nothing, {&
I also raided a couple of silent houses but they had already been broken
into & ransacked.} & I rested for the rest remainder of the daylight under
the trees in a shrubbery, being {in my enfeebled condition} too fatigued, in
to push on. All this /st/ time I saw no human beings & so no {signs of the}
Martians. I encountered a couple of hungry looking dogs, but both hurried
¥[54] away from my the advances I made them. {In Near <Byfleet>[55] I had
seen two human skeletons—not bodies, but skeletons picked clean, & in
the wood by me I found the *crushed & scattered* bones of several cats &
rabbits & the skull of a sheep. But though I gnawed *parts of* these in my
mouth there was nothing to be got from them.}

As the After the (C) sunset I struggled on, along the road to Weybridge
towards <Street Chobham Chobham[f] ¥ >[56]. {From As I crossed the summit
of St. George's Hill I looked back towards Weybridge.} (C) ¥[57] The aspect
of the place in the dusk was singularly desolate, blackened trees, <blackened

---

44. C–PRx: an anticipation.
45. PR: I drank a great <bulk of water /NY: deal of it>, & moved by an impulse gnawed
some fronds of red weed. But they were watery & had a sickly metallic taste.
46. C: but <it /L: the flood> evidently got deeper towards the river, {J•}and I turned
back <towards /P,AG: to>Mortlake.
47. C: {PR: occasional ruins of} <its villas /J•: the houses> and fences and lamps
48. C: presently
49. C–PP: {PR: I} got out of
50. J•: the canal
51. C: and made my way
52. <C: to the hill going up towards Roehampton, /J•: up the hill toward Inwood> and
came out on <Putney Common. /J•: the high ground overlooking the river.>
53. PR: the scenery changed from the strange & unfamiliar, to the wreckage of the familiar,
shapes of ground patches of ground exhibited the might the devastation of a cyclone, & in a
few {score} yards one came I would come upon perfectly fam undisturbed patches spaces,
houses with their blinds {trimly} drawn, & doors closed, as if they had been left for a day by
the owners or as if their inhabitants slept within. It h I had a curious The red weed was less
abundant, the {tall} trees along the lane were free from the red creeper.
54. PR: circuitously
55. C: Roehampton
56. C: Putney, where I think the heat ray must have been used for some reason.
57. PR: And in a garden {<near /L: beyond> Roehampton} I found a nu number got a
quantity of immature immature potatoes sufficient to stay my hunger. {From this garden one
<saw /NY: looked> down upon <the town & river /L: Putney and the river>}.

desolate>[58] ruins, {& <beyond these>}[59] the sheets of the flooded river, red tinged with the weed; & over it (PRx) all————silence. It filled [me] with a kind of (PRx) ¥[60] terror to look at it all, & (PRx) think how swiftly that desolating change had come. <For a moment the mad thought came into my mind>[61] that all (PRx) ~~the~~ mankind had been swept out of existence, & that I stood there, {alone} the last man left ~~behind~~ alive.

~~It was with intense relief that {presently near Street Cobham} I~~ *came* ~~at last suddenly heard human voices~~ [126]

{<Striking the road towards Street Cobham I ~~came~~ stumbled>[62g] upon another skeleton with the arms, [sic] dislocated & removed several yards from the rest of the body.}[h] [Unpublished segment of MS begins here.] It was after dark that I {first} came upon ~~the first~~ men. ~~I was then in a lane towards the S~~ It was in a little lodge {in the gateway to Pain[s]hill Park}. I saw a ruddy light in the window, & with an exclamation of thankfulness staggered towards this. In the room were men moving about. "Halt", cried ~~a~~ {an unfriendly} voice from the shadow of the porch.

"For God's sake give me food", I said {stopping *involuntarily at the tone of command*}.

"Give you food eigh?" said the voice. Then the door opened, & I saw it was a man. He thrust his head into the room. "Here's a chap", he said, "says he don't mind joining us." He laughed, & there was an answering laugh from the room.

He slammed the door. "Get", he said. I stood irresolute. Something clicked in the shadow {, *it was* the cocking of a gun}. ~~At that~~ I was so overcome by physical ~~misery~~ wretchedness, that I suddenly dropped on my knees, &— ~~misery~~ so misery unmans one—burst into tears.

"You'd better get out", said the voice, not quite so harshly.

"I don't care", I said.

"Poor beggar!" said the voice,$_\phi$—& then, "Damn it! Let's have a look at you."

He came out of the shadow, & stepped towards me, I saw the dim light along the barrel of ~~his~~ the gun with which he kept me covered. He peered at me. "Jack", he called over his shoulder.

The door opened again. [127]

"This isn't a confounded soup kitchen you know", said the second man in the doorway.

---

58. P•: stark and blackened
59. C: down the hill
60. PR: indescribable
61. C: For a time I believed
62. <C–P•: I went down Putney High Street, and at the corner of the upper Richmond Road came /PR: Hard by {the top of} Putney ~~Bridge~~ Hill [J•: Inwood Hill] I came>

"It's a bad case", said the man by me. There was a little hesitation. "I have had nothing", I said, "not a scrap, for four days." ~~In~~ They argued about me as though I was a ~~dead~~ starving kitten. "Fetch him in", said Jack at last. "We'll spare the poor swine the cooking water anyhow." So it was {by ~~a~~ the transient generous impulse of a stranger that} I was saved from starvation.

These men I found were ~~both armed with guns~~ brothers & had ~~two women~~ their wives ~~with~~ & a little girl with them. ~~Three days before they had found a pony~~ One was a carriage painter, the other was a board school teacher. They had been stopping together at the house of the former in Ripley, when the Martians came ~~up~~. {They had fled the house in a panic *a fortnight ago*. Afterward they had returned & found it sacked, & cleaned of its provisions. They had been unable to purchase food, because all the shops were deserted & empty & for a day or so they had starved. Then they had killed a sheep in the fields, & got some ~~yams~~ potatoes, & a day or so since they had shot a pony. *They had wandered about, finding the country deserted for the most part, save for necessitous stragglers like themselves.* All the food supply of the ~~country~~ country was disorganized, all the shops were closed, all the railways still, at least on this side of London. The Martians had gone to & fro over the country, using the heat ray only to kill soldiers & destroy guns, ~~&~~ but the people had ~~hid~~ fled before them. They crushed & killed people when they saw them, *so that* men ~~hid in~~ crawled into thickets & ditches *&) drains &)into* the cellars of houses when they came by. So these people told me.} ~~They~~ They received me with curious {& unfriendly} looks as I came in {& no wonder, for I was *horribly* attenuated, unwashed, & with a bristly beard *now* sixteen days old.} On the fire a saucepan boiled & ~~gave~~ diffused a fragrant smell. I sat down, & until I had eaten I was scarcely able to answer the questions {with which} they plied me ~~with~~. It was afterwards that they told me of the Martians.

~~For the last three or f In all~~ Ten ~~shots~~ cylinders in all had fallen upon the earth, all of them falling [128] into the county of Surrey ~~except~~ except the ones at Hounslow & Hampton Court. The furthest south was the one at Merrow, the most easterly that at Wimbledon, the westward one fell at Bagshot. When one considers the enormous distance across which these cylinders were fired, this is an amazing precision. A bulls eye {at a thousand yards} a million times running would scarcely compare with it. Each had disgorged Martians, & about each ~~it seems~~ a pit had been made, & for ~~a time~~ several days the Martians, save for occasional short raids had confined themselves to the irregular polygon traced by the shots. Then they had marched north to London. Of course I did not learn all this from these generous people. They were only able to give me a vague idea of the Martian movements. The thing that was more present in their minds was the {panic

&} famine, for famine {& fear} reigned now over the whole of Surrey_↓, albeit an enormous multitude of people had fled the county. Everywhere {a residue of} men & women {& children} ~~were~~ {who had failed to get away were} starving in their cellars, or prowling in search of food.

{~~The panic~~ For the most part the [129] people ~~had f~~ of the *southwestern* suburbs had ~~escaped through tracked~~ gone northward through London, taking with them every available beast of burden, while the ~~people~~ inhabitants of south Surrey & had made for the sea ~~coasts & for~~ ports of Sussex & Kent.} ¶ But[i] ~~the account~~ an account of the exhausting ~~scenes~~ scenes along the south coast {& down the *mouth of the* Thames}, where ~~thousands of~~ countless ships were presently embarking the terror-stricken multitudes, at exorbitant charges, ~~need scarcely take~~ scarcely falls within the scope of my personal experiences. Nor ~~will~~ need I tell here of the ~~ex extraordinary~~ tremendous disturbance of the social body that resulted from the torrent of Londoners which was suddenly poured northward, by rail {& road. It is calculated that} {the London & North Western alone carried over one hundred & ~~fifty~~ seventy thousand people {~~including my brother~~} ~~from East~~ out of Chalk Farm ~~to /D/~~ on the Monday of the panic} ~~& road~~. They say that London was swept clear of vehicles by midday on Tuesday, & that ~~huge~~ the fields about St. Albans were "crowded" with sleeping people who had tramped ~~off~~ afoot out of the doomed city. At Rugby, {on Monday} ~~a~~ {my brother has told me} glass{es} of water were sold for a shilling & {half-a-dozen} dry biscuits brought the same amount. ~~My brother has described elsewhere the~~

Neither is this the place to tell of ~~th~~ how two Martians walked across Sussex to the sea {at Bognor}, & how they {waded into the water and} fought with three ironclads from Portsmouth, searing holes in their sides with the Heat Ray & sinking them all three. That story ~~is~~ must be told {sooner or later,} by those who actually saw the scene. And of the sinking of the flotilla in the Solent, I can ~~say~~ add nothing {to what has been already written}.

But {~~here again I anticipate.~~} these ~~good~~ people {in the lodge} had chiefly to tell me of the state of the country about me. Of wolfish men banded together to get food, {&} of an awful rumour of cannibalism from ~~Leatherhead~~ Sutton. "~~Leatherhead!" cried I.~~ "We went as far as Leatherhead", said the [130] man called Jack. "Ah!" said I, {with a piece of ~~meat in my~~ horseflesh half way to my mouth} "that was what I have to ask you?. ~~For there~~ That is where I am going. There—"

I stopped, as they looked at one another. "The place was burnt by a Martian a week ago", said the woman.

I dropped the food & stood up. "*Why?*" He had done it as wantonly as a boy takes a nest. "My wife!" I said, & I heard the woman murmur sympathy. "Is there no way against them?" I cried, "no way of revenge.

[sic] Surely guns, mines, pitfalls—there are charges of dynamite! Are these things to walk over the world of men & ~~kill~~ destroy as they will?" And then in a passion of wrath & despair I swore to kill one Martian before I died. "A life for a life", I said. ["]They have destroyed all that makes life worth living to me, the social order, the security & comfort of life, art will vanish, letters, all the amenities of life. {Manufacture must cease, cities, [sic] vanish[,] *law & order must disappear*.} We shall soon be driven back to the woods & forests, to lairs & hiding places, to ~~the~~ the wilderness & the incessant struggle for food & life. We shall go back to the {communism of} beasts from whence we arose. It shall not be. [131] It shall not be. {All my cunning, all my strength, all the courage in my feeble body, shall ~~go~~ be given to the war₅ *against this /stifling/ tyranny. If I can die with a Martian dead upon me, then I will die, thanking God."*} ~~And so~~ So I devoted myself to the faint hope of the war.

And I was not the only man who took such views. Afterwards it was ~~the~~ found that hundreds of men, [sic] had like myself, been driven past fear, by the agonies of that time. Even as I spoke ~~like that~~ this in Street Cobham, there were scores of desperate men, lying in the fields of ~~Heref~~ Hertford & ~~Buckingham~~ the home counties, or slowly ~~crawling~~ tramping Londonward, {armed with ~~explosives bid~~ /the worst/ infernal machines, of ~~nitroglycerine~~ dynamite & ~~others~~ & explosives that the chemists of Birmingham made for them} & praying to heaven {only} than [sic] some Martian might come near enough to share the death they sought. Several were killed by accidents with their own ~~burthens~~ burdens, martyrs, if ever martyrs were, ~~in~~ to the cause of mankind. ¶ ~~Sitting~~ The {provisional} government{s} in Oxford & Birmingham, {for the official government at Westminster had vanished,} were indeed inviting men to volunteer in this enterprise. {A premium was set upon the manufacture of explosives.} A strange ~~reversal~~ inversion ~~of from since the days when~~ {, it seemed,} of the state of affairs in the days {of the Anarchists} when law & order had been assailed by these very weapons. But {of course} I did not know of these fellow workers at the time of my resolved [sic]. [132]

Exhilarated by the food I had eaten, & by ~~this~~ my desperate resolution, {& eager to put it into execution,} I left these people that night, & ~~pushed~~ pursued my way through Esher, where {sentinels were watching the sky for the approach of Martians &} numerous houses were occupied, to Kingston. I reached Kingston about the dawn, & found {that} here ~~was a V~~ too was a population {, watchers, ~~at all the chief points~~ upon the roofs & church towers} & a Vigilance Committee, which had {searched all the houses,} seized all the available provisions & was giving them out ~~only to~~ {*daily* in small rations} to the proper inhabitants of the place. I could ~~get~~ buy no {solid} food here, ¶ {though in that hope I waited for the distribution at ten. *Beer however was for sale in several public houses.*} ~~I~~ Here too nothing had been seen of the Martians for the last ~~four~~ three days. The{ir} last ~~seen~~ appearance near Kingston had been {in} a body of four, marching ~~over~~ over {Twickenham & scaling} the crest of Richmond Hill,. & {Each, *it seems,* was} carrying a heavy ~~mass of metal~~ & burden of metals & other substances. It was supposed that they had been moving their gear {from the pit about the Hounslow cylinder,} to a new & larger encampment in London.

~~I found *some a house* cottage {locked up &} apparently undisturbed in Kingston Vale, & by breaking a pane of glass, I opened a window & got into the house. In a pan under the kitchen dresser was some mouldy bread, & in the pantry two uncooked *kippers* herrings which refreshed me very greatly.~~

{London[k] I learnt was not destroyed, although the Martians, *it was said,* had established themselves in the northern heights about Highgate. A black & suffocating ~~cloud~~ fog had hung over the city & west end for two days & had then disappeared, *again.* It was said to have been produced by firing rockets which disengaged an inky black smoke, & it destroyed every living thing that breathed *it.* Afterwards they had fired other rockets through this & it had slowly rained down in the form of fine powder. I was told this by a man who said he had actually seen the fog from Putney Hill. For my own part *I can witness that* there ~~p~~ certainly was a blackened powder, about half an inch deep in Brompton & Oxford Streets, & also near St. John's Wood Station, & wherever this powder occurred, there also lay dead bodies, *in the streets.* But about nothing are we quite so much in the dark as about the black powder.}

~~While~~ I presently learnt that the Provisional Committee ~~had some~~ was making some bombs and, after an interminable enquiry, found myself in the presence of a short dark man of about fifty, ~~sitting in~~ sitting in the managers [sic] office of the London & County Bank. This was Marriott,[m] the head of the {Kingston} provisional government. He cross-examined me rather austerely, for not everyone who had a passing fancy for bomb-throwing at the Martians was entrusted with this duty. Finally {he accepted me, with an air of great magnanimity, & after certain instructions which need not be repeated here} I was given three metal cases the size,[sic] of pineapple tins, carefully packed in a handbag. "The sooner you get ~~over the Thames~~ out of Kingston, the better!" said Marriott. I was {then} allowed {to eat} bread, but not to take any with me. "Surely that's provisions enough!" said Marriott. [133]

~~The Martian howling ulla ulla ulla~~

XVIII

The Desolation of London

London Derelict

There were people too in Putney & one of the public houses at the top of the High Street was open. {Here I tried to get ~~information~~ news of the Martians, but *none of* the men drinking in the bar were sober enough to tell me anything definite. All the grocers shops had been sacked, & there were *dozens of empty tins of* corned beef, salmon, lobster & so forth, scattered ~~on~~ up & down the road. One shop had evidently caught fire & the house was gutted.} Near the bridge I ~~saw~~ heard people singing {drunkenly} in a house. {"Where are the Martians?" I said to a *yellow faced* man *loitering* on the bridge. He nodded his head northward. "I am going to kill one", said I *holding up my bag*. "I am going to sacrifice my life ~~to~~ for one." "Oh‚!" said he, & spat over the parapet into the river.} The river was flowing quietly in its bed here; it was only afterwards that the red weed came down & the floods at Fulham {Wandsworth} & Lambeth ~~took place~~ occurred. [End of unpublished segment of MS.] <Across the bridge the streets were very quiet>[63].n ¥[64] Some way towards Walham Green, ¥[65] a <whole>[66] terrace of houses was (C) on fire, ¥[67] & two or three people {with apathetic faces} watched ~~it stupidly~~ them burning, ~~without endeavouring to save them.~~ ~~Ther~~ A man there told me there was {no} water in the mains, "& if there is", ~~said~~ added he, "what's the good of it? {It's only putting things off *for* a day or so."} (C) Going on towards Brompton, the streets <became quieter {& quieter}>[68]. {Here <it was that I first came>[69] upon *the* black powder in the streets, & ¥[70] dead bodies. I saw altogether about a dozen in the length of the Fulham Road. They had been dead <some>[71] days <&>[72]

---

63. C–P•: I crossed the bridge {PR•: —the Red weed rose in bulging masses above the parapet,} and {PR• I} found a man {PR•}at last, lying at the corner of the lane to Putney Bridge {PR•: Station}. [See note n.]

64. C: He was as black as a sweep with the black dust, <and /PR: alive, but> helplessly and speechlessly drunk. {PR: I could get nothing from him but *curses & furious lunges at my head*. I think I should have stayed by him, but for the brutal <type /A: expression> of his face.} There was black dust along the roadway from the bridge onwards, and it grew thicker in Fulham. The streets were horribly quiet. I got food {<PP–P•: sour and mouldy, but still quite eatable / PR: sour, hard, & mouldy, but quite eatable>} in a baker's shop here.

65. C: the streets became clear of powder, and I passed

66. C: white

67. C: —the noise of the burning was an absolute relief.

68. C: were quiet again

69. C: I came once more

70. L: upon

71. PR: many

72. <C•: so /PP: so that>

I hurried ¥[73] past them. The black powder covered them over & softened
<the outlines of their bodies>[74]. One or two had been disturbed by dogs.}
~~It was It was save for these b~~ Where there was no black powder it was
{curiously} like a Sunday ~~in places~~ in the city, with the closed shops, the
houses locked up & the blinds drawn, the desertion & the stillness. In some
places plunderers had been at work {but ~~only~~ rarely at ~~the~~ other than the
(C•) *provision &* wine shops}. ~~But ¶ None of this part of London was destroyed. For the most part~~ A little (PR) jewelers window had been broken
open in one place, but {apparently} the thief had been disturbed & a number
of gold chains & a watch <were>[75] scattered on the pavement. I did not
trouble to touch them. Further on was [134] a tattered woman sleeping
(PRx) {in a heap} on a doorstep; ~~her~~ the hand that hung over her knee was
gashed & ¥[76] bled {down her rusty brown dress}, & a smashed magnum
of champagne formed a pool across the pavement. ¥[77]
     ¥[78]o

The further I penetrated into London, the profounder grew the <
silence>[79]. <It was not {everywhere}>[80] the stillness of death, it was the
stillness of suspense, of expectation. Somewhere to the north were the Martians & over it all hung the Heat Ray (C). ¥[81] At any time the destruction
that had (C-P•) ¥[82] already singed the northwestern borders of the metropolis, {& had annihilated Ealing & Kilburn,} might ~~begin~~ strike among
these houses {& leave them smoking <ruins.} ~~It~~ So that it>[83] was a city
condemned & derelict. ¥[84] ~~But it was {not} a~~ The remnant of the people
had fled east {& west, north}, ~~west~~ & south. ¶ Men wondered, men still
wonder, that the wilderness of houses endured from day to day. (C)
     {In South Kensington the streets were clear of dead & of black powder.}
It was near South Kensington that I first heard the howling. It crept almost
imperceptibly upon my senses. It was a ~~rasping~~ sobbing alternation of two
notes, *"ulla, ulla, ulla, ulla"*, keeping on perpetually. When ~~one~~ I passed

---

73. C: quickly
74. PP: their outlines
75. AG, E: lay
76. P•: had
77. PR: She seemed asleep but she was dead. ~~Perhaps it was her first champagne.~~
78. C: {PR: As I proceeded} I became more and more convinced that the extermination
of mankind was, save for such stragglers as myself, already accomplished in this part of the
world. The Martians, I thought, had gone on and left the country desolated, seeking food
elsewhere. Perhaps even now they were destroying Berlin or Paris, or it might be they had
gone northward. {PR: ~~End of Book II~~} [See note o.]
79. L: stillness
80. C: But it was not so much
81. C-PRx: Somehow I felt that this was not the end. [C-PR•] I had a sense of things still
impending. [C-PRx] Suppose the Martians were, after all, at hand.
82. PR: had
83. C: ruins. It
84. C-PRx: That, at any rate, would be completion.

streets that ran northward it grew in volume, & ~~where~~ houses & buildings
seemed to {deaden &} cut it off again. ~~At~~ I[t] came <in>[85] a full tide down
Exhibition Road. I <stopped staring>[86] towards ~~the~~ Kensington Gardens,
wondering at this strange {remote} wailing. It was as if that ~~deserted m~~
mighty desert of houses had a_ (C) found a voice for [135] its fear & ~~desolation~~
solitude. ~~At the sound of it my mood changed.~~

<"Ulla, ulla, ulla, ulla",> [with canceled underlining] ~~went that~~ wailed
~~these~~ that superhuman ~~voice note~~ note; great waves of sound, sweeping
down the {broad} empty (C) {sunlit} roadway,, between the tall buildings on
<either>[87] side. I turned northward, marvelling, towards the iron gates of
Hyde Park. {I had half a mind to break into the Natural History Museum,
& find my way up to the ~~towers~~ summits of the towers, in order to see
across the Park. But I decided to keep to the ground, where *quick* hiding
was possible & *so* went on up *the* Exhibition Road.} All the large mansions
on <either>[88]side of the road were empty & still,, & my footsteps ~~eechoed~~
echoed ~~along~~ against the sides of the houses. At the top, near the park gate,
I came upon a strange sight, a <bus>[89] ~~overturned~~ overturned & the
skeleton of a horse picked clean. I puzzled over this for a time, & then went
on to the bridge over the Serpentine. The Voice grew stronger & stronger,
though I could see nothing ~~over~~ above the housetops on the north side of
the park, save a haze of smoke to the northwest.

<"Ulla ulla, ulla, ulla"> [with canceled underlining] ~~cried the voice.~~
cried the voice, coming as it seemed to me from <somewhere ~~near~~ beyond
Baker Street>[90]. The desolating cry worked upon my mind. The mood that
had sustained me passed. {The wailing took possession of ~~my mind~~ me.} I
found I was intensely weary, footsore, & now again hungry & thirsty. It
was already past noon. ¥[91] After all what was the good of the expedition?
What chance had I? {And} if one {more} Martian [136] were killed, what of
that? It would only spur the others on, to complete the massacre of humanity. (C)p

I came into Oxford Street by the Marble Arch, & ~~going in~~ {here again
<was>[92] black powder, & several bodies & an evil ominous smell from

85. L–NY•: to
86. L: stopped, staring
87. NY: each
88. NY: each
89. C–L•: 'bus
90. PR: the district ~~towards Primrose~~ about Regents Park
91. C: Why was I wandering alone in this city of the dead? Why was I alone when all
London was lying in state and in its black shroud? I <was /L: felt> intolerably lonely. My
mind ran on old friends that I had forgotten for years. I thought of the poisons in the chemists'
shops, of the liquors the wine merchants stored. I recalled the two sodden creatures of despair
who, so far as I knew, shared the city with myself. (C–PRx) We were the last of men.

the gratings of the cellars of some of the houses. I ~was~ grew very thirsty after the heat of my long walk.} With infinite trouble I managed to break into a public house & get ¥[93] drink. I ¥[94] went into the parlour behind the bar & slept on a black horsehair sofa I found there.

I awoke to ~hea~ find that dismal howling still in my ears {; "ulla, ulla, ulla, ulla"}. It was now dusk, & after I had ~found~ routed out some biscuits & a cheese in the bar—there was <cold beef there also {in a safe} but it was too bad to eat>[95]—I <went>[96] on through the silent residential squares to Baker Street {—Portman Square is the only one I can name—}, & so came out at last upon Regents Park. And as I emerged from the top of Baker Street, I saw far away over the trees {in the clearness of the sunset,} the hood of the Martian giant from which this howling proceeded. ¥[97] I watched him for some time but he did not move. He appeared to be standing & yelling, for no reason that I could <conceive>.[98]

I ~watched~ tried to formulate a plan of action. That /~protracted~/ perpetual sound {of}, "ulla, ulla, ulla, ulla", confused my mind. ¥[99] I turned back away from the park & struck into ~the bye back streets to the west~ Park Road, <intending to skirt the Park {under shelter of the terraces} & get>[100] a view of this {stationary} ¥[101] Martian from the direction of St. John's Wood. [137] A couple of hundred yards out of Baker Street I heard a yelping chorus, & saw, first a dog with a piece of {putrescent} red meat in his jaws & coming {headlong} towards me, & then a pack of starving mongrels in pursuit {of him}. ~The~ He made a wide curve to avoid me, & ~the~ as though he feared I might prove ~one~ a fresh competitor. As <their>[102] yelping died away down the silent road, the wailing sound of "ulla, ulla, ulla ¥[103]," reasserted itself.

I came upon the wrecked Handling Machine half way to ~the~ St. John's Wood Station. At first I thought that(L) ~the~ a house had fallen across the road; it was only as I clambered among the ruins that I saw {with a start} this mechanical Sampson lying, {with its tentacles} bent & smashed {&

---

93. C: food and

94. C: was weary after eating, and

95. PR: a meat safe, but it contained nothing but maggots

96. C: wandered

97. C: I was not terrified. I came upon him as if it were a matter of course.

98. C: discover

99. C: Perhaps I was too tired to be very fearful. Certainly I was <C•, NY: more curious to know the reason of this monotonous crying than afraid. /P•: rather curious than afraid to know the reason of this monotonous crying. /PP–L•: rather curious to know the reason of this monotonous crying than afraid.>

100. <C•: and went along under shelter of the terraces, intending to skirt the park and get /PP: intending to skirt the park, (L) and went along under shelter of the terraces and got>

101. C: howling

102. C: the

103. L: ulla

twisted} among the ruins it had ~~created~~ made. The forepart was shattered.
It seemed as if it had driven {blindly} straight at the house, & had been
overwhelmed in its overthrow. It seemed to me {then that} this might have
happened by a Handling Machine escaping from the guidance of its Martian.
I could not clamber among the ruins to see it, & the twilight was no[w] so
far advanced, that the blood with which its seat was smeared & the gnawed
gristle of the Martian {that the dogs had left}, <was>[104] invisible to me.
Wondering still more, at all ¥[105] I had seen, I ~~pr~~ pushed on towards Primrose
Hill. Far away, through a gap in the trees, I [138] saw a second Martian,
¥[106] motionless as the first, standing in the Park towards the zoological
gardens ¥[107]. A little beyond the ruins about the smashed Handling Machine I came upon the red weed again, & found the (L•) Regents Canal a
spongy mass of dark red vegetation.

~~Suddenly~~ Abruptly (NY) {as I crossed the bridge}, the sound of "ulla,
ulla, ulla ¥[108]", ceased. It was {as it were} cut off. The silence came ~~high~~
like a thunderclap.

Unaccountable as it may seem, I began to feel frightened. (C) The dusky
houses about me stood faint & tall & dim, the trees towards the park were
~~becoming~~ growing black. ¥[109] Night the mother of fear & mystery was
coming upon me. ~~And suddenly~~ But while ~~tha~~ that voice <sounded the
solitude, & the desolation had>[110] been endurable; {by virtue of it} London
had still seemed alive ~~& now~~ & the sense of life about me had upheld me.
Then suddenly ¥[111] a stillness that could be felt. Nothing but this gaunt
quiet of death! (PRx)

London about me gazed at me spectrally. The windows in the white
houses were like the eye sockets of skulls. ~~The~~ About me my imagination
found a thousand noiseless enemies moving. Terror seized me{, a horror of
my temerity}. {In front of me the road I saw (C) became pitchy black as
though it was tarred, & I saw a contorted shape lying across the pathway.}
{I could not bring myself to go on.} I turned ~~to the~~ down St. John's Wood
Road, & ran headlong [139] from this unendurable stillness, towards Kilburn. I hid <all night>[112] until ~~the dawn~~ long after midnight in a cabmen's
shelter in the(NY) [H]arrow [R]oad. But ~~with~~ before the dawn my courage

---

104. C•: NY: were
105. C: that
106. NY: as
107. C: , and silent
108. NY: , ulla
109. PR: All about me the Red Weed clambered among the ruins, writhing to get above
me in the <PR–L•: dim /NY: dimness>.
110. <C•, NY: sounded the solitude, the desolation, had /PP–PR•: [no second comma] /
L•: [three commas, including one after "sounded"]>
111. C: a change, the passing of something—I knew not what—and then
112. C: from the night and the silence

returned, & {while the stars were still in the sky} I turned once more towards
~~the~~ ¥[113] Regents Park. I missed my way among the streets & presently saw
{down a long avenue,} in the half light of ¥[114] {early} dawn, the <summit>[115] of Primrose Hill. On the summit, towering up to the fading stars,
was a third Martian, ~~still~~ erect & motionless like the others.

~~The~~ <A strange fascination seized>[116] me. ¥[117] I marched on <
resolutely>[118] towards this Titan, & ¥[119] as {I drew nearer &} the light
grew, I saw that a multitude of <{black} birds>[120] was {circling &} clustering about the hood. At that my heart gave a bound & I began running
~~towar~~ along the road. I ~~hurried~~ hurried through the red weed that choked
St. Edmund's terrace~~, & before the sun rose~~ {<a torrent of water>[121] was
rushing down from the waterworks ~~to the~~ towards the Albert Road} and
emerged upon the grass before the rising of the sun. Great mounds had been
heaped ¥[122] about the crest of the hill, making a huge redoubt of it, ¥[123]
& ~~from~~ from behind <them>[124], rose a thin smoke against the sky. Against
the skyline an eager dog ran & disappeared. ¥[125] I felt no fear [140] only
a wild ¥[126] exultation, as I ran up the hill, towards the motionless monster.
Out of the hood hung lank <bleeding shreds>[127] at which the hungry
birds {pecked &} tore.

In another ~~moment~~ <minute>[128] I had scrambled up the earthen rampart & stood upon its crest_φ, & the interior of the redoubt was below me.
A mighty space it was, with gigantic machines here & there within it, huge
mounds of <material>[129], & <rough-hewn>[130] shelter places. And ~~som~~
scattered about it, some in their overturned war machines, some in the
{now} rigid Handling Machines, & ~~some~~ a dozen of them stark & silent &

---

113. C–PR•: the
114. L: the
115. C: curve
116. <C–P•: A strange insanity seized upon /PR: An insane resolve possessed>
117. C: I would die and end it; and I would save myself even the trouble of killing myself.
118. C: recklessly
119. C: then
120. C•: blackbirds
121. PR: I waded breast high across a torrent of water that
122. C•: up
123. PR: —it was the final & largest place the Martians <made— /NY: had made—>
124. PR: these heaps there
125. C: The thought that had flashed into my mind grew real, grew credible.
126. PR: trembling
127. C: shreds of brown
128. C: moment
129. C•: materials
130. PR: strange

laid in a row, were the Martians—*dead!*—Slain by the putrefactive {& disease} bacteria against which their systems were unprepared, ¥¹³¹ slain {, after all man's devices had failed,} by the humblest things that God ¥¹³² has put upon this earth. ¶ ¥¹³³ Here & there they were scattered, nearly fifty altogether in that ~~pit mighty cavern~~ great gulf {they had made}, overtaken by a death, that must have seemed to them as incomprehensible as any death could be. <But ~~all this~~ how they had died I did not know at this time>¹³⁴. All I knew was that these things that had been alive & so terrible to men, were dead. For a moment [141] I believed that the ~~miracle~~ destruction of Sennacherib had been repeated<, ¥ &>¹³⁵ that the Angel of Death, had slain them in the night.

I stood staring into the pit, & my heart lightened gloriously, even as the {rising} sun struck the world to fire about me with his rays. The pit was {still} <u>sunk</u> (L) in darkness, the mighty engines, so great & wonderful in their power & complexity, {so unearthly in their tortuous forms,} rose ~~dark~~ weird ¥¹³⁶ & strange out of the shadows ¥¹³⁷. <The>¹³⁸ dogs {I could hear,} fought over the bodies that lay {darkly} in the depth of the pit, far below me. ¥¹³⁹ Then (PRx) at the sound of a cawing overhead I looked up at the huge Fighting Machine, that would fight no more forever, at the tattered red shreds of flesh that dripped down ~~toward~~ upon the overturned seats <of>¹⁴⁰ the summit of Primrose Hill.

I turned & looked down the slope of the hill, to where, enhaloed {now} in birds, {stood} those other two Martians that I had seen overnight, just as death had overtaken them. The one [142] had died, even as it had been

---

131. PR: slain ~~even as the Red Weed~~ ~~was to be~~ was being slain;

132. PR: in his wisdom,

133. PR: For so it had come about, <as I indeed /L: as, indeed, I> & many men might have foreseen, had not terror & disaster blinded our minds. These germs of disease have taken toll of humanity since the beginning of things—taken toll of our pre human ancestors since life began here. But by virtue of ~~the~~ this natural selection of our kind we have developed resisting power, to no ~~disease~~ germs do we succumb without a struggle, & to many ~~germs~~, those that cause putrefaction {in dead matter} for instance, our ~~living~~ living frames are {altogether} immune. But there are no bacteria in Mars, & directly ~~they arrived~~ these invaders arrived, directly they {drank &} fed, ~~their~~ our microscopic allies began to work their overthrow. Already when I watched them they were irrevocably doomed, dying & rotting even as they went to & fro. It was inevitable. By the toll of a billion deaths, man has {bought} his birthright of the earth, {& it is his, against all comers, it would still be his} were the Martians ten times as mighty as they are. {<PR•: For men neither die nor live in vain. /L: For neither do men live nor die in vain.>}

134. PR: To me also at that time ~~their deaths~~ this death was incomprehensible

135. C: ; that God had repented;

136. PR: ~~dubious~~ & vague

137. PR: towards the light

138. PR: A multitude of

139. PR: Across the pit on its farther lip {flat & vast & strange} lay the great flying machine ~~upon~~ with which they had (L) <u>still</u> been experimenting upon our denser atmosphere when decay & death arrested them. Death had come not a day too soon.

140. C: on

crying to its companions, perhaps it was the last to die, & its voice had gone on perpetually until the force of its machinery was exhausted. They glittered now, harmless ~~towe~~ tripod towers of shining metal in the brightness of the rising sun.

~~Beyond them~~ All about the pit, & saved <by this>[141] miracle from {everlasting} destruction stretched the great mother ~~city~~ of cities.[q] [143]

~~Description of the Martian encampment upon P H~~ [Primrose Hill]

~~They too were dead. One had been gnawed by some large carnivore.~~

~~*XXIII*~~

~~*So* Thus it was that I came to stand alone upon Primrose Hill in the quiet of the early morning, the first man, so far as I knew then, to realize that the destruction of mankind *had* was averted, that the hand of the destroying angel was stayed. How it was accomplished I did not know, did not attempt to imagine {then}. These *little* creatures {that had been} so active intelligent & malignant were now no more than dead vermin putrefying upon the hill slopes. Above me, an empty symbol {now}, fluttered the purple streamer, about me gilded by the morning sun were their peculiar light *engines tha* artillery & cases {(as I judged)} of the evil explosive[r] that had done such infinite damage.~~ Those who have ~~never~~ <only seen London>[142] ~~save under~~ veiled in <its>[143] ¥[144] robes of smoke, can scarcely imagine the naked clearness ¥[145] of the silent wilderness of houses. Eastward over the {blackened} ruins of the Albert Terrace & the ~~wreckage~~ splintered spire of the church, {the sun blazed dazzling in a clear sky & here & there some facet in} the great wilderness of roofs ~~blazed~~ caught the light & glared with a white intensity. <There is a>[146] round ~~tower~~ store place for wines by the Chalk Farm Station & ¥[147] vast railway yards, marked <not>[148] with a graining of black rails but red lined ¥[149] with the quick rusting of a fortnight[']s disuse ¥[150]. (NY) [144] Northward <Kilburn & Hampstead rose>[151] blue, & crowded with houses, westward the great city was haze (L)

141. C: as by a
142. C•: seen London only
143. C: her
144. PR: sombre
145. C: and beauty
146. L•: It touched even that
147. L•: the
148. C–L•: once
149. C–L•: now
150. L•: , with something of the mystery of beauty.
151. L: were Kilburn and Hampstead

dimmed, & southward {across beyond the Martians the green <wash>[152] of Regents Park, the Langham Hotel,} the dome of the Albert Hall, the Imperial Institute /towers/ (C) & the giant mansions of the Brompton Road came out clear & little in the sunrise {with(L) the jagged ruins of Westminster ¥[153] beyond}. Beyond them Far away <the Surrey Hills rose up>[154] & the towers of the Crystal Palace glittered like two silver rods. The dome of St. Pauls was dark against the sun rise & shattered injured I saw for the first time by a huge gaping cavity on its <westward>[155] side. And as I looked at this wide expanse of houses & factories & churches, silent & abandoned, as I thought of the multitudinous hopes & efforts, the innumerable < host>[156] of lives that had gone to build this human reef {& of the *swift & ruthless destruction that had hung over it all*}, when I thought realized that the shadow had been rolled back & that men might still live again {in < its>[157] streets} & this dear {vast dead} city of mine be once more th alive & powerful *in the again the desolate desperation brooding despair of my mood was changed lightened* & I felt a wave of emotion {that was} near akin to tears.

The torment was over. Even that day the healing would begin. < The>[158] multitudes hundreds of thousands <millions of people>[159] scattered over the southern <home counties>[160], like {leaderless, lawless, foodless, like sheep without a shepherd,} the thousands who had fled by sea, would begin to return; the pulse of life, growing stronger & stronger, [145] would beat again in the empty streets, & pour across the vacant squares. ¥[161] All the gaunt wrecks about me that stared {the blackened skeletons of houses that stared so dismally at the sunlit grass of the hill} would presently be ringing {echoing <under>[162] the hammers of the restorers &} ringing with the noise <tintinnabulations>[163] of <the>[164] trowels. {<I lifted my hands above my head>[165], & began thanking God. In a year, thought I— ¥[166] <and then I thought of the dead. {with>[167] overwhelming force came the thought ¥[168] of my wife & the *old* life ¥[169] that <I thought had ceased>[170] forever.}

---

152. <C•: water /PP: waves>
153. L: rising hazily
154. <C•: the Surrey hills arose /L: and blue were the Surrey hills>
155. L: western
156. C: hosts
157. L: the
158. C•: When the
159. C: survivors of the people
160. C: country
161. C: Whatever destruction was done, the hand of the destroyer was stayed. {PR–L•: The hand of the destroyer was stayed.}
162. L: with
163. PR: tapping
164. AG: their
165. C: At the thought, I extended my hands toward the sky
166. C: in a year—

~~Keen & sharp my personal trouble came home to me, as the thought~~
~~of returning to the old routine of life entered my mind. In the last week~~
~~as the world had grown stranger~~ {& more terrible}, *I had then as the string*
~~stream of skirmishes & murders that had begun at Horsell, had flowed wider~~
~~& deeper~~ {darker & deeper} ~~until it seemed to be overwhelming humanity~~
~~in one black destruction[,]~~ *my home & my wife had been lost sight of in*
that rapid succession of monstrous disasters in that rapid succession of
monstrous disasters I had wellnigh lost sight of my home & my wife altogether. ~~It was~~ My old life seemed something ~~so as~~ remote, ~~so as~~ far off,
{~~so as alien to all my immediate surroundings as~~} *like* a distant glimpse of
a sunlit hillside {would be} to a man *perishing* freezing to death in the rigging
~~of some castaway ship~~ wave whipped wreck. ~~To~~ That my dear ~~wife should~~
~~have died & b~~ escaped the horrors of these last days seemed a matter that
~~scarcely called for regret. But now with the dead Martians about me I~~
~~realized that~~ {the old order was saved, that the final consummation of their
attack was averted & that} I must [146]

<*XIX. The Selvage of the Story*>[171s]

But here the story that will interest the ¥[172] reader {, the story of the
Martians,} ends. ¥[173] ~~It is on~~ This is indeed no history, it is a mere ¥[174]
narrative of my own personal ~~experiences of them~~ adventures during this
strange time ¥[175]. Such narratives we must have first in abundance & afterwards the History may be written. In the fact that I was among the first
to see the Martians at their arrival, & the second man—{indeed} I had fancied
myself first—to discover them dead, I have presumed to think my impressions might be of value. ¥[176] But {to tell} of the torrent of people that
{presently} flowed back into London, chiefly from the <northwards,>[177]
¥[178] {of the riots & <plundering>[179] & murders, of the restoration of

---

167. <L–NY•: And then, with /AG: With>.
168. C: of myself,
169. PR: of hope & tender helpfulness
170. <PP•: I imagined had ceased /P•: I had to imagine done with /PR: had ceased>
171. <C–P•: XXII. "The Epilogue" /PR: ~~"Home Coming"~~>
172. C–P•: general
173. C–P•: The rest, the return, the thanksgiving, has been written by a thousand pens.
174. P•: clumsy
175. C–P•: eked out {P•: by my brother's experience} where the gaps were too great
176. C–P•: And by an odd coincidence, of the four Martians killed by man, I saw the
death of one and my brother the overthrow of two others.
177. C–P•: north—
178. C–P•: —for the Martians had never gone farther than forty miles in that direction—
179. C•: plunderings

government, of the terrific explosion of the Heat Ray powder that wrecked the north of London} hundreds are better qualified than I. ¥ [180] ~~I stayed in L~~ I ~~went down~~ plundered a grocers shop in Camden Town ~~in~~ <on the morning of my discovery for food> [181], & afterwards tramped down to the docks {with the idea of spreading the good news there}. In Shoreditch I ~~found~~ met people again, & told them ~~my news~~ what I had seen & it was from ~~Bethnal~~ the general post office, ~~that the~~ by a Jewess who had learnt the trade of a telegraph operator, that [147] the news was first ~~tel~~ flashed out of London, to Paris first, & then to certain English towns. I remember ~~how~~ that I laughed hysterically until I cried, ~~at th~~ when after infinite trouble {& muddling}, we managed the telephone, & heard the French operator say over & over again as though ~~it was~~ they were his only words [italics in original], {Dead! *Nom de Dieu.* A} *Tousand* <'Gomgratulation'>. [182] ¥ [183] {*Vive l'Angleterre!* Hooray!} Its ~~amiable~~ kindly insipidity <was> [184] ~~so blankly~~ such an infinite contrast to the {half dozen} haggard yellow faced dirty {& hungry} people who crowded into the room. ¥ [185]

The thing that was of greatest moment to me will be of small concern to the reader. (C) I lingered in London ten days, <dreading> [186] to go back to where (C) my house stood (C) desolate among the ashes of ~~Woking~~ Maybury Hill, the house in which I had <trusted> [187] to live the best part of my days. I believed my wife was dead. I <dreaded> [188] to find a ~~silent~~ solitude that should confirm my fears. But at last {urged by the police} I induced myself to ¥ [189] ~~board~~ go to Waterloo (C) & return by one of the ~~free~~ government trains [148] by which people were taken back {free of charge} to their proper dwelling places. ¥ [190] ¥ [191t] I descended at Byfleet

---

180. C–P•: Nor have I any qualification to speak of the distresses in the home counties, the famine, the violence, even, it is said, the cannibalism, the disappearance of all law and order during the fortnight of the war, and afterward the struggle with the pestilence. It speaks eloquently for the lesson that humanity had learned that no attack was made on our <wounded /P•: stricken> Empire during the <weeks /PP–P•: months> of <restoration /P•: reconstruction>.
181. C–P•: for food on the morning of my discovery
182. <C–PP•: Comgratulation /P•: Congratulation>
183. C–P•: You have kill dem?
184. C–P•: offered
185. C–P•: That night, I have heard since, Paris, by no set contrivance, but of its own impulsive emotion, was a fairyland of <playing /PP–P•: blazing> illuminations from end to end, and ten thousand thronged cities in Europe and Asia and America shouted aloud and held festival at the news of the world's release.
186. C–P•: serving as a special constable. I dreaded
187. P•: hoped
188. C–P•: feared
189. C–P•: return [PP–P: resign] my white badge and staff
190. C–P•: The Surrey country was pitifully scarred and blackened on either side, and every water course was scarlet with the <weed /P•: red weed.>
191. PR: The line {on the London side of Woking Station} was still undergoing repair, so

Station, & took the <Maybury Road>,[192] ~~passin~~ going out of my way to view once more the red choked pit in which I had been imprisoned so long. Thence I pushed on, with a deepening melanchol~~iay~~, (C) past the place where <I & the /sap/ artilleryman>[193] had talked to the huzzars, & on by the spot where the Martian had ~~first~~ appeared to me in the thunderstorm. Here again (C) ¥[194] I turned aside, to find ¥[195] the {~~rim of the~~ warped & broken dogcart & with [the]} whitened bones of the horse, scattered & gnawed. ¥[196] Then I returned through the {pine} wood, ¥[197] to <find>[198] the landlord of the <Coach & Horses>[199u] had already found burial, & so came (P•) home, past the College Arms. {A man standing at an open cottage door greeted me ¥[200] as ~~he~~ I passed.}

I looked at my house with a quick flash of hope that faded immediately. The door had been forced {; it was unfastened} & ~~yawned open~~ was opening slowly as I approached. {<Then it>[201] slammed again.} The curtains of my study ~~blew~~ fluttered out of the open window from which <I ~~had~~ & the artilleryman>[202] had watched the dawn. [149] ¶ {No one had closed < it>[203] since.} The smashed bushes were just as I had left them ~~a fortnight~~ nearly <three>[204] weeks ago. I ~~went~~ stumbled into the hall, & the house felt empty. ¶ The stair carpet was ~~still~~ ruffled & discoloured where I had crouched & wept (C) {, soaked to the skin from the thunderstorm,} on (C)[205] the night of the catastrophe <, & our>[206] muddy footsteps {I saw still} went up the stairs. {I} ¥[207]

---

192. C: road to Maybury
193. C•: the artilleryman and I
194. PR: moved by curiosity
195. C: , among a tangle of red fronds,
196. PR: For a time I stood regarding these vestiges. . . .
197. C: neck high with <weed /PR: red weed> here and there
198. <C•: learn that /P•: find that /PP: find>
199. C: Spotted Dog
200. C: by name
201. PR: It
202. C•: the artilleryman and I
203. L•: that window
204. PP: four
205. P•: on
206. C: . Our
207. PR: I followed them to my study, & found lying on my writing table still, with the <ammonite /L: selenite paper weight> upon it, the sheet of work I had left on the afternoon of the opening of the cylinder. For a space I stood <weighing /L: reading over> my abandoned arguments. ~~Morals & civilization indeed! I had some new lights now. . . .~~ {It was a paper on the *probable* development of ~~'Morals'~~ moral ideas with the ~~complication~~ development of the civilizing process & the *last* sentence ~~ended~~ was the opening of a prophecy. 'In about two hundred years,' I had written, 'we may expect—' The sentence ended abruptly. I remembered my inability to fix my mind that ~~afternoon~~ morning, scarcely <two months ago /L: a month gone by>, & how I had broken off to get ~~the~~ my *Daily ~~News~~ Chronicle* from the newsboy. I remembered how I went down to the garden gate as he came along, & how I had listened to his *odd* story of <"Men /L•: the "Men> from Mars."}

<I went into the dining room & there>[208] <was>[209] the mutton & the bread, ¥[210] & a beer bottle overturned just as <I & the artilleryman>[211] had ~~half~~ left them. ~~I stared at them.~~ ¥[212] And then a strange thing occurred. "It is no use", said a voice. "The house is ~~desolate~~ deserted. {No one has been here these ten days.} {Do not stay here to torment yourself.} No one escaped but you? [sic]" I was startled. Had I spoken ¥[213] aloud? I turned, & the ~~Ve~~ {French} window was open behind me. {I made a step to it & stood looking out.} And there amazed & afraid, even as I stood amazed & afraid, ~~stood~~ were my cousin & my <wife. ¥>.[214] {She gave a faint cry. < ¥ "I knew", she said. "Knew—">[215]} <u>The colour vanished from her face. (C)</u> ¥[216] <I dashed out & caught her in my arms.>[217v] [150]

---

208. PR: I came down & went into the dining room. There
209. C•, PR: were
210. C: both far gone now in decay,
211. C•: the artilleryman and I
212. C: My home was desolate. I perceived the folly of the faint hope I had cherished so long.
213. C: my thought
214. C: —my wife, white and tearless!
215. C: "I came," she said. "I knew . . . knew . . ."
216. C: She put her hand to her throat—swayed.
217. PR: ~~I caught her in my arms as she fell.~~ I made a step forward and caught her in my arms. PR•:The End.

NOTES

a. See *WW* in *The Collector's Book of Science Fiction by H. G. Wells*, edited by Alan K. Russell (1978).

b. See Anthony West, *H. G. Wells*, pp.341, 351. A similar problem involves Henry Davray's standard French *WW*—first published in 1899–1900 in the *Mercure de France*, where five years later (Vol. 56, 635–636), Davray bragged that his many, sometimes large alterations, expansions, and omissions in translating Wells's works were incurred by Wells, his virtual collaborator. In fact, Davray's highly divergent *Island of Doctor Moreau* closely reflects revisions by Wells in a copy at Illinois. But Davray's *WW* rarely strays from the Heinemann text. Until and unless 149 of Davray's letters to Wells now being procured by Illinois reveal a collaboration, Davray's changes are not worth noting. Some place names disappear, and, e.g., it is unusual and quite remarkably lengthy when Davray revises the first two sentences of Book II. Also excluded is Tauchnitz (1898), a faithful resetting of Heinemann for India and the colonies.

c. In C–P, the title "After the Fifteen Days" is retained and does double duty, covering what MS covers under that title and the next, "London Derelict." PR reverts to two titles: "The Work of Fifteen Days" and "Dead London," with the new "Man on Putney Hill" in between. But from PR on, "Fifteen Days" begins three paragraphs later than in MS–P (in MS lumped together as the opening paragraph), and the new chapter cut causes the three paragraphs to conclude the preceding chapter, "The

Stillness" (created in PR by splitting off, enlarging, and renaming the second half of PP's "Death of the Curate"). But the new chapter cut was not Wells's first idea. At the old cut, he wrote and canceled "On Putney Common" (see above, note 18), as if thinking of amalgamating the stuff of "Fifteen Days" and "Putney Hill" under that head.

d. MS contains twenty-eight 8 x 10 inch sheets, some cut off, some with paste-ons. In numbering, Wells skipped 6, repeated 24 and 25, and so ended with 27. The Illinois numbering of *WW* manuscript sheets is unreliable, too, but is necessary for designation and retrieval and is used here.

e. Here J omits some sentences, resuming with the last sentence before MS's unpublished segment (see note g).

f. Should be "Street Cobham" (as it is a few lines later). See map for locations of the towns.

g. J resumes (see note e).

h. Here, C–P skips "Marriott" and instantly realigns with MS some lines into the first paragraph of MS's next chapter, "London Derelict," but no new chapter head appears (in C–P, "Dead London" is part of "Fifteen Days"). In PR, though, the typist is here instructed to shift C–P's third-to-next paragraph (identified in note o) to this point to the end of "Fifteen Days"; then to "Insert the ms marked K" ("Putney Hill"); and after "K," to insert, "~~VIII XXIV~~ VII. Dead London." All texts after PR are so set up, though with number "VIII" (see note n). Indeed, the interpolation of "Putney Hill" perhaps led Wells into toying with three, rather than two, "book" divisions. Before the instruction to insert "K," Wells wrote and canceled: "End of Book II," and on PR's title page is inscribed: "Book I. The Coming of the Martians. ~~Book II. The Nearer View. The Martians. Book III.~~ Book II. ~~The Martians Prevail.~~ The Earth Under the Martians."

i. From here to the end of the paragraph, a vertical line and a notation tell the typist: "omit this in copy B & insert a blank sheet." The tail of the line hooks under the text but is scissored off and actually hooks under the next paragraph, which is pasted in. Both the line and the tail are canceled, as are the directions. This may have been done by the typist; she apparently often crossed off directions after complying.

j. These final lines of sheet 11 (misnumbered "12") can be made out under a paste-on (itself numbered "28"). Since MS ends with "27," it is likely "28" was ready but not needed and was utilized here to cover, supersede, and extend the bottom of sheet 11.

k. Wells squeezed in this paragraph after writing the next one. The two fill the paste-on cited in note j. For simplicity, this paragraph is treated as an interpolation and the next one as straight text.

m. Wells had dedicated *The Stolen Bacillus and Other Incidents* to his friend and admirer, H. B. Marriott Watson, literary editor of the *Pall Mall Gazette.*

n. The "Putney Hill" draft includes the heading "Dead London" and a few opening words to that chapter which Wells used instead of an alternative opening in PR (see the textual note here). Under "Dead London" (numbered "VIII," as it is from L on, and not "VII," as in PR), he wrote: "After I had parted from the artilleryman I went down the hill, & by the <straight road /L: High Street> across the bridge to <Lambeth /E: Fulham>. The red weed was tumultuous at that time, & nearly choked the bridge roadway, but its fronds were already whitened (L)& shrivelled in patches, by the spreading disease, that presently removed it so swiftly. At the corner of the lane that runs to Putney Bridge Station [a curlicue at the end of the sheet ties this to PR's] I found a man lying" (for which see textual note). J now drops from the collation because, after the head "Dead New York City" and the words "After I had parted from the artilleryman I descended the hill toward Fort George," J reverts to C with "I found a man lying."

o. From PR on, this passage on "the extermination of mankind" is made to form the conclusion of "The Work of Fifteen Days" (see note h).

p. The artilleryman voices the same sentiments: "All that's happened so far is through our not having the sense to keep quiet" (see p. 173).

q. Sheet 21 (bottom) is blank, sheet 22 (top) is canceled, and the cancel may signal an earlier state; see note r.

r. The deleted "purple streamer" and "evil explosive," found nowhere else, evidently refer to descriptions that were in an earlier state of MS or in the otherwise missing complete draft of which MS is the conclusion.

s. For the next paragraph and a half (see note t), the collation of MS ceases with P. In PR, Wells substituted the paragraphs below (Illinois 96–97). They correspond closely to L and are transcribed here without collation since they are entirely of a later date than MS:

~~The wound *had healed*~~ would heal, the life of the city would come again. ~~But what healing was there for me?~~

~~V~~   ~~IX~~   XXII [as in P]   VIII
~~Home coming to Ruins~~   ~~Ashes~~   Wreckage

And now comes the strangest thing in my story. And yet perhaps it is not altogether strange. I remember, clearly & coldly & vividly, all that I did that day until the time that I stood weeping & ~~raising~~ praising God upon the summit of Primrose Hill. And then I forget.

Of the next three days I know nothing. [Paste-on begins.] I have learnt since that so far from my being the first discoverer of the Martian ~~overthrow~~ overthrow, several ~~distin wanderers like~~ such wanderers as myself had already discovered this on the previous day. ~~The~~ One man had gone {to St. Martins le Grand} & while I sheltered in the cabmen's hut, had {contrived to} telegraphed Paris. Thence the joyful news had flashed all over the world—a thousand cities chilled by ghastly apprehensions suddenly flashed into frantic illumination, they knew of it in Dublin, Edinburgh, Manchester, Birmingham, at the time {when} I stood upon the verge of the pit. Already men, weeping with joy as I have heard, {shouting, & staying their work to shake hands & shout,} were making up trains, even as near as Crewe, to descend upon London. {The church bells that had ceased a fortnight since, suddenly ~~awoke~~ caught the news until all England was bell ringing.} Men on cycles, lean faced, unkempt, tore along every country lane, shouting of the ~~great news of God's~~ unhoped deliverance, {shouting} to ~~the~~ {crouching gaunt staring} figures of despair. And for the food! ~~When To think of those Frenchmen, heedless of pay, Across the Atlantic~~ Across the Channel, across ~~St. Georges~~ the Irish Sea, across the Atlantic, corn, & bread & meat was tearing to our relief. All the shipping in the world seemed going Londonward in those days. And ~~though~~ of all this I have no memory. {I ~~drove~~ drifted,—a demented man} [Paste-on ends] ~~& then~~ I found myself in a house of kindly people, who had found me {on the third day} wandering, weeping & ~~raving~~ raving through the streets of Saint Johns Wood. They have told me since that I was singing some inane doggerel about "{The} Last Men left Alive {Hurrah! The last man left alive."} ~~I am not~~ Troubled as they were with their own affairs these people, whose name I may not even give here, much as I would like to ~~shout m~~ express my gratitude to them, nevertheless cumbered themselves with me, sheltered me & protected me from myself. Apparently they had learnt {something of} my story from me during the days of my lapse. ~~They avoided my questions at first.~~

~~At last very gently, seeing I would not be denied, they broke it to me that Leatherhead was destroyed. A Martian had destroyed it out of mere wantoness as it seemed{, on the seventh of the fifteen days. . .}~~

I was a lonely man & they were very kind to me. I remained with them four days. {I was a lonely man & a sad one & they bore with me.} ~~And~~ All that time I felt a vague ~~desire~~ {a growing} craving to /land/ once more in whatever remained of the little life that seemed so bright & happy in my past. {It was a mere hopeless desire to feast upon my misery. They dissuaded me. They did all they could to divert me from this morbidity.} But at last I could resist the impulse no longer, & promising faithfully to return to them, [96] {parting from these four day friends as I will confess with tears, I} went out, {again} into the streets that had lately been so dark {& strange & empty}. {Already they were busy with returning people, in places even there were shops open, & I saw a drinking fountain running water.}

~~I was consumed by my own sorrow.~~
~~All over England~~
I remember how mockingly bright the day seemed as I went back {on my melancholy pilgrimage to} ~~to~~ the little house at Woking, how busy the streets & vivid the {moving} life about me. So many people were abroad everywhere, ~~buses running again, workmen at work, shops reopened~~ busied in a thousand activities, that it seemed incredible that any great ~~section~~ proportion of the population could have ~~died~~ been slain. But then I noticed how yellow the skins of the people I met, {how shaggy the hair of the men} how large & bright the eyes, & every other ~~person I passed was dressed in black~~ ~~wore~~ & every other man still wore his dusty rags. {The faces seemed all with one of two expressions, a leaping exultation & energy, or a grim resolution. Save for the expression of the faces London seemed a city of tramps. The vestries were indiscriminately distributing bread *sent us by the French government.*} The ribs of the /lean/ few horses showed {dismally. *Haggard Special constables with white badges stood at the corners of every street.* ~~But~~ I saw little of the mischief wrought by the Martians until I reached Wellington Street, & then I saw the red weed clambering over the buttresses of Waterloo Bridge.}

[Side paste-on begins.] ~~In Wellington Street~~ At the corner of the bridge too I saw one of the most grotesque contrasts of all that time, a sheet of ~~coars~~ paper flaunting against a thicket of red weed, transfixed by a stick that kept it in place. It was the placard of the first newspaper to resume publication,—The Daily Mail. I bought a copy for a {blackened} shilling I found in my pocket. Most of it was in blank, but the solitary compositor {who did the thing} had amused himself by making a grotesque scheme of fragments of advertisement stereo on the ~~last~~ back page. The matter he printed was emotion—the news organization had not {as yet} found its way back. I learnt nothing fresh except that already in one week, the examination of the Martian mechanisms had yielded astonishing results. Among other things the ~~Daily M~~ article assured ~~us~~ me, what I did not believe at the time, that "The Secret of Flying" {was} discovered[.] [Side paste-on ends.] At Waterloo I found, {the free trains that were taking people to their homes.} ~~as I had been led to expect, were still running~~. The first rush was already over. [Lower portion of bottom paste-on begins.] There were few people in the train & I was in no mood for casual conversation. I got a compartment to myself, & sat with folded arms, looking greyly at the sunlit devastation that flowed past the windows. [Lower portion of bottom paste-on ends.] ~~And directly beyond Vauxhall I began to see traces of the~~ ~~And~~ Just outside the terminus, the ~~railway~~ train jolted over temporary rails, & ~~the~~ on either side of the railway the houses were blackened ruins. To Clapham {Junction} the face of London was grimy with the powder of the Black Smoke in spite of two days of {thunderstorms &} rain, & at Clapham Junction, the line had been wrecked again {, there were hundreds of *out of work* clerks & shopmen working ~~wit~~ side by side with the customary navvies} & {we} were jolted over a hasty relaying. All down the line from there the aspect of the country was ~~strange~~ gaunt & unfamiliar, Wimbledon particularly had suffered. Walton by virtue of its unburnt pinewoods seemed the least hurt of any place along the line. [Top portion of bottom paste-on begins.] {The Wandle, the Mole, every little stream ha was a heaped mass of Red Weed, in appearance between butcher meat & pickled cabbage. The sandy pine woods were too dry however for the festoons of the red climber.} At Beyond Wimbledon within sight of the line in certain nursery grounds were the heaped masses of the earth about the sixth cylinder. A number of people were standing about it, & some sappers & were busy with constr in the midst of it. Over it flaunted a Union Jack, flapping cheerfully in the morning breeze. The nursery grounds were everywhere crimson with the weed, a wide expanse of lurid colour, cut with purple shadows, & very painful to the eye. Ones eyes went with infinite relief from the {scorched} greys & sullen reds of the foreground to the blue green softness of the eastward hills. [Top portion of bottom paste-on ends.] [97]

t. Here continuity of descent from MS through E resumes (see note s), as does the full collation.

u. By June 12, 1896, under title "The Man at the Coach and Horses," *The Invisible Man* was two-thirds complete, and Wells had sent it to his agent, Pinker.

v. Here ends MS. A coda of a few pages, a draft of which is at Illinois, concludes C–P. It is canceled in PR, and "The End" is written instead, but a revision of it forms "The Epilogue" of subsequent texts, except NY.

APPENDIX II

The War of the Worlds *in the Yellow Press*

DAVID Y. HUGHES

Ever since the Mercury Theatre's Halloween prank electrified a million Americans back in 1938,[1] Orson Welles is often credited with originating the invasion from Mars. Actually, of course, he performed a brilliant adaptation of a brilliant romance by H. G. Wells, written 40 years earlier, *The War of the Worlds*. Wells himself was not delighted. "I am deeply concerned at the effect of the broadcast," he cabled. "Totally unwarranted liberties were taken with my book."[2] Incidentally, two South American versions of the broadcast in 1944 and 1949 again provoked dangerous panics, one in Chile, and a second, which claimed at least 15 lives, in Ecuador.[3]

Wells sounds rather petulant worrying about his copyright in the face of a major panic, but the fact is that the Mercury Theatre broadcast must have seemed to him to be simply a tiresome repetition of a copyright infringement of 40 years earlier. In 1897 and 1898, just before book publication, *The War of the Worlds* was serialized twice in unauthorized, lurid versions, one of them localized to New York City—like Orson Welles's—and the other to Boston. The organs of publication were two of the country's most aggressive yellow journals, the New York *Evening Journal* and the Boston *Post*, both of which enlivened their texts with daily sensational illustrations.

Now, since this yellow journalism phase of *The War of the Worlds* has escaped previous notice by historians, my purpose here is simply 1) to inquire briefly into the circumstances of the newspaper serializations and 2) to survey their contents as compared to that of the authorized serial text (which had appeared already in *Pearson's Magazine* in England and in *Cosmopolitan* in America).[4]

The immediate circumstances of the newspaper serializations were set forth by Wells early in 1898 in an open letter that he dispatched to America to the *Critic*. No doubt one of the rarer letters that an author has been goaded into writing, it is quoted here for the first time and quoted in full.

The Editors of the Critic:
I have received a rather startling cutting from the Boston *Post* through the Authors' Clipping Bureau. The cutting is dated Dec. 27, the accom-

Reprinted from *Journalism Quarterly* 43/4 (Winter 1966):639–646.

panying invoice is dated Dec. 31, the Boston post-mark is Jan. 7, and it
has reached me here today. From it I learn that my story "The War of
the Worlds" "as applied to New England, showing how the strange voy-
agers from Mars visited Boston and vicinity," is now appearing in the *Post*.
This adaptation is a serious infringement of my copyright and has been
made altogether without my participation or consent. I feel bound to
protest in the most emphatic way against this manipulation of my work
in order to fit it to the requirements of the local geography.

Yet it is possible that this affair is not so much downright wickedness
as a terrible mistake. The story originally appeared simultaneously in the
American *Cosmopolitan* and the British *Pearson's Magazine*. Mr. Dewey
of the New York *Journal* called upon me in November last and arranged
for its serial republication in the evening edition of that paper. In our
agreement (of which I have his signed memorandum) it was stipulated that
the publication should be with the consent of the American publishers
and that no alterations in the text of the story should be made without
my consent. On Dec. 26 I received a cablegram from the Boston *Post*
making an offer for the serial reproduction of "The War of the Worlds"
"as New York Journal." To this I cabled "Agreed." And now I find too
late that my story has been flaunted before the cultivated public of Boston
disguised and disarrayed beyond my imagining. What has been done to
it? I fail to see how a rag of conviction can remain in it after this outrage.
I do not know what a remote Englishman may do in such a matter. At
any rate I beg you will give me the opportunity of disavowing any share
in this novel development of the local color business.

H. G. Wells

Heatherlea, Worcester Park, Surrey, England.
21 Jan., 1898.[5]

It seems that the wording "as New York Journal" might have suggested to
Wells that what the *Post* was doing for Boston the *Journal* might already
have done for New York. But the idea that one great newspaper would
deliberately lie to him and that another would deliberately trick him was
perhaps more than a "remote Englishman," unacquainted with American
newspaper enterprise, could have been expected to imagine.

What the newspapers wanted was circulation, of course. In September
of 1897 Arthur Brisbane had assumed the editorship of the *Journal* under
the now famous agreement linking his salary to circulation, and he was
developing the techniques which, aided by the rising fever for war with
Spain, were to boost sales within a year from a hundred thousand to a
million.[6] Similarly, the *Post* was rapidly building up the largest morning
circulation in the country.[7]

And simply and solely from the point of view of circulation *The War
of the Worlds* would be a good bet for two reasons. The first was John
Brisben Walker. As editor of *Cosmopolitan*, he had achieved a spectacular
success because, as one admirer put it, "he has introduced the newspaper

ideas of timeliness and dignified sensationalism into periodical literature."[8] If Walker liked the story for his audience, it was probably a good choice for the similar, if much less literate, audience of the sensational newspapers.

The second indication that *The War of the Worlds* might pull circulation would come with a glance at its ingredients. While war with Spain was only a splendid possibility, here was a war indeed. Many astronomers thought the Martian "canals" to be artificial, and Percival Lowell had recently staked his reputation on the inference that Martian civilization must far surpass our own.[9] Yet—rather curiously—no one before Wells had conceived that these alien intelligences might have designs on the earth. Thus, *The War of the Worlds* is the original tale of extraterrestrial invasion by bug-eyed monsters.[10] Wells's Martians, to be more exact, are a sort of big leathery octopus or simple cerebral sac endowed with tentacles and possessing an awesomely advanced weaponry. Incidentally, they are vampires. Yet Wells rationalized all these attributes in up-to-date scientific language.

Nothing could be more adaptable to the requirements of yellow journalism (as listed by Mott): the scarehead, the screaming illustration, the appeal to the pseudoscientific.[11] How adaptable, may be seen from the three drawings [originally] reproduced with this article including not only the two scenes of violence but also the cutaway of the machine directed—according to the caption—by Martian "mind power" (a bit of pseudoscience of the illustrator's very own, it would seem, since no trace of this magical Martian faculty appears in the story itself). Thus, the escalation of sensationalism proceeded apace.

It was good business all round. The *Cosmopolitan* version was manipulated by the *Journal*; the *Journal* version in turn was manipulated by the *Post*; and afterwards both papers undertook a sequel, "Edison's Conquest of Mars" by Garrett P. Serviss and Thomas Alva Edison (so the titlepiece stated), depicting the swift revenge of Yankee ingenuity against the Red Planet.[12]

Coming now to the question of the texts themselves, the newspapers in general aimed at a detailed account of painful and eccentric horrors having a special immediacy and "reality" for New Yorkers (or Bostonians) on account of the home locale. If they did not attempt a hoax, it was probably because they did not think they could bring it off; or perhaps they preferred the continuing notoriety promised by several weeks of daily serialization.

At any rate—aside from the mechanics of substituting American locales for the English one—the papers 1) ruthlessly cut passages that deviated from the straight chronicle of death and destruction, and 2) interpolated long passages enumerating fresh Martian marvels and atrocities. The additions were mostly the work of the *Post*; the preliminary task of deletion was accomplished mostly by the *Journal*.

A reader of *The War of the Worlds* today is attracted by Wells's cunning and deliberate admixture of normality with calamity, familiarity with grotesquerie, the human with the bizarre. To the *Journal*, however, the ordinary, commonplace scenes were padding to be cut as fast as they appeared in the text, and in the earlier installments the cutting must approach fifty per cent. Here are a few samples, taken almost at random, of the more human types of scenes which were deleted from *Cosmopolitan*.

The first is a sample of commonplace humor. After fainting during the lightning-like carnage of the initial encounter with the Martians, the hero comes to and stumbles onto a group of people as he dashes into town:

> "What news from the common?" I said.
> "Ain't yer just *been* there?" asked the man.
> "People seem fair silly about the common," said the woman over the gate. "What's it all about?"
> It seemed impossible to make these people grasp a terror upon which my mind even could not retain its grip of realization. "Haven't you heard of the men from Mars?" said I.
> "Quite enough," said the woman over the gate; "thanks," and all three of them laughed.[13]

The newspapers likewise deleted the following passage. The commonplace humor broadens:

> "Ain't they got any necks, then?" asked a third [soldier] abruptly, a little, contemplative, dark man smoking a pipe.
> I repeated my description.
> "Octopuses," said he; "that's what I calls 'em. Talk about fishers of men—fighters of fish it is this time."
> "It ain't no murder killin' beasts like that," said the first speaker.
> "Why not shell the damn things strite off and finish 'em?" said the little dark man. "You carn't tell what they might do."[14]

At another level, Wells might state the persistence of the commonplace as an underlying psychological datum. This passage, too, was deleted:

> My terror had fallen from me like a garment . . . as if something turned over and the point of view altered abruptly. There was no sensible transition from one state of mind to the other. I was immediately the self of every day again—a decent, ordinary citizen. The silent common, the impulse of my flight, the starting flames was as if it were a dream.[15]

Finally, here is a deletion where the principle of the persistence of the commonplace has achieved the level of a basic sociological datum:

> The most extraordinary thing . . . was the dovetailing of the commonplace habits of our social order, with the first beginnings of the series of events

that was to topple that social order headlong. If, on Friday night, you had taken a pair of compasses and drawn a circle with a radius of five miles, . . . I doubt if you would have had one human being outside it, . . . whose emotions or habits were at all affected by the newcomers.[16]

Such are some of the more strictly human types of passages cut by the papers with the effect of diminishing the artistic (novelistic) side of the work in favor of a sort of directory of terrors. Moreover, it was a treatment which could be administered with a minimum loss of physical continuity because of the loose structure of *The War of the Worlds*. Since the story is narrated throughout by a supposed eyewitness who speaks in the first person, it was only necessary to retain his more bloodcurdling adventures but to excise the "padding" of commonplace observation, speculation and dialogue.

Turning now to the equally large category of additions, it should be noted to begin with that Wells himself wrote a major interpolation for the *Journal* and the subsequently published book—the only authorized departure from *Cosmopolitan*—the episode of the drunken artilleryman who proposes in about five thousand words that men recapture the earth by first disappearing into drains and sewers.[17] Both papers printed it in virtually the form in which it was soon to appear in the published book. They did so presumably because it occurs towards the end of the story and neither paper bothered to edit extensively after the first half. It is ironic that thus one of the most purely human chapters in *The War of the Worlds* first saw print in the gaudy newspaper versions.

Just as the loose, first person narrative structure of the story enabled the *Journal* to cut novelistic matter out, so, too, it enabled the *Post* to pump "yellow" matter in. Actually, the *Journal* pioneered the latter procedure, too, in a modest way. The trick was to seize a moment when the Martians were entering a town, and, ignoring the fact that the narrator was running for his life, require him to describe the destruction of the community tree by tree and brick by brick. Doubtless the childlike audience of these papers never noticed that the narrator was meanwhile stranded in a state of suspended animation. Such interpolations were one hundred per cent the inspiration of the newspapers.

In this fashion, the *Journal* interpolated a bird's-eye view of the wanton destruction of Brooklyn Bridge . . . and of other Manhattan landmarks. It is a short addition compared to several in the *Post* but already indicates the distinctive types of targets favored by the Martians. I do not refer to the bridge, which, after all, might have some military potential. During their New York outing, the Martians defaced or destroyed numerous specimens of five types of targets of a very different sort: of churches, St. John's Cathedral, St. Patrick's Cathedral and Grace Church, "carrying out the Martians' purpose that the people forget their God"; of institutions of learning,

Columbia University, whereat "priceless manuscripts from the library were blown over the ground like dead leaves"; of historic mansions, many along Fifth Avenue; of historic monuments, Grant's Tomb and the patriotic statues in Madison Square and Union Square, "as if the Martians wished that the people forget their heroes"; and, finally, of government buildings, the city hall.[18]

The Bostonian Martians, too, it could be shown, everywhere attacked the same five types of targets. Only they found many more of them because Boston is so rich in history. "The Martians, in going from Concord to Lexington," the *Post* asserted, "had in a general way followed the route which the English soldiers had taken in 1775."[19] And both Concord and Lexington of course contained almost limitless fodder for the heat ray. Concord offered, for example, the statues of the "Minute Man" and of the first redcoat who fell under "the shot that was heard around the world"; and then there were the homes, among others, of Emerson, Thoreau and Hawthorne; and there were several churches and the historic city hall and library.[20] In Lexington there was more of the same. But a quotation of some length alone can give the effect of such a sheer bulk of hackneyed detail:

> As they entered Lexington by way of Monument Street the heat ray was turned on with deadly effect. The first building to be destroyed was St. Bridget's Catholic Church, which crumbled into ruins as if it were a pile of match wood. On they came to the Common, around which clustered so many associations dear to the hearts of the people of Lexington. The tall spire of the Unitarian Church, at the western side of the Common, attracted immediate attention.
>
> The heat ray flashed on it, and the wooden spire and building became a mass of flame. On the southern border of the Common stood the Congregational Church. It was built of stone, but it collapsed as quickly as if it had been a house of cards.
>
> All the famous memorials on the Common disappeared in the common [!] ruin. The old monument on the west side erected in 1797, had been regarded as one of the oldest memorials of the revolution in the country. It was of granite, about twenty feet high, and the inscription was by the Rev. Jonas Clark, the patriot priest. The heat ray struck the shaft and it shivered into atoms. To the rear of the monument was the stone vault into which the remains of Lexington's martyrs to freedom were transferred on the sixtieth anniversary of their death. At the touch of the heat ray the vault split open and the resting place of the dead became a funeral pyre.[21]

And there is much, much more. Afterwards, the Martians went on to Waltham and finally to Boston, repeating their unholy depredations as they marched. In these industrial centers, too, they destroyed factories, railroads and shipping.

The Martians of the sensational newspapers are simply the antichrist rampant, and the Boston readers' appetite for such fare may well have been great. Yet it makes a bloodless narrative. The editors felt the need of a blow struck for humanity, something spectacular and military—and particularly so since the Martians finally succumb quite tamely to terrestrial disease germs, against which their systems have no defenses. However, Wells had provided at least the beginnings of a blood military action in his London version, describing how an armored naval ram smashed two of the tripods as they waded offshore near the Thames estuary. The *Post* liked the idea enough to use it twice, once with the *Katahdin* (the only ram then in the U.S. fleet) and in the next installment with the *Kearsarge*, our biggest and latest battleship (not completed, actually, until later in 1898).[22] Both ships sank with all hands, of course, but not before inflicting heavy damage.

Then came the climax. An undamaged tripod still wading about Boston Harbor happened to turn its heat ray on Governor's Island, the ammunition dump. Honeycombed with caves full of high explosives, the island blew to smithereens, smashing the tripod, "Samsonlike," amid the debris and raising a fifty foot tidal wave which hit the waterfront with a regular insurance inventory of damages.[23]

It was left to the next installment to itemize the destruction of the interior of the city—rather anticlimactically—after which the remaining half of the story was allowed to take care of itself except for the perfunctory editing of English names. Both newspapers probably felt that few new readers could be attracted while the old ones were safely hooked. Or maybe some poor alcoholic hack had simply run out of steam.

At any rate, thus ends this chronicle of the first Martians in America.

In the publishing history of *The War of the Worlds*, the affair is no more than a queer episode and an odd foreshadowing of the events of 40 years later, when broadcasting so far outstripped the newspapers in immediacy of impact that people imagined that—in a matter of half an hour—the Martians landed, erected their tripods and wiped out thousands of troops deployed between them and New York City while they were reported in all these activities by ever-vigilant CBS.

In the history of American journalism, it is a garish episode considering the later fame of the victimized H. G. Wells—and all the more garish for being forgotten for 70 years.

In the history of yellow journalism, it must have been a rather characteristic episode. The yellow journals systematically distorted fact to suit a melodramatic outlook, until, as Will Irwin remarked: "From this to outright falsehood was but a step, taken without perception by men no longer capable of seeing the truth."[24] This refers to truth to fact, truth to the news. The idea of "truth" in a piece of fiction—the idea that fiction can be falsified—would be far harder for such men to see. Besides, hadn't they bought the story? And didn't they own it? And who ever heard of this H. C. Wells anyway?[25]

NOTES

1. Hadley Cantril, *The Invasion from Mars: A Study in the Psychology of Panic. With the Complete Script of the Famous Orson Welles Broadcast* (Princeton: Princeton University Press, 1940) pp.58–59.

2. Quoted by Peter Noble in *The Fabulous Orson Welles* (London: Hutchinson & Co., Ltd., 1956), p.117.

3. "Those Men from Mars," *Newsweek*, November 27, 1944, p.89; *Time*, February 21, 1949, p.46; New York *Times*, February 14, 1949, p.7.

4. April–December 1897 respectively in vols. 2–3 and in vols. 22–24. Cosmo Rowe's illustrations gave the newspapers their model for the Martian tripods.

5. Vol. 29 (March 1898), p.184.

6. Will Irwin, "Yellow Journalism," in Edwin H. Ford and Edwin Emery, eds., *Highlights in the History of the American Press* (Minneapolis: University of Minnesota Press, 1954), pp.277–278.

7. Frank Luther Mott, *American Journalism, A History: 1690–1960*, 3d ed. (New York: The Macmillan Company, 1962), p.560.

8. Quoted in Frank Luther Mott, *A History of American Magazines: 1885–1905* (Cambridge: Harvard University Press, 1957), p.482.

9. Percival Lowell, *Mars* (Boston: Houghton, Mifflin and Company, 1895), pp.208–209.

10. Mark R. Hillegas, "The First Invasions from Mars," *Michigan Alumnus Quarterly Review 66* (Winter 1960):107–112.

11. Mott, *American Journalism*, p.539. Besides scareheads, illustrations and pseudoscience, Mott lists sympathy with the "underdog" and the use of the Sunday supplement as the five identifying features of yellow journalism.

12. Started January 12 and February 6 respectively. Edison's collaboration is more than doubtful since the *Post* claims it but the *Journal* does not. [For a recent discussion of "Edison's Conquest of Mars," see H. Bruce Franklin, *War Stars: The Superweapon and the American Imagination* (New York: Oxford University Press, 1988), pp.64–68.]

13. May 1897, p.6.

14. June 1897, p.216.

15. May 1897, p.6.

16. Ibid., p.8. But the *Journal* retained the second sentence, December 17, p.11.

17. A notation from Wells to his typist on the margin of the manuscript of *The War of the Worlds* states that the pages of the artilleryman episode are "wanted to send to America (where the story is now appearing in a New York paper)." The manuscript is in the Wells Archive of the University of Illinois. For a critical edition of it, see the author's unpublished Ph.D. dissertation, "An Edition and a Survey of H. G. Wells' *The War of the Worlds*," University of Illinois, 1962.

18. December 25, p.9.

19. January 13, p.5.

20. Ibid.

21. Ibid.

22. January 20, p.5; January 21, p.5. For ship data, see Fred T. Jane, *All the World's Fighting Ships* (London: Sampson, Low, Marston and Co., Ltd., 1904), pp.203, 222.

23. January 21, p.5.

24. In Ford and Emery, p.279.

25. The *Post's* daily title-pieces credited "H. C. Wells" from start to finish. . . . The *Journal* started with "H. G." but then misprinted "H. C." on December 18 and thereafter.

APPENDIX III

Of a Book Unwritten
("The Man of the Year Million")

H . G . W E L L S

Accomplished literature is all very well in its way, no doubt, but much more fascinating to the contemplative man are the books that have not been written. These latter are no trouble to hold; there are no pages to turn over. One can read them in bed on sleepless nights without a candle. Turning to another topic, primitive man in the works of the descriptive anthropologist is certainly a very entertaining and quaint person, but the man of the future, if we only had the facts, would appeal to us more strongly. Yet where are the books? As Ruskin has said somewhere, *apropos* of Darwin, it is not what man has been, but what he will be, that should interest us.

The contemplative man in his easy chair, pondering this saying, suddenly beholds in the fire, through the blue haze of his pipe, one of these great unwritten volumes. It is large in size, heavy in lettering, seemingly by one Professor Holzkopf, presumably Professor at Weissnichtwo. "The Necessary Characters of the Man of the Remote Future deduced from the Existing Stream of Tendency" is the title. The worthy Professor is severely scientific in his method, and deliberate and cautious in his deductions, the contemplative man discovers as he pursues his theme, and yet the conclusions are, to say the least, remarkable. We must figure the excellent Professor expanding the matter at great length, voluminously technical, but the contemplative man—since he has access to the only copy—is clearly at liberty to make such extracts and abstracts as he chooses for the unscientific reader. Here, for instance, is something of practicable lucidity that he considers admits of quotation.

"The theory of evolution," writes the Professor, "is now universally accepted by zoologists and botanists, and it is applied unreservedly to man. Some question, indeed, whether it fits his soul, but all agree it accounts for his body. Man, we are assured, is descended from ape-like ancestors, moulded by circumstances into men, and these apes again were derived from ancestral forms of a lower order, and so up from the primordial protoplasmic

As reprinted by Wells in *Certain Personal Matters* (1898), from *Pall Mall Budget*, November 9, 1893.

jelly. Clearly, then, man, unless the order of the universe has come to an end, will undergo further modification in the future, and at last cease to be man, giving rise to some other type of animated being. At once the fascinating question arises, What will this being be? Let us consider for a little the plastic influences at work upon our species.

"Just as the bird is the creature of the wing, and is all moulded and modified to flying, and just as the fish is the creature that swims, and has had to meet the inflexible conditions of a problem in hydrodynamics, so man is the creature of the brain; he will live by intelligence, and not by physical strength, if he live at all. So that much that is purely 'animal' about him is being, and must be, beyond all question, suppressed in his ultimate development. Evolution is no mechanical tendency making for perfection according to the ideas current in the year of grace 1897; it is simply the continual adaptation of plastic life, for good or evil, to the circumstances that surround it. . . . We notice this decay of the animal part around us now, in the loss of teeth and hair, in the dwindling hands and feet of men, in their smaller jaws, and slighter mouths and ears. Man now does by wit and machinery and verbal agreement what he once did by bodily toil; for once he had to catch his dinner, capture his wife, run away from his enemies, and continually exercise himself, for love of himself, to perform these duties well. But now all this is changed. Cabs, trains, trams, render speed unnecessary, the pursuit of food becomes easier; his wife is no longer hunted, but rather, in view of the crowded matrimonial market, seeks him out. One needs wits now to live, and physical activity is a drug, a snare even; it seeks artificial outlets and overflows in games. Athleticism takes up time and cripples a man in his competitive examinations, and in business. So is your fleshly man handicapped against his subtler brother. He is unsuccessful in life, does not marry. The better adapted survive."

The coming man, then, will clearly have a larger brain, and a slighter body than the present. But the Professor makes one exception to this. "The human hand, since it is the teacher and interpreter of the brain, will become constantly more powerful and subtle as the rest of the musculature dwindles."

Then in the physiology of these children of men, with their expanding brains, their great sensitive hands and diminishing bodies, great changes were necessarily worked. "We see now," says the Professor, "in the more intellectual sections of humanity an increasing sensitiveness to stimulants, a growing inability to grapple with such a matter as alcohol, for instance. No longer can men drink a bottle full of port; some cannot drink tea; it is too exciting for their highly-wrought nervous systems. The process will go on, and the Sir Wilfred Lawson of some near generation may find it his duty and pleasure to make the silvery spray of his wisdom tintinnabulate against the tea-tray. These facts lead naturally to the comprehension of others. Fresh raw meat was once a dish for a king. Now refined persons scarcely touch meat unless it is cunningly disguised. Again, consider the case of turnips; the raw root is now a thing almost uneatable, but once upon a time a turnip must have been a rare and fortunate find, to be torn up with delirious eagerness and devoured in ecstasy. The time will come when the change will affect all the other fruits of the earth. Even now only the young of mankind eat apples raw—the young always preserving ancestral characteristics after their disappearance in the adult. Some day even boys will regard apples without emotion. The boy of the future, one must believe, will gaze on an apple with the same unspeculative languor with which he now regards a flint"—in the absence of a cat.

"Furthermore, fresh chemical discoveries came into action as modifying influences upon men. In the prehistoric period even, man's mouth had ceased to be an instrument for grasping food; it is still growing continually less prehensile, his front teeth are smaller, his lips thinner and less muscular; he has a new organ, a mandible not of irreparable tissue, but of bone and steel—a knife and fork. There is no reason why things should stop at partial artificial division thus afforded; there is every reason, on the contrary, to believe my statement that some cunning exterior mechanism will presently masticate and insalivate his dinner, relieve his diminishing salivary glands and teeth, and at last altogether abolish them."

Then what is not needed disappears. What use is there for external ears, nose, and brow ridges now? The two latter once protected the eye from injury in conflict and in falls, but in these days we keep on our legs, and at peace. Directing his thoughts in this way, the reader may presently conjure up a dim, strange vision of the latter-day face: "Eyes large, lustrous, beautiful, soulful; above them, no longer separated by rugged brow ridges, is the top of the head, a glistening, hairless dome, terete and beautiful; no craggy nose rises to disturb by its unmeaning shadows the symmetry of that calm face, no vestigial ears project; the mouth is a small, perfectly round aperture, toothless and gumless, jawless, unanimal, no futile emotions disturbing its roundness as it lies, like the harvest moon or the evening star, in the wide firmament of face." Such is the face the Professor beholds in the future.

Of course parallel modifications will also affect the body and limbs. "Every day so many hours and so much energy are required for digestion; a gross torpidity, a carnal lethargy, seizes on mortal men after dinner. This may and can be avoided. Man's knowledge of organic chemistry widens daily. Already he can supplement the gastric glands by artificial devices. Every doctor who administers physic implies that the bodily functions may be artificially superseded. We have pepsine, pancreatine, artificial gastric acid—I know not what like mixtures. Why, then, should not the stomach be ultimately superannuated altogether? A man who could not only leave his dinner to be cooked, but also leave it to be masticated and digested, would have vast social advantages over his food-digesting fellow. This is, let me remind you here, the calmest, most passionless, and scientific working out of the future forms of things from the data of the present. At this stage the following facts may perhaps stimulate your imagination. There can be no doubt that many of the arthropods, a division of animals more ancient and even now more prevalent than the vertebrata, have undergone more phylogenetic modification"—a beautiful phrase—"than even the most modified of vertebrated animals. Simple forms like the lobsters display a primitive structure parallel with that of the fishes. However, in such a form as the degraded 'Chondracanthus,' the structure has diverged far more widely from its original type than in man. Among some of these most highly modified crustaceans the whole of the alimentary canal—that is, all the food-digesting and food-absorbing parts—form a useless solid cord: the animal is nourished—it is a parasite—by absorption of the nutritive fluid in which it swims. Is there any absolute impossibility in supposing man to be destined for a similar change; to imagine him no longer dining, with unwieldy paraphernalia of servants and plates, upon food queerly dyed and distorted, but nourishing himself in elegant simplicity by immersion in a tub of nutritive fluid?

"There grows upon the impatient imagination a building, a dome of crystal, across the translucent surface of which flushes of the most glorious and pure prismatic colours pass and fade and change. In the centre of this transparent chameleon-tinted dome is a circular white marble basin filled with some clear, mobile, amber liquid, and in this plunge and float strange beings. Are they birds?

"They are the descendants of man—at dinner. Watch them as they hop on their hands—a method of progression advocated already by Bjornsen—about the pure white marble floor. Great hands they have, enormous brains, soft, liquid, soulful eyes. Their whole muscular system, their legs, their abdomens, are shrivelled to nothing, a dangling, degraded pendant to their minds."

The further visions of the Professor are less alluring.

"The animals and plants die away before men, except such as he preserves for his food or delight, or such as maintain a precarious footing about him as commensals and parasites. These vermin and pests must succumb sooner or later to his untiring inventiveness and incessantly growing discipline. When he learns (the chemists are doubtless getting towards the secret now) to do the work of chlorophyll without the plant, then his necessity for other animals and plants upon the earth will disappear. Sooner or later, where there is no power of resistance and no necessity, there comes extinction. In the last days man will be alone on the earth, and his food will be won by the chemist from the dead rocks and the sunlight.

"And—one may learn the full reason in that explicit and painfully right book, the 'Data of Ethics'—the irrational fellowship of man will give place to an intellectual co-operation, and emotion fall within the scheme of reason. Undoubtedly it is a long time yet, but a long time is nothing in the face of eternity, and every man who dares think of these things must look eternity in the face."

Then the earth is ever radiating away heat into space, the Professor reminds us. And so at last comes a vision of earthly cherubim, hopping heads, great unemotional intelligences, and little hearts, fighting together perforce and fiercely against the cold that grips them tighter and tighter. For the world is cooling—slowly and inevitably it grows colder as the years roll by. "We must imagine these creatures," says the Professor, "in galleries and laboratories deep down in the bowels of the earth. The whole world will be snow-covered and piled with ice; all animals, all vegetation vanished, except this last branch of the tree of life. The last men have gone even deeper, following the diminishing heat of the planet, and vast metallic shafts and ventilators make way for the air they need."

So with a glimpse of these human tadpoles, in their deep close gallery, with their boring machinery ringing away, and artificial lights glaring and casting black shadows, the Professor's horoscope concludes. Humanity in dismal retreat before the cold, changed beyond recognition. Yet the Professor is reasonable enough, his facts are current science, his methods orderly. The contemplative man shivers at the prospect, starts up to poke the fire, and the whole of this remarkable book that is not written vanishes straightway in the smoke of his pipe. This is the great advantage of this unwritten literature: there is no bother in changing the books. The contemplative man consoles himself for the destiny of the species with the lost portion of Kubla Khan.

APPENDIX IV

Intelligence on Mars

H. G. WELLS

Year after year, when politics cease from troubling, there recurs the question as to the existence of intelligent, sentient life on the planet Mars. The last outcrop of speculations grew from the discovery by M. Javelle of a luminous projection on the southern edge of the planet. The light was peculiar in several respects, and, among other interpretations, it was suggested that the inhabitants of Mars were flashing messages to the conjectured inhabitants of the sister-planet, Earth. No attempt at reply was made; indeed, supposing our Astronomer-Royal, with our best telescope, transported to Mars, a red riot of fire running athwart the whole of London would scarce be visible to him. The question remains unanswered, probably unanswerable. There is no doubt that Mars is very like the earth. Its days and nights, its summers and winters differ only in their relative lengths from ours. It has land and oceans, continents and islands, mountain ranges and inland seas. Its polar regions are covered with snows, and it has an atmosphere and clouds, warm sunshine and gentle rains. The spectroscope, that subtle analyst of the most distant stars, gives us reason to believe that the chemical elements familiar to us here exist on Mars. The planet, chemically and physically, is so like the earth that, as protoplasm, the only living material we know, came into existence on the earth, there is no great difficulty in supposing that it came into existence on Mars. If reason be able to guide us, we know that protoplasm, at first amorphous and unintegrated, has been guided on this earth by natural forces into that marvellous series of forms and integrations we call the animal and vegetable kingdoms. Why, under the similar guiding forces on Mars, should not protoplasm be the root of as fair a branching tree of living beings, and bear as fair a fruit of intelligent, sentient creatures?

Let us waive objections, and suppose that, beginning with a simple protoplasm, there has been an evolution of organic forms on the planet Mars, directed by natural selection and kindred agencies. Is it a necessary, or even a probable, conclusion that the evolution would have culminated in a set of creatures with sense-perception at all comparable to that of man? It will be seen at once that this raises a complicated, and as yet insoluble,

Reprinted from *Saturday Review*, April 4, 1896, pp.345–346.

problem—a problem in which, to use a mathematical phrase, there are many independent variables. The organs of sense are parts of the body, and, like bodies themselves and all their parts, present forms which are the result of an almost infinite series of variations, selections, and rejections. Geographical isolation, for instance, has been one of the great modifying agencies. Earth movements, the set of currents, and the nature of rocks acting together have repeatedly broken up land-masses into islands, and, quite independently of other modifying agencies, have broken up groups of creatures into isolated sets, with the result that these isolated sets have developed in diverging lines. He would be a bold zoologist who should say that existing animals and plants would have been as they are to-day had the distribution of land and water in the Cretaceous age been different. Since the beginning of the chalk, all the great groups of mammals have separated from the common indifferent stock, and have become molded into men and monkeys, cats and dogs, antelopes and deer, elephants and squirrels. It would be the wildest dream to suppose that the recurrent changes of sea and land, of continent and islands, that have occurred since the dawn of life on the earth, had been at all similar on Mars. Geographical distribution is only one of a vast series of independently varying changes that has gone to the making of man. Granted that there has been an evolution of protoplasm upon Mars, there is every reason to think that the creatures on Mars would be different from the creatures of earth, in form and function, in structure and in habit, different beyond the most bizarre imaginings of nightmare.

If we pursue the problem of Martian sensation more closely, we shall find still greater reason for doubting the existence of sentient beings at all comparable with ourselves. In a metaphysical sense, it is true, there is no external world outside us; the whole universe from the furthest star to the tiniest chemical atom is a figment of our brain. But in a grosser sense, we distinguish between an external reality and the poor sides of it that our senses perceive. We think of a something not ourselves, at the nature of which we guess, so far as we smell, taste, touch, weigh, see, and hear. Are these senses of ours the only imaginable probes into the nature of matter? Has the universe no facets other than those she turns to man? There are variations even in the range of our own senses. According to the rate of its vibrations, a sounding column of air may be shrilled up, or boomed down beyond all human hearing; but, for each individual, the highest and lowest audible notes differ. Were there ears to hear, there are harmonies and articulate sounds above and below the range of man. The creatures of Mars, with the slightest anatomical differences in their organs, might hear, and yet be deaf to what we hear—speak, and yet be dumb to us. On either side the visible spectrum into which light is broken by a prism there stretch active rays, invisible to us. Eyes in structure very little different to ours might see, and yet be blind to what we see. So is it with all the senses; and, even granted that the unimaginable creatures of Mars had sense-organs directly comparable with ours, there might be no common measure of what they and we hear and see, taste, smell, and touch. Moreover it is an extreme supposition that similar organs and senses should have appeared. Even among the animals of this earth, we guess at the existence of senses not possessed by ourselves. Our conscious relations to the environment are only a small part of the extent to which the environment affects us, and it would be easy to suggest possible senses different to ours. With creatures whose evolution had proceeded on different lines, resulting in shapes, structures and relations to environment impossible to imagine, it is sufficiently plain that appreciation of the environment might or must be in a fashion inscrutable to us. No phase of anthropomorphism is more naive than the supposition of men on Mars. The place of such a conception in the world of thought is with the anthropomorphic cosmogonies and religions invented by the childish conceit of primitive man.

APPENDIX V

The Things that Live on Mars

A description, based upon scientific reasoning, of the flora and fauna of our neighboring planet, in conformity with the very latest astronomical revelations

H . G . W E L L S

What sort of inhabitants may Mars possess?

To this question I gave a certain amount of attention some years ago when I was preparing a story called "The War of the Worlds," in which the Martians are supposed to attack the earth; but since that time much valuable work has been done upon that planet, and one comes to this question again with an ampler equipment of information, and prepared to consider it from new points of view.

Particularly notable and suggestive in the new literature of the subject is the work of my friend, Mr. Percival Lowell, of the Lowell Observatory, Flagstaff, Arizona, to whose publications, and especially his "Mars and its Canals," I am greatly indebted. This book contains a full statement of the case, and a very convincing case it is, not only for the belief that Mars is habitable, but that it is inhabited by creatures of sufficient energy and engineering science to make canals beside which our greatest human achievements pale into insignificance. He does not, however, enter into any speculation as to the form or appearance of these creatures, whether they are human, quasi-human, supermen, or creatures of a shape and likeness quite different from our own. Necessarily such an inquiry must be at present a speculation of the boldest description, a high imaginative flight. But at the same time it is by no means an unconditioned one. We are bound by certain facts and certain considerations. We are already forbidden by definite knowledge to adopt any foolish fantastic hobgoblin or any artistic ideal that comes into our heads and call it a Martian. Certain facts about Mars we definitely know, and we are not entitled to imagine any Martians that are not in accordance with these facts.

When one speaks of Martians one is apt to think only of those canal-builders, those beings who, if we are to accept Mr. Lowell's remarkably well-sustained conclusions, now irrigate with melting polar snows and cultivate what were once the ocean-beds of their drying planet. But after all they cannot live there alone; they can be but a part of the natural history of Mars in just the same way that man is but a part of the natural history of the earth. They must have been evolved from other related types, and so we must necessarily give our attention to the general flora and fauna of this world we are invading in imagination before we can hope to deal at all reasonably with the ruling species.

Does Life Exist on Mars?

And, firstly, will there be a flora and fauna at all? Is it valid to suppose that upon Mars we should find the same distinction between vegetable and animal that we have upon the earth? For the affirmative answer to that an excellent case can be made. The basis upon which all life rests on this planet is the green plant. The green plant alone is able to convert really dead inorganic matter into living substance, and this it does, as everybody knows nowadays, by the peculiar virtue of its green coloring matter, chlorophyl, in the presence of sunshine. All other animated things live directly or indirectly upon the substance of green-leaved plants. Either they eat vegetable food directly, or they eat it indirectly by eating other creatures which live on vegetable food. Now upon this earth it is manifest that nature has tried innumerable experiments and made countless beginnings. Yet she has never produced any other means than chlorophyl whereby inorganic matter, that is to say, soil and minerals and ingredients out of the air, can be built up into living matter. It is plausible, therefore, to suppose that on Mars also, if there is life, chlorophyl will lie at the base of the edifice; in other words, that there will be a vegetable kingdom. And our supposition is greatly strengthened by the fact upon which Mr. Lowell lays stress, that, as the season which corresponds to our spring arrives, those great areas of the Martian surface that were once ocean-beds are suffused with a distinct bluish green hue. It is not the yellow-green of a leafing poplar or oak-tree; it is the bluish green of a springtime pine.

This all seems to justify us in assuming a flora at least upon Mars, a green vegetable kingdom after the fashion of our earthly one. Let us ask now how far we may assume likeness. Is an artist justified in drawing grass and wheat, oaks and elms and roses in a Martian landscape? Is it probable that evolution has gone upon exactly parallel lines on the two planets? Well, here again we have definite facts upon which to base our answer. We know enough to say that the vegetable forms with which we are familiar upon the earth would not "do," as people say, on Mars, and we can even indicate in general terms in what manner they would differ. They would not do because, firstly, the weight of things at the surface of Mars is not half what it would be upon the earth, and, secondly, the general atmospheric conditions are very different. Whatever else they may be the Martian herbs and trees must be adapted to these conditions.

Probable Appearance of the Martian Flora

Let us inquire how the first of these two considerations will make them differ. The force of gravity upon the surface of their planet is just three-eighths of its force upon this earth; a pound of anything here would weigh six ounces upon Mars. Therefore the stem or stalk that carries the leaves and flowers of a terrestrial plant would be needlessly and wastefully stout and strong upon Mars; the Martian stems and stalks will all be slenderer and finer and the texture of the plant itself laxer. The limit of height and size in terrestrial plants is probably determined largely by the work needed to raise nourishment from the roots to their topmost points. That work would be so much less upon Mars that it seems reasonable to expect bigger plants there than any that grow upon the earth.

Larger, slighter, slenderer; is that all we can say? No, for we have still to consider the difference in the atmosphere. This is thinner upon Mars than it is upon the earth, and it has less moisture, for we hardly ever see thick clouds there, and rain must be infrequent. Snow occurs nearly every-where all the year round, but the commonest of all forms of precipitation upon Mars would seem to be dew and hoar frost. Now the shapes of leaves with which we are most familiar are largely determined by rainfall, by the need of supporting the hammering of raindrops and of guiding the resulting moisture downward and outward to the rootlets below. To these chief ne-cessities we owe the handlike arrangement of the maple- and chestnut-leaf and the beautiful tracery of fibers that forms their skeletons. These leaves are admirable in rain but ineffectual against snow and frost; snow crushes them down, frost destroys them, and with the approach of winter they are shed. But the Martian tree-leaf will be more after the fashion of a snowfall-meeting leaf, spiky perhaps like the pine-tree needle. Only, unlike the pine-tree needle, it has to meet not a snowy winter but a dry, frost-bitten, sunless winter, and then probably it will shrivel and fall. And since the great danger for a plant in a dry air is desiccation, we may expect these Martian leaves to have thick cuticles, just as the cactus has. Moreover, since moisture will come to the Martian plant mainly from below in seasonal floods from the melting of the snow-caps, and not as rain from above, the typical Martian plant will probably be tall and have its bunches and clusters of spiky bluish green leaves upon uplifting reedy stalks.

Of course there will be an infinite variety of species of plants upon Mars as upon the earth, but these will be the general characteristics of the vegetation.

The Animal Kingdom

Now this conception of the Martian vegetation as mainly a jungle of big, slender, stalky, lax-textured, flood-fed plants with a great shock of fleshy, rather formless leaves above, and no doubt with as various a display of flowers and fruits as our earthly flora, prepares the ground for the consideration of the Martian animals. It is a matter of common knowledge nowadays how closely related is the structure of every animal to the food it consumes. Different food, different animals, has almost axiomatic value, and the very peculiar nature of the Martian flora is in itself sufficient to dispel the idea of our meeting beasts with any close analogy to terrestrial species. We shall find no flies nor sparrows nor dogs nor cats on Mars. But we shall probably find a sort of insect life fluttering high amidst the vegetation, and breeding during the summer heats in the flood-water below. In the winter it will encyst and hibernate. Its dimensions may be a little bigger than those ruling among the terrestrial insecta; but the mode of breathing by tracheal tubes, which distinguishes insects, very evidently (and very luckily for us) sets definite limits to insect size. Perhaps these limits are the same upon Mars. We cannot tell. Perhaps they are even smaller; the thinner air may preclude even the developments we find upon the earth in that particular line. Still there is plenty of justification if an artist were to draw a sort of butterfly or moth fluttering about, or antlike creatures scampering up and down the stems of a Martian jungle. Many of them perhaps will have sharp hard proboscides to pierce the tough cuticle of the plants.

No Fish on the Planet

But, and here is a curious difference, there are perhaps no fish or fishlike creatures on Mars at all. In the long Martian winter all the water seems either to drift to the poles and freeze there as snow or to freeze as ice along the water-courses; there are only flood-lakes and water-canals in spring and summer. And forms of life that trusted to gills or any method of underwater breathing must have been exterminated upon Mars ages ago. On earth the most successful air-breathing device is the lung. Lungs carry it universally. Only types of creatures that are fitted with lungs manage to grow to any considerable size out of water in our world. Even the lobsters and scorpions and spiders and such like large crustacean and insect-like forms that come up into the air can do so only by sinking their gills into deep pits to protect them from evaporation and so producing a sort of inferior imitation of a lung. Then and then only can they breathe without their breathing-organs drying up. The Martian air is thinner and drier than ours, and we conclude therefore that there is still more need than on earth for well-protected and capacious lungs. It follows that the Martian fauna will

run to large chests. And the lowest types of large beast there will be am-
phibious creatures which will swim about and breed in the summer waters
and bury themselves in mud at the approach of winter. Even these may
have been competed out of existence by air-inhaling swimmers. That is the
fate our terrestrial amphibia seem to be undergoing at the present time.

Here then is one indication for a picture of a Martian animal: it must
be built with more lung space than the corresponding terrestrial form. And
the same reason that will make the vegetation laxer and flimsier will make
the forms of the Martian animal kingdom laxer and flimsier and either larger
or else slenderer than earthly types.

Much that we have already determined comes in here again to help us
to further generalizations. Since the Martian vegetation will probably run
big and tall, there will be among these big-chested creatures climbing forms
and leaping and flying forms, all engaged in seeking food among its crests
and branches. And a thing cannot leap or fly without a well-placed head
and good eyes. So an imaginative artist may put in head and eyes, and the
mechanical advantages of a fore-and-aft arrangement of the body are so
great that it is difficult to suppose them without some sort of backbone.
Since the Martian vegetation has become adapted to seasonal flood conditions there will be not only fliers and climbers but waders—long-legged
forms. Well, here we get something—fliers, climbers, and waders, with a
sort of backbone.

Climatic Conditions

Now let us bring in another fact, the fact that the Martian year is just twice
the length of ours and alternates between hot summer sunshine, like the
sunshine we experience on high mountains, and a long, frost-bitten winter.
The day, too, has the length of a terrestrial day, and because of the thin air
will have just the quick changes from heat to cold we find on this planet
on the high mountains. This means that all these birds and beasts must be
adapted to great changes of temperature. To meet that they must be covered
with some thick, air-holding, non-conducting covering, something analo-
gous to fur or feathers, which they can molt or thin out in summer and
renew for the winter's bitterness. This is much more probable than that
they will be scaly or bare-skinned like our earthly lizards and snakes; and
since they will need to have fur or down outside their frameworks, their
skeletons, which will be made up of very light slender bones, will probably
be within. Moreover, the chances are that they will be fitted with the best
known contrivances for protecting their young in the earliest stages from
cold and danger. On earth the best known arrangement is the one that
prevails among most of the higher land animals, the device of bringing forth
living young at a high stage of development. This is the "hard life" ar-

rangement as distinguished form the easy-going, sunshiny, tropical, lay-an-egg-and-leave-it method, and Martian conditions are evidently harder than ours. So these big-chested, furry or feathery or downy Martian animals will probably be very like our mammalia in these respects. All this runs off easily and plausibly from the facts we know.

The Ruling Inhabitants

And now we are in a better position to consider those ruling inhabitants who made the gigantic canal-system of Mars, those creatures of human or superhuman intelligence, who, unless Mr. Lowell is no more than a fantastic visionary, have taken Mars in hand to rule and order and cultivate system-atically and completely, as I believe some day man will take this earth. Clearly these ruling beings will have been evolved out of some species or other of those mammal-like animals, just as man has been evolved from among the land animals of this globe. Perhaps they will have exterminated all those other forms of animal life as man is said to be exterminating all the other forms of animal life here. I have written above of floods and swamps and jungles to which life has adapted itself, but perhaps that stage is over now upon Mars altogether. It must have been a long and life-molding stage, but now it may be at an end. Mr. Lowell, judging by the uniform and orderly succession of what he calls the "fallow" brown and then of the bluish green tints upon the low-lying areas of Mars, is inclined to think that this is the case and that all the fertile area of the planet has been reclaimed from nature and is under cultivation.

How Like Terrestrial Humanity?

How far are these beings likely to resemble terrestrial humanity?

There are certain features in which they are likely to resemble us. The quasi-mammalian origin we have supposed for them implies a quasi-human appearance. They will probably have heads and eyes and backboned bodies, and since they must have big brains, because of their high intelligence, and since almost all creatures with big brains tend to have them forward in their heads near their eyes, these Martians will probably have big shapely skulls. But they will in all likelihood be larger in size than humanity, two and two-thirds times the mass of a man, perhaps. That does not mean, however, that they will be two and two-thirds times as tall, but, allowing for the laxer texture of things on Mars, it may be that they will be half as tall again when standing up. And as likely as not they will be covered with feathers or fur. I do not know, I do not know if anyone knows, why man, unlike the generality of mammals, is a bare-skinned animal. I can find, however, no necessary reason to make me believe the Martians are bare-skinned.

Will they stand up or go on four legs or six? I know of no means of answering that question with any certainty. But there are considerations that point to the Martian's being a biped. There seems to be a general advantage in a land-going animal having four legs; it is the prevailing pattern on earth, and even among the insects there is often a tendency to suppress one pair of the six legs and use only four for going. However, this condition is by no means universal. A multitude of types, like the squirrel, the rat, and the monkey, can be found which tend to use the hind legs chiefly for walking and to sit up and handle things with the fore limbs. Such species tend to be exceptionally intelligent. There can be no doubt of the immense part the development of the hand has played in the education of the human intelligence. So that it would be quite natural to imagine the Martians as big-headed, deep-chested bipeds, grotesquely caricaturing humanity with arms and hands.

But that is only one of several almost equally plausible possibilities. One thing we may rely upon: the Martians must have *some* prehensile organ, primarily because the development of intelligence is almost unthinkable without it, and, secondly, because in no other way could they get their engineering done. It is stranger to our imaginations, but no less reasonable, to suppose, instead of a hand, an elephant-like proboscis, or a group of tentacles or proboscis-like organs. Nature has a limitless imagination, never repeats exactly, and perhaps, after all, the chances lie in the direction of a greater unlikeness to the human shape than these forms I have ventured to suggest.

How wild and extravagant all this reads! One tries to picture feather-covered men nine or ten feet tall, with proboscides and several feet, and one feels a kind of disgust of the imagination. Yet wild and extravagant as these dim visions of unseen creatures may seem, it is logic and ascertained fact that forces us toward the belief that *some such creatures are living now*. And, after all, has the reader ever looked at a cow and tried to imagine how it would feel to come upon such a creature with its knobs and horns and queer projections suddenly for the first time?

Martian Civilization

I have purposely abstained in this paper from going on to another possibility of Martian life. Man on this earth has already done much to supplement his bodily deficiencies with artificial aids—clothes, boots, tools, corsets, false teeth, false eyes, wigs, armor, and so forth. The Martians are probably far more intellectual than men and more scientific, and beside their history the civilization of humanity is a thing of yesterday. What may they not have contrived in the way of artificial supports, artificial limbs, and the like?

Finally, here is a thought that may be reassuring to any reader who finds these Martians alarming. If a man were transferred suddenly to the surface of Mars he would find himself immensely exhilarated so soon as he had got over a slight mountain-sickness. He would weigh not one-half what he does upon the earth, he would prance and leap, he would lift twice his utmost earthly burden with ease. But if a Martian came to the earth his weight would bear him down like a cope of lead. He would weigh two and two-thirds times his Martian weight, and he would probably find existence insufferable. His limbs would not support him. Perhaps he would die, self-crushed, at once. When I wrote "The War of the Worlds," in which the Martians invade the earth, I had to tackle this difficulty. It puzzled me for a time, and then I used that idea of mechanical aids, and made my Martians mere bodiless brains with tentacles, subsisting by suction without any digestive process and carrying their weight about, not on living bodies but on wonderfully devised machines. But for all that, as a reader here and there may recall, terrestrial conditions were in the end too much for them.

APPENDIX VI

A Strange Light on Mars

Since the arrangements for circulating telegraphic information on astronomical subjects was inaugurated, Dr. Krueger, who is in charge of the Central Bureau at Kiel, certainly has not favoured his correspondents with a stranger telegram than the one which he flashed over the world on Monday afternoon:—

"Projection lumineuse dans région australe du terminateur de Mars observée par Javelle 28 Juillet 16 heures Perrotin."

This relates to an observation made at the famous Nice Observatory, of which M. Perrotin is the Director, by M. Javelle, who is already well known for his careful work. The news therefore must be accepted seriously, and, as it may be imagined, details are anxiously awaited; on Monday and Tuesday nights, unfortunately, the weather in London was not favourable for observation, so whether the light continues or not is not known.

It would appear that the luminous projection is not a light outside the disc of Mars, but in the region of the planet not lighted up by the sun at the time of observation. The gibbosity of the planet is pretty considerable at the present time. Had there been evidence that the light was outside the disc, the strange appearance might be due to a comet in the same line of sight as the planet. If we assume the light to be on the planet itself, then it must either have a physical or human origin; so it is to be expected that the old idea that the Martians are signalling to us will be revived. Of physical origins we can only think of Aurora (which is not improbable, only bearing in mind the precise locality named, but distinctly improbable unless we assume that in Mars the phenomenon is much more intense than with us), a long range of high snow-capped hills, and forest fires burning over a large area.

Without favouring the signalling idea before we know more of the observation, it may be stated that a better time for signalling could scarcely be chosen, for Mars being now a morning star, means that the opposition, when no part of its dark surface will be visible, is some time off.

Reprinted from *Nature*, August 2, 1894, p.319.

The Martians, of course, find it much easier to see the dark side of the earth than we do to see the dark side of Mars, and whatever may be the explanation of the appearances which three astronomers of reputation have thought proper to telegraph over the world, it is worth while pointing out that forest fires over large areas may be the first distinctive thing observed on either planet from the other besides the fixed surface markings.

WORKS CONSULTED

The War of the Worlds

WW MANUSCRIPTS AND PROOFS
(UNIVERSITY OF ILLINOIS, URBANA-CHAMPAIGN)
Ms sheaf "MS." c. January–April 1896. Atlantic edition counterpart: "Book II," end of Chapter V through Chapter IX (but Chapter VII corresponds to its MS counterpart only in physical position).

Ms sheaf "CD (coda)." c. 1896. Atlantic edition counterpart: "The Epilogue."

Paste-up sheaf "PR1." c. summer–fall 1897. First six and a half installments (April–October 1897) of the *Pearson's* serial "War of the Worlds," pasted up and revised. Atlantic edition counterpart: "Book I."

Paste-up sheaf "PR2." c. late fall 1897. Last two and a half installments (October–December 1897) of the proofs of the *Pearson's* serial "War of the Worlds," pasted up and revised, with last three and a half pages torn off and "The End" written instead. Atlantic edition counterpart: "Book II" (except Chapter VII), with the three and a half pages restored and revised as "The Epilogue."

Ms sheaf "PR3." Late 1897. Atlantic edition counterpart: Book II, Chapter VII, "The Man on Putney Hill."

Galleys of the Atlantic edition (1924), corrected for the Atlantic and further corrected for the Essex edition (1927).

GENEALOGICALLY SIGNIFICANT PUBLISHED VERSIONS OF WW
"The War of the Worlds." *Cosmopolitan: A Monthly Illustrated Magazine* 22 (April 1897):615–627; 23 (May–October 1897):2–9, 215–224, 251–262, 391–400, 541–550, 601–610; 24 (November–December 1897):79–88, 162–171.

———. *Pearson's Magazine* 3 (April–June 1897):363–373, 486–496, 598–610; 4 (July–December 1897):108–119, 221–232, 329–339, 447–456, 558–568, 736–745.

———. *The Collector's Book of Science Fiction by H. G. Wells: From Rare, Original, Illustrated Magazines*. Edited by Alan K. Russell. Secaucus, NJ: Castle Books, 1978. Photo-reproduction of *Pearson's*.

"Fighters from Mars: The War of the Worlds." *New York Evening Journal*, December 15, 1897–January 11, 1898.

The War of the Worlds. London: William Heinemann, 1898.

———. New York: Harper & Brothers, 1898.

———. *The Works of H. G. Wells*, Atlantic edition. Vol. III. London: T. Fisher Unwin, Ltd, 1924.

———. *The Collected Essex Edition*. Vol. XIII. London: Ernest Benn Ltd, 1927.

OTHER WW TEXTS
"Fighters from Mars: The War of the Worlds in and near Boston." *Boston Post*, January 9–February 3, 1898.

The War of the Worlds. Leipzig: Bernhard Tauchnitz, 1898.

"La Guerre des mondes." Translated by Henry Davray. *Mercure de France* 32 (December 1899):577–633; (January–March 1900):120–176, 405–445, 703–755.

"The War of the Worlds." *Strand Magazine* LIX (February 1920):154–163. Condensed and with an introduction by Wells.

The War of the Worlds. Rev. ed. [toned down for the school market]. London: William Heinemann, Ltd, 1951.

"An Edition and a Survey of H. G. Wells's *The War of the Worlds.*" Edited by David Y. Hughes. Ph.D. diss., University of Illinois at Urbana-Champaign, 1962.

The Time Machine, The War of the Worlds. Introduction by J. B. Priestley. Illustrations by Joe Mugnaini. New York: The Heritage Press, 1964.

——— . Introduction by Isaac Asimov. Greenwich, CT: Fawcett Publications, Inc, 1968.

The War of the Worlds. Oxford Progressive English Reader Series. Hong Kong, Kuala Lumpur, Singapore, Tokyo: Oxford University Press, 1972.

H. G. Wells: "The Time Machine"; "The War of the Worlds"; A Critical Edition. Edited by Frank D. McConnell. London: Oxford University Press, 1977.

The War of the Worlds. Adapted by Malvina G. Vogel. Illustrations by Brandon Lynch. New York: Moby Books (Playmore Inc.), 1983.

——— . Introduction by James Gunn. New York: Tom Doherty Associates, Inc, 1988.

TRANSLATIONS

[*The War of the Worlds* in Irish] Cogadh na reann. Translated by Leon O'Broin. Dublin: Government Publications Office, 1934.

[*The War of the Worlds, When the Sleeper Wakes, The First Men in the Moon* in Rumanian] *Razboiul lumilor; Cînd se va trezi cel-care-doarme; Primii oameni în luna.* Bucharest: Editura Tineretului [1963].

[*The War of the Worlds* in Japanese]. Translated by Isamu Inoue. Songen Suiri Bunko, 1969.

[*The War of the Worlds*] *Válka Svétu.* Moscow: Foreign Literary Handbooks Publishing House, n.d. English text, with notes in Czech by C. A. Krejnesova.

Writings by Wells

BOOKS BY WELLS

Volume numbers, as far as possible, refer to the Atlantic edition (London: T. Fisher Unwin, Ltd, 1924–1927); original dates are in brackets.

Anticipations of the Reaction of Mechanical and Scientific Progress upon Human Life and Thought. IV [1901].

Certain Personal Matters. A Collection of Material Mainly Autobiographical. London: Lawrence & Bullen, Ltd, 1898.

The Desert Daisy. Edited by Gordon Ray. Urbana: University of Illinois Press, 1957.

Early Writings in Science and Science Fiction by H. G. Wells. Edited by Robert M. Philmus and David Y. Hughes. Berkeley: University of California Press, 1975.

An Englishman Looks at the World, Being a Series of Unrestrained Remarks upon Contemporary Matters. London and New York: Cassell and Co., Ltd, 1914.

Experiment in Autobiography: Discoveries and Conclusions of a Very Ordinary Brain (since 1866). New York: The Macmillan Co, 1934.

The First Men in the Moon. VI [1901].

The Food of the Gods and How It Came to Earth. V [1904].

H. G. Wells in Love: Postscript to An Experiment in Autobiography. Edited by G. P. Wells. Boston and Toronto: Little, Brown and Co., 1984.

H. G. Wells's Literary Criticism. Edited by Patrick Parrinder and Robert M. Philmus. Totowa, NJ: Barnes & Noble, 1980.

The Holy Terror. New York: Simon and Schuster, 1939.

In the Days of the Comet. X [1906].

The Invisible Man: A Grotesque Romance. III [1897].

The Island of Dr. Moreau. II [1896].

The Island of Dr. Moreau. Edited by Robert M. Philmus (forthcoming).

Little Wars: A Game for Boys from Twelve Years of Age to One Hundred and Fifty and for that More Intelligent Sort of Girls Who Like Boys' Games and Books. With an Appendix on Kriegspiel. London: Frank Palmer, 1913.

Love and Mr. Lewisham. VII [1900].

The Man with a Nose and the Other Uncollected Short Stories of H. G. Wells. Edited by J. R. Hammond. London: The Athlone Press, 1984.

Mankind in the Making. London: Chapman and Hall, Ltd, 1903.

A Modern Utopia. IX [1905].

The Outline of History: Being a Plain History of Life and Mankind. 2 vols. New York: The Macmillan Company, 1920.

The Scientific Romances of H. G. Wells. Introduction by Wells. London: Gollancz, 1933.

The Shape of Things to Come: The Ultimate Revolution. London: Hutchinson & Co., Ltd, 1933.

A Short History of the World. XXVII [1922].

The Short Stories of H. G. Wells. London: Ernest Benn Ltd, 1927.

Star Begotten. A Biological Fantasia. London: Chatto & Windus, 1937.

Text-Book of Biology. London: W. B. Clive & Co, University Correspondence College Press, 1893.

The Time Machine: An Invention. I [1895].

The Time Machine: An Invention. Preface by Wells. New York: Random House, 1931.

The Definitive "Time Machine": A Critical Edition of H. G. Wells's Scientific Romance. Edited by Harry M. Geduld. Bloomington: Indiana University Press, 1987.

Tono-Bungay. XII [1909].

The Way the World is Going: Guesses and Forecasts of the Years Ahead. London: Ernest Benn Ltd, 1928.

When the Sleeper Wakes. II [1899].

ARTICLES NOT REPRINTED BY WELLS

"Ancient Experiments in Co-operation." *Gentleman's Magazine*: 273 (October 1892):418–422.

"The Democratic Culture" [review of George Warrington Steevens, *Land of the Dollar*]. *Saturday Review* 83 (March 13, 1897):273–274.

"H. G. Wells, Esq., B.Sc." *Royal College of Science Magazine* 15 (April 1903):221–224.

"Intelligence on Mars." *Saturday Review* 81 (April 4, 1896):345–346. See this edition, Appendix IV.

"Local Color According to Taste" [letter complaining of localization of *The War of Worlds* to Boston]. *The Critic: A Weekly Review of Literature and the Arts* 29 n.s. (March 12, 1898):184.

"The Mind in Animals" [review of Lloyd Morgan, *Introduction to Comparative Psychology*]. *Saturday Review* 78 (December 22, 1894):683–684.

"Mr. Le Gallienne's Worst and Best" [review of Richard Le Gallienne, *Prose Fancies (Second Series)*]. *Saturday Review* 82 (August 1, 1896): 113–114.

"The Newly Discovered Element." *Saturday Review* 79 (February 9, 1895):183–184.

"On Extinction." *Chambers's Journal of Popular Literature, Science, and Art* 10, 5th series (September 30, 1893):623–624.

"Peculiarities of Psychical Research" [review of Frank Podmore, *Apparitions and Thought Transference*]. *Nature* 51 (December 6, 1894):121–122. Rejoinder by

Oliver J. Lodge. *Nature* 51 (January 10, 1895):247. Rejoinder by Wells. *Nature* 51 (January 17, 1895):274.
"The Protean Gas." *Saturday Review* 79 (May 4, 1895):576–577.
"The Things that Live on Mars." *Cosmopolitan Magazine* XLIV n.s. (March 1908):335–342. See this edition, Appendix V.

Unpublished Wells Letters and Documents

(University of Illinois Collections)
Wells, to Arthur Morley Davies. December 15, 1887.
Henley, W. E., to Wells. September 5, 1895.
Pinker, J. B., to Wells. June 12, 1896; July 9, 1896; August 25, 1896.
Heinemann, William, to Wells. October 13, 1897; October 15, 1897.
Watney, Charles, to Wells. November 8, 1897.
Pawling, Sidney S. [of Heinemann publishers], to Wells. December 22, 1897.
Wells, to J. B. Pinker. Transcript. January 1900.
Insurance inventory of Wells's library. 1931.

Collections of Critical Essays

Bergonzi, Bernard, ed. *H. G. Wells: A Collection of Critical Essays.* Englewood Cliffs, NJ: Prentice Hall, 1976.
Huntington, John, ed. *Critical Essays on H. G. Wells.* Boston: G. K. Hall & Co., 1991.
Parrinder, Patrick, and Rolfe, Christopher, eds. *H. G. Wells under Revision: Proceedings of the International Wells Symposium, London, July 1986.* Selinsgrove, PA: Susquehanna University Press; London: Associated University Presses, 1990.
——— , ed. *H. G. Wells: The Critical Heritage.* London and Boston: Routledge & Kegan Paul, 1972.
Suvin, Darko, and Philmus, Robert M., eds. *H. G. Wells and Modern Science Fiction.* Lewisberg, PA: Bucknell University Press; London: Associated University Presses, 1977.

Publications on Wells

BOOKS AND ARTICLES RELATING TO *WW*
Bugeja, Michael J. " 'Culture and Anarchy' in *The War of the Worlds.*" *North Dakota Quarterly* 54 (1986):79–83.
Connor, Peter J. *Penguin Passnotes/The War of the Worlds.* Harmondsworth: Penguin Books, 1986.
Eisenstein, Alex. "Very Early Wells: Origins of Some Major Physical Motifs in *The Time Machine* and *The War of the Worlds.*" *Extrapolation* 13/2 (1972):119–126.
Gibbons, Tom. "H. G. Wells's Fire Sermon: *The War of the Worlds* and the Book of Revelation." *Science Fiction: A Review of Speculative Literature* 6/1 (1984);5–14.
Greely, C. E. C. "*The War of the Worlds* in the Classroom." *Wellsian* 8 (Summer 1985):27–28.
Hillegas, Mark R. "The First Invasions from Mars." *Michigan Alumnus Quarterly Review* 66 (Winter 1960):107–112.
——— . "Martians and Mythmakers: 1877–1938." In Ray B. Browne et al, eds., *Challenges in American Culture.* Bowling Green, OH: Bowling Green University Popular Press, 1970.

——— . "Victorian 'Extraterrestrials.' " In Jerome H. Buckley, ed., *The Worlds of Victorian Fiction*. Cambridge: Harvard University Press, 1975.

Hughes, David Y. *"The War of the Worlds* in the Yellow Press." *Journalism Quarterly* 43/4 (Winter 1966):639–646. See this edition, Appendix II.

Hume, Kathryn. "The Hidden Dynamics of *The War of the Worlds." Philological Quarterly* 62 (1983):279–292.

Lake, David J. "The Current Texts of Wells's Early SF Novels: Situation Unsatisfactory." *Wellsian* 11 (Summer 1988):3–12.

Pagetti, Carlo. *I Marziani alla Corte della Regina Vittoria: "The Invisible Man," "War of the Worlds," "When the Sleeper Wakes" di H. G. Wells*. Pescara: Edizioni Tracce, 1986.

Parrinder, Patrick. "H. G. Wells and the Fiction of Catastrophe." *Renaissance and Modern Studies* 28 (1984):40–58.

——— . *Notes on "The War of the Worlds"* (York Notes 103). Harlow, Essex: Longman York Press, 1981.

Shelton, Robert. "The Mars-Begotten Men of Olaf Stapledon and H. G. Wells." *Science-Fiction Studies* 11/32 (1984):1–14.

Simpson, Anne B. "The 'Tangible Antagonist': H. G. Wells and the Discourse of Otherness." *Extrapolation* 31/2 (Summer 1990):134–147.

Wakeford, Iain. "Wells, Woking and 'The War of the Worlds.' " *Woking History Journal* 2 (Spring 1990):4–15. Reprinted, slightly abridged in *Wellsian* 14 (Summer 1991):18–29.

PUBLICATIONS RELATING TO WELLS'S SCIENCE FICTION

Bellamy, William. *The Novels of Wells, Bennett and Galsworthy: 1890–1910*. New York: Barnes & Noble, 1971.

Bergonzi, Bernard. *The Early H. G. Wells: A Study of the Scientific Romances*. Manchester: Manchester University Press, 1961.

Crossley, Robert. *H. G. Wells*. Mercer Island, WA: Starmont, 1986.

Davray, Henry. "Oscar Wilde posthume." *Mercure de France* 56(1905):634–638.

Draper, Michael. *H. G. Wells*. Houndsmills and London: Macmillan, 1987.

Hillegas, Mark R. "Cosmic Pessimism in H. G. Wells's Scientific Romances." *Papers of the Michigan Academy of Science, Arts, and Letters* 46 (1961):655–663.

——— . *The Future as Nightmare: H. G. Wells and the Anti-Utopians*. New York: Oxford University Press, 1967.

Hughes, David Y. "The Garden in Wells's Early Science Fiction." In Suvin and Philmus, eds., *H. G. Wells and Modern Science Fiction*.

Huntington, John. *The Logic of Fantasy: H. G. Wells and Science Fiction*. New York: Columbia University Press, 1982.

——— . "Problems of an Amorous Utopian." In Huntington, ed., *Critical Essays on H. G. Wells*; and in Parrinder and Rolfe, eds., *H. G. Wells under Revision*.

LeMire, Eugene D. "H. G. Wells and the World of Science Fiction." *The University of Windsor Review* II/1 (Fall 1966):59–66.

Loing, Bernard. *H. G. Wells à l'œuvre: le début d'un écrivain (1894–1900)*. Paris: Didier, 1984.

McCarthy, Patrick A. *"Heart of Darkness* and the Early Novels of H. G. Wells: Evolution, Anarchy, Entropy." *Journal of Modern Literature* 13/1 (March 1986):37–60.

McConnell, Frank D. *The Science Fiction of H. G. Wells*. London: Oxford University Press, 1981.

Ower, John. "Theme and Technique in H. G. Wells's 'The Star.' " *Extrapolation* 18/2 (May 1977):167–175.

Rose, Mark. "Filling the Void: Verne, Wells, and Lem." *Science-Fiction Studies* 8/ 24 (1981):121–142.

Russell, W. M. S. "Folktales and H. G. Wells." *Wellsian* 5 (Summer 1982):2–18.

Stearns, R. T. "Wells and War: H. G. Wells's Writings on Military Subjects before the Great War." *Wellsian* 6 (Summer 1983):1–15.

Stover, Leon. "Applied Natural History: Wells vs. Huxley." In Parrinder and Rolfe, eds., *H. G. Wells under Revision*.

———. *The Prophetic Soul: A Reading of H. G. Wells's "Things to Come," together with his Film Treatment "Whither Mankind" and the Postproduction Script.* Jefferson, NC and London: McFarland & Co., Inc., 1987.

Sussman, Herbert L. *Victorians and the Machine: The Literary Response to Technology.* Cambridge: Harvard University Press, 1968.

Vernier, Jean-Pierre. "Evolution as Literary Theme in H. G. Wells's Science Fiction." In Suvin and Philmus, eds., *H. G. Wells and Modern Science Fiction*.

——— "H. G. Wells at the Turn of the Century: From Science Fiction to Anticipation." *H. G. Wells Society Occasional Papers* 1. London: H. G. Wells Society, 1973.

Weeks, Robert P. "Disentanglement as a Theme in H. G. Wells's Fiction." In Bergonzi, ed., *H. G. Wells*.

West, Anthony. "The Dark World of H. G. Wells." In Bergonzi, ed., *H. G. Wells*.

Williamson, Jack. *H. G. Wells: Critic of Progress.* Baltimore: The Mirage Press, 1973.

GENERAL PUBLICATIONS ON WELLS

Batchelor, John. *H. G. Wells.* Cambridge: Cambridge University Press, 1985.

Beresford, John Davys. *H. G. Wells.* London: Nisbet, 1915.

Hammond, J. R. *An H. G. Wells Companion: A Guide to the Novels, Romances and Short Stories.* New York: Barnes & Noble, 1979.

Haynes, Roslynn D. *H. G. Wells: Discoverer of the Future: The Influence of Science on His Thought.* New York and London: New York University Press, 1980.

Kagarlitski, Julius. *The Life and Thought of H. G. Wells.* Translated by Moura Budberg. London: Sidgwick & Jackson, 1966.

Kemp, Peter. *H. G. Wells and the Culminating Ape.* New York: St. Martin's Press, 1982.

Mackenzie, Norman and Jeanne. *H. G. Wells: A Biography.* New York: Simon and Schuster, 1973.

Parrinder Patrick. *H. G. Wells.* Edinburgh: Oliver and Boyd, 1970.

Raknem, Ingvald. *H. G. Wells and His Critics.* Oslo and London: Allen & Unwin, 1962.

Reed, John R. *The Natural History of H. G. Wells.* Athens: Ohio University Press, 1982.

Smith, David C. *H. G. Wells Desperately Mortal: A Biography.* New Haven and London: Yale University Press, 1986.

Wagar, W. Warren. *H. G. Wells and the World State.* New Haven: Yale University Press, 1961.

West, Anthony. *H. G. Wells: Aspects of a Life.* New York: Random House, 1984.

West, Geoffrey [Geoffrey H. Wells]. *H. G. Wells. A Sketch for a Portrait.* New York: W. W. Norton & Co., 1930.

Wilson, Harris, ed. *Arnold Bennett and H. G. Wells: A Record of a Personal and a Literary Friendship.* Urbana: University of Illinois Press, 1960.

Young, Kenneth. *H. G. Wells.* Writers and Their Work, 233. Harlow, Essex: Longman Group Ltd, 1974.

314   **Works Consulted**

PRIMARY AND SECONDARY WELLS BIBLIOGRAPHIES

Hammond, John R. *Herbert George Wells: An Annotated Bibliography of His Works.* New York and London, Garland, 1977.

Hughes, David Y. "Criticism in English of H. G. Wells's Science Fiction: A Select Annotated Bibliography." *Science-Fiction Studies* 19 (November 1979):309–319.

Scheick, William J., and Cox, J. Randolph. *H. G. Wells: A Reference Guide.* Boston: G. K. Hall, 1988.

West, Geoffrey H. [Geoffrey H. Wells]. *The Works of H. G. Wells: 1887–1925.* London: George Routledge & Sons, Ltd, 1926.

General Science Fiction. Criticism, Commentary, and Reference.

Amis, Kingsley. *New Maps of Hell: A Survey of Science Fiction.* New York: Harcourt, Brace and Company, 1960.

Bailey, James Osler. *Pilgrims through Space and Time: Trends and Patterns in Scientific and Utopian Fiction.* New York: Argus Books, 1947.

Clareson, Thomas D. *SF: The Other Side of Realism.* Bowling Green, OH: Bowling Green University Popular Press, 1971.

Geduld, Harry M., and Gottesman, Ronald, eds. *Robots, Robots, Robots.* Boston: New York Graphic Society, [1978].

Henkin, Leo Justin. *Darwinism in the English Novel: 1860–1910: The Impact of Evolution on Victorian Fiction.* New York: Corporate Press, 1940.

Ketterer, David. *New Worlds for Old: The Apocalyptic Imagination, Science Fiction, and American Literature.* Bloomington: Indiana University Press, 1974.

Moskowitz, Sam. "The Jew in Science Fiction." *Worlds of Tomorrow* 4 (November 1966):109–122.

Parrinder, Patrick. *Science Fiction: Its Criticism and Teaching.* London: Methuen & Co., Ltd, 1980.

——— , ed. *Science Fiction: A Critical Guide.* London: Longman Group Limited, 1979.

Philmus, Robert M. *Into the Unknown: The Evolution of Science Fiction from Francis Godwin to H. G. Wells.* Berkeley: University of California Press, 1970.

Rose, Mark. *Alien Encounters: Anatomy of Science Fiction.* Cambridge: Harvard University Press, 1981.

——— , ed. *Science Fiction: A Collection of Critical Essays.* Englewood Cliffs, NJ: Prentice-Hall, 1976.

Scholes, Robert, and Rabkin, Eric S. *Science Fiction: History, Science, Vision.* London: Oxford University Press, 1977.

Stableford, Brian. *Scientific Romance in Britain: 1890–1950.* New York: St. Martin's Press, 1985.

Suvin, Darko. *Metamorphoses of Science Fiction.* New Haven: Yale University Press, 1979.

Imaginative Literature Related to WW

WW SPIN-OFFS, ANALOGUES, AND DESCENDANTS

Anvil, Christopher. "The Gentle Earth." *Astounding Science Fiction* 60 (November 1957):9–58.

Asimov, Isaac. *The Martian Way and Other Stories.* Greenwich, CT: Fawcett Crest Books, 1955.

Bradbury, Ray. *The Martian Chronicles.* New York: Bantam Books, 1958.

Brown, Fredric. *Martians, Go Home.* New York: Ballantine Books, 1976.

Burroughs, Edgar Rice. *A Princess of Mars* [first of eleven Mars novels, 1917; serialized 1912]. New York: Ballantine Books, 1974.

Carter, Lin. *The Man Who Loved Mars*. Greenwich, CT: Fawcett, 1973.

Christopher, John. *The White Mountains* [first of three "tripod" novels]. New York: The Macmillan Company, 1968.

De Courcy, Dorothy and John. "Rat Race." In Groff Conklin, ed., *The Big Book of Science Fiction*. New York: Crown Publishers, 1950.

Farmer, Philip Jose. *Jesus on Mars*. Los Angeles: Pinnacle Books, 1979.

Graves, Charles Larcom, and Lucas, Edward Verall. *The War of the Wenuses: Translated from the Artesian of H. G. Pozzuoli, Author of "The Treadmill," "The Isthmus of Dr. Day," "The Vanishing Lady," etc., etc.* Bristol: J. W. Arrowsmith, [1898].

Gregg, Percy. *Across the Zodiac: The Story of a Wrecked Record: Deciphered, Translated, and Edited by Percy Gregg*. 3 vols. Hamburg: Karl Grädner, 1880.

Kneale, Nigel. *Quartermass and the Pit*. London: Arrow Books, 1979.

Lasswitz, Kurd. *Two Planets: Auf Zwei Planeten* [1898]. Translated by Hans H. Rudnick, abridged by Erich Lasswitz. Afterword by Mark R. Hillegas. Carbondale: Southern Illinois University Press, 1971.

Leinster, Murray [Will Jenkins]. "Nobody Saw the Ship." In Groff Conklin, ed., *The Big Book of Science Fiction*. New York: Crown Publishers, 1950.

McNelly, Willis E., and Hipolito, Jane. *Mars, We Love You: Tales of Mars, Men, and Martians*. Introduction by Isaac Asimov. New York: Doubleday & Company, 1971.

Priest, Christopher. *The Space Machine: A Scientific Romance*. New York: Harrow, 1976.

Serviss, Garrett Putnam. "Edison's Conquest of Mars." *New York Evening Journal*, January 12–, 1898; reprinted, with an introduction by A. Langley Searles, Los Angeles; Carcosa House, 1947.

Smith, George H. *The Second War of the Worlds*. New York: Daw Books, Inc., 1976.

Strugatsky, Arkady and Boris. *Far Rainbow: The Second Invasion from Mars*. New York: Macmillan Publishing Co., 1979.

Verne, Jules. *De la Terre à la Lune: trajet direct en 97 heures 20 minutes*. Genève: Editions Connaître, 1958.

Wellman, Manly W. and Wade. *Sherlock Holmes's War of the Worlds*. New York: Warner Books, 1975.

Wyndham, John. "The Revolt of the Triffids." *Collier's Magazine* 127 (January 6–February 3, 1951).

FUTURE INVASION STORIES AND RELATED CRITICISM

Bergonzi, Bernard. "Before 1914: Writers and the Threat of War." *Critical Quarterly* 6 (Summer 1964):126–134.

Briggs, Asa. *The Battle of Dorking Controversy*. London: Cornmarket, 1972.

[Chesney, George T.] *The Battle of Dorking: Reminiscences of a Volunteer*. Edinburgh: Blackwood, 1871.

Clarke, I. F. *The Pattern of Expectation: 1644–2001*. New York: Basic Books, 1979.

———. *Voices Prophesying War: 1763–1984*. London: Oxford University Press, 1966.

Curties, Captain Henry. *When England Slept*. London: Everett & Co., 1909.

Ferréol, P. *La Prise de Londres*. Paris: Boulanger, 1891.

Forth, C. *The Surprise of the Channel Tunnel*. Liverpool: H. Whightman & Co., 1883.

Le Faure, Georges. *La Guerre sous l'eau*. Paris: E. Dentu, 1892.

Lester, H. F. *The Taking of Dover*. Bristol: J. W. Arrowsmith, 1888.

Peddie, James *The Capture of London*. London: General Publishing Company, [1887].

Suvin, Darko. "Victorian Science Fiction, 1871–85: The Rise of the Alternative History Subgenre." *Science-Fiction Studies* 10/30 (July 1983):148–169.

Tempera, Mariangela. "Popular Literature and Propaganda in the Future War Tale (1871–1915)." Ph.D. diss., Indiana University, Bloomington, 1984.

LITERARY WORKS RELATING TO *WW* AS BACKGROUND OR SOURCE

Burton, Robert. *The Anatomy of Melancholy*. Edited by Arthur Richard Shilleto. 3 vols. London: George Bell & Sons, 1893.

Defoe, Daniel. *A Journal of the Plague Year*. Edited by Arthur Wellesley Secord. New York: Doubleday, Doran and Co., 1935.

Flammarion, Camille. "The Last Days of the Earth." *Contemporary Review* 19 (April 1891):558–569.

Heine, Heinrich. *The Prose Writings of Heinrich Heine*. Edited by Havelock Ellis. Camelot Series. London: Walter Scott, 1887.

Hood, Thomas. *Selected Poems of Thomas Hood*. Edited by John Clubbe. Cambridge: Harvard University Press, 1970.

Le Gallienne, Richard. *The Quest of the Golden Girl: A Romance*. London: John Lane, 1896.

Lucian. *Icaromennipus*. In *Lucian*, vol. II. Edited by Austin M. Harmon. Loeb Classics. London: William Heinemann, 1929.

Marx, Karl, and Engels, Friedrich. *The Communist Manifesto*. Translated by Samuel Moore, [1888]. Harmondsworth: Penguin Books Ltd, 1967.

Works of Science, Philosophy, and History

Adams, Henry. *The Degradation of the Democratic Dogma*. New York: Macmillan Co., 1919.

Anon. "The Light on Mars." *Black and White* 8 (August 25, 1894):244.

Anon. "Science Gossip." *Athenaeum* 3485 (August 11, 1894):199.

Anon. "A Strange Light on Mars." *Nature* 50 (August 2, 1894):319. See this edition, Appendix VI.

Clarke, Arthur C. *Voices from the Sky: Previews of the Coming Space Age*. New York: Pyramid Books, 1967.

Dampier, Sir William Cecil. *A History of Science and Its Relations with Philosophy and Religion*. 4th ed. New York: The Macmillan Co., 1949.

Darwin, Charles. *The Origin of Species by Natural Selection or the Preservation of Favoured Races in the Struggle for Life*. New York: Collier Books, 1962.

Denning, William F. *Telescopic Work for Starlight Evenings*. London: Taylor and Francis, 1891.

Flammarion, Camille. *Lumen*. Translated by A. A. M. and R. M. New York: Dodd, Mead and Company, 1897.

———. "Mars and its Inhabitants." *North American Review* 162 (May 1896):546–557.

———. *La Planète Mars et ses conditions d'habitabilité*. Paris: Gauthier-Villars et Fils, 1892.

Franklin, H. Bruce. *War Stars: The Superweapon and the American Imagination*. New York: Oxford University Press, 1988.

Gray, John. *Electrical Influence Machines. A Full Account of their Historical Development, and Modern Forms, with Instructions for Making them*. London: Whittaker and Co. and George Bell and Sons, 1890.

Hobbes, Thomas. *Leviathan or the Matter, Forme and Power of a Commonwealth, Ecclesiastical and Civil.* Edited by Michael Oakeshotte. Oxford: Basil Blackwell, 1946.

Hoyt, William Graves. *Lowell and Mars.* Tucson: University of Arizona Press, 1976.

Huxley, Leonard. *Life and Letters of Thomas Henry Huxley.* 2 vols. New York: D. Appleton, 1901.

Huxley, Thomas Henry. *Darwiniana: Essays.* New York: D. Appleton, 1896.

———. *Essays upon Some Controverted Questions.* New York: D. Appleton, 1892.

———. *Evolution and Ethics and Other Essays.* New York: D. Appleton, 1896.

———. *Lay Sermons, Addresses, and Reviews.* New York: D. Appleton, 1871.

———. *Method and Results.* New York: D. Appleton, 1896.

Jackson, Francis, and Moore, Patrick. *Life on Mars.* London: Routledge and Kegan Paul, 1965.

Jackson, Holbrook. *The Eighteen Nineties: A Review of Art and Ideas at the Close of the Nineteenth Century.* London: Jonathan Cape, 1927.

Jonas, Doris and David. *Other Senses, Other Worlds.* New York: Stein and Day, 1978.

Kendrick, Sir Thomas Downing. *The Lisbon Earthquake.* Philadelphia: J. B. Lippincott Company, [1957].

Ledger, Edmund. *The Sun: its Planets and their Satellites. A Course of Lectures upon the Solar System. Read in Gresham College, London, in the Years 1881 and 1882 Pursuant to the Will of Sir Thomas Gresham.* London: Edward Stanford, 1882.

Ley, Willy. *Exotic Zoology.* New York: The Viking Press, 1959.

———. *Rockets, Missiles, and Space Travel.* New York: The Viking Press, 1957.

Lockyer, William James Stewart. "Bright Projections on Mars' Terminator." *Nature* 50 (September 20, 1894):499–501.

Lowell, Percival. *Mars.* Boston: Houghton, Mifflin and Company, 1895.

Macvey, John W. *Space Weapons, Space War.* Briarcliff Manor, NY: Stein and Day, 1985.

Merz, John Theodore. *A History of European Thought in the Nineteenth Century.* 4 vols. London: William Blackwood and Sons, 1896–1914.

Miller, Dayton Clarence. *Sparks, Lightning, Cosmic Rays. An Anecdotal History of Electricity.* New York: The Macmillan Company, 1939.

Newcomb, Simon. *Popular Astronomy.* 6th ed. New York: Harper and Bros., 1890.

Richards, I. A. *The Philosophy of Rhetoric.* New York: Oxford University Press, 1936.

Riehn, Richard K. *1812: Napoleon's Russian Campaign.* New York: McGraw-Hill, 1990.

Salisbury, Frank. "The Inhabitants of Mars." In Edward Hutchings, Jr., ed., *Frontiers in Science, a Survey.* New York: Basic Books, 1958.

Schiaparelli, Giovanni Virginio. "The Planet Mars." *Astronomy and Astrophysics* 13 (1894):635–640, 714–723.

Singer, Charles, et al, eds. *A History of Technology.* Vol V: *The Late Nineteenth Century: c. 1850–c. 1900.* London: Oxford University Press, 1958.

Smith, Arthur E. *Mars: The Next Step.* Bristol and New York: Adam Hilger, 1989.

Spencer, Herbert. *The Data of Ethics.* New York: D. Appleton and Company, 1899.

Thomson, Sir William [Lord Kelvin]. "The Age of the Earth as an Abode Fitted for Life." *London, Edinburgh, and Dublin Philosophical Magazine and Journal of Science* 47, 5th series (January 1899):66–90.

———. *Popular Lectures and Addresses.* 3 vols. Vol. I: *The Constitution of Matter.* London: Macmillan and Co., 1889.

318   **Works Consulted**

Willey, Basil. *Darwin and Butler: Two Versions of Evolution.* New York: Harcourt,
Brace and Company, 1960.

General Reference Works

Altick, Richard Daniel. *The English Common Reader: A Social History of the Mass
Reading Public: 1800–1900.* Chicago: University of Chicago Press, 1957.
Malden, Henry Elliot, ed. *Victoria History of the County of Surrey.* 4 vols. and
index. In H. Arthur Doubleday, ed., *The Victoria History of the Counties of
England.* London: Constable and Company, Limited, 1902–1912.
Pound, Reginald and Harmsworth, Geoffrey. *Northcliffe.* London: Cassell, 1959.
Royal Commission on Historical Monuments. *An Inventory of the Historical Mon-
uments in Middlesex.* London: His Majesty's Stationery Office, 1937.
Royal Society of London. *Catalogue of Scientific Papers.* Vols. 13–19. Fourth Series
(1884–1900). Cambridge: Cambridge University Press, 1914.
Thorne, James. *Handbook to the Environs of London.* 2 vols. London: John Murray,
1876.
University of London. *The Calendar for the Year 1898–99.* London: Darling and
Son, Ltd, 1898.

Adaptations by Theatre, Radio, Film, and Television
(Texts, Commentary, and Translations)

Adamson, Joe. *Byron Haskin.* Metuchen, NJ: Scarecrow Press, 1989.
Anon. "The Day Orson Frightened the World." *Film Culture* 27 (Winter 1962/63).
Biskind, Peter. "War of the Worlds." *American Film,* December 1983, pp. 37–42.
Brady, Frank. *Citizen Welles: A Biography of Orson Welles.* New York: Scribners,
1989.
Breitinger, Eckhard. "A Halloween Boo! Selbstironisches Spiel mit dem Medium
Rundfunk im Orson Welles Adaptation von H. G. Wells' 'War of the Worlds.' "
In *Literatur im Fremdsprachenunterricht.* Frankfurt am Main: K. Schröder and
F. R. Weller, 1977. Pp. 142–158.
Cantril, Hadley. *The Invasion from Mars: A Study in the Psychology of Panic.
With the Complete Script of the Famous Orson Welles Broadcast.* Princeton:
Princeton University Press, 1940; reprint with Preface by Cantril, New York:
Harper Torchbook, 1966.
Draper, Michael. "The Martians in Ecuador." *Wellsian* 5 (Summer 1982):35–37.
Duffield, Brainerd. *The War of the Worlds.* Dramatized by Brainerd Duffield from
the novel by H. G. Wells. Chicago: The Dramatic Publishing Company, 1955.
Fabun, Don. "Science Fiction in Motion Pictures, Radio and Television." In Reginald
Bretnor, ed., *Modern Science Fiction: Its Meaning and Its Future.* New York:
Coward-McCann, Inc, 1953. Pp. 43–70.
Faulstich, Werner. *Ästhetik des Fernsehens. Eine Fallstudie zum Dokumentarspiel
"Die Nacht, als die Marsmenschen Amerika angriffen" (1976) von Joseph Sar-
gent.* Tübingen: Gunter Narr Verlag, 1982.
——— . *Filmästhetik: Untersuchungen zum Science Fiction-Film "Kampf der Wel-
ten" (1953/54) von Byron Haskin.* Tübingen: Gunter Narr Verlag, 1982.
——— . *Jeff Wayne. "The War of the Worlds": Analyse und Interpretation einer
Popmusik-Oper.* Tübingen: published by the author, 1982.
——— . *Medienästhetik und Mediengeschichte mit einer Fallstudie zu "The War
of the Worlds" von H. G. Wells.* Heidelberg: Carl Winter Universitäts Verlag,
1982.
——— . *Radiotheorie: Eine Studie zum Hörspiel "The War of the Worlds" (1938)
von Orson Welles.* Tübingen: Gunter Narr Verlag, 1981.

————. " 'The War of the Worlds' and the Styles of the Media: The History of the Adaptation of a Literary Classic." *Reports of the DFG*, March 1982, pp. 22–25.

————, trans. *"The War of the Worlds"/"Der Krieg der Welten": Vier Hörspiele.* Tübingen: Gunter Narr Verlag, 1981. [German translations of the 1938 radio adaptation, the 1955 Hollywood Radio Theatre production, and the 1974 Wonderland Imagination Theatre production (phonograph record: see below), together with "Der Krieg der Welten," the 1974 Westdeutschen Rundfunk radio adaptation by Klaus Schöning.]

Gilbert, James B. "Wars of the Worlds." *Journal of Popular Culture* 10 (1976):326–336.

Haskin, Byron. *"Kampf der Welten"/"The War of the Worlds."* Translated by Werner Faulstich. Tübingen: Gunter Narr Verlag, 1982. [German translation of Haskin's 1953 film adaptation.]

Herzog, Herta. "Why Did People Believe in the 'Invasion from Mars'?" In Paul F. Lazarsfeld and Morris Rosenberg, eds., *The Language of Social Research.* Glencoe, IL: The Free Press, 1955. Pp.420–428.

Houseman, John. *Run-Through: A Memoir.* New York: Simon and Schuster, 1972.

Koch, Howard. *The Panic Broadcast. The Whole Story of Orson Welles' Legendary Radio Show Invasion from Mars.* With an introductory interview with Arthur C. Clarke. New York: Avon Books, 1970.

Morson, Gary Saul. "The War of the Well(e)s." *Journal of Communication* 29/3 (Summer 1979):10–20.

Pal, George. "Filming *The War of the Worlds.*" *Astounding Science Fiction* 52/2 (October 1953):100–111.

Sack, Marie Helga. "Science Fiction als Radiospiel." Civil Service Examination Paper, Neuere Deutsche Literaturwissenschaft Universität, Heidelberg, 1974.

Sargent, Joseph. *Die Nacht, als die Marsmenschen Amerika angriffen/The Night that Panicked America.* Translated by Werner Faulstich. Tübingen: Gunter Narr Verlag, 1982.

Strangis, Gregg. *War of the Worlds: The Resurrection.* New York: Pocket Books (Simon & Schuster), 1988. [Novel based on the 1988 TV series.]

Phonograph and Cassette Recordings

Jeff Wayne's Musical Version of The War of the Worlds. New York: CBS Records. Columbia Stereo. C2 35290 A two-record LP set. [Stars Richard Burton.]

The Lux Radio Theatre Presents War of the Worlds. The Radiola Co., 1979. LP MR-1101. Science Fiction series 2, release 101. [An adaptation based on George Pal's 1953 film. The record includes Orson Welles's interview with H. G. Wells, heard originally over station KTSA, San Antonio, Texas, November 7, 1940.]

Orson Welles' War of the Worlds. Evolution Stereo 4001, n.d. A two-record LP set.

War of the Worlds. New York: Wonderland Records, 1974. LP-299. [An adaptation for children.]

The War of the Worlds. New York Records, Inc. LP TIL-505. [Adaptation performed by unspecified cast and with sound effects and music.]

The War of the Worlds: Invasion from Mars. Audio Rarities LP 2355. n.d. [An abridged version of the Welles broadcast.]

The War of the Worlds Starring Orson Welles. New Rochelle, NY: Nostalgia Lane, n.d. NLC 5029. Audio cassette.

The War of the Worlds Starring Orson Welles and the Mercury Theatre On the Air. New York: M. F. Distribution Co., n.d. MF 201/2. A two-record LP set.

DAVID Y. HUGHES is Professor of Humanities at the University of Michigan. He is co-editor of *H. G. Wells's Early Writings in Science and Science Fiction* (1975).

HARRY M. GEDULD, Professor of Comparative Literature and Chair of the Comparative Literature Department at Indiana University, has published numerous books on literature and film. He is the editor of several internationally known series of film books, including *Filmguides*, *Film Focus*, and *The New York Times Film Encyclopedia*, and has also published in a variety of journals.